D1554355

YUKON AUDIT

A Novel

Ken Baird

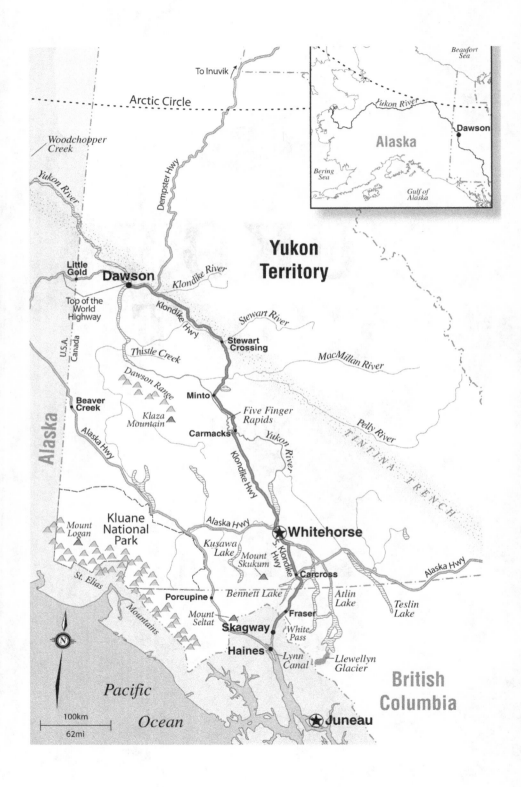

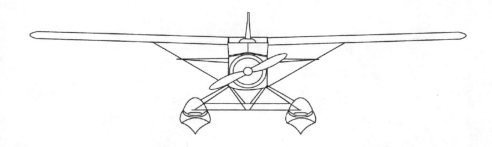

DeHavilland Canada DHC-2

General Characteristics

Crew: one pilot
Length: 30 ft 3 in (9.22 m)
Wingspan: 48 ft 0 in (14.63 m)
Height: 9 ft 0 in (2.74 m)
Wing area: 250 ft² (23.2 m²)
Empty: 3,000 lb (1,360 kg)
Loaded: 5,100 lb (2,310 kg)
Useful load: 2,100 lb (950 kg)
Powerplant: 1 Pratt & Whitney R-985 Wasp Jr. radial engine, 450 hp (335 kW)

Performance

Cruise speed (w/floats): 110 mph (180 km/h)
Range: 455 miles (732 km)
Rate of climb: 1,020 ft/min (5.2 m/s)
Service ceiling: 18,000 ft (5,500 m)

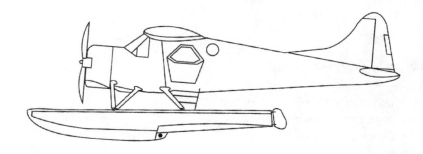

Yukon Audit
Copyright © 2016 by Ken Baird
All rights reserved

This book is a work of fiction. Names, characters, places, and incidents either are products of the author's imagination or are used fictitiously. Any resemblance to actual persons, living or dead, events, business establishments, or locales is entirely coincidental.

Third Edition

ISBN: 978-0-9973175-0-3

Cover Photo: Yukon River Sunset by Mark Dornblaser
Cover Design by Stillwater Graphics
Map by Chrismar Mapping Services
Formatting by Streetlight Graphics

This is the law of the Yukon, that only the Strong shall thrive;
That surely the Weak shall perish, and only the Fit survive.

—Robert William Service

For My Father

ONE

I met her in the spring.

A steady south wind had blown all night and the morning broke clear and mild. The valleys were green, the rivers swollen, the snow in the forests soft and wet. I was still putting a log on the fire before bed, but the harbingers of another short sweet summer were everywhere. It was a Monday, the first day of June, and the beginning of those two months when we can always count on three things.

Mosquitoes, twenty four hours of daylight, and tourists.

I live in the Yukon, just off the Klondike Highway, a few miles south of a place called Minto. The Klondike Highway connects the Yukon's capital city of Whitehorse, a hundred and fifty miles south, and the gold rush city of Dawson, a hundred and eighty miles north. It's a two and a half hour drive from my cabin to the nearest traffic light. I know, heard it before, the middle of nowhere.

Suits me fine.

Among other things, I'm a mechanic, and the only one for forty miles with a vehicle repair shop. So I'm the guy to see if you have a bad car day in the middle of the Klondike Highway. I remember that morning, raising the overhead door, walking outside, scanning the lot, hoping there'd be something to work on.

There was.

Someone had dropped off an old Toyota. The fifteen year old Corolla had Alaska tags, a big dent in the front bumper, and a lot of miles on the clock. It was unlocked. I opened the driver's door and leaned inside.

The entire handbrake assembly had been torn off the car's floor. It was lying on its side over a hole between the seats, still tethered to the brake cable. The keys and some paperwork were on the passenger seat. A handwritten note said 'please fix muffler, brakes and front seat by six o'clock today, thank you'. The note was signed by an 'S. Marsalis'. Under the note was a vehicle inspection report issued by our one man police force. The report had checkmarks in the boxes beside the words 'brakes', 'exhaust', 'handbrake' and 'seats'. 'Unroadworthy' was scrawled in the comment section at the bottom. 'Unroadworthy' meant that until the repairs were duly approved, the little car wasn't to leave my shop under its own power. Police extortion. And work for me.

I started the little car and it roared like an old tractor. I drove it inside, closed the overhead door, and raised it up on the lift. Mufflers generally fail because they've rusted out. But not this one. The muffler on this car had been crushed and the rest of the exhaust system was badly damaged. This car had run over something. The front brakes had deep gouges in the rotors and needed replacing. The handbrake assembly could be straightened out with a little bending and pounding in the vise. I could make it gorilla proof by remounting it with oversize bolts and washers. The front seats seemed to work fine.

I walked over to the bench, picked up my one and only telephone, and dialed the last independent parts store in Whitehorse. I ordered a muffler, a tail pipe, some straight pipe, some brackets and clamps, brake rotors and pads. My favorite parts guy said everything would get put on the morning bus to Dawson.

I went back to the lift, lowered the car, and checked the seats again. I still couldn't find anything wrong so just greased the levers and rails. I straightened out the handbrake in the vise, drilled some oversize holes in the floor, remounted it with heavy duty hardware, and had it working like new in an hour. At noon I made the half mile walk down to my cabin, ate a sandwich, fed my dogs, then walked back to the shop and did a little spring cleaning.

At two o'clock I drove up to the highway and waited for the bus from Whitehorse. Twenty minutes later there were four empty boxes on my work bench. I got to work. All afternoon I wondered if the owner of the little car could pay for the repairs, let alone would turn up to claim it. It wasn't worth very much.

But at six o'clock sharp a car growled over my gravel lot and stopped out front. If it was the owner, they were going to have to wait a little while longer. I still needed to bleed the brakes and check my work. I always check my work, and always, *always*, do a road test after working on brakes.

Two car doors opened and closed. I heard heavy footsteps, then light foot steps, then the thump of a trunk lid. No voices. Ten seconds later the side door opened and in walked the entire Minto police force – Constable Daryl Pageau of the Royal Canadian Mounted Police – all six foot five and two hundred and seventy pounds of born and bred Yukon cop. He lumbered over to me, stopped, glared up at the car on the lift, but said nothing. I could tell Daryl was in a good mood, though, his chin was high and his chest puffed out. He looked unusually dapper too, resplendent in his highly starched R.C.M.P. uniform and glossy-black, boat-sized shoes. I smelled aftershave. Someone else walked in.

A woman.

She was bent forward at the waist, struggling under the load of two backpacks: a large one slung on her back, a small one clutched in her arms. She set the small one down. I ducked out from under the front suspension for a better look. She arched her back, straightened her arms, gave a little hop, and lowered the large one to the floor. I noticed it had zipper locks on its bulging compartments. She straightened up, adjusted her clothes, brushed herself off, and gave her hair a flip. I gave her 'the up and down', that one second head-to-toe appraisal men have been known to give women they've never seen before. She caught me and stared back with a tired look, apparently used to such appraisals. It was easy to see why Daryl had got up early to polish buttons and perfume up.

She was stunning.

Her complexion was flawless. She had clear brown eyes, short auburn hair, a terrific figure. Slim. Great shape. Maybe five eight. Healthy. Athletic. Immaculate. Her hairstyle probably cost more than her car was worth. But more than beautiful, there was an aura about her, a charisma she exuded like an exotic perfume. She had that palpable self-assuredness that instantly fills a room, the kind that ivy league executives use to glide through life. My guess was she must be an actress, or a television personality, maybe a professional of some kind, perhaps a senior executive, or even a rising politician. Or maybe she was just from big money. She looked about thirty five. Whatever she was, whoever she was, the woman was clearly out of my league, and for that matter, definitely out of Daryl's.

"Constable Pageau," I said formally, nodding once with feigned respect.

"Brody," said Daryl, tipping his hat, eyeing me with his best cop glare. "This lady here's the owner of that car on your lift. Ms. Marsalis, meet Brody."

"Hello, Brody," she said. "Sarah Marsalis." She walked over to us, extended her hand to me, then had second thoughts when I showed her the state of mine. She gave me an understanding smile instead. Of course she would have to have a great smile to go with the rest of the package. Make that a perfect, dazzling white smile. I stared at her in awe. Get a grip. Quit staring. And if your mouth is open, now would be a good time to close it.

"Will my car be ready soon?" she asked with her eyebrows raised.

"Soon," I said, trying to swallow and looking back at her car. "Twenty minutes or so. Have to bleed the brakes and do a road test. You can wait at the café while I finish. I'll drive over and pick you up when it's done."

Daryl said, "Brody, is it fixed or not? I gotta be somewhere else."

"Yeah, Daryl, it's fixed, like I said, twenty minutes."

"Twenty minutes," he muttered. He leaned his enormous head in close to me and murmured discretely, "I'll sign the vehicle inspection report now so she can be on her way when you're done. But that car doesn't leave here until it's right, clear?"

"Very clear." *And not until the bill's paid too.*

Daryl turned to the woman and said, "Ms. Marsalis, as soon as Brody here's finished, you can drive your car again. I'll take you back to the café now. You can wait there."

"Thank you, officer," she said, "but I'd prefer to wait here, if that's alright."

She looked at me, then at Daryl. He nodded. I shrugged.

"So where's the inspection report, Brody?"

"On the bench."

"On the bench," he growled. The big cop walked over to the bench, surveyed the clutter, knocked some empty boxes to the floor, found the report under an old brake pad, flicked it aside with his pen, and scribbled something. "Have a safe trip, Ms. Marsalis," he said, touching his cap.

"Thank you very much, officer," she said, though I sensed she didn't mean it.

Daryl carefully navigated through a minefield of rusty old exhaust parts on his way to the door. Neither of us said a word until we heard his cruiser start, and gravel spit and crunch as he drove off. Ever notice that sensation of relief you get after the cops have left?

"There's a picnic table out back," I said. "If you want, you can sit outside in the Yukon sun while I bleed the brakes. Shouldn't be long."

"Actually, I've had enough sitting for a day, mind if I watch?"

"Suit yourself."

"How do you bleed brakes by yourself?"

"Huh? Oh, with a vacuum pump, on the calipers."

"Isn't it easier with someone helping? Someone inside the car pumping the brake pedal?"

"Well, it can be." Though it depends on who's pumping the pedal, I thought cynically.

"I know how to bleed brakes, how about I help you?"

I hesitated for a second, then without much conviction said, "Okay."

I lowered the car and held the driver's door open. She got in and I watched her lovely long legs slide under the steering wheel. I raised the car again and we did the 'down, hold, up, wait' thing with the brake pedal for each front wheel. In a couple of minutes there was crystal clear fluid flowing out of both brake calipers. I lowered the lift and said, "Good job, thanks."

She jumped out looking pleased with herself and flashed me another dazzling smile that almost buckled my knees. I put the front wheels back on her car, lowered it to the ground, and swung the lift arms out from under the frame. I filled the master brake cylinder, then checked the oil, the radiator and the battery, like I always do, on every car I work on.

"All done?" she asked, standing next to me.

"All done," I said, closing the hood.

"Is the bill ready? Can I pay you now?"

"No. First I do a road test. Then I write up your bill."

"Oh. Well could we just settle up now and skip the road test today? I'm kind of in a hurry."

"Actually," I said, wiping my hands on a rag and treating her to my best smile, "I always like to do a road test before preparing a bill. That way, if a car runs really good, I can charge a little extra."

Don't know why I said that. Well maybe I do. What a stupid thing to say. What a pathetic attempt to break the ice with a woman who I already had a supreme crush on. A woman way out of my league. *Idiot*.

She acknowledged my lame sense of humor with a perfunctory smile, sighed, nodded, then said, "Alright, go do your road test."

I dropped my coveralls, washed my hands in the laundry tub, and opened the overhead door. I got in and started her car.

"Wow, it's quiet now," she said, looking down at me with her hands on her knees.

I nodded, avoiding her eyes, and that smile.

"Back in five."

I backed out of the garage, drove out to the highway, turned south, and accelerated up to forty-five miles an hour. After checking the rearview mirror I braked hard, down to ten miles an hour, then accelerated again, back to forty-five, and braked hard again. I repeated the process a couple more times to cure the new brake pads, then turned around and drove nice and easy back to the shop.

I pulled in the lot, turned off the engine, and took a good long look through the windshield at Sarah Marsalis. She was staring back at me, calm and confident, leaning against the bleached wood building with her long legs crossed at the ankles, her hands in the pockets of a fleece pullover, its zipper open halfway to reveal her bosom. The wind was playing with her thick shiny hair. She was wearing perfectly tailored blue jeans, a snug fitting T-shirt, and short hiking boots. Everything she had on was brand new and high quality. The scene felt surreal. It was like watching a photo shoot for an L.L. Bean catalogue cover. Something about her driving an old Corolla didn't jive with the image in front of me. At the very least, this woman ought to be driving a brand new Subaru, definitely forest green, with a couple of kayaks on the roof and a 'Save the Whales' bumper sticker. I rolled the window down when she walked up to my door.

"Everything okay?" she asked.

"Yeah, brakes are good, runs nice and quiet."

"Great! Does that mean you're going to charge me 'a little extra', Mr. Brody?" She tilted her head and looked down at me with that nice smile of hers. Nice woman. Well, maybe a nice woman.

"It's just Brody, and no, I was only kidding about that."

I got out and we walked into the shop and over to the bench. I found the parts bill, scribbled a few lines, and added up two columns of numbers. I stapled it to the inspection report and handed them to her.

She scanned my paper work and said "Where's the total?"

I pointed at the two addition columns with my pen. "Two-fifty for parts and two-fifty for me, that's five hundred."

"Does that include the tax?"

I had to pause, wondering who the hell asks about *the* tax, then said, "Yeah, *the* taxes are included."

"Good. May I pay you with a credit card? Do you take credit cards?"

"I do, but we've got to go up to the café for that. They've got internet. I'm not set up for credit cards here."

She hesitated. "Well, could I wait here? I really don't want to go back to that café."

That café?

"Look, it's no big deal Miss, Mrs., Ms. – Ms. Marsalis. It's only a short drive, but you need to come with me. You need to sign the charge slip up there." She still seemed undecided so I said, "Hey, it's real simple. We drive over, we walk in, we scan your card, you sign the slip, we drive back, you're on your way. Fifteen minutes, tops."

She looked me in the eyes and said, "It's Miss."

"Miss," I mumbled, dropping my eyes like a shy kid.

"Okay," she said, "But if I go back to that café with you, would it be alright if I wait outside? Could I sign the charge slip outside?"

I nodded and looked at her carefully.

"Yeah," I said. "I guess we could do that."

That café.

TWO

We walked out to my old Chevy pickup. *Miss* Marsalis got in. I dropped the tailgate, turned to the trees, and blew my loudest whistle. Ten seconds later two Jack Russell terriers came charging out at warp speed, leapt into the back of the truck, and skidded up to the cab window. I closed the tailgate, gave each a quick mussing, and got in behind the wheel. We drove slowly out to the highway with a cloud of dust in pursuit, then turned left and headed north.

"Your dogs?" she asked.

"Yeah. Russ and Jack. Russ is the older one. I live on the river, down that road behind the shop. Whenever they hear my truck start, they come running. If I leave without them, they'll run out to the highway and chase me for miles. So rather than tie them up today, I figured we'd go for a nice family drive to the café."

The dogs were staring at Sarah Marsalis through the cab's rear window. I wondered what she was thinking about. I wondered what the dogs were thinking about. Neither of us said another word as we gazed out at the brilliant purple fireweed and an endless sea of spruce trees. Five minutes later the café came into view on our right.

The 'café', as it's called around here, is actually a poorly aging, two story timber hotel built in the early fifties. The gray weathered building sits in the middle of a long and dusty gravel lot on the east side of the Klondike Highway. The second story started to list over about ten years ago and the six hotel rooms upstairs were condemned when the plumbing started to break. I think a good wind's going to blow the second story off the café one of these days. Highway travelers are now accommodated in one of six log cabins behind the hotel, or at one of ten campsites, each replete with its own rickety picnic table and a circle of rocks for a fire pit.

The café has two large windows facing the highway. Patrons seated at the front windows have a panoramic view of the highway and two ancient gas pumps. Hand painted signs on the old single hose pumps say 'Pay Inside'. At the south end of the lot is a diesel pump, a cage full of propane tanks, a stack of barrels containing aviation gas, and a heating oil storage tank. Scattered along the back of the lot are the rusty relics from local ventures long gone bust: a fuel truck with no tank, a bulldozer with no tracks, a tow truck with no wheels, a plane with no wings, several wrecked cars, a hard rock drill, and a myriad of other non-descript junk no one wants to own anymore.

Across the highway is a dirt airstrip. A tattered and faded windsock swings and creaks all day on a canted steel pole, marking the mid-point of the north-south runway. Outfitters' horses wander freely up and down the strip, keeping the wild grass in check.

I drove past the café, turned right into the north entrance, then idled back and parked at the side of the building.

I looked over at Sarah Marsalis and held out my hand.

"I'm guessing you still don't want to come inside, so I'll need your card."

She slid a hand inside her jacket and pulled out a credit card. "Five hundred, right?"

She handed me the card.

"Five hundred, be right back."

I walked around the corner of the building and through the front door. The usual crowd of working men was seated for dinner at tables along the front windows. They wore ball caps, checked shirts, blue jeans and work boots, and all were deeply immersed in conspiratorial conversations while maintaining an ever vigilant lookout for new action at the pumps. I've never understood why watching strangers fill their vehicles with gas can be such compelling entertainment, but then I guess I have a life.

"Brody!" an enormous native woman hollered, waving at me from behind a long dining counter at the back of the restaurant. "Gotta talk to you, hon!"

"Hey Minnie, gotta talk to you too!"

Minnie McCormack manages the café from her usual station, a tall swivel stool behind the cash register. On the register is a sign that says 'Pay for gas here'. Behind her is an open window to the kitchen. A dark hall leading back to the bar runs down the left wall. On a shelf behind Minnie are a pair of two way radios – a police band radio to call Daryl on the highway – and a VHF radio to monitor airport and SOS calls. Above the radios hangs a greasy plastic sign that says 'We Don't Give a Damn How They Do It Outside'. At the right end of the dining counter is an upright cooler full of beer. A hand written sign taped to its glass door says 'No beer for miners must be 19'. On the right wall are two long white freezers that hum and buzz away 24/7. They're the old kind, the ones with a big lid on top you lift up. Someone used a felt pen to write 'Meat' on the lid of the first one, and 'Fish' on the lid of the other. At the center of both concave lids someone else had written, 'No sitting on here', and underneath that, 'No staring in the freezer ask for Help'. Beside the freezers are two shelving units stocked with a variety of basic pantry items and an excellent assortment of junk food. A petrified layer of dust keeps the shine off everything in the cafe, even the chips and pretzels.

I walked up to the cash register and handed Minnie the credit card.

"Five hundred, Minnie, credit my account."

Minnie adjusted her eyeglasses and held the card out at arm's length, inspecting it carefully like it might be forensic evidence. Then her eyes got huge. She slapped a hand to her chest and looked at me with astonishment.

"This is her, Brody! This is S. Marsalis! Where is she? Do you know where she is? That poor woman! She's so pretty. Did you fix her car? Did you hear what happened here last night?"

Then she broke into laughter, a belly shaking, table pounding laughter that shook the walls. She only stopped because she started to cough, then gathered herself and began wiping the tears from her eyes. She looked at me in agony, trying to resist another outbreak.

"Minnie, I don't know what's so funny but Miss Marsalis is outside waiting. Could we please run her credit card?" I could feel every eye in the room on my back, and heard chuckling and muttering.

"She's outside? Oh!" She swiped the card through a reader, punched in a bunch of numbers, heaved a great sigh, then started laughing again.

"Minnie! What's so funny?"

"Okay, okay," she said, wiping her eyes again. "Well! Last night about dinner time this little green car pulls up to the pumps. Reginald and Arlo and Arnie and Hank and Charlie and some of the boys from the highway department are eating their dinner over there by the windows, just talkin' their usual nonsense. So then this real pretty woman gets out of the little green car and starts gassing up. And then the whole place goes real quiet, 'cuz all the boys noticed how skinny and pretty she was, right? So they're starin' at her, lookin' out the windows, watchin' her gas up, and then she comes in to pay for her gas, and they're still all starin' at her with their mouths hangin' open when she walks past them, 'cuz oh my, she was so pretty Brody..."

"Minnie, the card, is it going through?"

"It'll start printing when it's gone through, hon. Anyway, so the woman pays me for her gas, then she asks if there's a pay phone and I told her down the hall. So she goes down the hall to the phone and she starts talkin'. So she's talkin' and talkin', real quiet like, I guess she was tellin' secrets or somethin'. So then this big RV pulls in on the far side of the pumps, and the man drivin' the RV gets out, and he starts gassin' up, and then Daryl pulls in and rolls up right behind the woman's little green car, 'cuz he's wantin' to gas up too, right? So now there's this big traffic jam out there to gas up, and Daryl's waitin' for the little green car to move out of his way, and he's waitin' and waitin', but that woman's still talkin' on the phone down the hall. So after a while Daryl gets out of his car and stomps in here all flustered like, 'cuz I guess he was in a big hurry to get gas. So he asks me who owns the little green car parked at the pumps, and I told him the woman back there on the phone. So Daryl walks down the hall to the phone and says something to the woman, and I guess she told him to go ahead and move it himself, must have, 'cuz then Daryl goes stompin' out of here with her keys in his hand, and he doesn't look all too pleased about movin' her car, mind you, but I guess he was in a real hurry to get gas, so then…"

"Minnie, the credit card."

"Brody, you know it's telephone internet. It's slow! I told you it'll print when it goes through! Anyway, where was I? Oh! So Daryl goes back out to the pumps and he squeezes himself into her little green car and then he starts rockin' back and forth, like I guess he's trying to adjust the seat, right? But I guess he can't get the seat to slide back, so there's Daryl in that big puffy coat of his, hugging the steering wheel with his hat mashed up against the roof, and he decides to try to move it anyway, even if he can't get the seat to move back. So he starts to drive ahead, like real slow, I mean like real, real slow, Brody. And then the little car starts jerkin' and buckin', and then it really starts jerkin' and buckin', go, stop, go, stop, go, stop, like about two miles an hour, and there's Daryl all squished up inside, buckin' back and forth like a rodeo cowboy, I guess 'cuz the seat came loose and now it's slidin' back and forth, right? So then he turns it out toward the highway, like he's plannin' on parkin' it at the edge of the lot. But Brody? That little green car just kept on buckin' and buckin', and goin' and goin', and it just wouldn't stop! It just kept on goin' and goin' and Daryl drove it straight into the ditch. Then pow! He hit the light pole! Like pow! We heard him hit it in here!"

Minnie burst into another roaring bout of laughter and everyone behind me joined in. I found myself laughing with them.

Two enormous hands the size of bear paws flopped down on the counter beside me. Without turning I said, "Hey, Reggie."

"Hi, tell him the rest, Ma. That little car had a stick shift, Brody. Daryl got his feet stuck in the pedals."

"That would have been my guess, Reg."

Reggie is Minnie's son. He looks like a cross between Minnie and an Alaskan brown bear. If you put a red and black checked shirt on an Alaskan brown bear, you'd know what I mean. Reggie isn't fat, he's just brown and big, thick and wide, and incredibly strong. He easily weighs three hundred pounds though he's less than my six feet. His leathery face is impossibly wide and bony, and there are thick scars under his eyebrows. Everyone is good at something and Reggie's specialty used to be prying the caps off beer bottles with his eyes. Ever since they put twist caps on beer bottles, Reggie has been looking for a new calling in life. In the meantime, he drives the café's tow truck.

The credit card machine started printing the ticket. Minnie raised her head off the cash register, sighed with exhaustion, wiped her eyes again and said "Oh, Brody, you gotta hear the rest." She tore the ticket out of the machine and handed it to me.

"Minnie, hang on a sec. I'll be right back."

She started to laugh again. So did everyone else.

I walked down the hall toward the bar, past the pay phone and out the emergency exit door. I walked over to my pickup and tapped on the passenger window. My dogs gave me a quick glance, then resumed staring at Sarah Marsalis with their tails wagging. She cracked the door open, grabbed the ticket and a pen from my hand, and muttered, "Mosquitoes". She closed the door, scribbled a signature, then opened the door again, just a crack, barely enough to slide the ticket and pen back to me.

"Are we done?" she asked through the window. Her impatience was palpable.

"Just about," I said.

I turned toward the front of the building but saw Reggie and four other men were holding the emergency door open. They stood in a line, shoulder to shoulder, staring at my truck.

"Hey. Thanks for holding the door, guys. Appreciate your thoughtfulness."

They dropped their heads like scolded school boys and retreated back inside. I followed them down the hall to Minnie and handed her the credit card ticket. She handed me the credit card and a copy of the ticket.

Reggie asked, "Hey, Brody? You charge for my tow?"

"What tow?"

"I towed that lady's car to your shop last night."

"Ah Reggie, we've talked about this before. When you tow a car to my shop, you've got to leave your bill in the car! Otherwise, how am I supposed to know I should bill a customer for a tow?" I sighed.

Reggie dropped his head.

"How much was the tow, Reg?"

"Eighty bucks," he said, studying the floor.

I looked at Minnie and said, "Minnie, please pay Reggie for his tow and charge it to my account. And add two bottles of water and a tube of Pringles." I grabbed my bottled water and Pringles.

"So you want to hear the rest?" Minnie asked.

"Sorry, don't have time. Got to drive Miss Marsalis back to her car. Later."

As I turned to leave, the phone on the counter started ringing. I was almost out the hall door when Minnie yelled, "Brody, phone call!"

"Take a message!" I yelled back.

"It's Daryl, he says it's important!"

Damn. I hustled back to the cash register, put my groceries on the counter and took the phone from Minnie.

"Yes, Daryl."

"Is she gone?"

"Miss Marsalis?"

"Yes," he growled, "Ms. Marsalis."

"Not yet, she's still here. Just paid her bill. I'm on my way out the door. About to drive her back to the shop."

"Good. Listen to me carefully," he said. He paused, I assumed for dramatic effect. "Last night I ran an international drivers license inquiry on our Ms. Marsalis. Got the report right here in front of me, just came off the telex." He paused again and took a deep breath. "Brody, Sarah Marsalis is trouble. Understand? Big trouble. So you're gonna leave this one alone. Hear me? When you get back to your shop, you make sure she gets into that little car of hers and drives it out of here. Tonight. Are we clear on that?"

"Wow, Daryl, what did the telex say?"

"Never mind the telex, that's police business. Just make sure she leaves as soon as you get back to your shop. Got that?"

"Well I think that's what she's got in mind, Daryl."

"Brody?"

"Yeah, Daryl."

"Stay away."

THREE

I walked out to my truck and got in. Sarah Marsalis was sitting bolt upright with her arms folded, staring straight ahead. She wasn't happy. The quintessential pissed off woman.

"Hey, sorry that took so long. The internet was really slow today."

"I'll bet," she said, rolling her eyes.

I drove slowly past the front window of the café and out to the highway, treating the boys to a final glimpse of the beautiful and mysterious stranger, now a legend of the Minto Café.

"Got you a bottle of water." She took the bottle from me and drank half of it.

"Thank you," she said.

I opened the Pringles, shook some into my hand, then held the tube out in front of her.

"Want some?"

She looked at them with disdain and said, "No. But thank you."

"Are you sure? They're sour cream and onion. Very hard to find up here."

I held the tube of potato chips in front of her while I drove. She ignored me. I shook the tube. She took it from me. We crunched on chips for awhile.

Eventually she said, "So I suppose you heard the whole story in there while you were waiting on the *slow* internet."

I had to smile. "Yeah, well everything up to the part when Constable Pageau hit the light pole with your car."

"I didn't see it," she said, "but I sure heard it. There was a big bang, then a horn started blaring. When I saw everyone run outside, I did too. Do you know it took three men to pull him out of my car?"

I grinned at her and said, "Hey, I think the R.C.M.P. ought to pay your repair bill. Everything except the front brakes."

"There was nothing wrong with the front brakes! And you're damn right they should pay! And they can buy me a new bumper too! You know that cop crashed my car into that pole because his feet got stuck in the pedals? He should never have tried to drive my car with those sasquatch feet of his. He lost control! He was entirely to blame! And ripping the handbrake out of the floor? That was outrageous! And then he gets mad at me! Blames me for what happened! Tells me my car isn't roadworthy and has it towed away! What crap! Unbelievable! I lost a whole day because of that cop. And because of him I had to sleep in a leaky log cabin last night with no heat, no hot water, and a million mosquitoes!"

"Look," I said, wondering how to calm her down. "I understand why you're mad, but obviously the cop was embarrassed about what happened. So he reacted unreasonably. Cops are like that. But hey, you're out of here now, right?"

"Damn right I'm out of here!"

"Where are you headed?"

"Dawson."

"Dawson, huh? Business or pleasure?"

She hesitated before saying, "Business."

"Business? Hmmm. Well, just so you know, if you leave for Dawson now, you won't get there until midnight. And make sure you stop to eat before nine. All the diners on the highway close at nine. The Klondike Highway is a pretty lonely road at night. Just so you know."

She mulled that over for a moment.

"Well, I don't need to stop. Besides, I have to be in Dawson tomorrow morning."

"But you're hungry."

"How do you know I'm hungry?"

"Because women who look like you don't eat Pringles."

She turned and looked at me. "Oh, is that so?" she said, then looked back at the highway and put another chip in her mouth. "Well I still have to be in Dawson tomorrow morning, okay? So I'm leaving now, even if I might be a little hungry."

"Important stuff to do in Dawson?"

"Well actually, yes, it is important. Very important. I have a meeting tomorrow afternoon and I need to charter a plane in the morning."

Charter a plane.

"A little sightseeing?" I asked.

"You could call it that."

"And what would you call it?"

She took a moment before saying, "Reconnoitering."

I laughed. "I bet I can guess what you're reconnoitering if you're chartering a plane out of Dawson."

"What?" she asked, glaring at me.

I laughed again. "In the middle of gold mining country? You're looking for gold!"

She folded her arms, clearly irritated, and stared out the front window. A moment passed before she said, "Not that it's any of your business, *Mr.* Brody, but I am not looking for gold."

"Whatever you say, *Miss* Marsalis."

I slowed the truck down and turned off the highway, then drove slowly down the two rut lane to the shop.

"Could I give you a piece of advice, Miss Marsalis?"

"What?"

"Well, here's what you need to know about chartering planes up here. See, flying planes is what bush pilots do when they're not hanging around the bars. Now I'm not saying bush pilots are a bunch of drunks, but they like to talk, and usually they head to the bar as soon as they land."

"What on earth are you talking about?" she asked impatiently.

We stopped beside her car.

"What I'm talking about is that pilots are the biggest source of news around here, and news travels like wildfire through the bars in gold mining towns. So if you need to charter a plane to look for gold, I wouldn't charter one out of Dawson. Not if you don't want everyone knowing what you're up to."

She seemed to be thinking about what I'd just said when we got out of the truck and closed the doors.

"So where else can you charter a plane around here?" she asked from the other side of the hood.

"Lots of places, just depends on where you want to fly. If you want to reconnoiter south of Dawson, where most of the gold mining is, you're better off chartering out of here."

"That doesn't make sense. Dawson's miles north of here."

"By road, yeah, but most of the gold mining country is south of Dawson. Flying there from here is only thirty miles farther than out of Dawson."

"You keep talking about gold! And I told you I'm not looking for gold!"

"Okay, okay, I believe you," I said, holding up the palms of my hands. "But whatever it is you're looking for, it sure sounds to me like it's in the middle of gold mining country."

"Look, Mr. Brody, you don't have any idea what I'm looking for, or where I want to fly, so let's leave it at that."

"Hey. I get it. I have no idea where you want to fly, or what you're looking for, and you want to keep that a secret."

She looked around furtively. "It's not a secret. I want to fly over a place called Thistle Creek."

"Thistle Creek, huh? That's ninety miles northwest of here, seventy miles south of Dawson."

"How would you know that?"

"Well, I live here," I said, shrugging my shoulders.

Russ and Jack were panting with their paws on top of the tailgate. I went back and dropped it down. They jumped out of the box and ran behind the shop to their water bowls. I walked back to the hood of the truck. Sarah Marsalis was still standing on the other side. She was brooding and pensive, looking around, waving at the occasional mosquito. I leaned an elbow on my side of the hood and watched her for a while.

"So," she said, "do you know a pilot with a plane around here that could fly me to Thistle Creek in the morning?"

"Yup. Can even arrange it for you."

She took a deep breath and said, "Oh look, forget I asked. I'm not spending another night with a bunch of mosquitoes in one of those decrepit log cabins. I'm driving to Dawson tonight. But thanks for all your advice."

"Miss Marsalis?"

"Yes, Mr. Brody."

"Would you be willing to listen to a proposal of mine?"

She turned and looked directly at me, then put her hands on her hips. The dogs were back with wet snouts, sitting in front of the truck, staring up at her with adulation. "A proposal," she said. "First you have advice, now you have a proposal. Alright. But please make it fast. I'm leaving now."

"Great. But first you have to lean on the hood like this". I folded my arms and leaned on the hood on my side of the truck. I looked across at her. "Come on," I said, "Indulge me."

She gave me a suspicious look, shook her head, then folded her arms and leaned against her side of the hood.

"That's perfect form," I said. "Welcome to your first meeting at a genuine Yukon conference table."

"The hood of a truck?"

"Yeah. The hood of a truck. Up here we make deals over the hoods of pickup trucks, not at conference tables."

"Well, it's certainly a nice and warm conference table," she said, appreciating the warmth of the engine.

"Yeah, I think if they heated all the conference tables in this world, we'd have world peace in no time."

She shook her head again, tried not to smile, then said, "Look, Mr. Brody, you're holding me up. You have a proposal. I'm only curious, that's all, so let's hear it. I really need to get going."

"Oh, right. Well let's review your current situation, shall we?"

She rolled her eyes. I looked down at my feet and kicked some gravel around, then looked up at her again.

"Okay," I said, "you need to charter a plane tomorrow, right?"

She rolled her eyes again and exhaled loudly. "Right," she said.

"But if you were to charter a plane out of here tomorrow morning, you'd insist on a decent place to stay tonight, right?"

"Yes, definitely."

"And, you're really hungry, right?"

"Look, Mr. Brody, you're out of time, what's your proposal?"

"Well, here it is. I'll arrange a plane to fly you to Thistle Creek tomorrow morning. Eight a.m. sharp. Now upstairs, over my shop, there's a very comfortable and freshly cleaned apartment – hot and cold, great shower, electric heat – and, no mosquitoes. It's the best hotel room in Minto, you'd be very comfortable, and…"

"And?"

"I'll cook you dinner."

She lowered her chin onto her stacked fists and appraised me with her intelligent brown eyes, then asked, "And in your wildest dreams ever, you're hoping to get what in return?"

I looked down at my feet and kicked some more gravel against the front tire. "Well, here's what I'd like in return, Miss Marsalis." I cleared my throat and said, "Last night your car was towed over here from the café. I just found that out. So I didn't bill you for the tow. I want you to pay me for the tow…eighty dollars."

"That's it?"

"That's it."

"So you'll arrange a plane for me, *and* you'll let me stay in your apartment tonight, *and* you'll feed me, *and* all you want in return is eighty dollars for the tow?"

I held my arms out wide. "That's it. Eighty dollars."

She studied me with a suspicious look for a moment, then stepped back from the truck, folded her arms, took a deep breath, looked at the trees, then at my shop, then at me.

"That sounds like a pretty good proposal," she said, staring up at the window on the second story of my old building. I was holding my breath. So were my dogs.

"Alright, Mr. Brody. You have a deal."

"Great!"

"But."

"Yes?"

"Two things."

"What?"

"One, I want my credit card back. And two, don't even think about making a pass at me."

* * *

We walked into the shop through the side door. My dogs followed hot on her heels. She ignored them. I handed her two keys on a ring, one for the side door, the other for the apartment.

"Lock the side door from the inside when you come back from dinner," I said. "I'm going to put your car in the shop for the night. In the morning, pull down on one of those chains to raise the overhead door. Drive your car out, come back inside, close the door. Leave through the side door. You don't have to lock anything. Leave the keys on the bench."

"Why are you putting my car in your shop?"

"Because you don't want any visitors tonight."

"Right," she said. "So what time is dinner? And where's dinner?"

I looked at the clock over the bench. It was seven thirty. "You can head down the road in about half an hour. It's a fifteen minute walk. When you get to the river, look left, you'll see a path that goes up to my place. Or if you want, I can come back in the truck and pick you up in forty-five minutes."

"No, I'll walk, I need a walk," she said.

"Okay. Want some help with that pack?" I pointed at the steep stair case at the back of my shop.

"No, I'm fine, but thank you. I can have a shower, right?"

"Of course, make yourself at home. You'll find clean linen and towels in the closet in the bathroom. Coffee and sugar is on the counter. There's a thermostat on the wall for the electric heater. If you need to make a call, there's a phone over the work bench."

"Good. Thank you, Mr. Brody. I'll see you in forty five minutes," she said, formally.

"See you then, Miss Marsalis," I said, reciprocating her tone.

I opened the overhead door, drove her car into the shop, and closed it again.

"Let's go boys!" I yelled.

I walked out the side door, held it open, and waited. They weren't coming. I stepped back inside and looked at them. They were sitting at the foot of the stairs, wagging their tails, watching Sarah Marsalis climb. She disappeared into the apartment above them.

"Come on, let's go!" Russ and Jack gave me a glance, then looked up the stairs again. I shook my head and shut the door, got in my truck and drove carefully down the dirt track leading to the river. This was exciting. Dinner with a beautiful woman. 'Miss Marsalis is trouble'. Deciding what to cook. 'Stay away'.

Sorry, Daryl, but I have a dinner date with *Miss* Marsalis tonight.

At the river I parked my truck and got out. I began climbing the short path leading up to my cabin on top of the bluff, then stopped halfway to look down at the Yukon River. I always stop there, even for just a moment, just to marvel at all that pale green water rushing by, to listen to it hissing and frothing, to watch it flow past me at almost five miles an hour. From where I stood, all that water would flow for another fifteen hundred miles – northwest to Dawson, then west across the entire state of Alaska – all the way to the Bering Sea.

What impossible power.

FOUR

Wei Lee, president of the Lucky Star Trading Company, loved his new office. He loved the floor to ceiling windows. He loved how the thick blue carpet flowed like a river out to the windows, then disappeared over the edge, as though it was cascading into the ocean. He loved looking at the Pacific, especially the sunsets. But most of all he loved the sensation of height, the power of twenty-four stories of steel and concrete underfoot. It gave him such energy, an energy he could feel surging through the souls of his feet, filling him with a great strength. This is real height, he mused, though he was no taller than five feet four inches tall when standing on the street below. Even with the custom made lifts in his Bally shoes.

He peered through his telescope at the Pacific Ocean and three container ships climbing over the horizon, each about to start a gentle slide into the port of Long Beach. Each ship was carrying the bounty of the Asian economic miracle, each riding low in the water under the load of three thousand containers. Containers packed full of brand new consumer products. Boxes and boxes of clothes, electronics, furniture and household goods. Something for everyone, something new and exciting and chic to buy at the mall this weekend. 'New and improved', 'our best ever', and everything at a 'new lower price'. But in the end, all those products in all those containers would be bought only to be forgotten. It wouldn't be long before they were shoved into the darkest corners of garages and basements and closets, and ultimately the trash cans at the ends of millions of driveways. It was all destined for the landfills of America. With one exception.

Wei Lee wondered which ship carried his containers. His containers were different from the rest. His containers were unique because his cargo was unique. His containers were full of hopes and dreams and ambition. Wei Lee's containers had people inside them. Chinese people. Fifty or so in each one. Some young, some old, some married, some single, some men, some women. Very young women. Girls, really.

The people in Wei Lee's containers were peasants. The little plots of dirt they'd farmed for generations had never been theirs, but they'd proudly worked and cultivated them as though they were. The peasants had always paid their rent on time to the People's Party. They'd always grown enough to feed themselves, and sometimes a little more, profit they'd take to market and trade for things. If nothing else, they'd had their dignity and independence.

But one day the mayor of their village announced to the peasants that their plots had to be vacated. He told them the land they were working was needed for a new factory. You must leave your fields immediately, the mayor had said. There will be jobs for you when the new factory is completed. This is progress, it is the will of the Party. It is a decision made for the greater good of everyone. The Party's decision is just and it is right and it is final. And that was that. There would be no discussion, no hearings, no appeals no compensation. One day the peasant farmers had a livelihood and independence, the next day they didn't. Their lives had been stolen in a single day. For 'the greater good', there would be nothing for them to do until the new factory was in operation, more than a year away.

But within days of vacating their fields, a well dressed man had come to their village. He had a new and exciting opportunity. He gave them hope again.

I can help you, he told them. I can give you a new life. A better life. Of course there is a price to pay. You must pay me my fee. That's all you have? Oh, I'm sure you can find a little more. Perhaps I can loan you some money. You can repay me when you begin your new life. Because what I am offering is a dream, and my fee is very reasonable for a dream. If you pay my fee, I will take you to another world. To a much better place with a much better life. A life you've only dreamt about. A life where everyone has a big car, a big house, a beautiful family. A life in America. Where everyone is rich, where everyone is secure, where everyone is happy. But you must pay me my fee.

Today the people in Wei Lee's containers were sick – very sick – hungry, and scared. It had been eighteen days since the big steel doors had been closed on them. They'd stacked the cardboard boxes against the doors, just as they'd been told. A small hole in the roof would supply enough air to breathe. Then a deafening crash. A great shudder reverberated through the container when another container was dropped on top of theirs. The light that had once seeped in through the skylight was gone. It had been dark and hot ever since. Occasionally a whiff of fresh air would blow through the hole in the roof, but most of the time the people could smell only the ship's exhaust. Yesterday a wretched stink had started coming from the chemical toilet in the corner. And always there was the noise, the snapping and popping of steel as it expanded and contracted in the heat and cold, the groaning and creaking of other containers as the ship rolled over the ocean. The people knew this was not right. This was not what they had bargained for. This was not hope. This was not a dream. This was hell.

They had agreed to pay the man his fee. They had given the man all their money. They had agreed to borrow the money they didn't have. They had agreed to the terms of his loan. They had trusted the well dressed man. The well dressed man who worked for Wei Lee.

* * *

Lee gazed down at the port of Los Angeles to his right, and the port of Long Beach to his left. He counted six ships being unloaded. He looked at all the containers.

There were thousands and thousands of them, painted every color, stacked on top of one other like toy blocks, sprawled over hundreds of acres of pavement and concrete, sitting on ships, on trucks, on railway cars, dangling from cables under gigantic cranes. The loading and unloading of containers went on all day, every day, all year long. Lee was excited. His containers would arrive soon. Perhaps as early as tomorrow.

I must speak with Henry and Tommy right away, he thought. I need to make sure that everything goes smoothly when my containers arrive. Make sure that cockroach customs broker gets my containers released without problems. Without any of that inspection nonsense! Releasing containers without an inspection – how could anything be easier? Every year, six million containers were unloaded at these two ports alone. But every month that scumbag broker would call, always wanting more money, just to release a few containers without a customs inspection! What was his name? Perez? Yes, Perez. What had he told Henry? Something about new X-ray machines? Perez said the people operating the new X-ray machines were very thorough, but also very greedy. Perez said the cost of importing a container without a customs inspection was going up. It was like inflation, he said, there was nothing you could do about it. Wei Lee would have Tommy talk to this man Perez. Tommy would know how to put an end to inflation.

Lee went over to his enormous acrylic desk and pressed a button on his phone.

"Yes, Mr. Lee."

"Lynn, call Tommy and Henry. I want to see them right away."

"Yes, Mr. Lee."

He sat down in his chair and stared out at the Pacific. More people would be here soon. More girls. He felt a stirring in his loins.

They'd travelled so far and were now so thin. But today they were in a nice house to begin their recuperation. Don't worry girls, your parents are safe. Some paper work and processing has to be done, then you will be reunited. This separation is only temporary, it's just normal procedure, it's the American system. All that's important now is for you to get your health back. You must eat. You must sleep.

I am a doctor and will help you get well again. Each day you will receive an injection. Some vitamins for your health and something to help you sleep. Sleep is so important for you now. The man in the white coat would stroke their hair, cup a pale face in his hands, then take hold of an arm, squeeze until a vein appeared, and insert the needle. China Cat. The best, and only the best, for his girls.

Most of his girls didn't want the injection. The feisty ones would need a little slap. And perhaps another. And perhaps one more, just for good measure, the last one a little harder. They would all receive their first injection. Then they lay back and floated away, oblivious and numb. The next day some of the girls didn't want another injection. No doctor, please, your injection made me sick. Another slap. Then another, this one harder. And again, harder still. The second injection was much better. Floating, euphoria, numb, rendered weak with pleasure. A pleasure they'd never known. For the third injection, all the girls acquiesced. By the end of the first week they were injecting themselves. By the end of the second week they were begging for their injection. The man in the white coat was now examining them before each injection. You must remove your clothes dear. So young you are, what soft skin you have, so soft down there too. And look how healthy you've become! None of the girls liked their examinations. Not at first. But now it was alright. Nothing else mattered anymore. First the examination. Then the injection. Anything for the injection. Anything to please you, Doctor Lee.

"Mr. Lee, Henry and Tommy are here to see you."

"Send them in."

Henry Tai was the first to enter Wei Lee's office. Tai was refined and diminutive, a thin short man about sixty, impeccably dressed in a finely tailored suit. He had wire frame glasses and ornate cuff links that complimented his delicate hands. Henry was a fifth generation Chinese-American. His ancestors had been 'imported labor' during the 1849 California gold rush. But Henry was as American as apple pie. Born in San Francisco, he spoke English and Mandarin, had an MBA from Stanford, and was a CPA. Henry had a network of influential people in every ethnic and business community in LA. Wei Lee highly valued that network. Henry was his greatest asset. Henry had shown him the secret to wealth and tax avoidance. Borrowing. 'There is no tax on what you borrow', Henry liked to say. 'Whoever borrows the most, wins'.

Henry Tai's polar opposite struggled to get through the door. Tommy Kay took up his usual position, standing against the inner wall, just inside the door. Tommy didn't like tall buildings and he certainly didn't like being anywhere near those floor to ceiling windows in Mr. Lee's new office. Tommy was a second generation Korean-American, born and raised in east Los Angeles. Thirty years old, he was only medium height, but built like a linebacker on steroids. His head sat on his shoulders without any visible neck. His muscles were so overdeveloped he struggled to walk. Tommy spent three hours every morning pumping iron. He spent his afternoons at a fight club, sparring with professional cage fighters. His drooping eyelids, buzz cut, and reptilian stare exuded the menace of a professional enforcer. Tommy stood with his thick arms splayed out at his sides, waiting to be addressed by his boss.

"Tommy, whose suit are you wearing today?" Lee asked.

"Armani, Mr. Lee."

"Tommy, they look so tight on you, you look so uncomfortable in an Armani. You should wear a Boss, it's a much better cut for you."

"I like Armani, Mr. Lee."

"Henry, good to see you my friend, how are you?" Lee held out an open hand, beckoning his accountant to a plush chair in front of his desk.

"I am fine, Mr. Lee, but Lucky Star, it has… challenges."

"Challenges? You mean problems, Henry? We always solve our problems, right Tommy? Henry, what kind of problems does Lucky Star have?"

"Too much cash," Mr. Lee, "too much cash in Haines."

"Ah, too much cash in Haines, but a wonderful problem to have, right gentlemen?"

"Yes, Mr. Lee," said Henry.

"Yes, Mr. Lee," said Tommy.

"Too much cash in Haines," Wei Lee repeated to himself, pondering the concept for a moment. He walked over to the tall windows with his hands clasped behind his back, gazing at the layer of smog smothering Los Angeles. "Henry, do you know this cockroach Perez, our import broker?"

"Yes, Mr. Lee."

"Henry, why does Perez call me every month wanting to meet? He says he only wants to talk business, but always he asks for more money. His job is so simple. Just release a few containers each month for Lucky Star."

"It's the Homeland Security, Mr. Lee, they are making everything much more difficult now. They have new x–ray machines. They x-ray every container leaving the port. They are looking for bombs and weapons inside the containers."

Wei Lee turned and looked at Henry. "These x-ray machines can see inside a container?"

"Yes, they can see everything inside a container, they can even take pictures."

"Through steel, they can take pictures?"

"Yes, Mr. Lee."

Wei Lee turned and walked over to Tommy. "Tommy, do you know this man, Perez?"

"No, Mr. Lee."

Lee walked back to his desk but didn't sit down. "Henry, tonight I have a dinner meeting with this man named Perez. But you will go instead, Henry. Tommy, you will go with Henry. Henry, explain to Mr. Perez that Lucky Star will pay no more than our current monthly fee for his services. And Tommy, after dinner, explain to Mr. Perez what will happen if there are problems clearing Lucky Star's containers."

"Yes, Mr. Lee," they said in unison.

"Good. That problem is solved. You see gentlemen? When we solve problems together, we succeed. And when we can't solve problems, we eliminate problems, right Tommy?"

"Yes, Mr. Lee."

"Good. Now Henry, what is this problem with too much cash in Haines? How can too much cash be a problem? We are still flying our cash to the Yukon, are we not?"

"Yes, Mr. Lee. To Whitehorse. Whenever there is gold to buy, we fly our cash in Haines up to Whitehorse, in boxes of fish, in a small plane. But right now there is no gold to buy. That is the problem. So we must wait. Our fisherman in Haines has all our cash stored in his warehouse. That is a very big risk for us, to trust a fisherman in Alaska with so much of our cash."

"So the solution is simple. We need to find someone to sell us the gold we need. This should be easy. Then we can fly our cash to the Yukon."

"It is not so easy to buy gold in the spring, Mr. Lee. The mining season in Dawson has just begun and there has been very little gold production so far. Our gold buyer says it will be weeks before he has all the gold we want to buy."

"Then Henry, while we wait for this gold production, perhaps we should fly our cash directly to our mine, keep it there, stop packing it in boxes with fish and storing it in Haines."

"That will add risk, Mr. Lee," said Henry. "Our fish pilot does not know what's in the boxes of fish. Only the fisherman knows. Our fish pilot always clears Canadian customs in Whitehorse when he flies our cash into Canada. He thinks he is importing fish. The fewer people who know about our cash, the less the risk. If we fly our cash directly to the mine, there can be no customs inspection. The fish pilot may refuse to enter Canada without a customs inspection. We may have to tell him about the cash in the boxes. He would be one more man to trust."

Wei Lee looked at the ocean and was quiet for a moment.

"Henry, can we trust our mine manager with our cash?"

"I don't know, Mr. Lee."

"Our fish pilot, would he co-operate, would he fly our cash to the mine, with the right offer?"

"Perhaps yes, perhaps no, Mr. Lee. Perhaps he is the type of pilot who always insists on a customs inspection for his cargo. Or perhaps he will refuse to fly cash into Canada. Or perhaps he will be like our last fisherman."

"Oh? What happened to our last fisherman. Tommy?"

Tommy looked at Lee and shrugged.

"He was stealing. He had an accident."

Wei Lee nodded and walked back to his desk. The *last* fisherman had been working on his boat one evening in Haines. Apparently he had hit his head on something and been knocked out. He had fallen overboard into the harbor and drowned. The next morning his wife found him floating under the dock, right beside his boat. The newspaper had called it a tragic accident. Tommy had found a new fisherman.

"Who else, Henry? What about the man who sells gold to us? Our gold buyer in Dawson. Can he be trusted?"

"He may be our best choice, Mr. Lee. He is a discreet man and has excellent security."

"Then he is our man. The problem is solved. From now on we will fly all our cash from Haines to our gold buyer in Dawson. And there will be no more customs inspections. Now Henry, what is the name of our gold buyer in Dawson?"

"His name is Ralph, Mr. Lee."

"Tommy, do you know this man, this gold buyer named Ralph?"

"Yes, Mr. Lee."

"Good, Tommy. Tonight you will leave for Dawson, after you have dinner with Henry. Lynn will make the arrangements. My associate in Las Vegas is also sending a man to Dawson. You will meet this man from Las Vegas in Alaska. You will travel with him to Dawson. My associate also needs to buy gold. You will help his man buy some gold. And Tommy, find the pilot who flies our fish to Canada. Explain to him the new opportunity he must take advantage of. From now on, the fish pilot will fly all our cash directly to Dawson and deliver it to this man named Ralph. Tell the fish pilot that there will be no more flights to Whitehorse and no more customs inspections of our cargo. Make sure the fish pilot understands his new responsibilities and that he takes them very seriously. You will make all the arrangements, Tommy. And Tommy, business is very good now, we have a lot of cash coming in, we need to buy all the gold available. Tell our mine manager to produce more gold at the mine. And tell our gold buyer, this man Ralph, tell him that we will be buying all his gold this summer, whatever he can sell us, whenever it is available. Now Henry, do we have any more problems? We are here to solve problems. We always solve our problems."

"Well, Mr. Lee, yesterday I spoke with our mine manager."

"And?"

"He spoke about the pilot who has been flying our gold from Dawson to our mine. He says our gold pilot was seen talking to the police in Dawson. And also to another man, an American, perhaps also with the police."

"The police? Who is this pilot who flies our gold?"

"His name is Robert."

"What do you know about him?"

"That's all I know, Mr. Lee."

"Tommy, do you know this man Robert? Our gold pilot?"

"Yes, Mr. Lee."

"Good. When you get to Dawson, Tommy, talk to him. Find out if he has been talking to the police. If there is a problem, solve the problem. If you cannot solve the problem, eliminate the problem."

"Yes, Mr. Lee."

"Thank you, Tommy. You may go now. Call me from the Yukon."

Tommy Kay turned to leave.

"And Tommy?"

Tommy looked back.

"Try on a Boss. You will be much more comfortable in a Boss."

"Yes, Mr. Lee."

Tommy Kay squeezed through the door and walked down the middle of the hall, his massive arms and legs swinging in wide arcs as he made his way to the elevator.

"Henry," said Lee, gazing at the ships below him. "This pilot who flies our fish to Whitehorse, do you think we can trust him to fly our cash, *and* our gold?"

"I don't know, Mr. Lee."

"Have you met him, or spoken to him?"

"No, Mr. Lee."

"What is his name, our fish pilot?"

"His name is Brody."

FIVE

I had lots to do in the next half hour: light a fire, have a shower, feed the dogs, *and*, cook dinner. For two.

I climbed the steps to the deck, walked into the screened porch, grabbed an armful of firewood, and entered my cabin. I set the wood down beside the airtight stove in the corner, opened its doors, stuffed some newspaper and kindling inside, and put a match to it. I closed the doors and opened the vents so the fire would have air.

In my tiny U-shaped kitchen I opened the main valve for the propane range, set the oven temperature to four hundred, turned on a burner, filled a pot with water, dropped in six small potatoes, and put the pot on the burner.

At the back of my cabin is a closet full of electrical equipment and batteries. I opened the closet door and checked the gauges for my wind powered electrical system. The windmill on the pole outside was generating just under 200 watts, good, the bank of storage batteries had a charge of 13 volts, good, and the inverter output showed 122 volts. All good. I flipped the master switch and presto, there was 120 volt electric power throughout the cabin. Last, I looked up at the polystyrene water tank sitting over the rafters. It was full. Everything was copacetic. I went back to the wood stove, placed a couple of logs on the grate, and closed the door.

From my little propane fridge I grabbed a head of fresh romaine lettuce and a handful of cherry tomatoes, rinsed enough lettuce for two salads, and put it all in the dish rack to drain. Then I poured some olive oil and lemon juice into a wooden bowl, added lots of grated parmesan cheese, some dried ground garlic, a little black pepper, and gave it a stir.

I went into the bathroom, turned on the tankless water heater, got the shower running to a perfect temperature, stripped down, and stepped in for my standard four minute shower: two minutes for body and hair, and two minutes to shave. A long time ago a friend of mine told me that he shaved in the shower. One day last year I tried it myself. Practice makes perfect and I'm pretty good at it now. There's not a better place to shave than under a hot shower and I like the idea of being ready to go when I step out. I toweled off, brushed my hair, put on a clean pair of jeans and a fresh shirt, and went back out to the kitchen.

The pot of potatoes was boiling away. They'd be ready soon. In a coffee cup I mixed some Dijon mustard with mayonnaise and ground garlic, then opened the fridge and took out a fresh sockeye salmon. I cut off three good sized steaks, placed each one on a piece of foil, spread Dijon over two of them, wrapped them up, and put them in the oven. The clock on the wall said eight. Sarah Marsalis would be here in fifteen minutes. So far, so good.

I sliced the cherry tomatoes into halves, broke the lettuce into pieces, and dropped the works with some croutons into the wooden bowl.

The only alcohol in the cabin was a bottle of Riesling that I'd been keeping for a special occasion. I wondered if this was a special occasion. Then I wondered if it would be presumptuous of me to have an open bottle of wine on the counter when my guest arrived. Maybe if there was just one glass on the counter, it wouldn't be. On the contrary, perhaps it would simply convey the impression that I was just incredibly sophisticated. Whatever, I decided to open the wine, plucked a glass off a shelf, and poured myself a short one. Considering how long it had been in the cupboard, it wasn't bad. Not for ten bucks.

The dogs were leading the way, pattering across the deck in front of *Miss* Marsalis when she appeared in the big front window. Her hair was wet and her face flushed from the fresh air. She looked radiant.

"Come in," I yelled, before she could knock.

"Hey," she said, walking in behind the dogs. "Wow, this place is nice, it's so modern, what a great place to have a cabin! That river is amazing, it moves so fast! Just a beautiful color too!"

"That's the Yukon River, the fourth longest in North America. And the cleanest one."

"Really? Hey, it smells good in here," she said, "can I help with anything?" She was obviously feeling a lot better after her shower. She was dressed as I'd last seen her, though now she wore a white cotton turtleneck under her fleece jacket.

"Well, you could toss that salad on the counter, we're about ready here."

The potatoes were done. I turned off the burner, drained the pot, dropped in a hunk of herb butter, cut the potatoes into pieces, and gave them a quick stir. Then I opened the oven, took out the salmon, and put all three pieces on top of the stove. I opened the one without Dijon and poked it with a fork. Done to perfection. For the first time since they'd set eyes on Miss Marsalis, my dogs were actually interested in something else. They were sitting at my feet, wagging their tails, fixated on my every move. I went outside to retrieve their bowls and they followed me. I walked back inside and they followed me. I split the piece of salmon, mashed it up in their bowls, added some dog food, and carried their bowls outside. They followed me. They would have followed me off a cliff. They buried their noses in their bowls.

Back inside, I pulled two plates out of a cupboard, put a steak and some potatoes on each one, and poured the remaining butter in the pot over the potatoes.

"Salad on the plates?" she asked.

A wobbly nod was all I could muster when she smiled at me. What a smile.

She sat down at my table for two beside the kitchen window. I put the plates down and asked, "Water, wine or both?"

"Just water, please."

I filled a glass under my filtered water tap and brought it over to the table with my wine.

"This looks amazing, Mr., sorry…, Brody."

"Dig in," I said, sitting down. "Hope you enjoy it."

We were both hungry. Eating was a perfect distraction while thinking about an appropriate topic for a dinner conversation with a perfect stranger. We both gazed out at the river often.

Finally she spoke. "Where did you get this fresh lettuce, and these tomatoes? And the salmon, it's all excellent".

"Thanks. Well, the salmon I got in Alaska yesterday, and the vegetables came in today on the bus with the parts for your car."

"This lettuce came in with my car parts?"

"Yeah," I said. "The woman at the parts store in Whitehorse, she always sends me fresh vegetables with my parts orders. In fact, in August she sends me tomatoes that she grows in her own green house."

"This woman, does she have a name? She must be someone special." Sarah Marsalis was smiling, tilting her head with what might easily be construed as a playful tease.

"Yeah, her name's Christine. She's just a friend, that's all. She sends me vegetables when she sends me car parts, and I bring her salmon when I visit Whitehorse. I guess she's a special woman, who happens to live with a special guy, who isn't me."

"Look I didn't mean to…"

"Hey, that's okay. I mean if someone sent you a head of Romaine lettuce and a bag of cherry tomatoes in a box full of brake parts, well if you think about it, that could be construed as a very romantic gesture, certainly very suggestive."

She smiled. "Brody?"

"Yes?"

"Please call me Sarah. And may I have a glass of wine to finish this incredible meal?"

Wow. 'Call me Sarah'. And now she wants wine. Things were looking up. I got up and poured her a glass of wine. "There you go, *Sarah.*"

"Thanks, *Brody.*" She looked at me and drank. "Not bad," she said, though not like she meant it.

We both ate like we were hungry, which of course we were. When we'd finished everything on our plates, we leaned back and looked out the window to see two happy dogs with their noses pressed up against the glass, their tails wagging furiously, entirely blocking our view of the river, fixated on my dinner guest.

"They sure like you," I said.

"I noticed."

"Everything okay with the lodgings?"

"Yes, thanks. Great shower."

"Sorry that I didn't think to leave you a hair dryer," I said, admiring her shiny wet hair. "There's one in my tool box, I'll get it out for you later. How about we finish our wine outside?"

"Good idea," she said.

We cleared the table and went outside to the delight of the dogs. I looked at their bowls. They were polished to a sheen. I unfolded a couple of old aluminum patio chairs and set them down on the deck. We sat in silence for a while, watching and listening to the river, looking west at the mauves and magentas on the mountains. The dogs got a whiff of something, leapt off the deck, and charged off into the woods.

"It's still so bright outside. Will it get dark later?" she asked.

"No. You'll be able to read a newspaper outside any time of day for another eight weeks."

"That's unreal. It's like being able to see what the world looks like at night."

"Never thought of it that way."

"The Yukon River. Where does it go?"

"All the way to the Bering sea. If you wanted, you could put a canoe in the water right in front of us and paddle all the way across Alaska to the Pacific Ocean."

"Wow."

"Wow, indeed."

"How far to the Pacific?"

"About fifteen hundred miles."

"That's a long way."

"Yeah, a very long way. You know for seventy years that river in front of you was the only way to get to the Klondike gold fields, unless you walked in. The old paddlewheel steamboats used to carry passengers and supplies upstream all the way from the Bering Sea to Dawson. And some of them would continue on up to Whitehorse. If we were sitting here in the early fifties, we might have seen a paddle wheeler go past us tonight. They used to stop just down the river from here to load up with wood for their boilers. That's what put Minto on the Yukon map. When they finished building the Klondike Highway in 1956, that was the end of the paddle wheeler era, and the end of Minto."

"Interesting". She paused. "It's so beautiful here. You must like living here."

"I must. It's a mystical place. It draws you in like a magnet. It turns you into a philosopher, or at least it makes you philosophical. It has an attraction that can't be explained."

"What's that whirring behind us?" she asked.

"It's a windmill, generates electric power for the cabin."

"You don't have electricity?"

"Ah, but I do have electricity. I generate it with wind. The nearest power pole is up at the shop. They wanted too much money to bring power lines down here, so I put up a windmill."

"That is so cool." She was quiet for a minute. "So what brought you up here, Brody?"

"A job. A summer job. The old fellow who built the shop was an amazing and self-sufficient man. But his eyes and his body started failing him about six years ago. When he realized he needed some help, I happened to be the guy he hired. As it turned out, he had lots of work, but there were too many customers that weren't paying their bills, so he often couldn't pay me. He felt badly about that.

But I liked him, and liked life up here so much – had no where else to go anyway – so kept working for him the rest of the summer. I told him I knew he'd pay me when he could. That fall I went back down to Phoenix for the winter. Got a phone call one day from a lawyer in Whitehorse, told me the old man had died, that he'd left me everything. When his kids threatened to contest the will, I decided to try settling with them instead of going to court. So I raised some cash, got a bank loan, and paid the kids to go away. That was five years ago. Don't know why I felt compelled to keep the business going, but the old man had survived here ever since the highway opened. He seemed to have a viable business if customers would only pay their bills. So that's why I did, what I did. That's why I'm here."

"Do you stay here all year?"

"No, there's not enough business to make it worthwhile in the winter ,which is a great rationalization for going south in the fall."

"And your cabin? It looks new."

"Yeah, built it last year. I realized a couple of years ago that every time I felt stressed out about something, I'd find myself down here in this exact spot, just watching the river. It always helped me to put things in perspective. So I figured it would be a good place to call home. A First Nations band owns most of the land around here, so I made a deal with Minnie's husband, he was the chief of the local band, he's deceased now, he leased me the land. Minnie's the woman who runs the café…"

"First Nations band?"

"What Americans call an Indian tribe, here we call it a First Nations band. And the people that Americans call Indians, here we call them natives. Or aboriginals. All the land around us here is owned by a First Nations band."

We were quiet for a long time.

"My turn to ask you a question," I said.

She inhaled deeply, apparently not thrilled about the prospect.

"Go ahead," she said.

"Your car. It's getting up there in years."

She seemed to relax a little. "Is that your question?"

"I'm just curious why you'd be driving an old Toyota on a wilderness highway, when you look like you…"

"Might be driving something a little newer?" She laughed. "It's my brother's old car. He lives in Juneau. He bought it brand new fifteen years ago when he finished college and started his first real job back east. Two years later he was transferred to Juneau and took the car with him. He finally bought a new one last month. When I called him a couple of weeks ago and told him I was going to the Yukon, he insisted that I visit his family in Juneau. Told me that he'd lend me his old Corolla, that it was still reliable, that I should take the opportunity to do some sightseeing. So I flew to Juneau. He was out of town on business when I arrived, I knew he would be, but I had a nice visit with his wife and met my two nephews for the first time. Then I borrowed his car. Drove it onto a ferry in Juneau and cruised up to Skagway along the Alaska coast. It was an awesome experience, just like he said it would be. I left Skagway two days ago and should have been in Dawson by now, but got sabotaged by that local cop of yours. So that's it."

I sat there for a minute thinking about the breathtaking scenery along the inland passage from Juneau to Skagway, and then for some reason about the warning Daryl had laid on me earlier. *Stay away.* Why? She seemed so nice.

"One more glass of wine left, Sarah." I pointed at her empty glass.

"Better not," she said, "I really need to get some sleep. What time is it?"

I looked at the sun, still high in the western sky. "About ten."

"Ten? Really? Hey, I need to go," she said. "Did you arrange a plane for me?"

"It's all set. I'll drive you back to the shop. There's no phone down here and I need to make a call."

We got in my truck and idled up the dirt lane toward my shop. Halfway there the dogs appeared in the rearview mirror, loping along behind us in a cloud of dust, working off their gourmet dinner. When we went inside the shop, I walked over to one of my tool chests and rummaged around for my hair dryer, something I never use to dry hair.

"Here you are," I said, wiping it off with a rag. "You probably ought to dry your hair to avoid that porcupine look in the morning. And you really don't want to catch a cold, either. I need to call someone. How about you go upstairs and dry your hair, and I'll make my call. Then I'll show you where you need to go in the morning to meet your plane. Okay?"

"Sounds like a plan," she said. The dogs followed her to the back of the shop, sat down and watched her climb the stairs. Their tails were wagging. Mine would be too. Lucky dogs.

I dialed the bar at the café. It rang six times before Minnie's daughter, Leah, picked up.

"Leah, it's Brody, is Reggie there?"

"Reggie, phone!" she screamed. The phone went clunk on the counter. Not a 'just a moment', or a 'hang on', or a 'one moment please'. Just a clunk. I guess Minnie did enough talking for both mother and daughter put together. For a couple of minutes I listened to country and western music, and a lot of shouting and laughing.

"Hello."

"Reggie, it's Brody. Are you sober?"

"Yeah."

"Reggie, I'm serious, are you sober enough to take a barrel of gas out to the lake tonight?"

"Yeah."

"Good. Listen carefully. Fill the center tank and put the rest in the front, okay?"

"Okay."

"Reggie, repeat what I just said."

"One barrel, fill the center tank, the rest in front."

"Perfect. Thanks, Reg. You won't let me down?"

"Nope. Hey Brody?"

"What?"

"Daryl's looking for you."

"Well, if you see him, tell him I'll be back at noon tomorrow."

"He says it's really important. He wants you to call him right away."

"And I said I'll be back at noon, so tell him I'll call him then."

"Okay."

"Thanks, Reg."

"Okay."

Click.

Reggie was the greatest friend anyone could ever hope to have. He was so just so reliable and dedicated. What's more important than that? I pulled the phone line out of the wall jack so Sarah Marsalis wouldn't be disturbed tonight. Like by Daryl, for instance. I don't have an answering machine, and when I'm not here, I'm not here.

I was stooped over under the stairs, filling the big pan of drinking water for my dogs when Sarah Marsalis stepped out of the apartment above me. I stood up and hit my head, then swore.

"Everything okay down there?" she asked, starting down the stairs.

"Yeah, fine, sorry, bumped my head, that's all." I rubbed my head. Damn wine.

I went over to the bench, grabbed a pen, and tore a flap off a cardboard box. She followed and stood beside me.

"Okay, I'm going to draw you a map," I said. "Watch and learn." She leaned in close to my shoulder. I could smell the shampoo in her hair. *Just concentrate on what you're doing, fool.* "This is simple. You go out the lane here to the highway, turn left, and go seven miles north." I was drawing the map as I talked. "You'll see a big brown sign on your right for the government campground. Turn right into the campground, go to the back of the campground, and you'll see a road that goes down to the lake. It's a couple of hundred feet to the lake, then turn right, and you'll see the plane. You're expected at eight, so give yourself about twenty minutes to get there."

She took the map out of my hand, hiked up a hip, and slid it into a rear pocket of her tight jeans. It was an amazing sight to behold.

"It's a sea plane?"

"What? Yeah, a plane on floats, a float plane."

"Do I need a float plane?"

"It's what's available."

"What if I need to land?"

"There's a lot more water around here than airports, so if you need to land, there's always a place."

"Oh," she said. She stood back from the bench and looked at me. "Now then, Brody. We have some unfinished business." She reached into her jacket pocket and plucked out four twenty dollar bills with the first two fingers of her right hand. She held them up high, rotating her wrist back and forth. "You have something for me I believe?"

I reached into my shirt pocket and pulled out her credit card with the first two fingers of my right hand. I held it up high, rotating my wrist back and forth. We each reached out for the other's right hand with our left hand. We stared at each other, perhaps a little too long for strangers. The exchange must have looked like a tango step.

"Do I need to count it?" I asked.

"You should always count cash."

"I won't."

We looked at each other for a moment.

"Well, Brody," she said, "thank you very much for a wonderful dinner, and for fixing my car. I really enjoyed my evening. And I really enjoyed meeting you."

"Me too, Sarah. Hey, maybe on your way back, if you had time, you might drop in again, if you wanted to that is, I mean if you had time. I could cook Mexican."

"Mexican. I like Mexican. I might just do that," she said with a smile that I'm sure always got her what she wanted.

She extended her hand to me. I shook it. It was soft but strong. She put her hands in the front pockets of her blue jeans and looked at me for a moment. *What?* Then she stood on her toes, kissed me on the cheek, and turned for the stairs. I watched her walk away. Damn. *She just kissed me.*

When I'd fully recovered, I looked over at my dogs. They were sitting at the bottom of the stairs, wagging their tails, watching Sarah Marsalis climb up to the apartment. I opened my mouth to call them, then stopped. Never mind, I thought. You guys want to stay here tonight.

Who wouldn't?

SIX

I never get tired of admiring my plane.

It's a 1952 DeHavilland DHC-2, mounted on floats. The most iconic bush plane in aviation history.

Just after the Second World War, and after much consulting with the bush pilots who would fly it, DeHavilland Canada set out to build an aircraft specifically designed for the Canadian wilderness. It was to be the first all metal, short take off and landing aircraft made expressly for frontier flying. DeHavilland called their new plane the Beaver. As it turned out, for the next sixty years no aircraft became more synonymous with flying in the Canadian hinterland, and for that matter, in any other frontier, anywhere else in the world.

The Beaver was designed to fly half a ton of cargo into any remote location in the Canadian north, and to take off and land on any kind of terrain, in any kind of weather, at any time of year. If you need to land a Beaver on a lake or river, you put it on floats. If there's an airstrip where you're going, you put it on wheels. If there's ice or snow on the ground, you put it on skis.

DeHavilland made 1692 Beavers, all of them in Canada, the first in 1947, the last in 1967, and they were sold to customers all over the world. The US military bought 980 Beavers and nicknamed it the 'general's jeep' during the Korean war. There's a lake, a glacier and an island named after the Beaver in Antarctica, where the New Zealand government used them to map over a million square miles. Sir Edmund Hillary used a Beaver to outfit his expedition to Nepal, where he climbed Mount Everest in 1953. Fidel Castro's regimental plane during the 1959 Cuban Revolution was a Beaver, purportedly the first one to be fitted with a cigar lighter.

Though it's been over forty-five years since the last one was built, there are still more than a thousand Beavers flying all over the world. People might wonder why a plane designed in the 1940's, with an engine designed in the 1920's, can possibly still be in daily service. The answer is simple. The Beaver is still the best plane ever made to do a job that hasn't changed. It's strong, rugged, reliable, powerful, easy to maintain, *and*, will take off, fly and land with just about anything you can fit inside it, or tie to the floats outside. A Beaver pilot was probably the first to say 'If it fits, it ships'. Canadian bush pilots didn't call it the *flying half ton truck* for nothing.

I arrived at the lake at seven thirty. Two Spirit Lake is a small shallow lake that's a mile and a half long, and a little under a mile wide. It's longest section is roughly oriented east to west, but with a uniform shore line, an absence of islands, and low surrounding terrain, I can safely takeoff and land in almost any direction. Being shallow means that any wind will quickly blow up short choppy waves, but it rarely gets the big rolling ones that can flip a float plane over. But what's most appealing to me about Two Spirit Lake, other than being so close to home, is that I've rarely seen a motor boat roaring around it at high speed. My worst nightmare is always crossing paths with a boater who isn't paying attention, and can't hear me coming over the sound of his own engine. So far so good on the quiet little lake.

I surveyed the sky. It promised to be another clear day. I grabbed two canvas duffle bags out of the back of my truck and carried them over to the dock, then picked up a wooden plank and laid it across the front of the floats. I stepped out to the center of the plank, held on to the prop for support, and removed the cloth cover from the engine cowl. I poked my head in the cowl and looked around for bird's nests and oil leaks around each of the nine cylinders, then checked the oil cooler inlet underneath to make sure it was clear too. I ran my hands over the prop blades and inspected them for nicks or cracks, then stepped over to the right float, opened a hatch door, and took out a hand operated pump. I shuffled up and down both floats, pumping a little water out of each of their compartments. It's beyond me how water always manages to get into my floats, even though they're not supposed to leak. I stowed the pump, stepped back on the dock, picked up the plank, and slid it across the floats midway down the fuselage. With my knees on the plank, and using a clear plastic beaker designed for the task, I collected a sample of gas from each of the three fuel tanks. I held the beaker up to the sky and looked for any sign of water at the bottom. There was none. That was good, because internal combustion engines run very poorly on water. I lifted the plank off the floats and laid it down on the dock. Last, I opened a duffle bag full of ropes and took out the one on top – my favorite – a sixty foot nylon rope with clips braided into either end.

I unlocked the cargo door, shoved the landing rope under the left seat, climbed up the ladder, crawled into the cargo bay, and stored the duffle bags and the engine cover behind a net at the back. Then I stepped between the front seats and sat down in the left one. That's my seat. I unlocked both cockpit doors then leaned over to check the engine oil. It was full. A great feature of the Beaver is that you can actually check and add engine oil from inside the cockpit, even during flight. Is that a good idea or what? I turned on the master switch to check the fuel gauge. The center tank was full. Reggie hadn't let me down. I pushed the mixture lever ahead to full rich, pumped the primer five times, and hit the starter button. After the prop rotated a few revolutions, I turned on the mags. The big radial engine popped and coughed a few times, then roared to life. I set the idle at five hundred rpm and went through the pre-takeoff checklist. When heat was showing on the oil and cylinder temperature gauges, I turned the engine off.

I was studying a map spread out on the hood of my truck when Sarah Marsalis arrived in her little car. I pointed to where she should park. She got out with a perplexed look.

"Good morning. What are you doing here?" she asked with that radiant smile of hers.

"You wanted to fly today?"

"You know I wanted to fly today. Is the pilot here yet?"

"You're looking at him."

"You? You're the pilot?"

"Yup. I'm your pilot. And there's your plane. Ready to go?"

"Well, you son of a bitch! You set me up! You conned me!"

"Hey," I said. "That's *Captain* son of a bitch to you. And I didn't set you up and I didn't con you."

"Are you kidding me? All that friendly advice about chartering out of here instead of Dawson? That conference over the hood of your truck? Your proposal? Cooking me dinner? Putting me up for the night? You are so full of it! You hustled me for a plane charter! God! This place is diabolical! Crooked cops and con men!"

"I'm not a con man. All my advice yesterday was completely valid. And if you'd asked me who your pilot was, I would have told you. But you never asked, so I didn't say. So what? What difference does it make anyway?"

"Because you were not forthright with me!"

"Look, do you want to fly or not?"

She glared at me with her hands on her hips, considering her options.

"In that?" She pointed at my plane.

"Yeah, in that."

"Is it safe? It looks ancient."

"It's not ancient. It's just experienced, like me, and it's very safe."

"Oh, why ask you anyway?" she said, throwing her hands in the air. "Like you'd give me an honest answer. That thing looks like it belongs in a junkyard."

"Hey, you can say whatever you want to me, but leave my plane out of this."

"You are a case, Mr. Brody, a real case," she said, turning her back.

"Look, I'm sorry you feel you got hustled. But the way I see it, you need to make a decision. Fly with me now, then drive to Dawson this afternoon, *or*, drive to Dawson now, and see if you can find someone else to fly you this afternoon. And for a lot more money, by the way. Now what's it going to be?"

She had her arms folded and was staring out at the lake. I waited.

"Alright," she said finally. "We'll go. But don't talk to me. And you can bet your last dollar that we will definitely not be eating Mexican any time soon. Got that?"

"Got that. But I have to ask you a couple of questions if we're going flying."

"Like what?"

"Like where exactly do you want to go? How about you show me on this map over here."

She walked over to my truck, then yanked a glossy photograph out of her day pack and slammed it down so hard on my map it made the hood bounce. Hell hath no fury.

"There," she said, pointing to what looked like a mine in a narrow creek valley. Written in felt pen on the satellite photograph were the GPS co-ordinates, with an arrow pointing at the mine.

"That's Thistle creek. It runs into the Yukon River. So what do we do when we get there? Do you want to land?"

"No. I just want to take some pictures of that mine." She tapped the spot on the photograph. "You circle around the mine a couple of times, I'll take some shots, then we come back here."

"That's it?"

"That's it."

"Let's go then."

When we stepped on the dock she stopped, put her hands on her hips again, and looked disapprovingly at my plane.

"You're absolutely sure this thing's safe?"

"Absolutely sure."

"What are all those buttons on the outside?"

"They're not buttons. They're rivets."

"Why are there so many? What are they for?"

"They hold the plane together."

"They look like buttons."

"I guess they do," I said, holding the cargo door open for her. "After you, please. You sit up there, in the right seat." She turned and glared at me. Wow. Still mad as hell. I closed the cargo door after her and was about to climb the pilot's ladder when I saw it.

It was in a ziplock plastic bag wired to a rung on the ladder. I untwisted the wire and took it out of the bag. It was a copy of a page faxed to Daryl last evening from the RCMP detachment in Dawson. It was a SAR Alert. Now I knew why Daryl had been looking for me last night. He wanted to tell me that a 'Search and Rescue' was underway. I wondered if he'd driven down to the lake last night to deliver the notice. Hopefully it was Reggie who brought it down when he fueled the plane. Otherwise, Daryl would be angry with me. As usual.

I read the RCMP fax. Twice.

SAR ALERT
Issued 1 6 13 0600Z
NOCA Beaver, C-PYPY, 2 souls
YDA – 63 04N, 139 28W – JNA
JNA – 63 04N, 139 28W – YDA
ETD 1 6 13 1500Z
ETA 1 6 13 0200Z
OVERDUE

"Overdue," I murmured.

"What?"

"Nothing. Sorry."

"I said don't talk to me." She had her arms folded and was staring straight ahead at the console.

I put the note in my shirt pocket and looked at her. "Sorry, but I'm obligated to talk to you for just a minute." I pointed above her window. "Above your door is an inflatable lifejacket. If you need to use it, put it on, get out of the plane, pull the orange ball, and it will inflate. In front of you is a headset which you'll want to wear because the plane is loud. If you want to talk to me, press and hold down the button on the cord to speak. Release the button to listen. Fasten your seatbelt. There's a fire extinguisher behind your seat on the floor. I have bottled drinking water if you get thirsty. Under your seat is a first aid kit. There's an airsickness bag in your door pocket. Do you have any questions?"

"No."

"Good," I said.

I opened my door and stepped down on the dock. I untied the short rope from the front of the left float, walked to the rear of the float, untied another short rope, stood under the wing, grabbed the strut, and pushed the plane backwards down the dock. When it was almost at the end I gave it a good shove, stepped on the float, and climbed inside. A gusty wind was blowing out of the west. I waited until we'd drifted out twenty feet, then dropped the water rudders down, started the engine, stepped hard on the right rudder pedal, and gave it a little throttle. The plane turned and we headed east down the lake. I increased the engine speed to eight hundred RPM, set the flap control to 'takeoff', and pumped the lever beside my seat until the flaps were set. I turned on the GPS and entered the co-ordinates Sarah Marsalis had given me. I turned on the radios.

There was plenty of time to let everything warm up and go through the takeoff checklist. The wind would help push us down the lake, then we'd turn around and take off toward the west. I looked at my passenger again. She was leaning over to her right, watching the water splashing over the float below her. Everybody does that. I hoped she wasn't a nervous flier.

I plucked the SAR Alert out of my shirt pocket and read it again. I wondered if my friend Robert was the pilot. He flew a Beaver just like mine. His was owned by NOCA Air, a company based in

Dawson. Robert Duncan was a little younger than me, maybe in his mid-thirties, a very careful sensible pilot. I'd gone to Robert's wedding a couple of years ago in Dawson and knew he now had two mouths to feed. His wife Katy had given birth to a baby boy in January. Robert was a nice guy who worked hard at his craft. If he was the pilot of the overdue plane, I hoped he was alright.

I thought about the overdue plane's flight plan. The flight plan specified a round trip, about four hours each way. The SAR Alert said the plane departed the riverfront dock in Dawson yesterday morning at seven o'clock local time. Its destination was Juneau, Alaska, 435 miles south of Dawson. I noticed that the flight plan included a waypoint on the flight track to Juneau. The waypoint was seventy five miles due south of Dawson, almost exactly the same spot on Thistle Creek where I was flying Sarah Marsalis today. The NOCA plane was scheduled to have returned to Dawson by six o'clock last evening. I knew the skies had been perfectly clear all over the Yukon and southeast Alaska yesterday, so it was unlikely a weather related incident, and I doubted if Robert would ever make a mistake with fuel. It should be a straight forward search and rescue mission, and hopefully one with a happy ending. Even so, I wondered why anyone looking for the missing plane yesterday couldn't establish radio contact. Or hadn't picked up an SOS call, or an emergency locator transmission, or a satellite relay signal. Or had seen a flare. There was valid cause for concern.

When I reached the point halfway down the lake we were three thousand feet from the dock. I turned the plane around, pointed it into the wind, pulled up the handle to lift the rudders out of the water, pushed the prop lever all the way forward to fine pitch, the mixture lever ahead to full rich, checked my gauges one last time, pulled the yoke back a little, and pushed the throttle lever all the way forward. The engine roared and everything started to shake, like it always has and always will. Gobs of power pulled us forward. When the floats rose up on the water, I eased the yoke ahead and let the plane accelerate. At an airspeed of seventy miles an hour I pulled the yoke back.

It never changes no matter how many times you've done it. That thrill you get the instant you start flying. I looked over at *Miss Marsalis*. She was looking out her window and I doubt if she saw me smile. I looked down and watched the dock and our vehicles flash by, a few hundred feet below us.

I adjusted the elevator trim and the RPM, and when the airspeed indicator showed ninety miles an hour, pumped the flaps up to the climb setting. I eased the throttle back, started a slow turn toward the northwest, kept my eye on the GPS, and ended the turn at a compass heading of two hundred and ninety degrees. At thirty-five hundred feet I fully retracted the flaps – adjusted the elevator trim, the manifold pressure, and the prop pitch for level flight – then pulled the throttle back and slowed the engine to eighteen hundred RPM. I leveled off at four thousand feet with an airspeed of a hundred miles per hour. With a few more adjustments to the manifold pressure and prop pitch, my old plane was flying rock stable at a hundred and ten miles per hour. It was just before nine o'clock. I reached for the radio.

"Minto Café, this is Beaver, Papa Papa Alpha Golf." I waited a good minute before Minnie answered.

"This is Minto Café, go ahead Alpha Golf, over."

"Flight advisory, Two Spirit Lake now, to 63 04 North, 139 28 West, and return. ETA 2000 Zulu at Two Spirit Lake, two souls, over".

"Copy that, Two Spirit Lake to 63 04 North, 139 28 West, ETA 2000 Zulu, Two Spirit Lake, two souls, confirm, over."

"Roger that, thanks Minto, hey, is that SAR still active?"

"Affirmative, no news. Alpha Golf, who's your passenger? Over."

"See you at lunch, Minto Cafe. Over and out."

I counted ten seconds before I heard her growl, "Minto Café, over and out."

I knew it would drive Minnie crazy, wondering who I was flying with today. But soon enough she'd put two and two together and would start spreading the rumor of the day. Daryl would be mad, as usual, and he'd probably be waiting at the dock with a crowd of highway workers when we returned at noon.

"What's all that Papa Zulu SAR stuff?" came a voice in my headset that made me jump. I looked at my passenger. She had her thumb on the talk button. I flicked my thumb at her and she lifted her thumb off the button.

"I was just telling someone where we're going and when we're expected back. It's called a flight advisory. And a plane has been reported as overdue. There's a search and rescue underway, the letters S,A,R, – they spell SAR – search and rescue."

"What's Papa Zulu?"

"Papa Papa Alpha Golf is radio speak for P,P,A,G, the letters that identify this plane. And Zulu means Zulu time. That's the time in London, England. It's the universal time zone used in aviation. Wherever you happen to be, you convert Zulu time to your local time. I said we'd be back at 2000 Zulu, which is eight o'clock in the evening in London, and noon here."

She nodded once, said nothing, apparently unimpressed. I didn't think she was interested in radio jargon, or Zulu time. Maybe something else.

"Hey," I said, "did you know that all the land out there to our left is only three hundred million years old, but all the land out there to our right is over two billion years old?"

"Fascinating." She was getting the hang of the talk button.

"I'll tell you all about the Yukon's geology when we do Mexican," I said with a grin.

"Not going to happen," she said, shaking her head, though I caught her smiling when she turned away.

"Hey, did you let the dogs out?"

"Yes."

"Thanks. Hey, you want some water, or something to eat?"

"Stop talking. I told you not to talk to me. Be quiet."

I nodded. "Right. Sorry. Forgot."

I looked through the prop at the Pelly River, flowing in from the east, then the Yukon River, flowing up from the south. Once the two rivers have merged, the Yukon River becomes three times wider and carries twice the volume of water.

I'd flown this route hundreds of times. Whenever the weather is lousy, or the ceiling is low, I navigate to Dawson by following the Yukon River.

It always gets me there.

SEVEN

The GPS said ten miles to the mine. I adjusted the prop and throttle for descent, trimmed the nose down, and turned toward the top of the Thistle Creek valley.

"Five minutes," I said into my mike, "we'll turn left and fly due west down Thistle Creek to the Yukon River, then turn around, come back up the valley to the mine, and do a few circles. Ready?"

"Ready," she said, opening her backpack. She took out what looked like a high quality SLR camera with a zoom lens.

"Tell me if I'm too high or too low when we fly over the mine, okay?"

"Okay."

I figured a good height to take photos would be about five hundred feet. When we got to the top of the valley, I pulled the throttle lever back, pumped the flaps down to approach angle, and turned west. I watched the airspeed drop and the altimeter move as the plane descended. When we were five hundred feet over the valley floor, I lowered the flaps all the way down to the landing position, and put the plane into slow flight.

"Comin' up," I said.

A minute later the Thistle Creek mine appeared over the nose. The valley around the mine had been stripped bare of vegetation from one side to the other. On the north side of the creek was a camp. There was a large steel building – probably the maintenance shop – several personnel trailers, a couple of large orange fuel tanks, and numerous trucks of various type and size parked around the buildings. A dirt road skirted the north side of the valley and snaked its way through the camp, then disappeared into the trees below. I guessed it continued all the way down to the Yukon River. Four large bulldozers were crawling back and forth and three earth movers were hauling dirt to a large wash plant. Two excavators and two loaders were working around the plant. It had two rotating screen trommels and a large sluice box. A large water pipe ran from a man-made pond upstream down to the plant. The two trommels were rotating and foamy dark water was running down the sluice box. The excavators were busy feeding dirt into the trommels, and the loaders were taking away tailings from the end of the sluice box. It was a good sized Yukon gold mine and clearly in full operation.

"You can drop your window down now, all the way if you want, but hang on to your hat, it'll get windy in here," I said.

"Okay, when we do our circles." She had her camera out, pointing it at the ground, zooming the lens in and out, "A little lower if you can."

I descended another hundred feet and was flying due west now, straight down the center of the valley. We passed directly over the plant and I let the plane sink as we flew toward the Yukon River. I looked left and right at the hilltops on either side of the valley. The valley was shallow and wide, its sides sloping gently down to the creek at its center. There'd be enough room to safely make a three hundred and sixty degree turn over the mine site without knocking the tops off any trees.

I've never liked flying in low circles over anyone's private property, mostly because I wouldn't appreciate the intrusion myself. And I've never liked the idea of conducting surveillance four hundred feet off the deck because my plane's call letters can easily be seen by someone on the ground. I hoped no one from the mine cared, and at worst would assume the plane circling above them was just another bunch of busy bodies from the fisheries department. Whatever, I needed the business and the customer's always right.

A few minutes later I flew out of the valley, crossed the Yukon River, added some power, and put the plane into a thirty degree right hand turn. I looked over at Sarah to see if she felt comfortable with her new orientation to the ground below.

"That's what your circle will be like, okay?"

"Fine," she said, though I sensed she wasn't thrilled with the view of the ground rotating below her right shoulder.

When I finished the one hundred and eighty degree turn we were headed east, flying back up the creek valley along its north side. When the mine was over my right shoulder, I banked the plane over thirty degrees and held it in a steep right hand turn. She surprised me when she dropped her window down and a roar of cold air filled the cabin. She put the camera to her face and got busy, tapping her finger on the shutter button, moving the camera around. I concentrated on maintaining a flat continuous turn while watching our airspeed. When it comes to flying an airplane, nothing else matters without adequate airspeed. After the first three hundred and sixty degree turn was complete, she surprised me again by closing her window and giving me a thumbs up, though she did look a little pale. I held the plane over for another half turn, then leveled out and headed down the valley toward the river.

Sarah was looking at pictures on the camera's display.

"Get what you needed?" I asked.

She nodded.

"Hey, if you don't mind, I'd like to make a small detour," I said. "I won't charge you for the time, is that okay with you?"

"A detour ? Where? What for?"

"That SAR I told you about? The search and rescue? I just want to take a quick look down the river here to the north, just do my part to help out a little with the search. It'll only take about ten minutes. Okay?"

"Okay," she said, though without enthusiasm.

"Thanks. Appreciate it." I looked at her like I meant it. She didn't look at me. She had her head down and was scrolling through pictures on the camera display.

I kept the plane in slow flight, pumped the flaps all the way down to 'full', and reduced our airspeed to eighty miles per hour. I started a slow right turn to the north when I saw the Yukon River. We flew over a barge with a large fuel tank on its deck, moored to a dock. There was an outboard motor boat tied to the barge. I assumed they both belonged to the mine. I looked at the GPS. We were at the exact waypoint that Robert had filed in his flight plan. I descended gradually to a hundred feet off the river, leveled out, backed off the throttle a little more, and flew as slowly as I dared, about seventy miles an hour, heading due north along the right bank.

The Yukon River was wide in this section, perhaps a couple of thousand feet. To the west the land was flat and rolling, heavily treed, with a wide open shoreline. In contrast, the east shore on our right was rocky and narrow, littered with dead trees, and looked dark and foreboding in the shadows cast by steep, consolidated gravel cliffs rising almost straight up from the water, a hundred to a hundred and fifty feet high, and occasionally even more.

I surveyed the east bank as it rushed by. Tall, mature spruce trees that had fallen from the eroding cliffs were scattered and piled up everywhere along the river's edge. The tops of many fallen trees protruded well out into the river, their roots serving as great grapple hooks that anchored them to the rocks and boulders scattered along the shoreline, holding them steadfast against the incessant tug of the current. Large pieces of ice, remnants of the spring breakup, littered the rocky beach.

"What are you doing?" Sarah asked.

"Looking for a plane like this one. It's blue and white, but will look the same. It's on floats, too."

The river was wide and black and smooth but I knew the current would be at least five miles an hour. In the shadows of the high cliffs on our right, it was downright daunting. There were so many fallen trees littering the shoreline, I realized this area would best be explored with a boat, not with a plane going seventy miles an hour. I kept a vigilant eye on the river and my airspeed, all the while trying to scan every foot of the east bank as it streaked past in a blur of green. I'd been on search and rescue flights before and was never sure if I actually wanted to be the one who made what was often a tragic discovery. More often than not, there was no *rescue* in a search and rescue.

"There's a plane," she said, almost casually, pointing out her window.

"What? Where? Where's a plane?" I instantly raised my hand and punched the 'mark' button on the GPS. I looked back and saw nothing.

"Back there, in the trees, on the shore."

"What exactly did you see? What color was it?"

"I don't know, but it was a plane, it looked like this one. Maybe it was green, with some white. It was just parked in the trees."

"Parked? Are you positive?" I looked at her incredulously.

"Well, I saw a plane, that's for sure."

I pumped the flaps up to the climb position and pushed the throttle ahead. I accelerated to ninety and made a sharp left hand turn, heading west across the river. Seconds later I turned ninety degrees to the right, flew north for a minute, then made a long one hundred and eighty degree right turn, straightened out, and headed back up the river. I dropped the flaps down to 'full' again and was flying low, heading toward the co-ordinates I'd just marked on the GPS. We were heading south, less than a hundred feet off the water, in slow flight again. I had the east shoreline less than a hundred feet off my left wing, keeping my eyes peeled, watching the GPS for my mark, looking left out the cockpit door window.

Then I saw it. Just for an instant. A flash of white paint in a stack of trees. But there was no doubt about what I'd just seen. It was the missing NOCA Air Beaver. I punched the mark button on the GPS. Now I had the exact co-ordinates.

"Yes!" I shouted. "You found it! You found the missing plane!

Good eye!" I gave her a friendly elbow in the shoulder and a big smile. "Good eye!" I shouted again.

"Hey, easy there big fella! Now what?"

I wasn't sure but knew this had to be called in on the radio. I had no idea if landing near the NOCA plane was possible. The river bank was a mess, littered with trees and chunks of ice and large rocks, with a fast current rushing along its edge. It's not easy maneuvering a floatplane in a fast current, much harder than a boat with a prop in the water. So before you beach a plane on a fast flowing river like the Yukon, you better do your homework. You need to know the shoreline, the depth of the river next to the shoreline, the direction of the current, the direction of the wind, and you better have a precise target picked out to land, stop, and tie up. With twenty-two feet of wing sticking out from either side of a Beaver, you also need a landing spot where the surrounding terrain is flat. All those factors would make landing anywhere near the NOCA plane a challenge.

The general idea for landing a float plane against a strong current is to have the plane stop exactly where you want it to stop. Landing against a strong current requires that you get the floats to stop planing and settle down into the water just as you arrive at your target. The end game is to get the engine turned off, get out of the plane, and tie a rope around something secure before the current takes over and carries the plane backwards. I had no idea of the river's nuances or the lay of the land in this area. Other than the general direction of the current, *absolutely no idea.*

I looked at Sarah Marsalis and said, "I need to call this in. We need to climb for awhile."

I pumped the flaps up a notch and accelerated straight south for a minute, then turned west across the river and began climbing in a long right hand circle. It felt good when sunshine poured in the cabin as we rose above the cliffs. We needed to gain a lot of altitude if I was going to radio Dawson from here. I kept the plane in a climbing circle for over five minutes, until the altimeter read six thousand feet. The NOCA Beaver was now far below us and impossible to see. Too many trees and dark shadows from the cliffs provided it with a perfect camouflage. Sarah Marsalis had spotted it only because we'd been flying so low. Good eye, Sarah Marsalis, whoever you are.

I dialed channel 122.1 on the radio and pushed the transmit button on the yoke.

"Dawson, this is Beaver, Papa Papa Alpha Golf. Come in."

I waited. At this altitude I should be in radio range of the Dawson airport, sixty miles north of us. I kept circling at six thousand feet, looking down for a viable landing spot, and at the spot where I thought the missing plane was. Occasionally I thought I saw a flicker of light off a wing, but couldn't be sure. Then it struck me that something was amiss. If the plane was intact and floating down there in the trees with occupants on board, why hadn't they been out on the floats or the river bank, waving madly at us when we'd flown by? Or why hadn't they tried to raise us on the radio, or fired a flare? And for that matter, why wasn't the plane's ELT – the Emergency Locator Transmitter – broadcasting a radio distress signal? Or why wasn't a satellite tracking signal being transmitted? Had the plane been abandoned? Were the occupants inside and injured? Or worse?

"Beaver, Papa Papa Alpha Golf, this is Dawson ATC, go ahead."

"Dawson, I have located NOCA Beaver, Papa Yankee Papa Yankee. It's on the east bank of the Yukon River, five miles north of Thistle Creek, location co-ordinates are…" I looked at my GPS mark and recited them. "The plane appears to be intact, upright and floating, but no sign of life. No radio contact or flares seen. Rough and limited terrain near the plane. Suggest helicopter rescue with medical personnel. Over."

"Roger that, Alpha Golf, will notify Air Rescue and RCMP, over."

"Dawson, I am descending to investigate and land, will lose radio contact soon. Please cancel all flight advisories for Papa Papa Alpha Golf."

"Roger that, Alpha Golf, you are landing, will cancel your flight advisories, monitor 121.5, Dawson ATC, over and out."

"Alpha Golf, over and out."

It was decision time. I'd done my duty. But was it all I should do? Or could do? If the occupants were injured, they'd have to wait at least another hour before a helicopter from Dawson arrived. They'd have another hour of misery. I pulled back the throttle and let the plane sink in a wide circling descent. Perhaps landing near the plane was a possibility. I had to find out.

At a thousand feet off the river we were heading north, flying downstream along its west bank. I continued descending and turned right, out over the river toward the east, then turned south until we were going the other way, flying upriver along its east side. This would be my one and only attempt to find a place to land. I lowered the flaps all the way down, descended to a hundred feet off the water, held the nose high, and mushed along at sixty-five miles per hour with lots of power.

I saw only one viable spot to land, a couple of thousand feet downstream from the NOCA plane. Six or seven uprooted trees lay prone on the shore, piled up by the current into a thick entanglement, their root balls at the foot of the cliffs, their tops extending twenty feet out into the river, creating a breakwater of sorts. Downstream of the trees the water surface looked relatively calm and smooth, and the shoreline was open and flat. It would be as good a place as any to try a landing. Approach from the north into a light wind and against the current, touch down at just the right spot, glide up to the trees, and throw a rope around one of them. I figured it was worth a shot, but expected to get my feet wet.

I pumped the flaps up a notch and started another short climb, continuing south until my airspeed increased, turned right and crossed the river again, then made another right turn and flew north for a few minutes. Then I pumped the flaps all the way down, turned the plane around over the river, and headed south again, back toward my targeted landing spot. The east shoreline was now only fifty feet off my left shoulder.

"What are you doing?" came a voice over my headset.

"Landing."

"Landing? Your ten minutes were up a long time ago, Mr. Brody, and I don't feel very well. Why are you landing here?"

"Look, I'm really sorry, Sarah. I'm going to have you on the river bank in about a minute. But please let me concentrate now."

She'd just called me Mr. Brody and I'd just called her Sarah. It felt a little odd, I'd enjoyed the notion of familiarity with her when she was calling me Brody, though I understood her formal tone at the moment. I could empathize with her current situation. I have to admit that while doing all those maneuvers, I'd completely forgotten about the paying passenger beside me. A passenger who wasn't used to flying up and down and around and around in circles, about to land under precarious conditions in a plane she didn't trust, with a man she didn't trust. I vowed to make amends, but at the time I was about to try the kind of landing they don't teach in flying school.

I fixated on the pile of twisted trees ahead, now in clear view over the nose, about a thousand feet ahead. The water surface looked smooth and free of debris and I could only hope it would stay that way for another thirty seconds. Hopefully there were no submerged rocks or dead trees lurking just below the surface on my landing path. I let the plane sink down to the river, keeping the nose high with steady power, holding the airspeed at sixty miles per hour until the floats touched down about five hundred feet from the trees. I reduced power slowly and held the yoke back to keep the floats on plane as long as I dared. At the last second I pulled the throttle lever back to idle, the mixture lever back to full lean, and turned the mags and master switches off. The engine stopped. Everything was suddenly dead quiet except the water foaming over the floats as they plowed into the water. When I was certain we had enough momentum to reach the trees, I dropped the rudders and gave a little push on the left pedal. The objective was to beach the plane before the prop hit the branches. The plane veered left as we glided against the current, slower and slower as the trees and shore got closer. Ten feet from the trees I reached behind me and grabbed my landing rope from under the seat, opened my door, stepped down on the float, and clipped the rope to the front cleat. Then I leapt at the shore, landed short with a big splash in a foot of water, took another stride, and was on the beach. I made a mad dash to the trees with the rope paying out behind me. Just as the left float brushed the river bottom, I saw a space between two thick trees. With two steps into the icy river, I dropped the end of the rope over the top one, pulled it out from underneath, made one more wrap, and tied a quick knot. I took two more bitterly cold, soaking wet steps back to shore and dropped the rest of the rope on the beach. I'd done it!

Piece of cake.

I looked back at my plane. It had come to a dead stop just shy of the trees but now the current was taking over. It began moving away from me. The rope went tight. Tight enough to walk on. The trees creaked, the rope creaked, the plane stopped. I watched it and the trees for a good minute to see if either one might move. But the plane had settled into an equilibrium, barely swaying in the current, the river rushing past the floats as though it was being towed through the water. To my pleasant surprise it remained stationary, barely yawing, never getting closer than a few feet from shore. I assumed there must be a pretty good drop off under the plane because it seemed to be floating free and clear of the bottom. I looked back at the trees again, making sure they weren't about to get hauled away. They were rock steady. But a single rope tied to a bunch of fallen trees wasn't going to be good enough. I stepped onto the left float, opened the cargo door, and pulled out my canvas duffel bag full of ropes. I spent the next five minutes tying the left float securely to a couple of good size boulders on the shore.

Now my plane wasn't going anywhere.

It was time to see if two people in an overdue plane needed help.

EIGHT

"How do you feel?" I asked, standing on the float under the cargo door, leaning into the plane with my hands on the floor, looking up at Sarah Marsalis.

"Not great," she said, not turning around to look at me.

"Look, I feel bad about this. But it could be an emergency. There could be people in that plane up there that need help. I think if you got out and sat down on the shore for a while, got some fresh air, maybe you'd feel better. What do you say?"

"Yeah. Good idea."

She squeezed between the seats and stepped to the rear of the plane, climbed down the ladder, and stood on the float. I jumped on shore and reached my hand out to her. She looked down at the water rushing past her feet, deciding whether to take my hand. She made the right decision, grabbed my hand, and made a successful leap onto land.

"Watch above you for falling trees and stuff." When I said *stuff*, I really meant rocks and boulders. I got back in the plane and emerged with a duffle bag full of survival gear, then picked out a clear dry spot on the beach where there was some room to get organized, and for her to sit down. I opened the bag and dumped all its contents on the ground, sifted through the pile, and pulled out an empty backpack, a ground sheet, and a thick blanket for her to lie on.

"Make yourself comfortable with anything you can find in here," I said. "There's water and some dried fruit somewhere. You'll feel better in no time."

"Why are we here? What are you doing?" she asked.

"Well, I'm going to pack a few things into this backpack and walk up to that plane you spotted, see if anyone's in it. If there is, see if they need help. Should be back in about forty five minutes."

"Hey, Mr. Brody, I know you're doing your civic duty here, but I'm going to miss my meeting in Dawson, the way things are going. Just so you know."

"Look, first of all my name's Brody, not Mr. Brody. Second, I'm well aware of your schedule, and your patience and co-operation are really appreciated. But people's lives may be at stake. So really, thank you." I paused for a second. "Look, I thought when I got back, we could fly you straight up to Dawson. It's not far and you'd get to your meeting on time. You could even stay in Dawson tonight. I could get someone to drive your car up tomorrow."

"That might work," she said. "We'll see when you get back."

I climbed back in the plane with the backpack and started filling it with things for my hike upriver. I grabbed my favorite sharp knife and slid it into the holster on my belt, then packed a hatchet, a few tools, the first aid kit, a small tree saw, a couple of survival blankets, two bottles of water, and some vacuum packed survival food. The NOCA plane would be at least as well equipped as mine, so I didn't pack everything I might need. It was cold on this side of the river so I threw on a ski jacket and a pair of old leather gloves, climbed down the ladder and jumped back on shore. Sarah Marsalis was sitting on the bag of ropes, shivering under a blanket wrapped around her shoulders. I sat down beside her and pulled out a pair of dry socks.

"It's cold," she said.

"Yeah, I know, it's too bad we're not on the other side of the river, in the sun. But it will be out on this side soon, shouldn't be long. Hey, you have everything you need?"

"Yes."

"Good," I said, working the dry socks onto my wet feet. They would help a little – for about ten seconds. I put my wet boots on again and laced them up. "By the way, if you hear noises above you, look upand be ready to get out of the way fast. All the trees and rocks down here, they came from up there, right? So if things get too exciting where you're sitting, just get back in the plane, you'll be safe there. And please, be very careful if you decide to do that. Okay?"

"Okay."

I slung the backpack over my shoulders, climbed over three trees and started walking, hoping the hike to the missing plane wasn't going to be an endurance test. But from the outset it was clearly going to be a challenge. The footing was treacherous on the wet shore and sticky mud weighed heavily on my boots. Unsorted rocks of every size and shape were scattered everywhere and I had to concentrate on every step. Patches of dirty snow lay hidden from the sun under fallen trees and chunks of ice were wedged between the rocks, stubbornly surviving the late spring. I made steady headway for the first five minutes, weaving back and forth to navigate countless trees and obstacles, trying to stay optimistic that my pace would get me to the NOCA plane in another fifteen minutes. Wrong.

The first real challenge presented was another large entanglement of uprooted trees, this one piled high like the makings of a giant bonfire, completely blocking my way. It looked like a giant maze, a mix of bleached white driftwood, dead spruce trees, and broken branches with rusty colored needles. I pushed and pulled on several trees to see what would happen. They had the inertia of steel beams. It was going to be impossible to walk around or through them and there was no choice but to climb over them. I was glad to have a hatchet to hack off branches as I went up and over. When I stepped down on the other side, I took an inventory of personal damage.

There were a lot of good scratches on my face and neck, a tear in my favorite old ski jacket, and sticky spruce sap all over my jeans and gloves.

The second challenge presented itself the moment I looked up the shore. Another couple of hundred feet ahead was a dike of boulders, running from the foot of the cliff on my left all the way across to the river's edge on my right. The rocks and boulders had fallen from the cliffs above, then had subsequently been plowed into a compacted row, likely by an ice floe when the river broke up three weeks ago. A mixture of tree debris, snow, and chunks of ice filled the spaces between the rocks. When I started to cross the dike, it quickly became apparent that crab walking over the boulders was the safest way to navigate across, the footing between them simply too treacherous.

Crossing the boulder dike hadn't done my knees any good. I'd just stepped off the last one, my feet on open ground again, when I heard a yelp behind me. I knew exactly who had yelped, and to my dismay, knew it had come from the jam of trees. Which I'd just crossed. Before I'd crossed the boulders. Damn!

I crab walked back over the boulders, then walked back to the trees.

"Are you okay?"

"Yes."

"Do you need help?"

There was a long pause. "Yes."

"Where are you?"

"In here. I think I'm stuck."

"Hang on."

I walked along the pile of trees to where I'd heard her call.

"Say something, I can't see you."

"I'm in here."

I dropped my pack, took out the hatchet, and started to climb the trees. It was easier without the heavy backpack, but nonetheless slow going.

"Say something."

"Down here, I can see you."

She was five feet below me, straddling the trunk of a spruce tree, skewered by a branch that had caught under her collar and worked its way down her back, under and well inside her fleece jacket.

"How the hell did you manage to do that?" I asked.

"Please just help me, okay? It hurts like hell when I move."

"Well, why don't you just...". I was going to tell her to unzip her jacket and take it off. Then I realized her fleece jacket was a pullover with only a half zipper down the front. Her escape from purgatory would require my help, and my tree saw. "Be right be back, stay still."

I had to retreat to my backpack to get the tree saw. I climbed back to the top of the trees again and positioned myself above her, holding the saw in one hand.

"I'm going to cut that branch off and there's going to be a lot of wood dust, so close your eyes and don't breathe for a few minutes."

"Very funny," she said.

"It's a good thing I have this tree saw today. Usually I carry a chainsaw."

"Haw, haw."

I sawed through the dead branch in no time. She was now free, but the sawed off branch was still stuck inside her jacket.

"Thank you," she said, embarrassed and contrite.

"Stay still." I reached down and tried pulling the branch out but the stubble on the branch was embedded in the fleece.

"Owww!"

"Sorry. Can you make it out of there and get down to this side with that thing stuck in there?"

"I'll try, but it hurts."

"Okay try, otherwise we'll to have to cut the jacket off your back right here."

She climbed up, then descended the mound of trees to the ground. I couldn't help but smile at the sight of her walking toward me, hunched over at the waist, a long white deadwood branch sticking up from the back of her collar.

"What?" she said.

"Nothing. Turn around," I said, trying to suppress a chuckle. She glared, then turned her back to me. I knelt down on my knees behind her and slid both hands up and under her pullover. I worked the branch free with both my forearms pressed firmly against her back. Her turtle neck slid up as the branch moved up. I got a lovely view of the skin on her lower back. Almost made the whole delay worthwhile. "Okay, pull it out slowly." She reached behind her head with both hands, pulled the branch out, looked at it, then hurled it at the cliffs with obvious disgust.

"Thank you," she said, brushing herself off and straightening herself out.

"You're welcome. I kind of enjoyed that actually." Don't know why I thought the moment required any attempt at levity, but I'd gone ahead anyway and said something I probably shouldn't have, again.

"I'm sure you did," she said with a wry grin. "Look, I was bored, and cold, and thought I'd..."

"Yeah, I know. But you need to go back. You can't come with me."

"Why not?"

It was a good question, a question I didn't feel like answering, not honestly anyway. For some reason, I decided to give in.

"Alright. Now that you're this far, I guess you can come. But please be careful. And I can't wait for you if you get stuck again, understand?"

"Understand," she said.

"Let's go then." I put my backpack on and we walked in silence toward the dike of boulders. Then I laughed out loud.

"What?" she said.

"Nothing," I said, looking out at the river.

"Come on, what's so funny?" She stopped with her hands on her hips in an indignant pose.

I turned around and looked at her. "I don't know, I guess you kind of reminded me of Quasimodo back there, all bent over with that stick down your back. You know, like 'the hunchback of the Yukon River'. Get it?" I laughed again. She didn't. I turned around and decided to laugh later.

When we got to the boulders I said, "Careful here, walk on all fours to cross these, and take your time."

Sarah Marsalis was obviously athletic and had no difficulty getting over the rocks. We arrived on the other side at the same time. I gave her a subtle nod of approval and she reciprocated with an 'anything you can do' nod of her own.

I thought it couldn't be much farther to the NOCA plane, the sun was coming out and it looked like it was going to be an easy hike the rest of the way. I was feeling confident about the rest of the mission. Five minutes later we arrived at a point that jutted out into the river, walked a few yards around a gentle bend to our left, and there it was.

The NOCA Beaver was five hundred feet ahead, clearly visible, floating in the river at a right angle to the shore, wedged in a thicket of fallen trees. But with so many more rocks and prone trees between us and the plane, my confidence quickly waned.

The shore was much narrower past the point. A hundred feet ahead the sheer cliffs were virtually hanging over the river, with barely twenty feet of relatively flat ground to walk below them. The specter that just about anything falling from the cliffs above might be potentially lethal to someone below was patently clear. All of a sudden, after coming this far, I wasn't sure whether to continue. For some reason, though, I felt compelled to try.

Alone.

I looked back and said, "Look, I'm sorry, but you'll have to wait here. This is going to be dangerous. If something falls from up there, there's nowhere to hide down here."

"Jump in the river."

"No. Do not jump in the river. Not ever. Not unless you're on fire. The water is forty degrees, it will paralyze you instantly and the current will sweep you away. There'll be no one to rescue you. You'll be dead in five minutes. Jumping in the river is not an option. Look, I won't be long. So please, just wait here, okay?"

She mulled that over and raised her chin. "No, I'm going with you," she said.

"No, you're not going with me. You're staying here."

She gave me a glare but said nothing. I glared back at her like I meant what I'd said. She turned, retreated ten feet, and sat down on a tree, not happy.

"Thank you," I said. "I shouldn't be long."

I set off for the plane. My progress along the narrow shoreline went better than expected. I kept a wary eye and ear out for anything falling from the cliffs, but the only sounds came from the river, a few feet to my right. I concentrated extra hard on the rocks and the trees ahead of me. I didn't want to get injured. Not here. I don't want to say I was scared, so let's just call it damn nervous. *'There'll be no one to rescue you.'* I'd just said it, it was true, but kept going anyway.

I climbed up and over yet another tree, stepped down to the ground, and looked ahead. The NOCA Beaver was right in front of me.

It was in the water, perpendicular to the shoreline, pointing at the cliffs, entangled in a mishmash of fallen trees and branches, its floats pushing hard against the river bank. It was canted slightly in my direction, to the downstream side, the current forcing the left float under a prone tree that extended well out into the river. The top of another prone tree had speared the triangular space formed by the left wing strut, the left wing, and the fuselage. The tree was parallel to the fuselage and the strong current was forcing the plane hard against it, its thick branches completely obscuring the cabin's interior. On the other side of the plane, the right wing was riding up against another fallen tree, and the leading edge was badly damaged. The plane was rocking erratically in the current and there was a constant squeaking and screeching as hundreds of tree branches rubbed and scraped against the aluminum fuselage and wings.

The left side doors clearly couldn't be accessed, let alone opened, barred shut by the tree. I dropped my backpack and climbed over the two trees, stopped in front of the nose, and saw that one blade on the prop was badly bent. I couldn't see through the cockpit windshield, it was too high above me and the interior was pitch black.

My heart was pounding as I walked around the nose and approached the right float. I had yet to look into the plane, had no idea of what to expect, and desperately hoped the aircraft had been abandoned and was empty. That wasn't the case.

Still standing on the river bank, I made out the silhouettes of two men in the front seats. The passenger was leaning his head against his door window, looking like any typical air traveler catching a nap on a long flight. The pilot was perfectly still, looking down.

"Hey!" I yelled. "Hey, help is here! Are you guys okay?" With the noise from the trees scraping against the plane and the water gushing around the floats, I could barely hear my hollow sounding shouts. But surely the two men inside could hear me. Why didn't they respond? Now I was scared. My heart was pounding in my ears and temples. A surge of adrenaline weakened my legs.

I stepped on the right float and rapped on the passenger's window. Neither man stirred. I rapped harder. No reaction. I pounded on the door with the heel of my hand.

"Hey!" I yelled. Nothing.

I carefully unlatched the right cockpit door and opened it a few inches. A stench poured out like nothing I'd ever experienced. I gagged and coughed, turned away for fresh air, fought back nausea, then looked inside. The man in the passenger seat moved toward me when I'd opened his door. His head had slid down the window a few inches. I let the door out a few more inches. He stopped moving, held back by his seat belt. I let the door swing out some more, watched him carefully, then opened it all the way. His head dropped toward me. I looked straight into his eyes, just for an instant, then over at the pilot, then back at the man in the passenger seat. He was directly over me now, hanging from his seat belt, his face barely a foot from mine. I looked away, trying to process the image.

I swung the door past center until it stopped against the engine cowl, then looked at the two men again, as if somehow the whole scene might have changed.

The man in the pilot seat had his chin on his chest, his arms at his sides. He looked like he'd just nodded off. He looked relaxed and uninjured. He was my friend, Robert Duncan. I looked at him for what must have been a long time, watching to see if he was breathing. I tried to say something but couldn't open my mouth. Please, I thought, just move. But the truth was held in the ashen pallor of his face and his cloudy eyes. There could be no doubt about it. He was dead.

I looked again at the man above me. His left eye and left temple were missing, the side of his face destroyed. There was dried blood and tissue all over his face and chest, his right arm, the console in front of him, and inside his door. He was dead too.

On wobbly legs I shuffled back along the float, pushing aside and breaking off tree branches. This Beaver had passenger seats in the cargo bay. I opened the cargo door. The stench that hit me this time was overwhelming. I climbed into the plane holding my breath and sat down in one of the rear seats with my legs shaking. I buried my nose in the crook of my right arm, breathed slowly, stared ahead at the two men, and wondered: what had killed them? The plane hadn't hit anything hard. They were wearing seat belts.

But it was impossible to stay in denial. I could see the bullet wounds in the backs of their heads.

Each man had been shot.

Each man twice.

They'd been murdered.

NINE

"**So yesterday morning, up there in your Yukon territory,** two of our Special Agents get on some plane called a beagle, they're supposed to arrive here in Juneau at noon, the plane never shows up, our agents never show up, and you don't have a clue what happened to the plane or our agents. Have I got that right?" Special Agent in Charge Harry Polichek of the US Department of the Treasury stared at the phone on his desk, waiting for a response.

"SAC Polichek, I think the plane you're referring to is called a Beaver, not a Beagle," said Staff Sergeant Allan Robson of the Royal Canadian Mounted Police. "And yes sir, you are absolutely right. We don't know the whereabouts of any missing special agents, because no one told us about any missing special agents, so we haven't been looking for any missing special agents, *sir*. However, we do have a plane reported as overdue, that is true, and that overdue plane is a Beaver. A SAR notice was issued last evening for that particular aircraft and we're out looking for it as I speak. But you'll have to explain to me, sir, why you think your two missing agents might be on that particular missing aircraft, because according to the passenger manifest, there was only one passenger on board. Now SAC Polichek, may I suggest that if you're missing *two* agents, that you file a missing persons report. I think that would be the best way to get things started. And it would be very helpful if you would tell me a little about your missing agents, the nature of their business in Canada, and their recent movements around the Yukon territory."

"May I put you on hold for a moment, Sergeant Robson?"

"It's *Staff* Sergeant Robson, and yes sir, you may put me on hold."

Polichek punched the hold button on his speaker phone and groaned, then looked up at the two men standing before him in his makeshift Juneau office.

"Gentlemen, what the hell do we tell this Yukon cop? He doesn't have a clue. Jesus."

US Treasury Special Agent Stanley Kurtz spoke first. "Well sir, it is a joint international investigation, so proper protocol is in order. And if our agents are in danger, then time is a priority. Perhaps we should call our people in Ottawa working with us on this case, perhaps they're the best ones to help us out. Let them deal with the Canadian police. Let this Yukon cop scratch his head for a while."

FBI Special Agent David Owen spoke next. "I agree with Special Agent Kurtz, sir. We need to move quickly. We've got two agents in the Yukon missing now, and another one in LA disappeared two days ago. And all three are working on this very same case."

"Who's missing in LA?"

"Perez, sir," said Owen.

"Jesus. Our customs broker?" asked Polichek.

"Yes, sir. Perez didn't come home from work two days ago. His family is frantic. No one has a clue where he is. We've been trying hard to locate him. The LAPD and the LA Port Authority were notified and have been working hard to find him. But so far, nothing, sir."

"Jesus," said Polichek.

"SAC Polichek?"

"Yes, Agent Kurtz."

"Staff Sergeant Robson is holding, sir."

"Jesus. If we file a missing persons report with this small town cop, he'll be putting up pictures of our agents in the post office – beside the lost dog notices! This can't get out! I'm calling Ottawa right away."

"Good idea, sir," Stanley Kurtz said.

"Very good idea, sir," David Owen said.

Polichek hit the talk button on his phone. "Staff Sergeant Robson, I apologize for taking your time. I need to discuss this matter further with my colleagues. Let me call you back."

"Please do that, SAC Polichek. And please let us know anytime if we at the RCMP can be of service to your government. Goodbye, sir."

Polichek put his elbows on his desk, removed his eyeglasses, and rubbed his face. "Gentlemen, I'm going to call our people in Ottawa right now. I'll let you know what's going on as soon as I know. That's all for now."

Kurtz and Owen walked out of Polichek's office and were halfway down the hall when Kurtz stopped.

"What do you think?" he asked.

"I think we need to move fast," said Owen. "We need to get up to Dawson right away. Call the Skagway office. Tell them to drive a unit up to Whitehorse, and pronto. Get us a bunch of hotel rooms in Dawson. I'll call the airport. We'll take the jet. We fly to Whitehorse International in an hour. We'll pick up our unit there."

"Got it," Kurtz said, and started down the hall.

"Agent Kurtz?"

Kurtz stopped and looked back at Owen. "Yeah?"

"Call that RCMP cop, the one Polichek was just talking to. Tell him to expect us in Whitehorse this morning."

"Done."

"Thanks. Hey, Agent Kurtz?"

"Yeah?"

"What do you think of the new boss?"

Kurtz rolled his eyes. "I think he says 'Jesus' an awful lot."

* * *

Staff Sergeant Allan Robson pressed the intercom button on his desk telephone.

"Yes, sir."

"Mary, with pen and paper please."

"Yes, sir."

Robson leaned back in his chair and gazed out his big office window at the quiet streets of Whitehorse and Grey Mountain on the other side of the Yukon River. It was going to be a nice day, too nice a day to be inside. He knew there were only a couple of months up here when you could go kayaking in a T-shirt and shorts. Maybe he could get out this evening, spend a little time on the water, relax a bit.

"Sir?" A short, stern looking woman about fifty sat down in front of Robson's desk.

"Mary, I need the following, and fast. When and if anything comes in, you call me, you find me, you interrupt me, no excuses."

"Yes, sir."

"Number one. Call the Canadian Customs highway branches at Fraser, Porcupine, Beaver Creek and Little Gold, and the airports in Dawson and Whitehorse too. For the last forty-eight hours, I want a list of all US government personnel entering Canada carrying restricted weapons. Two. Fax all our Yukon detachments on the Klondike Highway. For the last forty-eight hours I want a list of all incidents, accidents and inquiries involving US citizens. Oh, and all US drivers license inquiries requested by our detachments. Three. Fax Yukon Flight Services. For the last forty-eight hours, I want all the flight plans filed for Beaver aircraft. Four. Call the Canadian Revenue Agency in Ottawa, their Criminal Investigations section. I want a list of all current joint operations going on in the Yukon between Canada and the US Department of the Treasury."

"Yes, sir." Mary stood up.

"Mary?"

"Sir?"

"You know I ask you to do all this because you're the best man I've got around here."

"Thank you, sir."

Mary walked out of Staff Sergeant Robson's office and got to work.

TEN

Tommy Kay poked at his salad. The lettuce wasn't fresh. Nothing was fresh.

He was in Dawson, sitting with his back to the wall in a crowded hotel dining room, at a table in the corner with Ricky, the moron who worked for Mr. Lee's associate. Tommy looked around the room at the other patrons, all of them tourists, exhausted after a morning of staggering up and down the wooden sidewalks of Dawson, scouring every souvenir shop for a bargain that didn't exist. The food was heaped high on their plates and they sat in silence, devouring mounds of meat and deep fried carbs, determined to clean their plates to get their money's worth. Tommy thought all that fresh air must have made them hungry. Fresh air that he'd had enough of in the last two days.

Two nights ago – the night they'd arrived – he and Ricky had spent ten hours on that damn Yukon River, travelling south against the current with some old Indian in a leaky plywood boat. The engine had quit three times. That had been a seventy mile river trip against the current, from some hick village in Alaska where their plane had dropped them off, all the way up to Dawson. They'd crossed the border into Canada in the middle of the night.

Then yesterday, another river trip, this one unscheduled. This one had been with the current, eighty miles down the Yukon River, travelling north from Thistle Creek to Dawson. Tommy and Ricky were supposed to have flown to Juneau yesterday, not go on another Yukon River trip. They were supposed to be home by now, not sitting here in an old wooden hotel with a bunch of tourists who kept asking them where they were from.

All that Tommy and Ricky were supposed to do yesterday was fly to the mine, land on the river, wait at the barge for the mine manager, hand over the briefcases, and take off for Juneau. But no, Ricky has to start yapping at the pilot, has to start asking him questions, questions that were none of his business. Ricky said he didn't like the answers he was getting, said he didn't like the pilot's attitude, said he'd lost patience, said he'd had no choice with the other guy. Who the hell did Ricky think he was? The pilot was none of his business. He'd been Mr. Lee's gold pilot. It was Mr. Lee's gold mine. Mr. Lee was not going to be pleased.

Next thing you know they had to 'borrow' a boat from the mine, had to go out on that damn river again, try to 'hide the plane'. Ricky said they had to tow the plane somewhere, to 'get it away from the mine'. But it wasn't long before they had to let the plane go, after it began to tow them. The wind and current took the plane away. They'd watched it drift into the shore, then disappear in some trees. Tommy didn't know where it had ended up. He didn't like that.

And so here he was, stuck in Dawson with a dumb wop named Ricky, looking for another plane to take them home. And they still had the two briefcases. Why does Mr. Lee make me work with a loser from Vegas? Why would he ask me to work with a scumbag, even if he does work for Mr. Lee's associate? The guy never shuts up and he's dumber than a box of rocks.

"You don't like your salad? Try the ribs, Tommy. You can't live on salad. A man has to eat meat. Try the ribs."

Ricky was yapping again.

"I like salad," said Tommy, glaring at Ricky with overt disdain. There's nothing more dangerous than a man high in confidence and low in brains, thought Tommy. What kind of an asshole wears a gold chain, a gaudy watch, and silk shirts on a trip to the Yukon?

And the hair. What's with the grease in the hair? When this was over, Tommy was going to take Ricky out for a big rib dinner in Vegas. Give him plenty to drink, then take him for a nice drive out into the Nevada desert. Tommy looked forward to watching Ricky beg for his life while he dug his own grave under the stars. The lizards would burrow down and eat his eyes out in the first week. The idea made Tommy feel much better.

"So Tommy, whatta we gonna do now? We stuck here or what?"

Tommy just stared.

"Well Tommy, while you're thinkin' hard about how to answer that simple question, I'm goin' out tonight to get laid. What are you gonna do? How we gonna get outta here anyway?"

"You're not going anywhere tonight. You're going to look after that briefcase at your feet. You stay in your room."

"Hey, nobody tells me what to do, Tommy. 'Specially you, Tommy. Now if I say I'm goin' out to get laid, I'm goin' out to get laid, get it?"

Tommy glared daggers at the man with the greasy hair and the plastic bib with painted lobsters tied around his neck.

"Look Tommy, I'm just gonna go out and have a little fun, that's all. I'll leave my briefcase with you, how's that? There'll be nothin' to worry about, right?"

Ricky picked up another big rib with both hands and sunk his yellow teeth into the meat.

"Hey, Tommy!" he said, chewing with his mouth open. "I asked you already, what are we gonna do now? Are we stuck here or what?"

"We're not stuck. I'm looking for another pilot so we can get out of here. Now shut up."

"Oh yeah? Another pilot? We maybe gotta whack him too?"

Tommy looked around the room to see if anyone might have heard Ricky. Didn't look like it. Lucky.

"I'm going to the salad bar," Tommy said.

Tommy heaved his massive body out of his chair. He picked up his plate, walked around the table, stood beside Ricky, then set his

plate down again. Ricky looked up at Tommy and grinned, holding
a juicy rib in his hands. Tommy gave Ricky a friendly pat on the
back with his massive right hand, slid it up to his shoulder, then
around his neck, and gave a little squeeze. Ricky went limp as a rag
and Tommy lowered his head gently into his meal. Then Tommy
dug his right middle finger in so deep, and squeezed so hard under
Ricky's collar bone, he could feel muscles and tendons rupturing.
Ricky's mouth opened but not a sound came out. His eyes went
white, rolling back in his head from the shock. Tommy stepped
behind Ricky and wrapped his arms around him, lifted him out of
his chair, and administered his personal version of the Heimlich
maneuver. When Tommy felt at least two ribs crack, he lowered
Ricky back into his chair, eased him forward, and returned his head
to the plate.

"Sir, is everything alright here? My goodness, what's wrong
with your friend, should I call an ambulance?" The matronly woman
who had served them was aghast. She stared at the unconscious
man whose face was lying in the lunch special.

"He was choking," said Tommy. "On a piece of meat. But it
came out. Nothing to worry about. See? He's breathing good now.
But I'm sure he feels bad. So don't mention this to no one. I'll take
him up to his room. He needs to rest. He'll be okay."

"Alright sir, but you're sure he'll be fine?"

"Yeah, like I said, he was choking on somethin'. But it came
back up. See? He's okay now. You won't say nothin' 'bout this,
right?" Tommy stared at her with his lizard eyes. No, she wasn't
going to say anything. Not for at least ten seconds.

Tommy reached into his pocket and dropped a hundred dollar
bill on the table. "I hope that takes care of everything. Keep the
change. Remember, don't say nothin' about this. Not a word. We
don't want to embarrass him."

"No sir. Of course not. Not a word."

The woman picked up the hundred dollar bill, walked to the
next table and began waving her arms, pointing at Tommy and

reciting her version of how that wonderful large man over there had just saved his friend's life with the Heimlich maneuver.

Tommy picked up the two briefcases under the table with his left hand. They each weighed over fifty pounds. He wrapped his right arm around Ricky and plucked him out of his chair like a stuffed animal. Tommy held Ricky upright, waiting for him to find his legs, watching him slowly regain consciousness. Then, arm in arm, the two men began to walk, one slow step at a time. Tommy might have been helping his grandmother cross the street. Knives and forks froze in mid-air as whispering filled the room, the news of a life just saved spreading like wildfire from table to table. The large lunch crowd craned their necks and watched with admiration as the big man led his poor friend out to the lobby.

Now there goes a hero.

ELEVEN

Her cry jarred me from a trance.

She was standing fifteen feet away, on the river bank to my right, staring in horror at the dead man in the passenger seat. She walked up to the plane, stepped on the float, grabbed the wing strut, and looked carefully at the man in front of me. Her hands went to her face.

"No, no, no!" she whispered, repeating the words over and over like a mantra. I was frozen in my seat and couldn't speak. She stepped back on shore, staggered a few steps, crumpled to her knees, put her hands on the ground, and heaved. Whatever was inside came out. She sat back on her heels, put her hands on her knees, raised her head, and looked up at the cliffs.

I forced myself out of my seat, climbed down the ladder, closed the cargo door, and shuffled up to the cockpit. I swung the door across me and pressed it against the man in the passenger seat. With a shove of my shoulder I forced his head and upper body back inside the plane, then latched the door shut. I turned around and took a deep breath of fresh air. I looked at Sarah Marsalis, still on her knees, her head hanging back on her shoulders, staring up at the sky. I stepped off the float and walked up beside her.

"I'm really sorry you saw that," I said. Under different

circumstances I might have asked her why she hadn't stayed at the point. "We need to go now, Sarah. It's dangerous here."

She dropped her head to her chest and went still. She was catatonic. I offered her my hand. She didn't react. I reached down and lifted her left hand off her knee. She didn't react. "Time to go," I said. I lifted her hand high enough to motivate her to stand. She looked back at the plane.

"Don't," I said. "Come on. Let's go. We need to get out of here. We need to get back to our plane." *Our* plane.

I led her over to my pack, picked it up, and let go of her hand. I started out for the point and glanced back. She wasn't moving, still fixated on the plane.

"Sarah, come on. Please! Walk with me. We need to get back to the point. We're in a lot of danger here."

"I know him," she whispered.

"The passenger?"

"Yes. I know him. Knew him."

"Well, will you walk with me for awhile and tell me who he is when we're in a safer place?"

She nodded once and followed. I couldn't wait to get out of there. The cliffs seemed a lot higher and a lot closer to the river than when I'd walked out to the NOCA Beaver ten minutes ago. We stepped over and went around the same uprooted trees and rocks that littered the way back to the point. The return trip seemed to take forever. It was a relief when we finally got around the point, clear of the imposing cliffs, and out of sight of the doomed plane.

"Do you want to sit and rest for a while?"

She moved her head slowly from side to side, her unfocussed eyes staring down at the ground. I figured we'd better stay on our feet and pick up our pace lest she changed her mind. I didn't want to have to carry her back. There was a long way to go and we still had to navigate the dike of boulders and the pile of trees.

It was another twenty minutes of hard work before we arrived at *my* plane. Somehow we made it without incident, crab walking over the boulders, climbing over the trees, our feet slipping the whole way in the soft sand and mud. We hadn't said a word to each other since we'd left the point, both lost in our private reflections of the horror we'd just experienced. We sat down exhausted, contemplating the previous hour of our lives in silence. I got out some water and fruit. She drank but refused my offer of food. I didn't feel like eating myself, but if I was going to fly, needed something in my stomach. I ate an apple, then began repacking the survival gear. It was time to move.

I finally broke the silence and said, "We need to leave. We need to report this. We need to fly to Dawson and tell the police what we found."

I stood up with the duffel bag in my hand. She stood too, facing me, blocking my path to the plane.

"No! No police! I'm not talking to the police right now. Take me back to the campground. I want to go back to my car."

"Look, we'll go back to your car after we talk to the police. Or like I said before, you can stay in Dawson tonight. We'll get someone to drive your car up tomorrow. Anyway, you have a meeting to go to. Right?"

"No. Not anymore."

"Why? Are you saying…?"

"Yes."

"Oh." I paused, looked out at the river and took a deep breath, then said, "Well, we probably should to go to Dawson anyway. We'll know for sure when I get on the radio and report what we found."

"No, Mr. Brody, this is my charter. I hired you to fly me where I want to go. Not the other way around. So you can call whoever you want on your damn radio on the way back to Minto, but we're not flying to Dawson. We're flying back to my car."

"Excuse me, *Miss* Marsalis, but neither you nor I should be avoiding the police right now. Our fingerprints and our footprints just happen to be all over that murder scene back there. So if the police want us in Dawson, we're flying to Dawson. Otherwise they'll get the air force out and chase us all the way back to your car, and we'll be greeted by a trigger happy SWAT team when we land."

She had her arms folded and was tapping the fingers of one hand on her arm, glaring at me as though deciding how to deal with a petulant child.

I'd had enough acrimony for the day, it was time to get going. I walked around her and threw the duffle bag into the plane. We needed to get untied and back on the river. I wondered how best to deal with Sarah Marsalis. I walked up behind her, put my hands in my pockets, and did my best to appear conciliatory.

"Sarah?"

She turned and faced me.

"What?"

"Look, whatever we decide, we both need to get in the plane and leave. What do you say we get in and discuss our options out on the river?" She gave a big sigh, or maybe it was a big huff, then brushed past me and climbed into the plane.

I set about untying all my previous rope work from the rocks on the shore, coiled the ropes, and stuffed them in the other duffel bag. There was only one left to be untied, the first rope I'd tied to the trees when we landed. It still looked secure, though now it was under increased tension, once again being the only rope holding the plane stationary against the force of the current. I threw the duffel bag full of ropes into the cargo bay and shut the door. I jumped back on shore, jogged up to the thatch of trees, then looked back down the shoreline, trying to judge where the current might take the plane. It should drift out into the river.

I coiled up the slack section of the rope hanging from the tree, gripped it in my left hand, then pulled back hard to keep the wrap from slipping. I untied the knot with my right hand and began walking backwards down the shore, pulling hard on the rope to maintain tension on the wrap, switching my grip from one hand to the other as it payed out. When I got to the plane, I jumped on the float and let the rope go. It whizzed around the tree as the current accelerated the plane backwards, then the end whipped out of the trees. We were free now and the plane was drifting with the current. Hand over hand I hauled the rope out of the water, then unclipped it from the float. I climbed into the cockpit with the soaking wet coil and tossed it behind the seats. I started the engine, stepped on the right rudder, and turned the nose out into the river.

It felt good to be off that river bank.

* * *

The 'whopping' noise was growing louder, buffeting the plane, shaking everything inside the cockpit. It was the distinctive sound of a helicopter's rotating wings beating the air. The helicopter has to be the most unique flying machine in all of aviation. With the invention of the helicopter, man finally had a veritable magic carpet, a proverbial sky hook, a flying machine that could take off and land anywhere in its own footprint.

It had approached us from behind and was now hovering on a cushion of air, twenty feet above the river, a hundred feet off to my left. It was a Jet Ranger 206, decked out in the red, black and yellow livery of the RCMP. A billowing mist was blowing everywhere, soaking my plane and all its windows. I could barely make out the three men in the helicopter. My radio crackled.

"Papa Papa Alpha Golf, this is RCMP helicopter, on your port side, come in."

"RCMP, this is Beaver, Papa Papa Alpha Golf, go ahead RCMP helicopter, over."

"Did you report locating the missing NOCA Beaver, over?"

"Roger that."

"Where is it, over?"

"Two thousand feet south of us, on the east bank, stuck in the trees, over."

"Have you been to the plane, over?"

"Roger that, I'm just leaving, over."

"Why are you leaving, over?"

"I needed to radio in what I discovered, but now that you're

here, I can tell you there will be no rescue, all souls on board are…
expired. The best recovery method will be with a boat, over."

"You say all souls are expired, confirm that Alpha Golf, over."

"All souls aboard the NOCA Beaver are expired, over."

"Roger that. Stand by Alpha Golf."

"Alpha Golf, standing by."

I looked over at Sarah who was clenching her jaw. She was
clearly not pleased with the situation.

"Alpha Golf, this is RCMP diver Constable Moore, how many
souls are on board the NOCA Beaver, over?"

"Two souls, over."

"Just two souls, confirm that sir."

"RCMP, two souls, over."

"Stand by Alpha Golf."

Why would 'just two souls' be any surprise to him? The SAR
Alert said two souls were on board the missing NOCA plane,
and that's what we found. A pilot and a passenger. I was irritated
already with his interrogation, let alone the torrential drenching of
my plane. I could barely see outside and wasn't happy about it as
we drifted blindly and backwards down the river.

"Alpha Golf, would you describe the scene and condition of the
aircraft, over."

I took a deep breath. This was something I had wanted to avoid
broadcasting over public airwaves. But what choice did I have?

"RCMP helicopter, the NOCA aircraft is floating against the
river bank, it has been damaged by trees, two occupants are on
board, they are both…expired. The aircraft is a crime scene, over."

"Alpha Golf, say again, over."

"RCMP helicopter, two souls are in the NOCA Beaver, two
souls are expired, the plane is a crime scene, over."

"Roger that, stand by Alpha Golf."

I could feel her eyes on me.

"What?" I said, looking at her. "What can I say? I'm answering
his questions. I'm giving him the facts."

"Why don't you tell him you have a charter passenger and you're flying back to Minto now. Tell him those facts."

The radio cackled again. "Alpha Golf, you are instructed to fly immediately to Dawson. Dawson RCMP will interview you there, over."

"RCMP helicopter, I have a charter passenger on board who has a schedule to keep. My passenger needs to return to Minto right away. Can we give our statements to the RCMP in Minto, over?"

"Stand by, Alpha Golf."

"Alpha Golf, standing by."

I waited for what seemed like a long time. An aircraft radio couldn't possibly transmit all the way to Dawson from this altitude, certainly not from under the shadows of the cliffs. I assumed that Moore was using a satellite phone to communicate with his superiors.

"Oh, let's go to Dawson," Sarah said in an acquiescent tone.

"Really?" I looked at her with surprise.

"Yes. Let's just go to Dawson and get this nightmare dealt with."

"Alpha Golf, I have instructions to order you to fly to Dawson immediately or you will face arrest in Minto, over."

"RCMP, did you say face arrest, over?"

"Roger that, Alpha Golf."

"RCMP helicopter, do you have a SAT phone on board, over?"

I waited a moment. I guessed Moore was thinking about whether to answer the question.

Finally he said, "That's affirmative, over."

"Then here's what I need, sir. You tell your superior if he wants to interview me in Dawson, then the RCMP must pay for two hours of charter time, and, book and pay for two rooms at a hotel in Dawson, one for me and one for my passenger. If that's agreed, I will fly to Dawson now. If not, I will fly my charter passenger directly to Minto and will report to Minto RCMP there on arrival, over."

Sarah looked at me as if I was crazy.

"Stand by, Alpha Golf."

"What are you doing?" she hissed, making big eyes at me.

I put a finger to my lips.

A minute later, I got my answer.

"Alpha Golf, that's agreed to, over."

"RCMP helicopter, one more thing, sir. Have someone in Dawson call the Minto café. Tell someone there to go feed my dogs, over."

"Alpha Golf, please confirm, did you say 'go feed your dogs', over?"

"Roger that, they're hungry, they haven't eaten since last night, over."

There was a long pause, then, "Copy that, will call Minto café, over."

"Thank you, sir. I'm on my way to Dawson, will arrive at the Dawson water aerodrome in an hour or so, over."

"Copy that Alpha Golf, someone will be waiting there to meet you, RCMP helicopter, over and out."

"Alpha Golf, over and out."

The helicopter tilted forward and accelerated up the river. It left us behind in a swirling windstorm and sheets of water drenched my plane.

"You are a real case, Mr. Brody," she said, looking at me cynically.

"Hey, how about that? I just got us free hotel rooms in Dawson."

She shook her head and turned away, close to tears.

With a film of water on the windshield I lifted the rudders, shoved the throttle forward, and took off for Dawson.

TWELVE

Somewhere high over the Yukon River, about half an hour from Dawson, I was feeling overwhelmed. I'd been trying to process a whole bunch of things and wasn't getting anywhere.

I was thinking about Robert Duncan, a young man and new father, murdered for reasons beyond my knowledge or comprehension, gone forever from the life of his wife and child. I wondered why on earth anyone would murder a pilot from a small town, who flew a small plane, for a small company. I wondered who was going to tell his wife about his murder. And when? *When* would they tell her?

Hopefully before I got to town. It would be a nightmare to run into Katy Duncan on the streets of Dawson, me knowing well her husband's fate, she full of hope he'd soon be found alive and well. What would I do or say if faced with that dilemma?

I wondered about Robert's murdered passenger, a man Robert had probably never met before he boarded his plane yesterday. A man who Sarah Marsalis said she knew. So who was he? And how might she know him? And for that matter, who was Sarah Marsalis? What was her connection to Robert's passenger? Were they colleagues, friends, lovers? Talk about a coincidence. A woman hires me to fly her over a mine to take pictures, and just happens to know one of two murdered men we find in a missing airplane in the middle of nowhere. I thought about what Daryl had told me last night.

'Marsalis is trouble', and 'Stay away'. Why would he say those things? What could he possibly know about Sarah Marsalis that would motivate him to warn me off? And why had Sergeant Moore in the RCMP helicopter given me the impression there might be more than 'two souls' to be accounted for on the NOCA Beaver? Though I don't do it very often, I thought a few stiff drinks might be in order tonight.

I looked over at my passenger. She'd had her face pressed against the window ever since we'd taken off. I had no idea what she'd been doing. Sleeping, crying, or thinking – or maybe all three.

We were total strangers when we met last evening, and I supposed we still were just eighteen hours later. But somehow I felt as if I'd known her for a long time, having watched her display so many emotions in less than a day. She was a beautiful woman, no doubt about that, obviously athletic too, judging by the way she'd climbed over those boulders. She was certainly assured and professional, and though she seemed to get angry often enough, there was always justification in the short time I'd known her. When she did get angry, she didn't lose control, she just made sure you knew it. She'd demonstrated great patience when I'd been flying up and down and back and forth across the river, looking for NOCA's missing plane. And last night at dinner she'd revealed a warm and gracious quality that I found extremely attractive. And oh yeah, she'd kissed me. Now that had been a surprise. So who was this woman sitting beside me? What was her business in Dawson? Why did she hire me to fly her over a gold mine to take pictures? And what was she up to, driving that little green Corolla up the Klondike Highway?

She was an enigma, that's what she was. An enigma.

* * *

Twenty million ounces of gold have been dug out of the hills southeast of Dawson.

On August 16, 1896, just a few miles outside of town, three prospectors discovered gold on what was then called Rabbit Creek.

A week later the creek was aptly renamed Bonanza Creek, and for good reason. Because what the prospectors discovered was indeed a bonanza. Reports that the gold lay six inches deep at the bottom of Bonanza creek quickly became legendary, and the seeds of the 1898 Klondike Gold Rush were sown.

News of the discovery reached a world mired in a severe economic depression and captured the imagination of thousands of unemployed men, yearning for any kind of opportunity, any kind of adventure, and if nothing else, something to do. Over the next two years a hundred thousand men set out for the land known as the Klondike, to scour the Canadian sub-arctic for gold, to live the dream of finding their own fortune. Gold fever would increase the population of Dawson from just five hundred in 1896 to over thirty thousand by the fall of 1898.

Today's Dawson has a population of only thirteen hundred people, and though there are still a number of small mines operating in the area, the city serves primarily as a memorial to the greatest gold rush in history. The history and legacy of the 1898 gold rush is well promoted by the city, and each year it provides a vicarious experience of gold rush fever to thousands of visitors.

When Dawson appeared over the nose, I pulled the throttle back and adjusted the plane's settings for descent. Dawson is situated on the northeast flats at the junction of the Klondike River, which flows in from the east, and the Yukon River, which flows north past the town. From miles away in an airplane you can see the tailings left by the enormous dredges that mined the Klondike River. Dredge tailings are the most visible legacy of the large scale gold mining that took place near Dawson from 1900 to 1966. Millions of tons of washed rocks, cleaned of their gold bearing pay dirt by the big dredges, now line the banks of the Klondike River, and the valleys of Bonanza and Bear Creeks.

The Klondike Highway ends when it reaches Dawson and runs into Front Street, the town's main drag. Front Street continues north for another few miles along the east bank of the Yukon River and terminates at the river's edge. There, highway travelers can board a vehicle ferry that will transport them west across the river to Highway Nine, better known as the Top of the World Highway. The Top of the World Highway meanders west toward Alaska through some of the most awe inspiring country you'll ever get to see from the seat of a family car. In the winter months, vehicles can cross the Yukon River from Dawson on a well plowed and nicely maintained ice road. I've never been on an ice road – never trusted them – though they're proven to be viable and safe.

I called Dawson air traffic control.

"Dawson ATC, this is Beaver on floats, Papa Papa Alpha Golf, five miles south of Dawson, inbound for landing at the Dawson Water Aerodrome."

"Papa Papa Alpha Golf, this is Dawson ATC, winds one ninety at eight, gusts fifteen, pressure thirty point two, no conflicting traffic reported, watch for ferry traffic on the river, over."

"Roger that, Dawson, thanks, Alpha Golf, over and out."

For the first time in almost an hour Sarah looked up. She was wearing sunglasses. I pointed at the view through the prop.

"Dawson," I said. She nodded.

"How are you feeling?" She nodded again.

The wind was out of the south so I needed to land heading south. I steered the plane over to the hills on the west side of the river and prepared to make a one hundred and eighty degree right hand turn. I looked down at the river on my right. There were two ferries working, serving a long line of parked vehicles, RV's, and highway trucks waiting on the Dawson side of the river. The lineup of vehicles extended south from the ferry landing at the north end of Front Street, well past the docks where I planned to tie up. People were standing outside their parked vehicles, waiting for the line to move, enjoying the afternoon sun, looking at the river, watching the two ferries that were currently loading and unloading on opposite sides of the river. With the river clear of ferry traffic it was a perfect time to land. After starting a descending right hand turn down to the river, I glimpsed two RCMP cruisers parked at the docks. They would have easily spotted my plane and would be watching us land. We *were* expected, after all.

With the ferries still loading vehicles on opposite sides of the river I trimmed everything for approach, dropped the flaps, and made a pretty good landing in front of a large audience.

The Dawson water aerodrome docks are strategically located where the river current is relatively slow. I dropped the float rudders down and had an easy time taxing up to the main dock, parallel to the river bank. A crisply dressed RCMP officer was standing on the dock. He was holding a rope in his hand. I turned the engine off with the mixture lever and glided in the last ten feet, stopping beside him. When the left float bumped against the dock, the cop looped the rope around the front cleat and tied a knot. I turned off the mags and the master switch, shut off the fuel supply, raised the rudders, and pumped the flaps up.

"We're here Sarah, grab your stuff, we'll go out the cargo door."

I climbed down to the dock, picked up a line, and tied it to the cleat on the rear of the float. Then I opened the cargo door, took her pack from her, and let Miss Sarah Marsalis step out in front of a growing and fascinated crowd. I offered her my hand but she wanted none of that, choosing to turn her back to the audience and climbing down the ladder to the delight of many of the male onlookers – I'm sure – who were treated to an excellent view of her finely tailored blue jeans.

"Good afternoon sir. I'm Constable Evans. Is your name Brody?"

Constable Evans stood in the middle of the dock, a few feet in front of me. A woman officer approached and stopped behind him.

"Yeah, that's me. Let me lock up the plane, I'll be right with you."

I locked the cockpit doors from the inside, checked the switches on the console one last time, climbed down the cargo ladder, and locked the door. I stepped on the dock and walked forward to check the knot on the front of the float. Constable Evans was apparently never a boy scout and I retied his knot.

I knew he was watching and looked up at him. "Don't take that the wrong way, sir, just like to do my own knots."

He smiled and said "I'm actually glad you checked. Now if you're ready, sir, would you follow me please? And you Mme.?" He looked at Sarah and gestured at his colleague. "Would you go with Constable LeMay, please?"

Sarah glanced at me, shrugged, picked up her pack and followed Constable LeMay.

"See you later, Sarah."

"See you later," she said, not looking back.

We all walked in a single file along the floating dock, then turned left and walked up the jetty to a small parking lot on the river bank. Constable LeMay led the way, then Sarah, then me, and Evans towed the rear. I cast my eyes up to a long line of people watching us with curiosity from Front Street above us. I wondered what they thought about the official police greeting given to this pilot and his passenger. I guess some would think we were with the police, others that the beautiful passenger might be some kind of VIP, and of course some would be suspicious and assume that Sarah and I were both criminals. Not that it mattered. They were all about to leave Dawson on a ferry for the other side of the river.

Evans gestured to the cruiser parked in front. He walked around me and opened the rear door on the driver's side.

"Make yourself comfortable," he said.

"The back seat, in the cage, really?"

"Sorry, standard procedure. But I didn't frisk you and didn't put you in cuffs, in case you're worried about what anyone up there might be thinking." He tilted his head at the gallery above us.

"Okay," I said, "Understand."

I looked back at Sarah who for some reason was allowed to get in the front seat of the cruiser behind me. I threw my pack on the seat, then glanced over the roof of the cruiser, scanning the crowd of curious onlookers for a familiar face. Everyone does that when they arrive at an airport. I recognized no one, just a stranger watching strangers.

But one imposing man did catch my eye. He was watching me intently. He was Asian, big and thick and strong. He had the build of a weight lifter and a menace in his stare. He was standing beside a thin man who had his right arm in a sling.

I got in the cruiser.

THIRTEEN

Wei Lee was sitting in the rear seat of his new Lincoln Continental Town Car, savoring its new car aroma, caressing its plush leather seats. He'd bought one of the last ones ever made. What a fine car, he thought, what a shame they've stopped making them. Milton, his driver for many years, drove carefully and smoothly in the heavy afternoon traffic. Lee loved the rarefied tranquility inside the big luxury car. The heat and noise of the Los Angeles freeway outside might as well be a million miles away. There's no greater comfort for the mind than peace and quiet, he mused. It lets a man think with clarity. Lee heard the phone purr in front of him. He leaned forward and took the phone from its cradle.

"Yes."

"Hello, Mr. Lee."

"Tommy! Is that you? How are you, Tommy?"

"I am fine, Mr. Lee."

"Good. How is our gold business?"

"We produced seven hundred and fifty ounces this week, exactly one million dollars as planned, Mr. Lee. But yesterday there was a problem, a tragic accident. We have lost our gold pilot and his plane. We could not deliver our gold. We will deliver the gold when we talk to our fish pilot. We are in Dawson waiting for him. But Mr. Lee, the accident, it should not have happened. The man I am working with, he…"

"Stop, Tommy." Wei Lee brooded over the news for a moment. "Tommy, you need to find our fish pilot right away. We need him to fly a load of fish this week. We have so much fish coming in now, Tommy. The fish pilot can deliver our gold too. Do you know where he is, our fish pilot?"

"Yes, Mr. Lee. He is here in Dawson, with his plane, but he was just taken away by the police."

"The police? Why was he taken away by the police?"

"I don't know, Mr. Lee. They took him away when he landed his plane. He was with a woman."

"A woman? What woman?"

"I don't know, Mr. Lee. A woman was with him in his plane. The police took them both away."

"Find out who the woman is, Tommy. She could be a problem, do you agree?"

"I agree, Mr. Lee."

"And find out why the police took away our fish pilot. You must find that out too."

"Yes, Mr. Lee."

"And Tommy. You know we need to deliver more gold, and you know we need to pick up more fish. Right away."

"Yes, Mr. Lee, I know."

"Good Tommy. Now this man you're working with. What is his name?"

"His name is Ricky. He works for your associate from Las Vegas. He is very hard to work with. He talks too much. He made a terrible mistake."

"Tommy, if this man Ricky is a problem then you know how to solve the problem, like you always do. I will talk to my associate."

"Thank you, Mr. Lee."

"Tommy, did you try on a Boss yet?"

"No, Mr. Lee."

Wei Lee put the phone back in its cradle and rubbed his thighs.

Nothing but bad news. There had been too many problems lately. Every time one got solved, a bigger one came up. No one could do business with the police hovering around. Lee wondered why the police were suddenly so interested in his Yukon pilots. And who was this woman in the fish pilot's plane, the one the police took away? Was she working with the police? Were the police investigating his gold mine and his fish business? He had to look at the big picture now. You don't eliminate a swarm of mosquitoes by swatting them one at a time. He picked up the phone.

"Lucky Star Trading Company, good afternoon."

"Lynn, find Henry, have him call me in the car."

"Yes, Mr. Lee."

Lee hung up the phone and wondered about the man Arturo Pistone had sent to Dawson. Arturo had justification to send his own man to carry his cash to Dawson, and to guard the gold he would buy. But why would Arturo send a loose cannon who would whack Wei Lee's pilot? Wei Lee owned the Yukon mine, not Arturo. None of Lee's gold mining operation was any of Arturo's business, and that included planes and pilots. The man Arturo had sent north to work with Tommy was now a liability. He would have to disappear. Tommy would take care of that. Wei Lee would explain the situation to Arturo. But things had to change. Lately, there were too many problems getting solved the hard way.

Like that cockroach customs broker, Perez. Perez had asked Henry too many questions at dinner, questions about things that didn't concern him. Perez could no longer be trusted. A change was made. Perez was gone now. Tommy had always been very good at eliminating problems. Henry had found Wei Lee a new customs broker. At least that problem was solved.

Lee rubbed his thighs again. He was agitated and didn't like the feeling. Things were getting complicated, the challenges growing in difficulty, even with outstanding people like Tommy helping to sort them out. Lee knew he couldn't succeed with mistakes like what had just happened in the Yukon. Especially now with the police talking to the fish pilot. People were always the problem.

Except his girls. His girls just did their jobs. His girls made him so much money. So much cash.

Weir Lee thought deeply. So what *is* the big picture? He rubbed his temples. The challenge wasn't how to make money. He was making lots of money. The challenge was what to do with all the cash. The big picture was that cash was getting packed into boxes of fish faster than he could fly it to Canada and buy gold. The car phone rang.

"Is that Henry?"

"Hello, Mr. Lee."

"Henry, how are you?"

"I am fine, Mr. Lee. How are you?"

"Henry, I am very concerned about problems with our business in the Yukon. Perhaps you can help."

"Of course, Mr. Lee."

"Henry, how much cash do we have in Haines now?"

"Three boxes full, Mr. Lee. And more will arrive tomorrow."

"Can we fly it all to Dawson next week?"

"Well, Mr. Lee, perhaps, but we can not use that cash to increase our gold production at this time. Not yet. No Yukon mine can produce so much gold in the first two weeks of a new mining season. The authorities know this. They would be suspicious if we were to report so much gold production so early in the year. You know we are reporting all our gold production to the government. That is why we always pay the export royalties. You know we must pay these royalties to document gold production from our mine. You know our bankers insist on this documentation, or we don't get our loans. So our gold production must be realistic, otherwise the authorities will become suspicious. That would not be a good thing, Mr. Lee. We must always avoid an investigation or an audit of our mine. We have to be patient and wait before reporting more gold production. We should not increase our gold production at this time. We must wait a few weeks."

"I cannot wait a few weeks, Henry. You know I am constructing a condominium building in Vancouver. We need to ship more gold right away to get our construction loans. And my associate in Las Vegas, he also needs gold. As my partner in this project, helping him finance his construction payments is good business. Do not forget that he provides a very important product to us. A product we need to do business. There must be a way to increase our gold production."

"Yes, Mr. Lee, but please, we should not be helping your partner to buy gold right now, not until we have enough for ourselves. As I have suggested to you before, you must buy another mine to increase gold production, or better still, buy a bank. A bank would make everything so much easier, much easier than flying fish and operating a gold mine."

"I will never buy a bank, Henry. Banking is a complicated and sleazy business. But perhaps you are right. Perhaps we should buy another mine. Is one available?"

"I will investigate that, Mr. Lee."

"Good. And Henry, perhaps we should buy our own plane. And hire our own pilot."

"I will investigate that too, Mr. Lee."

Wei Lee paused, thinking about what he'd just said.

"Yes, Henry. I think it would be an excellent idea to buy our own plane. And hire our own pilot."

FOURTEEN

I dug down to the bottom of my backpack and rummaged around for my cell phone. Yes, I have a cell phone. It doesn't work in Minto, but believe it or not, there are now a couple of places in the Yukon where it does work. The city of Whitehorse is one, Dawson is another. It also works in Haines and Juneau. Last winter I used it a few times in Phoenix. I've decided that cell phones can be pretty handy sometimes. Don't know my phone number, have never received a call, but last year I probably made a dozen calls out.

I bought my phone two years ago in a drug store in Juneau. It's called a 'pay as you go' phone and my 'plan' costs a hundred dollars a year. Don't know how many minutes that buys, but if I don't use them all, they stay in my account if I renew my plan for another year. I think there's a hundred and seventy dollars worth of minutes in my account right now. Someday I'm going to call an old friend of mine in Europe, talk for a couple of hours, and use up all those minutes.

My phone was at the very bottom of my pack. I brushed the sand and grit off it, then turned it on. The screen lit up and it said it was searching for something. It was a five minute drive to the RCMP detachment and a good time to call Minnie, make sure my dogs were being looked after. I stared at the screen and waited. And waited. My phone played a jingle. It found what it was searching for.

I dialed the café in Minto and pressed 'send'.

"Minto Café!"

"Hey Minnie, it's Brody."

"Brody! Where are you? The cops are after you!"

"I'm in Dawson, Minnie. Look, I may not be home tonight. Just called to make sure Russ and Jack are getting fed. What do you mean the cops are after me?"

"Are you in jail Brody?"

"No, I'm not in jail. Minnie, my dogs, is someone going to feed them?"

"Yeah. Reggie went down to your place after lunch. Hey Brody?"

"What?"

"You wouldn't believe what's been going on around here."

"Oh yeah? What's been going on?"

"Well, a couple of hours ago me and Reggie were in here goin' over some bills. It was real quiet, like it always is on a Tuesday morning, well you know that. But then two RCMP cruisers pulled into the parking lot, and then a minute later this big black SUV drives in and parks right behind the two cruisers. I think it was like one of those giant excapades or somethin' like that, it was huge, all black with black windows, Alaska plates, aerials stickin' out everywhere, very official looking. So anyway, four cops get out of the two cruisers, and then a couple more cops get out of the big black excapade, and they all come marchin' in here, and then this big one with a bunch of stripes on his shirt comes walkin' up to me at the counter and tells me that someone here should go feed your dogs, 'cuz he says you won't be back tonight. So like it takes two RCMP cruisers and an SUV and six cops comin' in here to tell me to go feed your dogs? Well no problem, I said, and I told Reggie to go feed your dogs. So there's these three other guys wearing street clothes waiting outside in the excapade, travelling with all the cops from Whitehorse, I can see 'em through the window, right?

They were just sittin' inside it, talkin' with the doors wide open. So then they decide to come in. They looked like Americans to me, I can always tell you know. Then two more cops get out of the two cruisers, and they come in too. So now there's all these cops in here, just standin' and walkin' around with their hands in their pockets, not saying a word. Like eight cops, Brody, plus those three American guys too, and they're all just walkin' around in here, lookin' at the walls like a bunch of aliens who've never been in a restaurant before. Then the big cop with all the stripes starts asking me all these questions, like do I know where you are, where did you go, were you out flying, where did you fly to, when did you leave, when were you comin' back, stuff like that, see? And oh yeah, one of the guys in street clothes wanted to know where that S. Marsalis is, I just told him she went flying with you, anyway…"

"Minnie, how do you know she went flying with me?"

"Oh, 'cuz some of the boys went down to the lake this morning and saw her car parked beside your truck. Anyway, listen to this Brody! Then Daryl comes burnin' into the parking lot in his cruiser, comes runnin' inside here, and whispers somethin' to the big cop with all the stripes. So the big cop whispers somethin' back to Daryl, and then Daryl goes over to Reggie and tells him to go down to the lake and tow that S. Marsalis' car over to his place! And then the big cop with all the stripes runs out of here like a bat out of hell, and all the other cops run out after him, and they all pile into their cruisers, and those three American guys ran out too, and they jumped in their big black excapade, and then Daryl runs out, and he jumps into his cruiser, and then all three cruisers and the excapade take off with their wheels spinnin' and their lights flashin', kickin' up clouds of dust, headin' north. It looked like a jail break out there! So Brody? Like, are you and that S. Marsalis in some kind of big trouble or what? Like what's goin' on?"

"Minnie, I don't know what's going on, but I intend to find out. You'll know when I know."

"Right. Sure, sure. Oh, hey Brody?"

"Yeah, Minnie."

"That Chinese guy named Charlie? The cook from Whitehorse? The one who works in the hotel and orders fish from Haines? Well he called here twice this morning. Says you've got to fly to Haines right away. Says there's a big load of fish ready to pick up."

FIFTEEN

I turned off my phone when Constable Evans slowed in front of the Dawson RCMP building. He angle parked between two other cruisers and got out. When he opened my door, I watched Constable LeMay and Sarah Marsalis drive past and turn down the alley. I assumed LeMay had her reasons to park at the back of the building, there were plenty of parking spots on the street.

The Dawson RCMP detachment is headquartered in a two story wood building clad in grey vinyl siding with white trim around its numerous small windows. A white billboard stands out front on a tiny patch of lawn, displaying the RCMP logo with the words 'Royal Canadian Mounted Police' printed on top. Lest anyone in the extreme northwest section of Canada is unaware that the country has two official languages, the French words 'Gendarmerie Royal du Canada' are printed underneath. A wide wooden sidewalk runs along the front of the building, and for the full distance up and down the long dirt street.

Wooden sidewalks are ubiquitous in Dawson, allowing pedestrians to stay high and dry off its unpaved streets, which quickly turn into muddy quagmires when it rains. Stand and look down the length of any Dawson sidewalk and you'll notice how it rolls and twists and undulates, as though it's floating on ocean swells.

In a sense Dawson's sidewalks are floating, because the town is built on a block of frozen mud hundreds of feet deep that hasn't thawed out for a hundred thousand years. The permanently frozen ground under Dawson precludes constructing just any type of building or house. Concrete buildings are definitely out of the question, because let alone their excessive weight, they'd conduct their heat down into the permafrost and melt it. And were the permafrost to melt, any building above would sink and shift and break apart. No one knows exactly how deep the permafrost is under Dawson, but I doubt anyone will ever build a high rise building with an underground parking garage here.

Maintaining the city's water and sewer lines – and its sidewalks – is a major annual expense for Dawson. Throughout the year the top few feet of permafrost is continuously thawing and freezing, shifting and heaving, moving everything around, including the sidewalks. So contrary to myth, Dawson does not purposely build its sidewalks with rolls and twists to help bar patrons stay on their feet.

I got out of the cruiser and slung my pack over my shoulder.

"Follow me please, Mr. Brody," said Constable Evans.

We could have walked fifty feet down to the corner, climbed some stairs to get on the sidewalk, then doubled back to the front door. But instead we did what most locals do when the streets are dry. We walked down into the shallow ditch in front of the cruiser, put our hands on the sidewalk, threw a leg up, and climbed on. We walked across the wide wooden sidewalk straight into the RCMP building.

"We're at the end of the hall", Evans said, brushing dust off his hands, leading the way, gesturing toward the back of the building.

I followed Evans past a large open reception area. A woman behind a desk was trying to accomplish something while a fat cop with a cup of coffee was leaning against a file cabinet, telling her something he thought was terribly funny.

"Is there coffee close?" I asked Evans.

"In there." He pointed into a small room on his right, then leaned against the far wall to wait for me.

"Thanks," I said, "I'll be quick."

I emerged from the room with a cup of foul tasting black water that can only legally be called coffee if it's free. I followed Evans to the end of the hall. He gave two short knocks with a knuckle on the last door on the left, then opened it.

"You're in here," he said.

"Thanks."

"Good luck."

I entered the room and heard the door close behind me. There were no windows. Five uniformed cops and two men in civilian clothes were seated around a long conference table. One of the cops was Daryl Pageau. I nodded at him. He nodded back. As I was lowering my pack to the floor the two guys in street clothes were hastily sweeping photographs and papers off the table, stowing them safely out of sight. No one got up to introduce themselves or shake my hand. The cop seated at the far end of the table gestured to the only unoccupied chair, the one at my end which faced him.

"Please sit down, Mr. Brody. I'm Staff Sergeant Robson. We appreciate you coming to Dawson. I see you've found the coffee so let's get started. We have a number of questions we hope you can answer. Your co-operation is much appreciated."

"Alright," I said, making myself comfortable, "but I have a couple of questions before you ask yours."

Robson stiffened, inhaled deeply, and gave me a long stern look, as if to convey that I was somehow way out of order. He looked like a man that was used to asking questions, not answering them. He was obviously the one in control of the meeting. He was an imposing figure, probably well over six feet tall, very strong and fit looking, with clear blue eyes and a brush cut that would get him into any army. He was about forty-five years old.

"Go ahead, ask your questions, but we are pressed for time today."

"Thanks," I said. "First question, did you get me and my passenger hotel rooms?"

"You're at the Downtown tonight. Booked and paid for. Any extras are on you."

"Great, thanks. Now, the RCMP agreed to pay me for two hours of charter time, who gets the bill?"

Robson was giving me his best deadpan cop stare now. "Send your invoice to the RCMP in Whitehorse, attention myself."

"I'll do that, thank you". I paused for a second, looked around the table, then back at Robson. "Sir, has the RCMP told Katy Duncan what happened to her husband?"

"What happened to her husband?" Robson replied.

Okay, so now the games start, I thought. "He was shot in the back of the head, sir, twice." I looked directly into his eyes. "He was murdered."

"Mr. Brody, by the time our meeting is over, Mrs. Duncan will have been told about her husband's passing. Now, if those are all your questions, can we get started?"

"Will you tell her he was murdered?"

"At this point, sir, there has not been an autopsy and our investigation has just begun. So we'll provide Mrs. Duncan with our standard description of his cause of death, which in this case is that we suspect foul play. I'm afraid that's all we can tell her at this time. Now, if you don't mind, *you're* here to answer *our* questions."

"But I have another question."

"*Yes*, Mr. Brody."

"Aren't you going to introduce me to your colleagues?"

Robson hesitated, then sighed in irritation.

"On my right is Corporal Harris, Whitehorse detachment, to his right is Constable Monahan, also Whitehorse detachment, I believe you know Constable Pageau from the Minto detachment. To my left is Sergeant Arcand, Dawson detachment, to his left is Mr. Kurtz, and to his left is Mr. Owen. Mr. Kurtz and Mr. Owen are... with the U.S. government."

"Really? The U.S. government? Like the FBI or the CIA or one of those three letter deals?" I leaned forward and looked at Kurtz and Owen.

"US Treasury Department," Kurtz said.

Owen said nothing. I leaned forward and looked at the two of them, hoping they'd explain their presence in a foreign country. But they simply held my eyes with the practiced dead pan stares of law enforcement professionals. They were both clean cut and neatly dressed in good quality shirts and pressed cotton slacks. They might have been pushing forty, and seemed very self assured.

"How did you get the scratches on your face?" Robson asked me, perhaps as an attempt to change the subject as fast as he could.

"Climbing through a bunch of trees on the way to that plane we found this morning."

"Who is *we*?"

"My passenger and I."

"What was your passenger's name?"

"Sarah Marsalis."

"What time did you scratch your face?"

"About eleven o'clock this morning."

"What did you do today before eleven o'clock this morning?"

"Well, I got down to the campground in Minto about seven thirty. That's where I keep my plane, at Two Spirit Lake. I found a SAR Alert on my plane and read it. It said the NOCA Beaver was overdue. The SAR said the Beaver's flight plan took it over a spot just west of where I was flying my charter passenger. Miss Marsalis, she was my charter passenger, she arrived at the lake about eight. We took off from the lake about eight thirty and headed for Thistle Creek. We got to the west end of Thistle Creek around nine thirty. She wanted me to fly some circles around a mine so she could take some pictures. When she was done taking her pictures, I thought we'd take a little time to look for the missing NOCA plane. So we flew down to the Yukon River from the mine and went north along the river. Miss Marsalis spotted the plane a few minutes later. I landed on the east bank of the river just north of the plane. That was about ten thirty. I was walking up the shore, heading to the NOCA plane, when I scratched my face climbing over some trees. So like I said, it was about eleven o'clock this morning."

"Was Sarah Marsalis with you when you scratched your face?"

"Yes, well actually no, she was back at my plane, waiting for me, so she didn't exactly see it happen."

"What was she doing back at your plane?"

"I don't know. I guess she was just sitting on the beach. I told her to wait there while I walked up the shore to the NOCA plane."

"And did she?"

"Did she what?"

"Did she wait for you?"

"Not for long."

"What did she do?"

"She decided she didn't want to wait at the plane and followed me. She eventually caught up to me, then we both walked up to the NOCA plane together."

"Did she see the men in the plane?"

"Yeah, she saw the *dead* men in the plane."

Robson paused and looked at the two men from the US government. They looked back at him. Robson took a long deep breath and exhaled loudly enough so that everyone heard him. Then he continued.

"Mr. Brody, how many men did you say you found in the plane?"

"Two."

"Just two."

Here we go again, I thought. "Yes. That's right, just two."

"You're sure."

"I'm sure."

"You saw no one else in the plane, or in the area of the plane, either alive or dead."

"No sir. Two dead men is what I saw. That's all. But you never know, there could have been another two men hiding on top of the wings, or lying on their backs submerged in the river, breathing through bamboo sticks. But I only saw two men."

Like all experienced cops, Robson didn't react to my sarcasm, let alone show any indication whether he believed any of my answers. I was hungry and irritable, but knew I better control my emotions if I wanted to walk out of the building after my 'interview'.

"Mr. Brody, right now I don't mind enlightening you a little on why we're so interested in how many men you might have found in the NOCA Beaver." Robson was speaking in a deliberate and careful manner, and had my interest piqued. "NOCA's manifest for their flight out of here yesterday listed only two souls on board the missing Beaver, the pilot and one male passenger. But we're a little unsure if that's actually the case. You see, all the ferry captains were issued the SAR Alert too, the same one you got. One of the ferry captains working on the river yesterday morning called us up this morning and asked why only two souls were listed as missing on the SAR. The ferry captain swears he saw four men getting into that Beaver yesterday morning. Unfortunately his view of the plane leaving the docks was from quite a distance away, so he couldn't give us a clear description of what the men looked like. But he's adamant he saw four men board that plane. Now obviously if there were two other men on the flight, we'd very much like to know who they are, where they are, and we definitely want to talk to them. We'll be asking for the public's help in identifying those two other men, so don't go thinking I've just spilled a kettle of fish here. Now, perhaps that information will help you adjust your attitude for the rest of this meeting."

"Sure," I said. "Thanks for explaining that."

It was a significant revelation. I was embarrassed and Robson had me exactly where he wanted me now.

"You're welcome, sir. Now, what did you do after you discovered the two dead men in the NOCA plane?"

"I got in it. I wanted to make sure the men were dead. I mean, they looked dead, but I wanted to make sure that they weren't just injured and unconscious, that there wasn't something I could do to help them. But they were both very dead. So Miss Marsalis and

I walked back to my plane. We untied it, got out on the river, and were about to take off when your chopper came up beside us."

"Where were you going to take off to?"

"Well, first I was going to climb up high enough to radio Dawson."

"Climb up high.," Robson said, with a cynical look.

"Yeah, climb up high, up to an adequate altitude to get into radio range of Dawson, to report what we'd found. But then your RCMP helicopter arrived and I told your man Moore what the situation was."

"And that's when you did your bargaining for hotel rooms and charter time, I understand."

"That's right."

Robson was nodding, staring at me intently. He didn't blink and he never looked away. Who knew what he was thinking? I wondered if he thought I was somehow a murder suspect. Maybe he was seeing if I'd falter or break down, or would offer up some incriminating information that he could sink his teeth into. I felt everyone's eyes on me while I tried to hold Robson's gaze. He was taking his time before his next move and I wasn't going to say a thing unless spoken to. He rubbed his chin and looked at Owen and Kurtz. They nodded at him.

"Mr. Brody," said Robson, "we're going to show you some photographs. Please tell us whether you recognize anyone in the photographs."

Owen reached down beside his chair and produced a stack of eight by ten, black and white photographs which he placed on the table, face down in front of him. He picked up the one on top, flipped it over, looked at it, then slid it over to me. The photo was of a short Asian man getting into a limo. A large black man in a chauffeur's uniform was holding the door for him. The photo was grainy, as though it might have been taken from a long distance away, or had been enlarged significantly. It had been taken on a busy city street in front of what looked like an entrance to a large office building.

"Have you ever seen either of these men, and do you know who they are?" asked Owen.

I looked carefully at the photo. The small Asian man was wearing a dark suit. The car looked like a big Lincoln. The chauffeurs face was barely discernible.

"No."

"Are you sure?"

"I'm sure."

Owen pulled the photo back and slid another one in front of me.

"How about this man?"

This one was a head and shoulder photo of an Asian man. He looked about forty five years old. He had strange eyes. The shot was probably a government ID photo that had been enlarged, perhaps from a driver's license or passport.

"No."

"Are you sure?"

"I'm sure."

"How about this one?" Owen slid another photo in front of me.

This photo was of a tough looking working man dressed in a red and black checked jacket and blue jeans. He was wearing a ball cap and tall rubber boots. He was pulling a large white box off the tailgate of a pickup truck. There were fishing boats tied up in the background. Once again, the photo looked like it had been taken from a fair distance away, or enlarged, or both, but I knew who it was. And I knew exactly where it had been taken.

"Yeah. I know that guy. That's Jack. That was taken in Haines."

"Jack who?" said Owen.

"I don't know. Something 'ski'. He only told me his last name once. But Jack is the guy they send down to the harbor in Haines with fish for me to pick up."

"Who is they?" asked Robson, now leaning forward with his arms on the table.

"The Panhandle Fish Company. That's the consignor's name written on the bills of lading and the customs docs. That's the company that supplies my customer in Whitehorse with salmon and crab. I fly down to Haines, load up my plane with boxes of fish and crab, and fly them up to Whitehorse."

"Fish," he said. "Do you ever see this fish or crab, do you ever look in the boxes?"

"No. They're packed on ice in styrofoam boxes. The boxes are sealed shut with plastic strapping and tape to keep the fish cold. They can only be opened for inspection by Canadian Customs in Whitehorse. They're about eighty pounds each, I should know, I've loaded enough of them. But I've never opened one because I have no business opening one. Why do you want to know what I do down in Haines?"

"Mr. Brody, how many boxes do you usually load into your plane when you pick up fish and crabs in Haines?" asked Kurtz.

"Usually ten, sometimes twelve."

"And you fly directly to Whitehorse with these boxes?"

"Yes."

"Always directly, you never make a stop anywhere else on your way up to Whitehorse?"

"No. I always fly directly to Whitehorse."

"How often do you fly boxes of fish and crabs from Haines to Whitehorse?" Kurtz asked, leaning forward to look around Owen. Don't know why, but I didn't like the look Kurtz gave me.

"From May through October, maybe twice a month, on average."

"When was the last time you flew boxes of fish from Haines to Whitehorse?" he asked.

"I flew ten boxes from Haines to Whitehorse two days ago. First trip of the year."

"How about from November to April? Do you fly fish from Haines to Whitehorse in those months?"

"No. I don't pick up any fish in those months, only during tourist season. Hey, what's with all these questions about my cargo business? I thought I was here to answer questions about the murdered men in that Beaver."

They all ignored my question. Again. Owen took back the picture of Jack and slid another one over to me.

"How about this man? Do you recognize him?" Owen tapped his finger on the photo.

This one was also taken with a long lens. I easily recognized this man too. He was standing beside a pickup truck, leaning against its hood, looking out at a lake. It was taken in Whitehorse beside Schwatka Lake, just south of the city above the power dam, where most of the float plane traffic going into the city lands. Me included.

"Yeah, I know him. His name's Charlie. He works for the Fifty Below Hotel. He's the guy who picks up the fish that I fly in from Haines."

"Charlie who?" asked Robson.

"I forget. Woo, I think, yeah, Woo. They'll know at the hotel for sure, he works in the kitchen."

"When you land in Whitehorse, Mr. Brody, do you meet anyone from Canadian Customs?" Kurtz asked.

"Well, yeah, of course I do. Every time. I have to. When I call Whitehorse tower for landing clearance, I always request a customs officer to meet me at the lake. A Canadian customs officer is always waiting with Charlie when I pull up to the wharf. I show him the paperwork for the fish, he stamps a few documents, looks at my passport and leaves. Then Charlie and I load the fish into his pickup truck. I hand him my invoice, he gives me a ride into town, and we say goodbye."

"You say 'he', and 'him'. Is it always the same customs officer?" asked Robson.

"Yeah, I guess it is, now that you mention it."

"Do you know his name?" Kurtz asked.

"No idea."

"Would you describe him please?"

"White, male, five eleven, one eighty, moustache, maybe sixty years old."

Owen flipped through a few photos, then pulled one out and held it up. "Mr. Brody, is this the customs officer you meet at the lake when you deliver fish in Whitehorse?"

He held up what looked like an enlargement of a Yukon driver's license photo of the Canadian Customs officer. It was the first time I'd ever seen him without his hat on, but it was definitely him.

"Yeah, that's him."

"Mr. Brody," Owen asked, "the invoice you give to this man Charlie, how is it paid?"

"He gives me a check."

"Who is 'he'?" asked Robson.

"Oh, well, I usually overnight in Whitehorse after I fly fish in from Haines. I need fuel when I land and can't get fuel delivered at the lake until morning. So the next day I go down to the hotel, walk in the kitchen, and Charlie hands me a check, and usually a couple of salmon or some crab as a tip. Then I go to the bank and deposit the check, buy some groceries, go back to my plane, and meet the fuel truck. Then, I fly home."

"But who is 'he', Mr. Brody?" Robson was in a full press now. "Whose name is on the check, the check you get from this man named Charlie?"

"I'm not sure. Something or another enterprises. I forget the whole name. But it has the word 'enterprises' on it. And the check is on a local Whitehorse bank and it always clears. That's all I care about. Look, are we just about done with these questions about my cargo business?"

"You said you give this man Charlie an invoice," Robson said, ignoring my question, again. "What is the name of the person or the company that you invoice for flying fish to Whitehorse from Haines?"

"The Fifty Below Hotel, that's the name of the consignee written on the bill of lading, and the importer named on the customs docs."

"But you get your check from a man named Charlie," Robson said, "he's the one who pays you at the hotel, even though the check is issued by something or another enterprises, right?" Robson was really pushing now, leaning toward me.

"That's right. Like I said, I walk in the kitchen at the Fifty Below Hotel where Charlie works, and he hands me a check. Look, what's with all these questions about my cargo business? What does any of this stuff about the checks I get for flying fish to Whitehorse have to do with two dead men in a plane?"

There was a pause and the men around the table were looking at each other.

Owen took away the photo of the customs officer and replaced it with another one.

"We're almost finished, Mr. Brody," he said. "How about this man. Do you recognize him?"

This photo was of a good looking Hispanic man with a moustache, maybe forty years old. The photo was also probably another enlargement taken from a drivers license.

I shook my head. "Nope."

"You're sure?" Owen asked.

"I'm sure. Don't know him," I said. "And you guys still haven't answered my question. So one more time, why are you so interested in my cargo business and the checks I get paid with?"

"As I just said, we're almost finished," Owen said with a polite smile. He pushed another photograph in front of me. "How about this man?"

I shook my head in frustration while waiting to look at his next offering. It was another drivers license photo. I didn't recognize the man in the photo, though there was something vaguely familiar about him. He was good looking, white, clean shaven, healthy, maybe late thirties. But no matter how hard I tried, I couldn't place him. I shook my head.

"Nope, can't say I know him."

"You're sure," said Owen.

"I'm sure."

Owen took the photograph back and slid another one in front of me.

"How about this man? Do you know him?"

This photo was of a man walking down a wooden sidewalk in front of a building with gray wood siding. There were patches of snow here and there and the streets were muddy. It had probably been taken in Dawson. It would be a good bet it was taken a few weeks ago when the weather was still pretty wet and cold. The man was bent forward under the load of a large backpack and he was carrying a briefcase. He had a full head of white hair and a neatly trimmed white beard. His clothes gave me the impression of a well heeled gentleman. He looked like my idea of a birdwatcher. I guessed his age at about sixty. His head was turned slightly toward the camera so his face was clearly visible. I'd never seen him before.

"No." I leaned back in my chair and folded my arms.

"You don't recognize this man?" Owen asked.

"No, I do not."

"You're absolutely sure?"

"I am absolutely sure."

"Alright Mr. Brody, last one". Owen slid another photo in front of me. "Do you know this person?"

I leaned forward and looked at the photo. I sure knew this one. It was another enlargement of a government ID photo. I probably studied it a little too long for my own good.

"Yeah. That's Sarah Marsalis."

SIXTEEN

I burst out the front door of the RCMP building and stopped on the sidewalk. I was suffocating. I threw my head back and hauled in a few lungfuls of fresh clean Yukon air. A minute later, I felt a whole lot better.

For over an hour I'd been held captive in a twenty by fifteen foot room with no windows, a closed door, and seven other men sharing a box full of air. It was a miracle no one had expired for a lack of oxygen. How do people do it? I've often wondered how half the western world can possibly like their jobs when they have to spend their days working in sealed buildings. It can't be healthy. I certainly couldn't do it.

I thought about what to do next. A shower would be nice but that would have to wait. First I had to eat something. Then visit Katy Duncan.

Robert and Katy Duncan had bought a little house in the northeast section of Dawson just after they got married two years ago. The house was six or seven blocks away. I didn't have a vehicle but had my feet and legs. I decided to head toward the Duncan's house and stop for something to eat on the way. That was the plan.

I turned left and started down the sidewalk, heading north, my boots clomping and bouncing over the wood planks. There are no traffic lights in Dawson and vehicle traffic is sparse at any time of day. Drivers here are rarely in a hurry. People in small towns know they can get their business done faster just by walking from one appointment to the next. When you step off a sidewalk in Dawson, vehicles usually stop for you, no matter who has the legal right of way. Nice town. Nice people.

I walked past the rear entrance to the Eldorado hotel and stepped off the sidewalk to cross the street. I looked to my right and saw a blue crew cab pickup truck approaching. It was going a little fast so I decided to wait and let it drive by. Then it stopped suddenly, right in front of me, blocking my way to the other side of the street. For an instant I thought that the driver may not have noticed me until the last second, then stopped to let me cross the street in front of his truck, perhaps as a belated courtesy. I waved it on, but the truck didn't move. I stepped to my right to go around behind it, then the rear driver's side door opened. There was no one in the backseat. The driver must have opened it. For me? I stopped and waited, not sure what to think.

Then from behind a powerful force accelerated me toward the truck. Without any idea of how or why my feet were suddenly off the ground. I flew through the air and landed with a bounce on the back seat of the truck. It had happened so smoothly, as though I'd been a small child picked up and playfully tossed onto a bed by a parent. The instant I sat up and tried to get my bearings, my backpack hit me hard on the left side of my face and knocked me over. The door I'd flown through slammed shut. I sat up again and the door to my right opened. A large Asian man got in beside me. He closed the door.

"Don't move," he said to me. "Go," he yelled at the driver.

The truck began moving. I looked around the cab. There was a driver in front of me and a man on my right. My disorientation quickly changed to anger when I realized what had happened.

"Hey!" I yelled. "Who the hell are you guys and what the hell do you think you're doing?"

I sensed more than saw a lightening like movement from my right side, then heard a resounding 'ping'. My vision shattered into a million tiny mirrors, glittering in front of me like a disco ball. My right ear began ringing like there was a giant tuning fork inside. It was all I could do to stare down at the seat between my legs and try to stay conscious. I couldn't lift my chin off my chest. I stayed still.

"You don't return your calls, Mr. Brody." I vaguely heard the words from a voice far away. The ringing was unbearably loud. I couldn't think or hear clearly. Things between my ears just weren't right.

"Hmmm?"

"You don't return your calls. Charlie called you today. Three times. You didn't call him back."

"Busy. Been busy. Flying." I sighed and kept staring at the seat. It was blue vinyl with white stitching. I wanted to say something but couldn't compose a sentence. Things were very hazy inside.

"Why are you talking to the police? What do they want? What do you say to them?"

"Pictures." I'd managed to articulate the complete word with a concerted effort. Inside it felt like I'd just recited the Gettysburg address.

"Pictures of what?"

"People."

"What people?"

"Charlie," I said. Don't know where that answer came from, but speaking of Charlie, I did for some reason recall being shown his picture in the meeting.

"Who else?"

I could barely hear him.

"What?"

He slapped me hard again on the side of my head. That didn't help me think or hear any more clearly, but it sure stung.

"Who else?" the big man yelled. "What other people in pictures?"

"Wait! Thinking!"

"Think fast."

"Okay." I thought hard about photographs and cops. "Jack."

"Jack who?"

"Jack. Haines in Jack. No. Jack in Haines."

"Who else?"

"That's all." I was working hard to think in the simplest terms. Deep inside things were slowly reorganizing. Then I had a couple of occurrences. How did this man know my name? And maybe if I tried hard enough, I could remember another photograph. Anything to stop him from hitting me again. But I couldn't recall any more of the photos those cops had shown me.

"Mr. Brody. Who else?"

I raised my head a little and looked at the driver in front of me. He had a full head of white hair. I looked in the rearview mirror at his face. He had a white beard. The bird watcher. My head dropped down to my chest again.

"Him," I said, pointing at the driver. "Picture of him."

I rolled my eyes to the right, just enough to view the man who'd thrown me into the truck with such ease. He was grotesquely thick, strong and muscular. I recognized him then. He was the man who'd been on the river bank, the one who'd watched me get into the RCMP cruiser.

"Who are you? What do you want?" I asked, then dropped my eyes and went back to studying the stitching on the seat.

"You don't ask questions," he said. "I ask questions. What other pictures did you see?"

"That's all."

"Who is the woman?"

"What?"

He slapped me on the side of my head again. It stung like hell. The ringing inside grew louder.

"Stop!" I yelled. "I can't hear you!" He waited. I breathed deeply.

"Mr. Brody. The woman in your plane today, who is she?"

That helped. A question with a clue.

"Marsalis," I muttered.

"Who?"

"Marsalis!"

"Who is Marsalis?" he asked. I knew things inside were clearing up a little because I'd just had an epiphany. If I didn't want to get slapped again, don't say 'what'.

"She takes pictures," I said.

"Pictures of what?"

"A mine."

"What mine?"

"Thistle Creek."

Things went quiet. The truck had been moving slowly since I'd been thrown inside, though I had no idea of where we were. We'd been going around corners, making left turns, maybe some right turns too, but there was no telling where we were. I could move my eyes but still couldn't lift my head high enough to look outside.

"Mr. Brody. Listen to me. Tomorrow morning at seven o'clock you will fly me to Juneau. Then you will fly to Haines. There you will pick up fish. You will fly the fish here, to Dawson, not to Whitehorse, to Dawson, okay? You will deliver the fish to this man here." He pointed at the driver. "We leave at seven o'clock tomorrow morning. Don't be late or your plane will sink. Do you understand?"

"Not at seven. Plane needs fuel. Wait until nine. Need fuel."

"Seven o'clock, Mr. Brody, or your plane sinks."

The powerful man leaned forward, put a hand on top of the front seat, looked ahead out the windshield. He scanned the street, then turned and looked through the rear window. The truck slowed down. He leaned across me and opened my door, put his left hand against my ribcage, and shoved me out of the truck. I landed hard on my left shoulder, bounced and rolled a few times, then stopped.

The fall knocked the wind out of me. I couldn't move, couldn't breathe, was gulping for air in a silent panic. The world was tilted over ninety degrees. I was lying on my side in the middle of a gravel street, watching a blue truck drive off. I glimpsed my backpack fly out the passenger window and roll into the ditch. Then finally – finally – the air roared back into my lungs.

Okay. Got it. Seven. Be ready to fly at seven.

I rolled onto my back, looked up at the sky, and groaned.

SEVENTEEN

"Brody? Is that you?"

It sounded remotely like Deborah Larabie. It took me a moment to match the voice to the face. She was leaning over me on her hands and knees, looking down into my eyes, her face inches from mine. There were people standing around, though it was hard to tell how many. I tried counting their feet and dividing by two, but couldn't do the math.

"Deb?" I gazed up at two beautiful blue eyes and an exquisite face, an angelic vision in a pale blue sky. Wisps of long blond hair tickled my face. Was this the end? Was I dying?

"Brody? What happened to you? Are you alright?"

"Yeah."

"Let's get you off the street, okay?"

"Okay."

I sat up and looked around. People were leaving. I wasn't dying.

She helped me stand and we staggered off the road, my hand on her shoulder, her arm around my waist. We sat down on the sidewalk with our feet in the ditch. I dropped my head into my hands and stared down at my boots, contemplating what had just happened, taking inventory of my mental faculties. Things were slowly improving between the good ear on the left and the bad one on the right, which was ringing like ghosts and goblins in a bad Halloween movie. A little boy trudged up to us, dragging my backpack by a strap.

"Is this your bag, Uncle Brody?"

"Bobby?" I looked up at the boy in front of me. "Hey, thanks, buddy." The boy smiled with pride. I managed to smile too, put my hands on his shoulders, looked at him carefully. He must be six years old now, a great kid, and a very good looking one too.

That's because Deborah Larabie is his mother. Deb and I met three summers ago and had a pretty good thing going for a while. Our 'thing' ended when her estranged husband reappeared in her life. The husband convinced her that he was a new man, that his days of hard partying were over. He'd asked for another shot. So Deb had to make a choice. Me, or the husband with the house and a regular job and a regular paycheck, and another chance to raise her son with his father. I lost that one. The girl of my dreams exited stage right. The search for a replacement has continued ever since.

I hadn't seen Bobby Larabie since the fall two years ago, but saw Deb a couple of times last summer. Deb owns a little soup and sandwich shop aptly named 'Deb's Soup Kitchen'. Every day but Sunday she makes two enormous pots of the greatest homemade soup I've ever tasted, and she's usually sold out by noon. I could never convince her that if she made three pots a day, she'd sell more soup, and make more money. She insisted it would ruin the allure of her niche. Maybe she was right. She was apparently still in business.

"Brody, you look God awful terrible! What just happened out here?"

"Not sure, Deb, but I could sure use a bowl of soup."

"Well today's your lucky day. There's a bowl of beef barley left. Come in and wash up. Want a piece of bread with that?"

"Does Roy sleep with Dale?"

"Who's Roy?" She always asks and I never tell her.

Life can be ironic sometimes. I'd planned to eat on my way over to Katy Duncan's house and that gorilla who'd just worked me over was kind enough to throw me out of his truck, right in front of Deb's Soup Kitchen.

Deb is eight years younger than me. I studied her face to see how she'd survived another long and cold, dark Dawson winter. The dry air of a sub-arctic winter is never kind to a woman's complexion. Her delicate skin did show signs of living in a harsh climate, but at her age, nothing that a couple of weeks in Hawaii couldn't fix. She was still drop dead gorgeous.

Deb is tall and lean with clear blue eyes and straw colored hair, and probably the most genuine woman I know. She rarely uses makeup, doesn't wear jewelry, doesn't dye her hair, and is usually dressed in jeans, a denim shirt, and an insulated vest. Like today. With her face and body she could have been a model, with her brains she could have been a doctor, but instead she ended up in the Yukon running a funky little eatery in Dawson. A woman who knew how and where she wanted to live. A genuine free spirit.

I still felt wobbly but managed to climb onto the sidewalk and walk with her into her tiny restaurant. Bobby followed us in. The bells on the door knob jingled when he closed the door behind us. I was in a warm and a cozy place that felt like home.

I've always loved the atmosphere in Deb's restaurant. The floors are weathered wood, the walls are weathered wood, and the ceiling is weathered wood. Against the front window are two small round tables and six bamboo chairs with lots of chips and nicks, no two the same, all with at least one rickety leg. Hardly anyone ever sits down anyway, most of Deb's customers buy their soup and sandwiches to go. Deb used to tell me how she'd never wanted a staff. She said it would compromise her objective which was strictly to be a purveyor of simple, healthy, honest, stick-to-your-ribs food, without any brass or plants in sight. I hate brass and plants in restaurants too. To me brass and plants means that the food is probably lousy, or the prices are twice what they should be, or both. There won't ever be a hostess to seat you in Deb's Soup Kitchen.

Her short and simple daily menu is written on a small framed chalkboard mounted on the wall behind the counter. It's where everyone orders and picks up. I had my eyes on the glass display under the counter. Deb also bakes pastries and rustic Irish soda bread from scratch, fresh every day. On that rare occasion when she hasn't sold out by closing time, she takes whatever's left to the women's shelter. There were two loaves of soda bread left. I planned to buy one before leaving.

"Go clean up," she said. "I'll get your soup." She walked back to her little kitchen.

I kicked my pack under the table in the corner and went down the hall to the unisex washroom, naturally the cleanest one in town. I looked at myself in the mirror. Deb was right. I did look 'God awful terrible', though you could hardly tell I'd just taken a few good licks to the head, other than my right ear which was glowing like a ripe apple. It hurt like hell, by the way, like it was on fire. The whole right side of my scalp hurt like hell too, where that monster had slapped me twice. Or was it three times? I'd completely forgotten about the scratches on my face from the trees, but could see some of them were starting to redden and swell. They felt tender to the touch. The left shoulder of my shirt had a big tear and the skin underneath was scraped raw and red. I had gravel and dirt and tree sap all over my face and clothes. And a whopping headache to boot. I was looking forward to my soup.

I did my best to clean up without making a mess of the sink, ran my hands through my hair, and walked back to the table. I was sitting quietly, feeling sorry for myself, picking gravel out of my clothes, when Deb appeared and presented me with a bowl of my favorite soup. Beef barley, served in a big heavy warm porcelain bowl with a chip on the rim. She put it down in front of me with a plate of thickly buttered bread and a glass of Dawson tap water. Let the games begin.

"Wow," I said.

Deb pulled up a chair and sat down across from me. "So Brody, are you going to tell me or not? What just happened to you out there?"

"Don't really know, Deb. But I can tell you my life was pretty good until about six o'clock last night. It's been going downhill fast ever since. Until you and this soup came along."

"So what's her name?"

"Huh?"

"Her name, Brody. This must have something to do with a woman. It always does with you."

"Let's forget about her name right now, if you don't mind. Hey Deb, any chance you'd like to get together with me for the rest of your life?"

She smiled. "Let me think about that. But keep checking, huh?" She smiled, put her hand over mine, gave it a squeeze, then folded her arms on the table.

"I'll do that," I said.

"Hey, did you hear anything about a missing plane?"

While thinking about how to answer that I dug into my soup. It was delicious. The best bowl of soup is always off the bottom of the pot. Deb was right. It was my lucky day in an ironic sort of way. I took a big bite of bread and savored the sweet butter. It was delicious, too. I was feeling better already.

Finally I took a break and said, "Yeah, heard about it this morning."

"They say Robert Duncan's the missing pilot, is that true? Have they found him yet?"

Deb is Katy Duncan's best friend. That's how I ended up at Robert's wedding, at the invitation of the prettiest girl in town. It wasn't going to be easy, but I had to tell her what happened.

"Deb. I have some really bad news. And I need you to do us a big favor."

She gasped, stared at me, clasped her hands together and put them to her mouth. She'd already made the leap. "What Brody, what happened?" she murmured through her hands.

"Mom?" a little voice piped. "Can I go to Larry's for dinner? They're having pizza."

She looked down at her son with compassion and said, "Not

today, honey. We're having dinner at home tonight. We're going home soon. You can have dinner with Larry some other night."

"Actually," I said, "Bobby having dinner at Larry's tonight would be an excellent idea. You need to do something really important now."

"What? What's so important?" she asked, almost breathless.

"Please, trust me, okay?"

"Bobby, go get Mommy's phone, it's behind the counter," she said, not taking her eyes from mine.

The boy ran behind the counter and returned with the phone. She called Larry's mom. Yes, it was fine that Bobby comes over for pizza tonight. Yes, we'll wait for you to bring him over. Great. Thanks. See you then.

The boy was waiting with his elbows on the table, his chin cupped in his hands, watching his mother, hanging on her every word. When she hung up he'd already figured out the outcome of the conversation. He was ecstatic.

"Yay," he cried out, jumping up and down.

"Honey," said his mother. "Go put some pastries in a box. We'll take them over to Larry's. And please wait for me behind the counter. Okay?"

"Okay." The little boy ran behind the counter. I watched him through the glass display while I ate. He seemed to know what he was doing. First he pulled a flat piece of white cardboard off the top of a tall stack and expertly folded it into a pastry box. Then he carefully took a piece of waxed paper off another stack and placed it in the bottom of the box he'd just assembled. Amazing kid. And I thought Deb didn't have help.

"Brody. Talk to me," she said.

I looked at her and put my spoon down, wiped my mouth, took a deep breath. "Well, Katy Duncan is going to need your help and support for a while. Starting tonight. You should be going over there now."

"Oh God, this *is* about Robert, isn't it?"

"It is. I'm sorry to tell you this, but Robert is dead."

She gasped. "Dead? He's dead?"

"Yes, dead." I paused. "What you and Katy need to know is that he didn't crash and he didn't make a mistake and that he was a really good pilot." I paused again, looked out at the street for a while, then back at her. "I found him this morning, on the Yukon River, sitting in his plane about seventy miles south of here. He was dead when I found him." I took a deep breath. "Look, there's no other way of saying this, he was murdered."

"What? Murdered? God! Why? How?"

I put my hand on hers. "Shhh. That doesn't matter now. It's just what happened. The police are working hard to find out why and how and who did it. They should know soon and will make an arrest. In the meantime, I'm going over to see Katy right now, so give me fifteen minutes before you head over. And please, not a word to anyone, okay?"

She didn't take her eyes from mine and nodded.

I looked at the phone in front of her and asked "Could I use your phone for a second?"

She pushed it over to me, got up, and went behind the counter. There were tears in her eyes when she crouched and hugged Bobby. I picked up my backpack and dug out a little black address book, and a bottle of Aleve. I took double the recommended dose and chased the pills down with a whole glass of water. Then I looked up Gilbert Mahoney's phone number – under 'K'. I dialed the number and pressed 'send'.

"Mahoney Fuel Services."

"Gilbert, it's Brody. How are you doin'?"

"Brody! Where the hell are you? How the hell are you?"

"I'm good. Look, Gilbert, I'm in Dawson. With my plane. I need a fill up. All three tanks. It's down at the docks."

"Perfect timing there, guy. Tomorrow morning I'm going down to the river. Can fill you up about nine. How's that?"

"Actually Gilbert, I need to leave real early tomorrow. I was thinking more like about six thirty."

"Six thirty in the morning? Hey give yourself a shake man, I can't do it that early, we're real busy this time of year out at the airport, you know that, sorry."

"Well, how about right now?"

"Let me check. Hang on." He put me on hold. Gilbert was thinking about it, or acting like he was thinking about it. Or checking his busy schedule, or acting like he was checking his busy schedule.

For years Gilbert and his brother Al have been pumping every kind of fuel into everything that uses fuel in the Dawson area. Houses, buildings, planes, helicopters, highway trucks, heavy equipment, you name it. Pumping fuel is all they do. And they pump a lot of fuel. The Mahoney brothers have a good sized tank farm ten miles south of Dawson, just off the Klondike Highway. They have ten fuel trucks of various shape and size that they drive around town all year, and up and down the creek roads to the mines in the summer. Mahoney Bros. trucks are an integral part of the Dawson landscape. They must be millionaires, I thought, though you'd never guess it. Gilbert and Al have lived for years in two side by side trailers in a mobile home park, just south of their tank farm. They wear the same ball caps, the same gloves and the same coveralls everyday of the year. I don't know when they gave up laundering their work clothes, but it must have been a while ago, because they always reek of fuel oil. Gilbert and Al Mahoney come honestly by their aptly earned moniker, 'the Kerosene Brothers'.

"Brody? You still there?" Gilbert had apparently checked his busy schedule.

"Still here."

"Good news. I can do it tonight, but there'll be an after hours delivery charge."

I sighed. "Yeah, I know Gilbert. But go ahead and do it tonight anyway. I guess I'll have to pay the extra hundred dollars. All three tanks, huh?"

"A hundred dollars? Where you been, man? Hamburger's ten bucks a pound. The after hour fee's been a hundred and twenty dollars for two years."

"A hundred and twenty dollars? The after hour fee's a hundred and twenty dollars?"

"Tell ya what, Brody. Just for you, 'cuz you just flew in from outer space, this one time only, I'll make it a hundred. How's that?"

"Thanks Gilbert. Appreciate that."

Like I said, they must be millionaires.

EIGHTEEN

I felt a lot better when I left Deb's place. My belly was full for one thing. That was good. And when I took off for Juneau in the morning, my plane would be full too. That was also good because I didn't want that gorilla to sink my plane. Mostly though, I felt a sense of relief in having told a friend about what had happened to Robert. Now I could deal with his death on my own terms.

I headed toward Robert and Katy Duncan's house. It was only three blocks away. I wasn't looking forward to the task at hand but it was something that had to be done. A pilot's thing, we're a brotherhood. As I walked I thought about what to say to Katy. There were no right words.

Two RCMP cars were parked in front of the Duncan's house. Across the street a dozen or so curious onlookers were assembled in a straggly line, staring at the little house, doubtless wondering what was going on inside. They were whispering and watching the front window when they saw me approaching. Great, I thought, an audience. At least there weren't four television vans with satellite dishes parked on the front lawn, and a bunch of Maybelline models milling about in high heels with microphones glued to their hands. Thankfully we still don't have local television stations in the Yukon.

It crossed my mind that it may not be the best time to make an unannounced house call at the Duncan's, then realized there was never going to be a best time, and pressed on with my mission, ripped shirt notwithstanding. When I stopped in front of their house, I was shocked.

Since my one and only visit two years ago, the changes and improvements were spectacular. The most striking improvement was parked in the driveway. On a street dominated with funky houses and muddy old vehicles it stuck out like a ballerina with a broken leg. It was big, fire engine red, shiny and clean. It was a brand new, four wheel drive pickup truck with a chrome roll bar, sitting high over huge white wheels and rugged tires. Nice truck. Fifty grand worth of nice truck.

I stood at the end of the driveway and looked around. The entire property had recently been sodded. A water sprinkler was hissing in the back yard, keeping the vivid green lawn soaking wet. New trees and shrubs were strategically planted in all the right places. There was a new steel fence enclosing the backyard and running out to the street along the property lines. The house had a new shingled roof, new gutters, faux window shutters, fresh paint, and a new front door. It was the perfect ginger bread house for a flourishing family. It made the situation all the more tragic.

I climbed the stairs to the front porch and peaked through the front window. People were inside though it seemed eerily quiet. I knocked on the door.

It was opened immediately by Constable LeMay.

"Good evening, Mr. Brody. This isn't the best time for a visit. Mrs. Duncan is being interviewed right now. Would you mind waiting outside, please?"

"With these mosquitoes out here? No thanks. I'll wait inside."

I feinted left and she casually stepped to her right to block me. As she opened her mouth to say something, I dodged to my right and slipped past her into the short hall. Two more strides took me into the living room. LeMay stomped around me in her big shiny shoes and shouted, "Mr. Brody! You stop right there!"

I *was* stopped, looking directly at Katy Duncan, seated at a large round dining table at the rear of the house. LeMay repositioned herself between me and the living area.

"Sir! I said stay right there! Not another step!" Now she was giving me that fearless glare they teach in cop school. LeMay was about five eight so I could easily see over her left shoulder and the entire living and dining areas beyond.

"Brody? Is that you?"

Katy Duncan was seated with two uniformed cops and a man in street clothes. They too were glaring at me. Katy jumped out of her chair at the same time as Staff Sergeant Robson. She easily outpaced him across the room and threw her arms around my neck. She began to sob. Robson stopped behind her, shook his head and glared at me some more. He said nothing, though, waved LeMay off, and returned to the kitchen table. Robson murmured something to Sergeant Arcand and Special Agent Kurtz, the man dressed in street clothes. What was he doing here?

"How could this happen, Brody? How could this happen?" Katy cried with her face buried in my neck.

I held her for a moment, then eased her away so I could look at her face. "I have no idea, but I'm going to find out. Now listen to me carefully. Okay?"

She nodded.

"Deb will be here any minute. You tell those cops over there that when Deb arrives, they're to let her in, make that clear to them, okay?"

"Okay," she said.

"Deb is going to help you get through this, okay?"

She nodded again.

"Katy, this is important. Whatever happens in the next two days you are not going to sign anything, no matter who asks, no matter what it is, you're not going to sign anything, got that?"

"Who wants me to sign things?"

"I don't know, but it's not a good time to be signing anything, so if anyone asks, just don't, not for any reason, okay?"

"Okay."

"Promise me."

"I promise."

"Good. Call me anytime of day if you need help. Whatever you need, anything at all. Deb knows how to get in touch with me. So don't hesitate. Anything."

She nodded. "Thank you."

"And if you have a family lawyer, call him now, wherever he happens to be. Get him off the golf course, out of a meeting, out of court, wherever he is, you need to tell him right away what happened. Okay?"

"Okay."

"Good. That's important. Now tell those guys back there they've got five minutes. Then they have to leave. Tell them they can come back tomorrow."

She nodded again and wiped her eyes. "Who did this, Brody? Why would anyone kill Robert? Why?" She fell into my arms and started sobbing again. I could feel her pain. There was a knock on the front door. I turned my head and watched LeMay open the front door. It was Deb.

"Looks like Deb's here. Tell that cop at the door to let her in."

Katy stepped around me and pushed her way past LeMay, then fell into Deb's arms. *Thank you, Deb.*

I needed to leave. The three men at the table were giving me the dirty eye. Robson was rubbing his forehead with both hands, clearly revealing his exasperation. I looked at the three cops for a moment, shrugged my shoulders, turned and squeezed past the girls in the hall, whispered to Deb that I'd see her tomorrow.

I stepped outside and walked out to the street.

"What's going on in there?" asked a man from the crowd.

"We've lost a good pilot," I said.

* * *

I needed a shave, a shower, and a new shirt. I headed toward my hotel. There'd be a couple of places on the way to buy a shirt.

The walk was a good time to do some thinking and there was

lots to think about. Like what tomorrow held in store. Like what was going to transpire tomorrow morning at seven a.m. down at the river. Like why did that goon want me to fly him to Juneau? Was I really going to have to spend four hours sitting beside a man who'd beaten me up? And who was he? Since when was he giving me instructions where to fly Charlie's fish? Should I tell the police about what he did to me this afternoon? And on the subject of cops, why were they so interested in my cargo business? What did flying fish from Haines to Whitehorse have to do with Robert's murder? Then there was long lost Sarah Marsalis. I kind of missed her. Actually, I really missed her. Now what was that about? I wondered how she'd made out with the cops this afternoon. I wondered how she was going to get back to her car. My new schedule would preclude me from flying her to Minto tomorrow. She'd have to find her own way back, and regardless of how she did that, she owed me money. I hate not getting paid for my work. If I never saw her again, I'd have no idea where to send my bill.

But mostly I was thinking about something else, something that bothered me more than anything. It was the Duncan's house.

What bothered me had nothing to do with all the cops inside, or seeing Katy Duncan in the state she was in, or the glare that Robson had given me on my way out.

It was the smell of fresh paint. It was the new truck. It was that everything inside the house was brand new – the flooring, the carpet, the furniture, the television, the stereo, the window dressings – everything. All brand new. That, and everything else they'd done to the property all added up to a lot of money, and an overt display of new found wealth.

Of course no one can ever really know everything about other people and their money. Times in the Yukon happened to be good. There was a lot of mining and mineral exploration going on. Property prices were high, interest rates were low, and the banks were on a lending spree. So maybe the Duncan's were simply all flash and no cash. Maybe they'd just mortgaged themselves to the hilt and maxed out their credit cards. Or maybe they'd won a lottery. Or maybe a long lost aunt had passed away and left them a tidy sum. Or maybe a parent had given them a generous wedding gift. I had no way to know. What I did know for sure, though, was that at his pay scale, Robert hadn't earned close to what he'd spent on his property in the last year. So not without a tinge of guilt, I had to consider the possibility that whatever he'd been up to while flying for NOCA Air, it may not all have been above board.

Then I thought about something else.

I needed a drink.

NINETEEN

I felt lucky to find a nice soft shirt in the drug store. It didn't have any gold rush slogans on the pockets or the sleeves or the lapels. That saved me twenty bucks. I picked out a nice new pair of wool socks, too.

The biggest drug store in Dawson doesn't actually have much to do with drugs anymore. Of course neither do the big drugstores anywhere in North America. I marveled at the selection of goods for sale in this one. It had everything from groceries to car wax, stationery to clothing, gardening supplies, electronics, makeup, and toys. Which is why it took ten minutes of wandering around before I found the first aid section and a bottle of rubbing alcohol to clean the scratches on my face.

I paid for my stuff and walked another two blocks to the Downtown Hotel. It's where I usually stay in Dawson because it's the closest hotel to the docks. I walked in and leaned on the front counter.

"Well hello there, Mr. Brody, how are things with you?" said Molly, a round and healthy looking woman about thirty-five, and a card carrying friend of the earth. Molly always greets me by name when I check in. She must work every day of the year because she's always behind the reception desk when I visit. Molly is usually dressed for winter, regardless of the season or the temperature outside. Today she was wearing a thick burgundy wool sweater with a high collar, and a matching wool hat. It was late spring and almost sixty degrees. I wasn't wearing a jacket.

"Well, things could be better Molly, but it's good to see you again."

"Oh, sorry to hear that, Mr. Brody. Perhaps a warm bath would do you good!" I suppose she couldn't help make that subtle suggestion, given how I must have appeared to her at the moment.

"Hey," I said. "No one in the history of the world has ever needed a shower more than I do right now. Have you got a reservation for me?"

"As a matter of fact, I do," she said. "It's already paid for so you're all set. Here's your key. Enjoy your stay with us in Dawson."

"Thanks, Molly." I took the key from her and was heading to the stairs when I had an occurrence and returned to the desk.

"Hey, Molly? Has a woman named Sarah Marsalis checked in yet?"

"Mr. Brody, you know I can't tell you that."

"How come? I just want to know if she's checked in. Not what her room number is."

"I'm sorry, I can't give out that information, you know it's the policy everywhere these days," she said.

"Right. No problem. Well, when she does check in, would you tell her my room number, if she asks?"

"Of course, sir."

I went up to my room, stripped down, and had a long hot shower. The scratches on my face burned when I shaved and so did my right ear under the hot spray. The whole time in the shower I was thinking about how to get even with that muscle bound son of a bitch who'd beaten me up. I felt like a new man when I stepped out to towel myself off.

I emptied the contents of my backpack all over the bed. Wherever I fly I need to carry aeronautical maps, documents, licenses, and permits for my plane. I also carry a thin waterproof jacket, a ball hat, a hairbrush, a toothbrush, a razor, a bottle of headache pills, a pen, a tiny LED flashlight, my cell phone, and a Swiss army pocket knife. And always, always, there's one more thing I keep rolled up in a small plastic bag at the bottom of my pack. Just in case, because you never know. I opened the plastic bag and admired two of the most beautiful things you'll ever lay eyes on when you're cold and wet and far from home. A pair of clean dry boxer shorts, and a clean dry T-shirt. 'Sleep dry, sleep well' is something I learned a long time ago.

I put them on. The boxers felt great. The T-shirt felt great. I went into the bathroom with the bottle of alcohol and spent five minutes torturing my face until all the scratches were clean and sterilized. My eyes were still watering from the alcohol when I held my blue jeans over the bathtub and shook the dried mud off them. They actually didn't look so bad when I put them back on. I walked out of the bathroom to the bed and tried on my new shirt. It felt pretty good and fit me well. I tried on my new wool socks. They felt great. I put my damp boots back on. Not so great. I brushed my hair. All dressed up and nowhere to go.

I repacked everything that was on the bed, then for the sake of being thorough, checked the small pocket on the left side of my pack. My wallet wasn't there. I checked the small pocket on the right side. My passport wasn't there.

I sighed and sat down on the bed and cursed, knowing exactly what had happened to my wallet and passport. That muscle bound gorilla who'd beaten me up this afternoon was no dummy. I wasn't going anywhere tomorrow without him. That made me angry. Really angry. I thought some more about having that drink. And getting even.

I'd just stood up, about to leave the room, when I saw the envelope poking out from under the door. My name was hand written on the outside. Might as well open it and take a look, see what it is, even if it's probably just a hotel receipt or coupons for horseback riding. I opened the envelope and pulled out a single piece of paper.

I'll be at Gerties at 10:00

I recognized the hand writing. The note was from Sarah Marsalis.

TWENTY

I had an hour to kill before heading to Gertie's, so instead of having that drink right away, decided to go down to the docks. To check on my plane. To see if Gilbert had fueled it up. To see if it was still floating.

When I stepped out of the hotel the sun was high and the air was warm, warm enough to be outside without a jacket. Lots of people were on the streets and sidewalks, taking pictures and peering in store windows, working off their evening meals, wobbling their way down to Front Street. It was a perfect time of day to buy some ice cream and go for a walk along the river. I fell in behind a group of tourists heading west toward the river, then turned right onto Front Street.

A somber crowd had gathered on the docks. People were throwing flowers in the water, hugging each other, having solemn conversations. News travels fast in a small town and most had heard about the loss of one of their own. I noted my plane was still floating while making my way down the short road to the parking lot. Several pilots from Dawson were congregated in a loose circle, including Dale Morrow, the owner of NOCA air. He was standing beside a woman who might be his wife.

I approached them and said, "Dale."

"Brody," he said, turning around. "Heard you're the one who found Robert."

"I did. A bad day." We shook hands.

"Brody, you remember my wife Sherry?"

I remembered being introduced to Sherry at Robert's wedding. We shook hands. She was a pleasant looking woman with a warm smile, about sixty years old, perhaps a few years younger than Dale. The two had lived in Dawson for years, building NOCA Air from a one pilot, one plane company into a six plane company with a staff of twenty and their own hangar at the Dawson airport. Of the six aircraft that NOCA operated, five were available for charter, and the other one, a DC3, flew a daily scheduled flight to Whitehorse.

Dale Morrow was one of those pilots who was so busy running an aviation company he hardly had time to fly any more. But you could tell by his eagle eyes and lean physique that he was still all bush pilot. He'd been a pilot for forty years and had amassed twenty thousand hours flying time in this northern frontier, including ten thousand hours in a DeHavilland Beaver. There wasn't a patch of the Yukon that he hadn't seen from behind the controls in the pilot's seat. His experience was revered by younger pilots like me.

Dale gave a subtle nod to Sherry, then gave me a nudge in the back. We walked fifty feet up the road for some privacy. When a man like Dale Morrow is in private conversation, there's no chance of being interrupted, not in this town.

"What happened to your face, Brody? Looks like you got in a fight with a cat. And the cat won."

I smiled grimly. "Climbing over some trees," I said, "this morning on the river."

"Where you found our plane," he said.

"Actually, it was my charter passenger who spotted it."

"But you managed to land on that river bank and get yourself up to our plane, that's what the cops told me."

"Yeah."

"Tough place to beach a plane. Appreciate you doing that."

"Anyone would have done the same. No big deal."

Dale gazed out at the river and asked, "So, do you think Robert was murdered?"

"Yeah, Dale. He was murdered. He was shot twice in the back of the head. So was the man beside him."

Dale took a deep breath and studied the river some more. "You know," he said, "if that's what happened, then I really can't say it's all that big a surprise to me."

"Oh?"

"Yeah, I mean as far as I'm concerned, some of Robert's customers in the last year were...I don't know...kind of shady you might say. Just my impression, mind you, never met any of them. But I could never figure out what that whole deal was with Robert flying back and forth to Juneau so often."

"What do you mean?"

"Well for one thing, the guy or the guys he was flying to Juneau always paid with cash. When they first started chartering our Beaver last spring, every two weeks or so, this one fellow would call the office at the airport and book the Beaver for a flight to Juneau. He always insisted that Robert had to be the pilot, or forget it he'd say. And for some reason he always wanted the Beaver, a plane on floats. I wondered a lot about that. I'd tell him that a float plane flies slower and burns a lot more fuel than a wheeled aircraft. I'd tell him that he'd save money flying to Juneau by chartering a plane on wheels. The difference can be a lot when you're going that far, as you well know. But this guy didn't seem to care about the extra cost. So Robert would fly him and whoever else down to Juneau in the Beaver, and the next day Robert would come into our office with a wad of US cash in an envelope. Now who pays cash for a charter flight anymore? It's a credit card world these days. The bill was always close to five grand with the stand by charges. That's a chunk of change to be carrying around in your jeans, don't you think?"

"A big chunk of change," I said.

"So why do you suppose anyone would insist on chartering a Beaver out of here to fly four hundred and thirty miles down to

Juneau? A charter costs four times as much as a 'sched' flight, and we both know they've got an 8,500 foot paved runway in Juneau. Hell, commercial jets land there every day. Now I'm not saying that the guy or guys Robert was flying were big shots who ought to hire a private jet because they can't stand flying with screamin' babies. But who wants to fly all the way down to Juneau in an old slow Beaver on floats?"

I almost laughed at the irony of his question but let Dale continue.

"Anyway, beginning of last summer that guy stopped calling our office to book his flights to Juneau. You might say Robert became his travel agent. Robert would call me at home late at night and tell me he had another charter to Juneau in the morning. He always asked me how much the invoice would be. I'd tell him how much and the next evening he'd come into the office and pay the bill with a wad of US cash. It was a really odd way to do business. It made me nervous." Dale paused for a moment to watch a gull do a low pass over the crowd on the dock. "You know, I never once met one of Robert's passengers for any of those flights to Juneau," he said. "Not one. Robert would give me their names over the phone the night before he'd leave, and I'd write them down on the passenger manifest. But I never met or saw one of them. Robert would always leave here real early in the morning, even in the fall when it was dark, and he'd always come back with an empty plane, real late in the evening. Every time I asked him about who he was flying to Juneau, he'd just shrug and mumble that he didn't really know them."

"Who do you think they were?" I asked.

"Who do I think they *are*, you mean". Dale paused and I waited for him. Then he said, "Actually, the fact is I don't know for sure. But you know, yesterday there was something different about the flight plan Robert filed. Something that got me to thinking about who his passengers might be, and what they might be up to. See, up until yesterday, Robert would always file a YDA to JNA direct flight plan. A straight shot, Dawson to Juneau. But for some reason yesterday, he added a way point to his flight plan. If you saw the SAR Alert you'd have noticed the waypoint he added was more or less around where you found him this morning. Around the mouth of Thistle Creek. Now why, after all those flight plans he'd previously filed when he flew to Juneau, would he add a waypoint yesterday? For the exact same route. His flight plan didn't specify he'd be landing at the waypoint, he just added it. And the waypoint he added is so close to the direct line of flight to Juneau, why bother? Why all of a sudden did he add that particular way point?" Dale looked at me with a knowing twinkle in his eyes. "If you ask me, I'd say Robert was leaving breadcrumbs. I'd say he went out and got himself mixed up in some real shady business with the people running that mine on lower Thistle Creek. And that things were starting to go sour for him. So yesterday I think he decided to give us a hint, let us in on what he was up to, you know, just in case."

I pondered what Dale had just said while watching a ferry loaded with campers and trucks crossing the river, struggling to hold a straight line against the current. Someone was crying on the dock.

"Dale, I was just over at Robert's house to see Katy. Looks like whatever business he might have got mixed up in was a pretty good one."

"You're not the only one to have noticed that. Everyone around town was talking about how much money the Duncan's were spending. The boys at the hangar were real envious of that fancy new truck of his. The first day he drove it up to the hangar he was joking he'd married for money. Told them Katy was paying for everything. How's she holding up anyway?"

"Not great. Deborah Larabie is with her now."

"You still with Deb?"

"Nope, she's back with her husband again. That's been over for awhile."

"Sorry to hear that. She looked like a keeper to me." We let that hang between us for a moment, then Dale asked, "So how's business in Minto these days?"

"Not bad. Don't fly much until August when hunting season starts. But I've got the shop, there are always lots of cars and trucks coming up the highway that need fixing, so I get by."

"You know Brody, I've just lost a pilot and a Beaver on floats. That leaves a big hole in our company. Business is good for float planes these days. I don't suppose you'd consider selling me that plane of yours. I'd pay you top dollar. And I'd love it if you'd fly it for me. I'd pay you well. You could live right here in the big city. There are a lot more pretty girls in Dawson than Minto, well I suppose you know that. And you could fly free to Whitehorse anytime time you wanted, courtesy of NOCA Air."

I smiled at him. "That all sounds great Dale, but you know I don't like big cities."

"Think it over, Brody. The offer stands until I get our Beaver back, and of course when it's airworthy again."

"When do you get it back?"

"Don't know exactly. The RCMP told me this afternoon they'll tow it down here when they're finished with their investigation on the river. Who knows how long that'll take. The cops told me it could be here as early as tomorrow morning, or as late as next week. But they warned me that it won't be released to us any time soon. They said it will take a long time to complete all the fingerprinting and forensics. So I've really got no idea about the timing for getting it back in service."

I nodded and thought about fingerprints. There would certainly be a lot on a charter plane. It beckoned my next question.

"Hey Dale, who was the man in the plane with Robert?"

"Don't know. Never met him. The name Robert gave me for the manifest was Delgado. Forget his first name. The guy had already flown once with Robert last week. Then a few days ago Robert said he'd be taking him out again, on a sightseeing trip to look at some mines south of here. The boys at the hangar told me the guy was new in town, only arrived here last week. He was staying at the

Eldorado and apparently telling people in the bar that he was some kind of mining consultant from the States."

I nodded and looked at the crowd of people in front of my plane, then asked, "Did the cops mention to you that there might have been three men who got on the Beaver with Robert yesterday morning?"

"As a matter of fact, they did. Didn't know what to make of that at first. Robert gave me just the one name for the passenger list. And he knew perfectly well that if more people climb on board at the last minute, you're supposed to call in their names – for the flight plan, Transport Canada, US customs – just the rules, you know? Well, you know the rules. Anyway, Robert never called me about any extra passengers he might have taken on. But I talked to old Harry this afternoon. Harry told me that early yesterday morning he was piloting the ferry coming from the other side of the river. He swears he saw four men get into our Beaver. Why do you ask?"

"The cops asked me how many men I found in your plane today. I said there were two, Robert and one other man. But the cops kept asking me if there was anyone else. They think there may be another two passengers who are unaccounted for."

Dale nodded. "Yeah, well Harry isn't getting any younger but he can still see. At least I hope he can see if he's a ferry captain. Anyway, right now I just don't believe anything that Robert ever told me, not after what happened yesterday, and not after talking to Harry this afternoon. For all I know, for the last two years Robert's been flying all over the damn territory, picking up and dropping off people all over the place, and not reporting any of it."

"Really?"

"Look Brody, put two and two together. The reason that guy – or those guys – always chartered a float plane is because they wanted to make a water landing somewhere on the way down to Juneau. And given where you found our plane this morning, I'd say that water landing was at or around the waypoint Robert added to his flight plan yesterday, near the mouth of Thistle Creek."

"Near the Thistle Creek mine," I said.

"Near the Thistle Creek mine," Dale said.

TWENTY ONE

Diamond Tooth Gertie's is a fun place to spend an evening. It's a combination gambling hall and cabaret, housed in a big old wood building at the corner of Fourth and Queen. Seven days a week and three shows a night – dressed in ruffles, flowers and feathers – Gertie's cancan dancing girls strut their stuff, singing and kicking up their legs to the accompaniment of a honky tonk piano. If you don't want to sit and watch the follies on stage, you can buy a drink at the bar, mingle with the crowd, lose a few bucks at the tables, or catch up with friends.

I paid the cover charge and joined the throng inside. Most of the patrons were young men, wandering around with a beer in their hand, hoping to see a long lost friend or meet a new girl. Gertie's girls were between shows so the stage was empty. I did a cursory scan of the large hall but didn't see Sarah Marsalis. I went to the bar and bought a beer. It tasted great. The blackjack tables were doing a good business, as usual. There was a pretty good crowd surrounding one particular table, so I walked over to see if someone was on a really good streak.

I should have known. Once you've cast your eyes on her, there's not another woman in the room. She was one of five players seated at the center of a semi-circular blackjack table, sandwiched between two men who looked more interested in gaining her attention than the cards being dealt to them. The man on her right was Kurtz. That guy is everywhere, I thought. To Kurtz's right was a short bald man wearing wire rim glasses. He was about sixty years old and appeared extremely nervous. He was tapping the fingers of both hands on the table, like he was playing a piano. I saw him lean over and murmur something to Kurtz who just shrugged. They seemed to relate to each other as though they were well acquainted. At the other end of the table was a short grey haired woman who looked like she was settled in for the night. In front of her was a pile of chips, two drinks, a clutch purse, a bowl of pretzels, and a large set of keys.

The man sitting on Sarah Marsalis' left looked familiar though I couldn't place him. His right arm hung unnaturally at his side. His jet black hair was combed straight back and he was wearing a shimmering silver sport coat over a grey silk shirt. He had a fancy watch and a gold chain around his neck. There was a gaudy turquoise ring on his left hand. The guy belonged in Atlantic City, not Dawson. There was an amber colored drink on the table in front of him. Kurtz had a beer. The nervous man had a beer. Marsalis was without a drink. I decided to watch her play a hand of blackjack and stood inconspicuously behind two big guys wearing identical ball caps. They were watching her too. She'd just split a pair of ten's.

I sensed that the guys with the ball caps were fixated on Sarah Marsalis – not the cards she was playing – like me and everyone else watching the table. She'd certainly cleaned up nicely since I'd last seen her and had obviously found some new clothes. In fact, she had that 'everything I'm wearing is brand new' look – again. To see her now you'd never guess she'd spent a really rough morning on the Yukon River. How did she do it? She was wearing a black blouse under a short black jean jacket. The only decorations she'd added were a pair of tiny diamond ear studs and a hint of makeup around her eyes. The overall result was world class eye candy. I assumed she was wearing new slacks from the same place she'd bought the rest of her new wardrobe. And there I stood, three rows back, happy to have found a new shirt in the drug store.

I watched Jersey Boy for a minute. He seemed to have a lot to say to Sarah. Several times he'd lean over and say something to her, laugh, then tilt his head at her with an exaggerated smile. She ignored him every time. I watched him lean forward a few times to get his face in front of hers, but she remained stoic, never acknowledging him, concentrating on her cards. Once, after he'd said something, he stretched his left arm across his chest and put his hand on her shoulder. She'd calmly turned to him, lifted a finger, said something short and sweet, and he withdrew his hand immediately. But the way he kept on talking and smiling at her didn't give me the impression he was about to give up.

The dealer dropped a seven on one of Sarah's ten's, and an eight on the other. She stuck and looked around. The dealer busted and dropped a stack of chips on each of her two bets. Jersey Boy whooped and smiled at her. She ignored him. Kurtz won a few chips. The bald guy did too. The grey haired woman had already busted. The dealer was out of cards and started to reshuffle. Then Sarah Marsalis looked me straight in the eyes.

Without a word to anyone she slid off her stool and stood. She slid a couple of chips to the dealer and scooped the rest into a pile using both hands, then stuffed them into every pocket in her new jean jacket. She bent down, picked up her pack, and deftly slipped a strap over a shoulder. The crowd of men parted like the red sea when she walked around the table and headed toward me. I watched her approaching, not sure what to expect. When she was a few feet away her mouth broke into that dazzling smile of hers. She threw her arms around my neck and gave me a big hug, then planted her lips on mine and delivered a long, sensual, and slightly wet kiss that made my legs buzz.

"You're late," she said, smiling with glee. "Let's get out of here."

She wrapped her left arm around my waist and gave me a solid shove in the direction of the exit.

"Whatever you say, dear," was all I could muster on wobbly legs. I was absolutely stunned but grinning ear to ear. I put my arm around her waist and rested it on her hip. It was exciting to feel her pelvis move under my hand as we walked stride for stride past a suddenly silent gallery of utterly perplexed men. I could feel a hundred eyes boring into my back and would have loved to look back to see their faces. Of course I didn't dare, and it didn't matter anyway. You know you've got it made when no one can fathom what the girl you're with might possibly see in you. Frankly, in this case, neither could I. Not this one.

She looked up at me through a frozen smile and murmured, "Put your hand on my ass and I'll break your arm."

"It would be worth it," I said, grinning at her like an idiot.

"Then I'll break both your arms," she said through the same frozen smile.

"Still worth it," I said.

When we got to the exit she let me go. She walked over to the cashier and dug into every pocket in her new jean jacket to fish out her chips. When she was done there was an impressive pile on the counter. A minute later she came bouncing over to me looking pleased with herself, fanning her face with a splayed stack of multi-colored Canadian bank notes.

"What's with this Canadian money anyway?" she asked as we walked out the building. "It's slippery, it feels like plastic, you can't fold it."

"Yeah, but it comes out of the laundry looking great."

She laughed then said, "Brody, I am famished, I have got to eat."

I said, "At this time of night, in this town, your choices are Chinese or pizza."

"What's closest?"

"Chinese."

"Then let's do Chinese." She started walking down the sidewalk ahead of me.

"Where are you going, Sarah?"

"To eat," she said, looking back at me, perplexed.

"Well seeing how the restaurant is the other way, and since I know where it is and you don't, what do you say you follow me?"

"Sorry," she said, "character flaw."

We headed to the Pure Gold Hotel, a block and a half north. It was still bright and light outside, even though it was almost eleven o'clock. She didn't have her arm around my waist anymore and kept a civilized distance as we navigated the wavy wooden sidewalks in silence. I guessed the game was over. It had been no more than a charade to let one or more men in Gerties know exactly where they stood. I suppose if you look like Sarah Marsalis, you can be forgiven for doing whatever it takes to keep the wolves at bay. All the same, I was a little depressed about her change in attitude. We walked into the hotel and stopped at a table for two in a quiet corner near the bar.

"This is a Chinese restaurant?" she asked, still standing and surveying the virtually empty room. The walls were decorated with dusty stuffed animal heads and plastic fish on glossy wooden plaques.

"It is. It's the hotel's bar, but they have a Chinese food kitchen in the back. Are you ready to sit down? Is this table okay?"

"Yeah, fine. I'm going to the ladies room. Order for me, okay? And get lots to eat. And get me a couple of vodka tonics too, and a glass of water."

She turned and started walking away.

"Sarah?"

She stopped and turned around. "Yes?"

"Please."

"What?"

"Say please. It will make me so much happier to do your ordering if you said 'please'."

She dropped her head and rubbed her forehead. I was surprised to see her eyes were a little moist. She composed herself, walked over to me and put her hand on my chest. "I am very sorry, Brody. It's been a terrible day for me. I am not a rude person. I'll be fine after I have a drink and something to eat. Please forgive me." She patted my chest and began walking away again.

"Sarah?"

She stopped and turned again.

"Yes?" she said, this time with a hint of impatience.

"The ladies room is that way." I pointed behind me.

A pretty young woman took my order. Five minutes later she brought over our drinks and set the table. Sarah still hadn't returned. For five seconds I contemplated whether to be a gentleman and wait for my 'date', or start into my Jack and Coke. I looked around at the tired furniture and all the dead creatures on the walls, then decided that chivalry probably wasn't practiced much in here. I was well into my second drink when she returned.

"Sorry. Had to make a phone call." She sat down and downed half her drink, then whistled and said, "Whew! I needed that." She downed the rest of it. All gone. Wow.

"Hey Sarah, we have a couple hours until last call. You can take your time, just so you know."

"Good, I'll take my time starting right now," she said, smiling at me.

The pretty bartender came back and placed three plates of Chinese food in front of us. I said, "You're looking at a number one, a number two, and a number three. Combination plates. I hope there's one you like. Help yourself."

"Wow, this looks great," she said.

We ate steadily for five minutes without a word. I was hungrier than I thought, even after a big bowl of soup five hours ago. She was the first to stop eating and leaned back.

"I'm done," she said. "What are we going to do with all this food?"

"You may be done, but I'm not. Ask again in ten minutes."

She smiled some more and watched me eat. She finished her second vodka tonic. "One more?" she asked.

"Yeah, one more. Then that's it for me."

She waved at our server who came over and took an order for

another round. I was still working on the last of the vegetable chow mein but thought it was time for some conversation.

"How was your visit with the RCMP today?" I asked.

She took a deep breath. I could sense a reticence in her demeanor. "Not bad. They asked me a lot of questions and showed me some photographs. Then they let me go. That was it."

"You're all dressed up, you've got new clothes. You look good."

"Thanks." She seemed to relax a little with the change of topic. "Constable LeMay gave me directions to a nice little woman's clothing store. I was pleasantly surprised at what I could buy here."

I nodded and said, "Then what?"

"What, then what?"

"What did you do then?"

"Well, I went back to my hotel, had a shower, had a snooze, watched some TV, then went over to your Gerties night club and won two hundred and sixty dollars. Then I saw you, and here we are."

"You left out the part about sliding a note under my door."

"Actually, I had that sent to your hotel."

"You're not at the Downtown?" I asked with surprise.

"No, I'm at the Eldorado, just down the street from the cop shop. Why?"

"Seems odd." I thought about that revelation for a moment, then said, "So if you were booked at the Eldorado, how did you know I was at the Downtown?"

She took another deep breath. "I asked Constable LeMay. She found out for me."

"Hmmm."

"What, hmmm?"

"Nothing". But I did wonder why Sarah Marsalis was in a different hotel. Why would the cops go to the trouble of booking us into two different hotels? The town wasn't that busy at this time of year, every hotel would have lots of rooms. I picked up a fortune cookie and tried to open the cellophane wrapper without using my teeth.

"So Brody, about tomorrow, and going back to Minto? My plans have changed. Actually, now I'd…"

I cut her off. "Actually, my plans have changed too, Sarah."

"They have? But you're still my pilot, right?"

"Well, technically yes, but after the cops let me go this afternoon, well I ran into this guy who… insisted I fly him to Juneau tomorrow morning."

"Perfect," she said. "Because that's exactly where I need to go too."

"Sarah, there isn't enough room in the plane for you to come with us."

She looked intensely at me and finished her drink. Her third.

"I don't believe you, Brody. You can make room for me in that plane of yours. There's lots of room."

"Yeah, but there are only two seats."

"I don't care about a seat. And you're still my pilot. I need to go to Juneau and you're taking me to Juneau."

She was adamant and emphatic. I sighed and finished my third Jack and Coke. I wasn't sure how to deal with the situation. She was obviously not the kind of woman to take 'no' for an answer. But there was no way she was going with me to Juneau tomorrow. That was not going to happen. Not with that gorilla who'd beaten me up and thrown me out of a truck this afternoon. I needed to change the subject. I had a couple of questions I wanted to ask her anyway. I decided to start with an easy one.

"Sarah, could I ask you a couple questions?"

"You *may* ask," she said formally, folding her napkin and dusting off her lap. She looked at me as if she was in total control of the situation. She was absolutely confident that I was going to fly her to Juneau.

"At Gerties…" I paused, unsure of myself. "Why did you kiss me?"

She smiled and seemed relieved. "Because I wanted to," she said.

"Come on Sarah, don't be flippant. Who were you sending a

message to? I know damn well that girls like you don't kiss mugs like this one in public places."

She chuckled. "I gave you my answer. I kissed you because I wanted to."

"Alright, whatever. Another question, why all of a sudden do you want to fly to Juneau tomorrow? What about your car in Minto?"

"Urgent family business, that's why. That's all I can tell you. Sorry. I'll deal with my car later."

"Okay. Last question," I said. "When we were on the river today, at that plane, you said you knew the man in the passenger seat. Who was he?"

She inhaled deeply. "I used to work with him." She looked down and rubbed her temples with both hands. "God, I shouldn't have told you that. I'm sorry, that's all I can tell you right now."

I mulled over her answers for a moment while studying my empty glass. This was depressing. She never yielded any information. I wanted to know more about her. Like what she was doing up here. The less she shared with me, the more curious I became. She was a mysterious, reticent woman, clearly making a conscientious effort to keep me in the dark. Why?

"How about one more drink?" she asked, perking up. "A night cap."

I was really feeling the effects of a beer and three cocktails, and wondered how she could ask me to have another drink when I must have been looking the worse for wear. In contrast, she looked like she was just getting started. I'd already broken the 'twelve hours bottle to throttle' rule for pilots, and regardless, the way things were going I might not be alive at the end of tomorrow anyway. What the hell, I thought, given my current maudlin attitude.

"Alright," I said, "One more. But that's it for me, then I'm calling it a night."

She got up and walked over to the girl behind the bar. After a lot of hand waving and conversation between the two, the young woman prepared two drinks and placed them on the bar. Sarah plucked out a wad of cash from her jacket pocket and thumbed a few Canadian bank notes onto the counter. The young lady seemed very pleased. Sarah came back with the two drinks and stood beside me. She leaned over the table, and with exaggerated ceremony, placed one in front of me. She looked into my eyes. I looked into hers. Her face was inches away from mine. I could smell her. It was intoxicating to be this close to her. I really didn't need another drink. She made my head spin.

"I guarantee you've never had one of these before," she said with a mischievous smile. "Tell me what you think."

The best I could do was utter a raspy, "Thank you."

She went back to her chair and sat down, more than pleased with herself. She was definitely back in control again, and knew it.

"So what's this?" I asked, holding up my glass, inspecting a coffee colored drink.

"My own concoction. It's a secret recipe. Hope you like it". She smiled, looked at me over the top of her glass, and took a sip. I tried mine. It was pretty good.

"Give me a hint," I said.

"Kahlua."

"And?"

"That's all I'm telling you."

"No coffee in it?"

"No coffee in it. Now drink up."

I did. She did. They were gone in a minute. I was feeling really good now. Too good to drive a car, that was for sure. I don't drink much anymore and rarely have more than two drinks when I do. But years ago, when drinking was an integral part of my lifestyle, I always took pride in being able to maintain a reasonably good sense of judgment, even when the alcohol in my blood was drastically affecting my co-ordination and eyesight.

"Sarah?"

"What?" She had her arms folded on the table, looking at me confidently. She leaned forward with anticipation.

"Who are you?"

She smiled broadly and said, "Just a girl from Virginia, Brody, just a girl from Virginia."

"Hmmm," I said, dejectedly.

She was staring at me and I was staring at her. It was one of those moments when nothing really had to be said anyway. Just two people sitting at a table with their bellies full, a few drinks the wiser, savoring the sight of one another, enjoying private thoughts.

"Brody?"

"Yes, Sarah."

"Would you care to listen to a proposal of mine?"

"You have a proposal?" I laughed. "Do we need a pickup truck with a warm hood to table your proposal?"

"No. Not for this one". She raised her eyebrows. "So, do you want to hear it or not?" she asked.

"Hey, I'm all ears. Tell me your proposal."

"Well. Let's review our situation, shall we?" She was leaning forward, her arms folded elegantly on the table.

"Alright, good idea, let's do that," I said, leaning forward too.

"Well, you're flying to Juneau tomorrow, right?"

"Right."

"And I want to fly to Juneau tomorrow, right?"

"Right."

"And you want to know more about me, right?"

"Right. A whole lot more, as a matter of fact." That last drink was beginning to make me brave.

She looked down at the table in front of her and began drawing figure eights with a finger through some water droplets. For the first time since we'd met, I sensed she was a little unsure of herself.

"Well," she said, "if you fly me to Juneau tomorrow, after we get there, I'll tell you everything about myself. Anything you want to know."

"That's it? That's your proposal? You'll answer my questions if I fly you to Juneau?"

She paused, looked down at her artwork for a while, then up again, straight into my eyes.

"And," she said, leaning in even closer to me.

"And?" I said, leaning in even closer to her.

"And, we could go to bed. You could take me back to your hotel tonight. If you wanted to, that is. We could go right now."

I must have looked like a deer in the headlights. I could do no more than stare at her with my mouth open.

"Well, *Mr.* Brody? What do you say? Does that sound like a good deal?"

TWENTY TWO

I woke with a start. The room was bright. Sunlight was pouring in the windows. I almost panicked, then remembered that at this time of year, sunlight is always pouring in the windows. I looked at the hotel alarm clock. Six a.m. I had one hour.

Sarah Marsalis was lying beside me, naked in spite of the chill in the room, sound asleep. I was naked too, lying on a bed with just a fitted sheet still clinging to the mattress at one corner. Everything else was on the floor – the blankets, the bedspread, the top sheet, the pillows. Our clothes were on the floor too, at least I hoped they were, mixed up with the bedding. The room reminded me of a television news image, one of those scenes of a house interior just after a tornado has ripped off its roof. If we'd been playing football last night, the score was tied after four quarters, we played another two quarters of overtime without a time out, and the game ended in a draw. I learned one thing about Sarah Marsalis last night. She was a hell of an athlete.

I rolled onto my side, propped my head up with an arm, and admired the shapes and curves of her body. We were spooned together, her buttocks molded into my hips, her hair under my face, my hand on her belly. She had a small red scratch on her shoulder, another in the middle of her back. I studied the side of her face, watched her breathe, watched her sleep, smelled her skin and hair. She looked peaceful and secure, in a bed with me.

If a man is lucky – really lucky – then at least once in his life he'll wake up with a beautiful naked woman sleeping beside him, marvel at the perfect primeval design of her body, and realize that it just never gets much better than that. I was tempted to let fate determine the future of my airplane, spend the rest of the day in bed, make love, order room service, make love again. I daydreamed about that scenario for a moment, then thought that surely there was going to be another night, just like last night, in another room, in another place, very soon. I decided to save my plane from sinking and got out of bed.

The pain hit me the instant my feet hit the floor. My battered ear was burning. My scalp was throbbing. My head was spinning and the ringing in my right ear was deafening. A searing fire was roaring in my temples and pulsating down the back of my neck. I staggered over to my pack and dug out a bottle of headache pills. I went into the bathroom, popped three pills in my mouth, and chased them down with a few handfuls of tap water.

I turned on the shower then tiptoed out to the bedroom to survey the battlefield. I needed my clothes. I picked up the top sheet with one hand, a blanket with the other, and gave them each a good shake. Clothes fell out but they weren't mine. I gently laid the sheet and the blanket over Sarah. She stirred, stretched, and yawned.

"Time is it?" she moaned.

"Six," I said. She rolled onto her stomach and buried her face in the mattress.

"Going now?" she mumbled.

"Soon. Go back to sleep. I'll see you tonight." I kissed the scratch on her shoulder and gave her a pat on the bum, then went back into the bathroom minus my clothes. I got in the shower, hoping the hot water would rejuvenate me and wash away my agony.

It didn't.

When I emerged from the bathroom my clothes were stacked in a neat pile on the corner of the bed. Sarah Marsalis was standing naked in front of me with the poise of a high class concierge. She raised her eyebrows and asked, "Finished in there?"

"Yes," I said, my mouth suddenly dry, fixated on the extraordinary sight before me.

"I won't be long," she said. "Wait for me."

"Sarah, I'm sorry, but you can't come with me to Juneau."

"Yes I can. We made a deal. Wait for me."

She disappeared into the bathroom and closed the door. I sat down on the bed, still naked, studying my clothes. I wasn't sure what to do. I had to file a flight plan and do my pre-flight inspections, that was for sure. I also needed to get moving right away if my plane was going to be ready to fly at seven – and not get sunk. But a deal's a deal. If I wasn't around when she came out of the bathroom, there'd be hell to pay. She'd come down to the plane and that wasn't an option. I had to avoid a scene at the docks and knew she could get down there well before I was ready to take off. I had to figure out a way to stop her, keep her away from that gorilla. There was no other option. This had to be resolved here and now. Our deal had to be renegotiated, notwithstanding how good a deal it had been for me, so far anyway, especially last night.

I got off the bed, went to the bathroom door, and listened. The shower was running. I knocked, opened the door a crack, and yelled in, "Sarah, you can't come with me. I'm leaving now."

"No you're not!" she yelled back from inside the shower. "Come in here!"

I could barely see anything with all the steam in the little bathroom. With modesty and feigned reverence for her privacy, I turned around and shuffled backwards toward the hiss of the shower, then said, "Look Sarah, I'm very sorry, but I really mean this, you can not come with me to Juneau. I didn't properly explain the situation to you. The man I'm flying with today is a thug and a criminal. Yesterday he threw me into a truck and beat me up, then he threw me out on the street. He threatened to sink my plane if I don't fly him to Juneau today. He's a dangerous man, Sarah. I can't have you get in my plane with him. So you can't come. That's final."

"I can't hear you, come closer," she shouted.

I shuffled backwards another two feet until one of my heels hit the side of the tub. I was about to repeat myself, then heard a swish as the curtains opened. She grabbed my arm and pulled. If I hadn't high stepped over the tub, I would have fallen in. Her hair was wet, her body was wet, and now I was wet. Again.

She swung the curtains shut, then wrapped her arms around my neck and kissed me hard. She slid her hands down my arms, pulled me close, and pressed her breasts against my chest.

"Brody?" she said, looking up at me through the steam.

"What?" I gulped.

"Right now the only man who scares me is you. Now wash my back."

* * *

I was pacing back and forth on the sidewalk in front of the hotel. Washing Sarah's back and everything else that entailed took another twenty minutes out of my morning. I'm not complaining mind you, there'd be few sympathizers. But it was twenty to seven and I was running out of time. When I'd left the room she was still steadfast on flying with me to Juneau. She said she had a plan. There was nothing I could say to change her mind. The best I could hope for was that no one got hurt today. I kept pacing – and pacing – and waiting.

I pulled my cell phone out of my pack and watched the screen as it began searching for things. I had to call flight services and file a flight plan. I decided to get that done before making a final appeal to Sarah not to fly with me this morning. I found the toll free phone number for Yukon flight services in my little black book, dialed the number, then filed the exact same flight plan to Juneau as Robert Duncan had two days ago, making sure to include the waypoint for Thistle Creek. But in contrast to Robert's flight plan, and with no intention to do so, I specified a landing at the waypoint, 'leaving breadcrumbs' as Dale had put it. I named just one passenger for the flight: a Mr. John Smith, aka, the gorilla. As I was closing my cell phone Sarah emerged from the hotel looking immaculate, healthy, and refreshed. I wasn't anywhere close to matching that image and my splitting headache had barely subsided, even after inhaling three potent painkilling pills.

"Ready to fly?" she asked, walking past me with a gait and pace that was hard to match. I hustled to catch her.

"Not really. You're absolutely crazy you know. This thing you've got for going to Juneau today, it's just asking for trouble. You're nuts."

"I'm not nuts. You worry too much, Brody. Everything will be fine. It's just another plane ride with another stranger."

"Sarah, it's not just another plane ride with another stranger. How can you be so naive? I've told you and I'm serious. This stranger's a thug. He'd kill us both without conscience."

"Brody, I have a plan, so just relax. Just fly your plane, okay?"

And that was that. End of negotiations. End of discussion. Appeal denied. Her mind was made up. She was coming with me. There was nothing else to say.

The streets were empty and we walked in silence, alone in a town still in a slumber. I looked at the river. It was dark and smooth and foreboding. The morning air was cool and crisp, the sky clear and blue, the wind light.

Experience told me that the weather in the western Yukon would be ideal for flying today, but I regretted not getting a weather report for Juneau this morning – when I'd had the chance – and the time. I'd been otherwise engaged in a hot shower with a hot woman in a Dawson hotel. That was no excuse, or a good excuse, depending on your point of view. But knowing the weather forecast for your destination is mandatory protocol in aviation. Flying into Juneau usually means flying into the clouds and swirling mists that more often than not shroud the coastal mountains in the Pacific northwest. Juneau is backed up against the mountains and is one of the most dangerous places I've ever flown into because the visibility is so variable and unpredictable. Without the benefit of having an instrument landing system, like the large commercial aircraft do, all you have for reference when landing a small plane is what you can see out the windows. Alaska panhandle pilots really earn their pay. The numbers don't lie and the statistics are clear. Flying in the Alaska panhandle is a dangerous job. Five times more dangerous than a cop's. For some reason, though, panhandle pilots don't make nearly as much as cops. Go figure.

We turned right onto Front Street at a brisk pace and headed toward the docks. It was ten to seven. A minute later I could make out the wings of my plane, gently rocking in the morning breeze.

TWENTY THREE

He was standing beside my plane, watching us as we turned off Front Street to head down the short gravel road to the parking lot. There were two briefcases and a small duffel bag at his feet. He looked bigger and thicker than I remembered. He was wearing a navy blue track suit with white stripes, white sneakers, and a US Navy ball cap. If you didn't know better, with his clean shaven face and buzz cut, you might think he was an authentic military man. Regardless of who he was, he didn't look like someone you'd want to mess with. He was glaring at me when we walked down the jetty and stepped on the dock. Then he glared at Sarah.

"Good morning," she called out, smiling ear to ear, striding confidently up to him with her hand extended.

Please no, do not shake his hand. He'll crush it.

"Pleased to meet you sir, I'm Sarah Marsalis with the Juneau Sentinel, Juneau's only daily newspaper, Sunday circulation 7,800. I'm with the travel section, are you familiar with our paper?" I couldn't believe her gall. She was fearless. He ignored her hand.

"What do you want?" he asked.

"Well sir, yesterday I hired Mr. Brody here and his fine airplane to do a little sightseeing around the Dawson area, take some pictures of the city and gold rush country, and of course the beautiful Yukon River. Well I just couldn't help myself, I took so many pictures,

I'm sure my editor will have a really hard time picking out the best ones for our Sunday feature section. And what a day it was for picture taking! You might say we had a picture perfect day for perfect picture taking." She chuckled at her contrived and very corny humor. The big man didn't. "Anyway, I'm doing a Sunday feature for the Sentinel on the unique history and sights to see around Dawson, definitely one place in the world our readers have to put on their 'must see list'. What an incredible place to visit. And what a great opportunity to meet our wonderful neighbors to the north. Absolutely the most friendly people here, don't you think? Oh, I'm sorry, I didn't catch your name."

"What do you want?" he repeated. He was glaring at her with a look of menace that would intimidate any sane person but Sarah just continued with her absurd spiel. Watching the two of them standing face to face conjured up an image of King Kong and Ann Darrow.

"Well sir, I'd like to return to Juneau today. Would you believe I took over two hundred pictures yesterday? It's certainly a feast for a photographer here, isn't this scenery just awesome? So anyway, I was wondering if I might join you today on your flight to Juneau. I'd be more than happy to split the cost of the flight with you. We'd have a win-win deal there, don't you think? Would that work for you? I certainly got all the pictures I needed yesterday, so there's no sense in spending any more of the Sentinel's money on another day in Dawson. If I could join you on your flight today, then I'd get home a day early. Always got to watch the old travel budget, right?" She laughed and flashed him another brilliant smile. "Just me and my little backpack here. I'm ready to go whenever you are, sir. Oh, would you like to see some of the pictures I took? You really have to see them, they turned out just great." She swung her pack around and unzipped the main compartment.

The big man was out of patience with the effervescent bubble head from the newspaper. She wouldn't shut up and he'd had enough. He yanked the pack off her shoulder and began digging inside. He squeezed all the compartments to assess their contents.

He pulled out her camera, then let the pack drop to the dock with a thump. Somehow she managed to keep smiling.

"Turn it on," he said, thrusting it in her face.

She stepped around to his side, reached over his enormous forearm, and pushed a button. The screen on the back of the camera illuminated. She pushed another button. I could make out a picture of Diamond Tooth Gerties. She hadn't mentioned anything last night about taking pictures when I'd asked about her day.

"Push this button here when you want to see the next one," she said, peering over his tree trunk arm at the camera. I marveled at how comfortable she seemed to be in such close proximity to him. He turned and glowered at me.

"What are you looking at," he said, "start the plane."

I shouldn't have hesitated but was reluctant to leave her alone with him. "Start the plane," he repeated when I didn't move, a little louder this time, and a definite warning.

I knew he wouldn't tell me again, not without some physical coaxing, and did what I was told. There was nothing I could to protect her from him anyway, not under the circumstances, not against his raw power and strength. I left them to their picture viewing and got down to the task of preparing my plane for flight.

I unlocked the doors, got in the pilot's seat, turned on the master switch, and checked the fuel gauge. All three tanks were full. The Kerosene brothers had delivered as promised. That was a big relief. I'd worried about fuel last night when I left the docks to go up to Gerties. I hadn't felt like checking then because of the crowd on the docks.

I opened the cargo door and left it open. With the cockpit and cargo doors both open, I was in easy earshot of my two unlikely passengers. I stole a glimpse of them, standing with their backs to me, just off the nose of the plane. The gorilla was rapidly flicking the camera button, scrolling through Sarah's pictures. I knew what he was looking for.

From the back of the cargo bay I dug out the fuel test beaker and climbed down the ladder to the float. I crouched and leaned under the fuselage, then drew a fuel sample from each tank.

"What are you doing?" he asked, glaring at me.

"Checking for water in the fuel," I said, turning my back to him.

"Start the plane!"

"I will in a minute, got to make sure there's no water in the fuel."

"Start the plane," he yelled again, louder this time, a final warning.

I risked taking the extra time to hold the clear plastic beaker up to the sky, searching for water at the bottom. There was none. But I'd been told to what to do and there probably wouldn't be any more warnings. So no preflight inspections today. I flicked the beaker at the shore and my sample splashed on the rocks. I got back in the plane through the cargo door and stowed the beaker, then squeezed between the seats and sat down to start the motor. I was about to yell at Sarah and the gorilla to move down the dock, away from the prop, when he delivered his decision.

"We're going now. You can't come. Leave." He picked up her backpack and threw it up the dock toward the jetty.

"Hey," she yelled, with her hands on her hips. "Was that necessary? That was very rude, do you know that? I'll have my camera back now, if you don't mind." She held out her hand.

"Get it later," he said. He tossed it in the river. It made a spectacular splash and disappeared in the dark water.

"Hey!" she yelled, throwing her hands in the air. "That was an expensive camera. Why did you do that? What is wrong with you?"

I gritted my teeth. I knew this would happen. This was real trouble brewing and about to get worse in a hurry if she didn't leave right away. She might be the next thing to get tossed in the water. *Please, Sarah, just go.*

She walked ten feet up the dock and picked up her pack.

We all saw him at the same time. He was walking down the jetty, heading our way. Now I could place him. Jersey Boy. The

man who'd been sitting beside Sarah last night in Gertie's. The
same man who'd been standing with the gorilla on Front Street
watching me climb into an RCMP cruiser. Today he was wearing
the same clothes he had on yesterday afternoon: a black fleece
jacket, blue jeans, and short hiking boots. He was carrying a gym
bag. His right arm wasn't in a sling today, but he was sporting large
purple bruises under his eyes and had cotton balls stuffed in his
nostrils. I could only guess who'd recently broken his nose.

"I told you to stay in the hotel," barked the gorilla, jabbing his
finger, lumbering toward the jetty. Jersey Boy stepped onto the
dock and without any reservation kept striding toward the plane.
Sarah was standing on the narrow dock between Jersey Boy and
the gorilla, looking back and forth at the two of them as they closed
in on one another. She had nowhere to go. They stopped to face off
with Sarah between them.

"Shut up, Tommy. I'm sick of you beatin' on me and I'm sick
of you telling me what to do. You're gonna be listenin' to me from
now on. From now on, I'm calling the shots." In a flash he pulled
a gun out of his pocket and pointed it at Tommy's head. So the
gorilla has a name.

Tommy.

To my horror, I realized these two men must be the 'two other
men' seen climbing into the NOCA Beaver two days ago. One or
the other had probably murdered Robert Duncan and his passenger.

Tommy held his ground but was looking down the barrel of
a gun. Jersey Boy looked intensely at Sarah. "Well, well, well,"
he said, smiling at her, "if it isn't the pretty little bitch I played
blackjack with last night. You and me honey, we're going flying
today. I got plans for you later. Now the two of you, turn around
and walk back to that plane. Get going, Tommy."

Tommy didn't move. Sarah didn't move. I wasn't sure if one of
them was about to try something heroic.

Jersey Boy swung the gun away from Tommy and pointed it
at Sarah's head. It looked like an old snub nose Colt revolver,

probably a .32 caliber. He pulled the hammer back and I heard the click fifteen feet away. My heart was in my throat.

"I said move bitch! Get over to that plane! Now! You too, Tommy! The both of you get goin' or I'll kill you both right here, right now!"

When Tommy turned around and started walking toward the plane, I knew he was taking Jersey Boy's threat seriously. Sarah stared at Jersey Boy with a defiant glare, then turned and followed Tommy. Jersey Boy followed them with the gun pointed at Sarah's back, the gym bag in his hand.

I'd been sitting in the cockpit, frozen in my seat, watching the drama unfold out of the direct line of sight of Jersey Boy. When they all arrived and stopped below me, Jersey Boy looked up and said, "Well, isn't this a surprise? Lover Boy is here too. You the pilot?"

"Yeah," I said, swallowing hard.

"Get down here," he said, waving the gun at the dock and jutting his chin at the back of the plane. "Go back there with your bitch girlfriend and wait. Do exactly what I say. Try anything and I'll shoot you. Understand?"

"Understand," I said, believing him. Whoever he was, he seemed awfully confident with a gun in his hand. While I climbed down the ladder, I sneaked a peak at the road above us and the parking lot. Hopefully someone would see what was going on and call for help. No such luck. The road was empty.

When I stepped onto the dock, the barrel of the gun went hard into my back and he gave me a shove. I grabbed Sarah's arm and pulled her down the dock. We walked ten feet behind the plane, then turned around to look at Jersey Boy and Tommy.

"Face the plane, Tommy. Put your hands behind your back." Jersey Boy had the barrel of his gun pressed hard into the small of Tommy's back. Tommy did what he was told.

"You're a dead man, Ricky. You are so dead right now."

"Shut up Tommy or I kill you right now."

Ricky. Tommy. Ricky and Tommy. Now we knew their names. But did they care? Were our fates already sealed?

Ricky looked down the dock at Sarah. "What's your name bitch?"

She looked at him defiantly. She certainly had courage. She waited for what seemed like a long time, then finally said, "My name is Sarah."

"Sarah. Sarah the bitch. Sarah the blackjack bitch. Come here, Sarah the bitch. Open this bag here."

He kicked his gym bag.

She walked up to him, knelt down and unzipped the bag. Ricky apparently knew what he was doing. He lifted Tommy's jacket at the waist and slid his gun hand underneath it. Tommy wouldn't dare try a fast move to disarm Ricky now, not with the certainty of getting shot in the back. Ricky looked down at Sarah and said, "Take out three ties, them big black ones, put one around each of his wrists, pull them tight, then tie them two together with another one." Sarah looped and fastened a tie around each of Tommy's wrists, then fed another tie through the ones on his wrists.

"Pull them all tight, real tight," he said. He watched her, then pulled the ties even tighter. "Go back there to lover boy," he barked at her, yanking the gun out from under Tommy's jacket, gesturing in my direction. She did.

"Where's my gun, Tommy?" Ricky asked.

Tommy said nothing.

Ricky jabbed the gun into the back of Tommy's neck. "I won't ask again, I said where's my gun?"

"In my bag. Where'd you get that one, Ricky?"

"Right here in town. From a friend, Tommy. I made a new friend in town last night. And you know what? He used to be your friend. What do you think of that? Now get in the plane. Sit down and shut up or I'll kill ya'. Get up front there, on the right. Move!"

I watched with amazement at how easily the big man climbed the ladder with his hands tied behind his back, then crouched and stepped into the plane, seemingly unaffected.

"Keep going, sit down, that's it, on the right," Ricky said, waving at the passenger seat.

This should be interesting, I thought. Tommy will never be able to get those massive legs through the narrow space between the front seats. But though he was crouched low under the ceiling, he easily swung his right leg up and over the left seat, put his foot down on the floor, then swung his left leg up and over and sat down. His weight and movements made the plane rock. He turned and glared at Ricky. If looks could kill.

Ricky knelt down and opened Tommy's duffel bag. He dug around with his left hand for a few seconds, watching Sarah and I as he did, always keeping the gun pointed in our direction. He smiled broadly at us when he pulled out a sock with a lumpy object inside. He reached in the sock and slid out a shiny Ruger pistol. Sarah gasped.

For some macabre reason, Ricky took a moment to admire the gun. It was small and compact, probably a .22, a popular caliber amongst professional hit men. Ricky shoved it down the front of his jeans.

Ricky looked at me. "So what about you lover boy, you got any guns? Any weapons? Maybe in there?" He gestured into the cargo bay.

"No," I said.

"Oh yeah? You got a flare gun?"

"Well yeah, there's a flare gun somewhere in the back, in a duffel bag."

"Get it out."

I walked up to the cargo door and had just put a foot on the ladder when he grabbed me by the collar and shoved the revolver hard into my ribs. "Lie to me again, I kill you," he said into my ear. "Understand?"

I nodded.

"Good. Now I'm gonna ask you once more. You got any weapons? A gun? A knife? Anything. Don't lie to me. Last chance."

"A knife," I said.

"Where a knife?"

"I have two. One on my belt, in a holster. And a little one in my backpack."

"What else?"

"Nothing."

He located the holster on my hip, opened it and pulled out the six inch knife. He looked it over. "Very nice," he said, slipping it into his jacket pocket. Now Ricky had two guns and a knife. He ran his free hand up and down my torso and legs. When he'd finished his search, he said, "Get in. I want that flare gun. You take it out of the bag real, real slow. You slide it to me on the floor. Point it at me, you die." He shoved me toward the ladder. "Move."

I climbed the ladder, got in the plane, and reached for the duffel bag holding my survival gear. I lifted it out from behind the cargo net. Ricky was standing on the ladder, leaning in the plane, holding the gun on me, watching my every move, occasionally stealing a glance at Tommy and Sarah. I shoved the duffel bag across the floor so that it was between us. I opened it, reached in, and pulled out the flare gun with two fingers. I laid it on the floor and slid it over to him. He picked it up and dropped it in the water between the floats. He stepped off the float, down to the dock.

"Alright," he said, "Time to load up. Drop one of these in the water, you're dead."

He picked up the first briefcase and swung it up at me. I could barely control it when I grabbed it at the peak of its arc. It fell to the floor of the plane with a resounding 'thud'. It was incredibly heavy. My first guess was gold. My second and third guesses would be gold. He swung the other briefcase up and I did a better job of controlling this one, but it too fell hard to the floor. He reached down to his gym bag and pulled out a long nylon tie.

"Tie them cases together and fasten them to his seat." He pointed at Tommy with his gun.

He watched me slide the two cases up to the passenger seat. I looped the nylon tie around the passenger seat frame and through the handles on the cases, then pulled it tight. I could hear Tommy breathing in front of me.

"Get in your seat," Ricky commanded, "start the motor, we're going". I stepped between the seats, squeezing past Tommy's massive shoulders, and sat down beside him. I didn't dare look at him. I leaned down to my left to pump the fuel primer and looked back to see what Ricky would do next. He was rummaging through my backpack, searching every pocket and compartment. He found my Swiss army knife and slipped it in his jeans. Now he had two guns and two knives. He picked up my pack and threw it into the rear cargo hold of the plane, then went through Sarah's backpack, being just as careful, checking every compartment for anything that could be used as a weapon. When he'd finished, he threw her pack after mine. Last, he rummaged through Tommy's duffel bag. When he seemed satisfied it had no weapons, he threw it into the back of the plane with the others.

"Hey you, Sarah the bitch," he said, waving his gun at her, "come here."

She strode up to him with a look that could kill. I kept stealing glimpses of the road as I pumped the fuel primer. A camper van rolled slowly by with an elderly man at the wheel, presumably on his way to catch the ferry, but he never looked down at the plane. That had been the only vehicle I'd heard or seen in the last five minutes. The road was quiet. No one was around. We were on our own.

"Stand there," Ricky said to Sarah, pointing at the float under the open cargo door. "Put your hands in the plane, flat on the floor. And don't you dare move." She stepped on the float and put her hands on the cargo bay floor. I looked back at her over my left shoulder. She was staring straight ahead, clearly furious. Ricky stepped on the float and straddled her from behind, his feet on either side of hers, then pressed his pelvis into her buttocks. He pressed the barrel of the gun into the right side of her neck, then took every liberty he could with his left hand, fondling her everywhere as he searched for a weapon.

"You fucking pig!" she screamed. He laughed with the right side of his face pressed against her left ear, then stepped back on the dock, reached his left hand out to her left buttock, and gave it a squeeze. "Get in the plane, Sarah the bitch. Up you go, move it." He laughed again, admiring her backside. "Can't wait for tonight, honey."

I was fixated on her, ignoring Ricky. Her face was beet red. She was livid. There was fire in her eyes. Hell hath no fury.

Sarah Marsalis put her left foot up on the first rung of the cargo door ladder and stepped off the float. Then she drove her right leg straight back with a mule kick. The heel of her boot caught Ricky flush in the face. Ricky's head snapped back and he toppled over backwards, landing hard on his back on the dock, losing his grip on the gun as he reached back to break his fall. The gun bounced and clattered, coming to rest five feet to his left, teetering on the edge of the dock.

"You fucking bitch!" he screamed, clutching his broken face with his left hand. He rolled over to his left and sat upright with a push. Then Sarah launched herself at him from the ladder, snapping another kick at his face, the heel of her left boot landing flush on the right side of his chin. Ricky's head snapped to his left. He gazed starry-eyed at his gun for a second, then groaned and fell back on his left side. After the second kick to his head, Ricky was down for the count. He lay motionless. Sarah's second kick and its inertia had carried her out to the far edge of the dock. She was bent over at the waist, waving her arms in big circles, desperately trying not to fall in the water. She buckled her knees, finally regained her balance, stepped to her right, and picked up the gun.

She whirled around and pointed it at Ricky's chest, stepped over him, and rolled him onto his stomach with a foot. Then she dropped her full weight on him, driving both knees hard into his back. I heard the air blast out of his lungs. She pressed the barrel of the gun against the side of his head.

"Don't move asshole! Don't even think about moving unless you want to die." Ricky wasn't going to move. He was still blinking his eyes, trying to figure out where he was, what had happened, why he could barely breathe, and where his gun had gone.

"Brody!" she yelled. "Get this asshole's bag down here. See if there are any more nylon ties inside. We need to tie him up. And get me a plastic bag."

I did what I was told. I climbed down the pilot's ladder to the float and climbed back inside the plane through the cargo door. I grabbed Ricky's gym bag, found a plastic bag, and climbed back down to the dock. I handed her the plastic bag, then found some more nylon ties in the gym bag. I tied Ricky's wrists and ankles together while Sarah kept the Colt trained on him.

Sarah put her left hand in the plastic bag and pulled the Ruger out from the waist of his jeans. She used the barrel of the Colt in her right hand to work the plastic bag down over the Ruger in her left hand, then set the bag down on the dock. She reached in and took my knife out of his jacket pocket, then rolled him over and pulled my pocket knife out of his jeans pocket. She put the two knives into the plastic bag with the gun, then tied a knot to seal it closed. She stood up and walked a few steps down the dock with the bag. She set it down, walked back, and crouched beside Ricky. She patted him down, head to foot, making sure he had nothing left to cut, stab or shoot anyone. She stood up with the gun trained on his back.

"Pull harder on those ties, Brody. Make them really tight," she commanded.

Once again I did what I was told. There was no doubt who was in charge. I stood and admired my work, watching Ricky for a moment. He was perfectly still, lying on his side, glassy eyed and pathetic looking. The cotton balls in his nose were now saturated with fresh blood and it was dripping on the dock. His nose was shifted unnaturally to the left. He was breathing heavily through his mouth. I stared in awe at Sarah Marsalis. She looked back and gave me a nod of approval.

Then she stepped over to the pilot's door and pointed the gun up at Tommy. He was staring out the windshield, apparently oblivious to all the Rambo-like action that had just taken place.

"You!" she yelled. "You owe me a camera. And if I see you get out of that seat, I'll shoot you." I was standing beside her, astounded at her bravado.

"Hey, Sarah, I want my passport back," I said. "That guy has my passport and wallet. Ask him where they are."

"We'll get your passport and wallet later. Come here for a second."

I followed her a few feet down the dock toward the tail of the plane. We stopped and looked at Ricky. He was still lying motionless on the dock. There was now a puddle of blood under his face.

"Do you have a cell phone?" she asked in a hushed voice.

"Yeah, in my backpack."

"Get it out. I'll watch these guys, you call the RCMP. Tell them we have the man and the gun that killed Robert Duncan and David Marsalis."

"Who's David Marsalis?"

She paused, looked furtively at the river for an instant, took a deep breath, then turned and looked me in the eyes.

"My brother," she said.

TWENTY FOUR

I could hear them coming. I slung my backpack on my shoulder and headed toward the jetty.

"Where are you going?" she called out.

"To get some sleep," I muttered, not looking back.

I stepped on the jetty and began climbing, watching the road above me. Seconds later a parade of police vehicles with blaring sirens and flashing lights came roaring down into the parking lot, fishtailing and spitting out gravel, churning up clouds of dust, skidding to a stop with their wheels locked. One cruiser, two cruisers, three cruisers, four cruisers – then a big black SUV. One after the other their doors opened and slammed shut with a cacophony of thumps and thuds that sounded like exploding artillery. Boots hit the ground, hands went to holsters, and a battalion of cops came running toward me. With a few hasty strides I managed to step off the top of the jetty just seconds before the first cop arrived.

"Get out of the way, Mr. Brody!" a gravelly voice bellowed from somewhere in the cloud of billowing dust. "Step aside and wait right there." A dozen uniforms in bullet proof vests stampeded past me, one after the other, their boots pounding the wood planks, their guns drawn, ready to shoot it out with the bad guys.

Staff Sergeant Robson emerged from the cloud of dust with the aura of a matinee gunslinger. He swaggered toward me with his thumbs rammed under his gun belt, stopping only when his face was inches from mine. I stood my ground. When he opened his mouth, I beat him to the punch.

"What the hell are you doing, Robson? What's with all the commando shit? See that woman down there? She wrapped this thing up ten minutes ago. I told you on the phone, the bad guys are totally under her control. You're way too late to be a hero here."

Robson scowled. "I need you to get in that unit over there right now, Mr. Brody," jutting his chin at the fourth car in line, "I'll be with you in a minute."

"No thanks," I said. "I'm out of here. I need some sleep. Got a terrible headache. See you later."

He straightened his back, stepped to his right to block my way, and glared daggers at me. "I'm not asking you, I'm telling you. Now get in that cruiser."

"No."

"Do you want me to arrest you? Don't test me. I've had enough of your antics and I'll arrest you if I have to. You'll spend the rest of the morning in a holding cell if you want to do it that way."

"If I can sleep, that'll be fine with me," I said. "And hey, if you arrest me, I don't have to talk to you, right?"

Robson laid on some more of his cop glare, then glanced at my plane. There were four cops with their pistols trained on Ricky, still lying motionless on the dock. Two other cops had Tommy covered in the plane. Things seemed to be under control. Just like they were before the cops arrived. Sarah no longer had a gun in her hand. She looked ready to leave.

"Now you listen to me," Robson said, leaning into my face again. "You get in that cruiser right now or I'll wrap so much yellow tape around that plane of yours it'll never fly again."

"Robson, you do that and I'll have to find someone to drive me home. Maybe I'll call a friend of mine at the newspaper. The three hour drive to Minto would be a great opportunity for us to catch up on what's been going on around town lately."

The big cop's face reddened and he was ready to explode.

"What's your problem anyway? You're obstructing the due process of a criminal investigation. All we're trying to do here is find out what happened."

"Ask her what happened," I said calmly, pointing at Sarah. "Her name's Sarah Marsalis. She's the only one you need to talk to, she's the hero, she did your job for you, and she knows exactly what happened."

"But we need *your* statement, Mr. Brody. Now when exactly do you think you might fit us into your busy schedule? Sometime today perhaps?" His eyes burned with disdain but he was clearly capitulating.

"Well, I don't want to sit down with a bunch of stuffed shirts in a sealed room again. What do say we meet in the park, across from the ice cream shop, say about one thirty? You'll find me sitting at a picnic table near the river."

I stepped around him and headed for my hotel.

"Staff Sergeant!" someone yelled from the dock.

* * *

I walked into my hotel and Molly was behind the counter. Today she was wearing a grey fisherman knit sweater and a matching toque with a big pompom. I'd just taken off my windbreaker.

"Hi Molly, I'm back, could I get another key for my room? My plans have changed. I need my room until checkout time."

"No problem, Mr. Brody, I'll activate another key for you." She swiped a card through a reader, typed a few numbers, and handed me a new key.

"Thanks. Hey, when's checkout time?"

"Noon," she said, "but we're not busy today so you can push that back to one o'clock. Just make sure you hang the 'Do Not Disturb' sign on your door."

"Great. I'll do that. And hey, could I have an eleven thirty wake-up call, please?"

"Of course, sir". She typed something into a computer then looked up. "Done," she said, smiling at me.

I smiled back at her. If only everyone was as easy to get along with as Molly.

"Oh, Mr. Brody?"

"Yes?"

"Did you hear all those sirens? Do you know what's going on out there?"

"Molly, I have absolutely no idea what's going on." I pinched at the pain under the bridge of my nose and headed for the stairs.

I walked into my room, hung the sign on the door, dropped my pack on the floor, waded through a mess of towels, sheets and blankets, and fell on the bed. I was asleep in five minutes.

* * *

When the phone rang I stretched out my arm, lifted the receiver an inch, and dropped it back on the cradle. Must be eleven thirty. I rubbed my face, stretched and yawned, opened my eyes, and analyzed the texture of the ceiling for a minute. I still felt tired but my headache was waning. Looked like I was going to live. The phone rang again. This time I picked it up, put it to my ear and waited for the recorded greeting.

"Brody?"

"Yes?"

"Why'd you just hang up on me?"

"Thought it was my wakeup call. Is that Sarah?"

"Yes, it's Sarah. Who else?"

"I don't know. What time is it?"

"Eleven twenty five. What are you doing?"

"Sleeping when you called. What are you doing?"

"I just left the police station. Want to have some breakfast?"

"It's lunchtime."

"Well then, do you want to have some lunch?"

"I have plans for lunch."

"Plans?"

"Yeah, plans. You know, things you intend to do."

"Okay, I get it. Hey, why are you giving Robson such a hard

time? He's just trying to do a job. Things would be so much easier if you just co-operated with him."

"Things would be so much easier if he just co-operated with me."

"So it's going to be like that, huh? Anyway, when can we get together?"

"One-thirty. At the park on the river. Across from the ice cream store."

"Okay. See you then."

"Hey, Sarah?"

"What?"

"Don't forget to bring my passport and my wallet. And my knives."

"I'm afraid you can't have your knives for awhile. They're evidence."

"Evidence?"

"Yes, evidence."

I hung up and went into the bathroom for another shower, thinking about *evidence*.

The only plan I actually had was to lose a headache and have a bowl of the best soup in the Yukon.

TWENTY FIVE

The bells on the door jingled when I walked into Deb's Soup Kitchen. I could smell fresh bread and a medley of mouth watering aromas. It was exactly noon.

Two women were standing in front of the counter. I didn't see Deb anywhere and looked down the hall. Bobby came walking out of the kitchen with a large paper bag cradled in his arms.

"Number sixteen!" a little voice chirped from somewhere behind the bag. He walked toward the women, carrying his precious cargo with the utmost care and concentration.

One of them gave him a big smile, took the bag from his arms and said, "Well, thank you very much, young man." Bobby smiled at her, then noticed me.

"Uncle Brody!" he cried.

"Bobby!" I said, mimicking his enthusiasm. "What are you doing working? Aren't you on summer holidays?"

"I'm helping my Mom today. She says it's a very busy day. She's in the kitchen."

"Well she's lucky to have you helping her. Hey, do you think I could sit down at that table in the corner?"

"Yup," he said, with the nod of a man in charge.

"Thanks." I walked ten feet to the corner table and kicked my backpack under the table. Bobby followed and watched me sit down. He folded his arms and leaned on the table, looking up at me with anticipation. It's nice to be someone's hero.

"Bobby!" came a voice from the kitchen. "Order up!"

"I have to go now," he said, deeply disappointed, resigned to doing some more heavy lifting. He walked down the hall and disappeared into the kitchen. A moment later he reappeared with another large paper bag with the number seventeen written in bold letters.

"Number seventeen!" he yelled to the only person standing at the counter. The woman smiled and said, "Thank you, dear." She took the bag and the door jingled behind her. Deb came out of the kitchen wiping her hands on a towel. She looked tired but still managed a warm smile when she saw me. She came over to the table.

"Hi," she said with a sigh, sitting down.

"Hey, Deb. How did things go last night?"

"Not so good. I didn't get home until two. A lot of tears, you know? Katy's mom will be here tomorrow, she's coming up from Toronto. That should make a big difference, with the baby and all."

"You're a good friend, Deb. Hey, when did the cops leave?"

"About twenty minutes after you did. I don't think any of them like you very much, just so you know, especially that older guy. Katy wouldn't sign some papers when he was about to leave. She told him you said not to, so she just refused. He was pretty mad about that and she got upset, but she wouldn't sign his paperwork. I guess she must trust you, Brody. You did tell her not to sign anything, right?"

"I did. Did she call her lawyer?"

"Apparently her father's going to find her one in Whitehorse."

"Good, the lawyer will tell her what to sign. To hell with the cops."

"Excuse me, your language please?"

Bobby was leaning on the table between us, resting his chin on his folded arms, absorbing our conversation. He smiled up at me mischievously. 'To hell'. Two new words for his vocabulary that he really didn't need at this stage of his life.

"Sorry. Hey Deb, do you know where can I find a tape recorder in Dawson?"

"No," she said with a perplexed look. "Why? No one uses tape recorders anymore."

"They don't?"

"Well, no. Everything's electronic now. I think what you're looking for is a voice recorder. And if you have a cell phone, you already have one."

"I do?"

"Yes. Do you have your cell phone with you?"

"Yeah."

"Give it to me."

I reached under the table, fished my phone out of my pack, and set it down in front of her. She slid it over to Bobby. "Bobby, show Uncle Brody how to use his voice recorder."

He picked up the phone in his little hands, held it impossibly close to his face, and began deftly working the key pad with his thumbs. Five seconds later he held it out to me with a big grin. The screen displayed the words 'Record', 'Start', and 'Stop'.

"Wow," I said, looking at him with genuine admiration, "That's amazing. Show me how you did that."

The front door jingled and Deb got up.

"Want something to eat?" she asked. "Broccoli or Vegetable? Bread?"

"Broccoli and bread."

"Two slices, lots of butter?"

"Does Roy sleep with…"

She rolled her eyes before I'd finished my rhetorical question and walked over to her customer. She took the order and disappeared into the kitchen. Bobby showed me the key strokes to turn on my 'voice recorder'. Over and over again he showed me. How to locate the voice recorder in the phone menu, how to start recording, how to stop recording, how to save the recording. It took a lot of tries before I could do it all by myself. I wasn't confident I could do it again, not without his help.

Deb called Bobby again and he ran off to the kitchen. He came out with another bag for the customer at the counter. Deb followed him out with my soup and bread. She set them down in front of me and sat down again.

"Your soup is the best, Deb. You know, if we were married, you could make me soup, and I could give you free car maintenance. Think about that."

"Brody, I think there's a little more to marriage than soup and car maintenance, but I'll consider those advantages."

I started in on my cream of broccoli soup with shredded parmesan on top, wondering what else might be required for a good marriage.

"Exceptional as usual, Deb. Remember, free car maintenance." She shook her head and barely smiled.

Bobby came back to the table after making his delivery and took up his usual position, standing at the table between us.

"Hey, Bobby," I said.

"What?"

"See that last loaf of bread over there behind the glass? Do you think you could put it in a plastic bag for me to take home?"

"Okay." He ran enthusiastically behind the counter. I looked at Deb.

"I think they caught the guy," I said, "the one who killed Robert. The cops took him away this morning."

"Really? That was fast. Where was he? Who is he?"

"They just arrested him here in town, but I don't know who he is. Look, I wouldn't be spreading the news quite yet, not until it's announced, but maybe you could tell Katy. She might feel a little safer knowing the guy's locked up."

"Sure". She paused then asked, "So how did you find out?"

"Well, actually it all happened down at the docks this morning, right in front of my plane. It's kind of a long story. The man was trying to force me to fly him to Juneau, but he…failed you might say. The cops came and took him away."

"Failed? What do you mean he failed? How did he fail? Did you stop him? Did you beat him up or something? And how do you know he killed Robert?"

I took a deep breath. "Actually, the person who beat him up was a woman I met a couple of days ago in Minto. I had nothing to do with his capture. She's the hero. Look, never mind about that right now, wait for the newspaper story, just be happy the guy's locked up."

"A woman beat him up? What woman? The one you met in Minto? The one who's been trying to ruin your life?" Deb leaned in toward me, obviously fascinated with the scenario.

"Never mind who she is. To tell you the truth, I don't have a clue myself."

She studied my face for a while, then her eyes got big and she smiled broadly. "You have a crush on her, don't you?"

"What? No. Don't be ridiculous."

"You are such a lousy liar, Brody. You have a crush on her. I can tell. It's all over your face. Can I meet her?"

"No, you can't meet her, she doesn't even live here."

Bobby returned to the table with my loaf of soda bread and heaved it on the table in front of me. "Thanks buddy," I said.

Deb was looking at me, grinning ear to ear.

"What?" I said. "Let me eat my soup, okay?"

The bells jingled again and Deb got up, still smiling at me.

I looked at Bobby. "Have your lunch yet?"

"Yup."

"Good. When I've finished my soup, maybe your Mom will let you come with me to the park for some ice cream."

He turned and bolted down the hall, catching his mother on her way to the kitchen. She listened to him with her hands on her hips, then turned to me and held up a finger. They both disappeared into the kitchen. I ate my soup.

Bobby delivered another bag of soup to the customer at the counter. A few moments later mother and son returned to my table.

"So I hear you want to go for ice cream," she said, sitting down again.

"Yeah, is it okay if he comes with me to the park?"

"Alright, but don't be long, he was up late last night at Larry's and he's tired. When will you be back?"

"About two."

"Alright, but no later, okay?"

"Okay."

"What's your phone number, Brody?" She took her cell phone out of her apron pocket.

"In Minto?"

"No, not in Minto, your cell phone number, in case I need to call you today."

"Why would you need to call me?"

"Brody, you're not going anywhere with my child unless I know how to call you."

"Oh."

"So what is it?"

"My cell phone number?"

"Yes, your cell phone number."

"I don't know."

"Give me your phone," she said with a sigh. I got out my phone again and slid it over to her. She held her phone in her left hand, picked up my phone with her right, and punched a bunch of keys with her thumb. Her phone rang once, she pressed a button, then put it down. She got busy with her fingers on my phone, put it down, then picked hers up and punched its buttons for awhile. She looked up and said, "There, now I have your phone number, and you have mine. Bobby, show Uncle Brody how to call me. And you guys better be back at two."

She stood up from the table and went back to the kitchen. She didn't look happy. I made big eyes at Bobby. He made big eyes at me. We smiled knowingly at each other. Mommy was angry about something.

I stood, stuffed the bread in my pack, and slipped some cash under my soup bowl.

"Come on buddy, let's go have some ice cream."

TWENTY SIX

We each decided on a single scoop of chocolate on a sugar cone. Half the fun for a kid in an ice cream shop is deciding which flavor to pick. Bobby spent a good five minutes perched on my back, looking over my shoulder through the glass display at all the buckets of ice cream. He was a lot heavier than he was two years ago. When he finally made his decision, I was relieved to let him slide down my back to the floor.

It was just before one o'clock when we crossed Front Street and headed into the park, licking our cones, looking for a table near the river. I was having second thoughts about bringing Bobby with me to the park, knowing perfectly well that he couldn't attend my meeting with the cops. I'd made some hazy rationalization that we'd run into someone to watch him while I met with Robson. I was regretting my judgment. There were very few people around. If I didn't soon find someone to watch him, I'd have to postpone my meeting and return him to his mother.

We found a table at the river's edge. I sat facing the street, a couple of hundred feet from the ice cream store, watching for cops. Bobby sat across from me. He was watching a ferry bellowing black smoke, crossing the river at a forty five degree angle in a battle against the current.

"Bobby," I said. "I might have to talk to some policemen for a minute. Do you see anyone around here that you know?"

He looked around, then pointed at an athletic young man playing with a large dog. "Him," he replied, pointing at the man a hundred feet away. I watched the dog charge after a well thrown ball.

"Who's he?"

"That's Mr. Kerry. He's our gym teacher. He likes my Mom. He always talks to her when she drives me to my school."

"Really," I said. It was no mystery to me why Mr. Kerry would enjoy talking to Bobby's mother. I didn't like him already.

I watched an enormous black SUV roll up and park in front of the ice cream shop on the other side of Front Street. It was the same one that I'd seen this morning at the docks. All four doors of the ominous looking vehicle opened at once. I recognized Kurtz when he emerged from the driver's door. Another man, older and vaguely familiar, got out of the right front door with a briefcase in his hand. Robson got out of the right rear passenger door. Owen got out of the left rear passenger door. He too was holding a briefcase. Then Sarah Marsalis emerged.

All five of them stood in a group behind the vehicle, scanning the park, doubtless searching for me. I wondered what Sarah was doing with them. I noticed how they would all cast their eyes on Bobby and me, then dismiss us and continue to scan the other picnic tables for a man sitting alone. I had no inclination to help them out with a wave of my hand. Eventually Sarah recognized me and made a gesture to the men. She turned her back and spoke to them, like a quarterback calling a play in a huddle. I was intrigued as to what her role might be in a meeting I'd scheduled with Robson. All of them except Sarah got back in the SUV. She began walking toward us.

It was a fair distance from the vehicle to our table and I enjoyed watching her for the whole two minutes it took her to reach us. She had on the same clothes as last night but was now wearing her fleece jacket. Her backpack swung at her side, slung from her left shoulder, held with a thumb under the strap, like she was carrying a purse. She looked freshly showered and groomed, no surprise there after what she'd been through this morning. I marveled at how she always managed to look so fresh and healthy looking. I guess certain people just have that persona. Bobby couldn't see Sarah approaching and didn't notice her until she stopped at the end of our table.

"Hello, Brody, who's your friend?"

Bobby looked up at her. She was leaning over him with her hands on the table, radiating a wide warm smile. He was instantly as intimidated as any red blooded male would be. He turned his head the other way, completely overwhelmed by her charisma and killer smile.

"Miss Marsalis, this is Bobby Larabie. Bobby, meet Miss Marsalis."

Bobby could do no better than stare at his cone. The ice cream was almost gone.

"Bobby, aren't you going to say hello?" I asked.

"Hello," he said, not looking at her.

"Hello, Bobby, nice to meet you," she said warmly, though not displaying any intention to join us. "Brody, could I have a word, please?"

I stood and said, "A word? Hey buddy, wait here for a sec. Miss Marsalis has to tell me some top secret spy stuff. I'll be right back, okay?"

"Okay," he said, happy to be left alone to work on his cone.

Sarah walked twenty feet away from the table and stopped at the edge of the bluff, looking down at the Yukon River below. I followed and stood beside her. Out of the corner of my eye I saw Bobby steal a peek at us. A light wind was playing with Sarah's hair and I had a fleeting urge to kiss her. But it clearly was not the time or the place, and regardless, she looked preoccupied and nervous, avoiding my eyes, then turning around and scanning the park. She was clearly upset about something.

"Hey, what's up Sarah? I'm really sorry about your brother. You can talk to me about it later, if you want, but right now I'm supposed to meet with those cops over there. Hey, what are you doing hanging around with them?"

I looked at the SUV in the distance and noticed that Kurtz was out of the truck again. He had on his Special Agent mirror sunglasses and was leaning against the front fender. His arms were folded and he was staring intently at us. Sarah was biting her upper lip, now standing with her back to Kurtz, looking at me with her arms wrapped around her chest, clutching her elbows.

"Brody? Why did you bring that little boy down here when you knew you had a meeting with the police?"

"Oh, he's my lawyer."

"Damn. Don't you ever take anything seriously? Did it not occur to you that you're involved in a situation with some very bad people? People who will think nothing of using a little boy to get what they want? Just being seen with you puts him in danger. Don't you realize that?"

"Whoa! What do you mean involved with bad people? What bad people? Aren't all the bad people in jail now? It's over, right?"

She shook her head and took a deep breath, then looked at her feet and took some time before answering. "No. It's not over. It's far from over. Right now only that guy named Ricky will be charged with anything. He'll stay locked up for a while. But the other guy, the big one named Tommy, he got himself all lawyered up this morning. Hasn't said a word since he was arrested. There's no evidence he had anything to do with the murder of those two men yesterday. The ferry captain couldn't positively identify him as one of the men who got on the NOCA plane yesterday. His pal Ricky won't say a word. And even if Kay's finger prints are found inside the NOCA plane, his lawyer will point out that he's been in that plane numerous times before. So right now there's only an assumption the two were working together. And you can't charge people based on assumptions. Tommy Kay will probably be released as soon as his lawyer from Vancouver arrives tonight. So now do you see why you shouldn't be hanging around with anyone who may be vulnerable to an abduction? Especially someone like that little boy over there?"

I was shocked at what she'd just spewed out and had no idea of how to respond. All I could manage was, "Who the hell are you, Sarah? How do you know so much about what's going on with those two goons who tried to hijack my plane? Are you some kind of a cop?"

She inhaled deeply, then sagged and looked down again with a vanquished pose.

"You don't like cops, do you Brody?"

"You mean those pot-bellied, trigger-happy slobs who sit in their cars all night guarding the donut shops? Or do you mean those two-fingered typists who pack handguns around the office in case someone tries to steal their stapler, or do you mean those guys who…"

"Okay, okay, I get the picture," she interrupted. She put her hands on her hips and looked around, took a deep breath, then swung her backpack in front of her and unzipped the main compartment. She shuffled inside the pack for a second then held it out to me, revealing a clear view of its contents. It was obvious what she wanted me to see. It was a gold badge in an open leather billfold, just like the ones you see in the movies.

"You wanted to know who I am?" She gave me a fierce look, her head held high in a defiant pose. "My name is Sarah Roberta Marsalis. I'm a Special Agent with the U.S. Department of the Treasury. That's who I am."

TWENTY SEVEN

"Shit! A Special Agent? You're a Special Agent?"

"Yes, I'm a Special Agent."

"Not an ordinary agent. A special agent."

"Come on Brody. Get over it."

"Hey, Special Agent Sarah. What do they teach in Special Agent school about sleeping with witnesses?"

"They say don't."

"Don't." I heaved a sigh and shook my head, then looked across the street. Kurtz was still watching us.

"Look," she said with exasperation, "can we hash this out later? Right now you need to give your statement to Staff Sergeant Robson. And I'd like to get this little boy safely back to his mother. Can we get those two things done first, as a matter of urgent priority?"

I looked out at the river and sighed again. "Yeah, as matter of urgent priority. Alright, you take him back to his mother. I'll go talk to Robson. But wait here for a second. And don't move."

I walked back to the picnic table and sat down across from Bobby.

"Bobby, I have to go and talk to the police about something very important. Would you mind taking Miss Marsalis back to the 'Kitchen' and introduce her to your Mom? She's a really nice lady and she needs you to show her the way there. She's really hungry and wants to try a bowl of your Mom's soup. Would you do that for me?"

He nodded, though I'm sure he was confused about the change of plans, and his new mission.

"Okay, thanks pal. Let's call your Mom and tell her who you're going to be with, and where you're going, okay?"

He nodded again, though clearly uncertain about the specter of leaving the park without me, and in the company of Sarah Marsalis, a complete stranger. No time like the present for a boy to learn what it's like to be alone with a beautiful woman.

I pulled my phone out of my backpack and slid it over to Bobby. "Can you call your Mom for me, and let me talk to her too, okay?"

"Okay," he said. He pushed some buttons with his sticky fingers and waited.

I listened to his side of the conversation. "Hi Mom. Yup. At the park. Chocolate. One. Yup. Sugar. Yup. Soon. Okay. Okay. Okay, here's Uncle Brody. Okay. Bye." He handed me the sticky phone.

"Hi Deb."

"Hi, Uncle Brody. You guys having fun?"

"We're having a great time. Listen Deb, I just ran into the police down here and they want me to give them a statement about what happened this morning. Is it okay if I send Bobby back with my new friend, that woman I was telling you about?"

"The one who beat up the murderer?"

"Yeah, her. She's actually very nice. Very much a lady."

"Is she the woman you met in Minto?"

"Yes."

"The one who's been making so much trouble for you?"

"She's not so bad."

"The one you have a crush on?"

"Deb, I don't have…" I stopped just in time. Sarah was beside me, listening.

"How old is she?"

"I don't know". I lowered my voice. "Older than you, I think."

"What's her name?"

"Sarah Marsalis."

"Brody, you hardly know her. Are you're sure she's responsible?"

"Absolutely, she's absolutely responsible. I wouldn't let her take Bobby anywhere if she wasn't."

"Why are you whispering?"

"I'm not whispering."

"Oh, she's beside you, isn't she?"

"Deb, please."

"Alright. When will they be here?"

"They're leaving right now. Ten minutes. And Deb?"

"What?"

"Do you have any soup left?"

"I think so, yeah."

"Great, I think she's hungry."

"Brody? Is everything alright?"

"Everything's just perfect, Deb."

I flipped my sticky phone closed and gave it a wipe. It didn't help much but I dropped it in my pack anyway.

"Alright Bobby, are you ready to go with Miss Marsalis?"

He nodded and shoved the last piece of his cone into his mouth using both hands. He had chocolate ice cream all over his face and hands. I pulled a bottle of water out of my pack and soaked a few napkins for him to clean up. He took the napkins from me and rubbed his face and hands roughly. He looked at me for approval. I nodded. There was a slight improvement. His mother could deal with the rest. We got up and I took his hand. We stood facing Sarah.

"Okay, you're headed to the corner of Third and Queen. Bobby knows the way, don't you?"

He nodded, though didn't look up at me, unsure of himself.

I looked at Sarah. "I said you'd be there in ten minutes so you'd better get going. I've got to go over to the Bat mobile to get my finger nails pulled out by those cops. See you later."

"I'm sure everything will be fine, *Uncle* Brody". She smiled at me with a sparkle in her eyes and took Bobby's hand.

"See you later, *Special Agent*. See you later Bobby."

"Bye," he said.

They started walking diagonally across the park toward the foot of Queen Street. I headed the other way, toward the cops. I watched Sarah and Bobby as our paths diverged. It looked like Sarah was doing all the talking. Bobby looked over at me often. I waved at him every time. He waved back every time.

It dawned on me then that the current flame and the ex-flame were about to meet for lunch. I thought what a perfect opportunity for the two of them to get acquainted, compare notes, appraise each other's physical attributes, make all the subtle personal comparisons – the hair, the clothes, the shoes, the makeup, their ages and weight – then move on to the really important stuff, like me, discussing my virtues and deficiencies as a potential mate, ad nauseam. The second worst nightmare for a single man was in my immediate future. Of course the worst will always be when she just happens to mention out of the blue that it's the six month anniversary of your first date.

I crossed Front Street to the big black SUV. Kurtz held the left passenger door open for me. Neither of us said a word as I got in and sat down beside Owen, who was sitting in the middle of a long and luxurious leather bench seat next to Robson. I recognized the guy in the front seat. He was staring straight ahead. Kurtz closed my door, got in behind the wheel, and started the engine. He backed the enormous SUV out into the street while watching a television screen on the dash. How ridiculous, I thought. You're thirty something. Turn your head around and use your eyes to see where you're going. Or use your outside mirrors, like a real trucker. Who comes up with these electronic gimmicks? And who's going to fix them when they quit working?

Owen's phone rang. He took it out of his jacket pocket, looked at the screen, put it to his ear, but said nothing. He listened for five seconds, then put the phone back in his pocket. He turned to his right and murmured something to Robson. Robson nodded. I guess some top secret message had just been delivered.

There was dead silence in the big quiet truck for the short drive over to the RCMP building. Kurtz drove down the alley and parked behind the building. We all got out.

"Follow me please, Mr. Brody," said Robson, climbing a short set of stairs.

He slid a card into an electronic reader mounted on the wall and there was a click. Everyone followed him through the back door of the building. I was relieved when he walked past the first room on the right, the one they'd used for my first interview. Robson opened the second door on his left and we all walked into a room with a large round table and six chairs. I was more than pleased to see a window with a view of the street, and a source of natural light. Already seated at the table was a stern looking woman about fifty. She had a stenotype in front of her. She looked poised and bored. Stenographers have heard it all.

Robson said, "Mr. Brody, this is Mrs. Hanlon. She'll be recording your statement. Sit wherever you like."

I waited for Robson to sit down, then sat down opposite him. Perhaps he knew I'd do that, that I would choose to sit precisely where he wanted me to. Smart cop. The other three men sat down.

"Mr. Brody, I think you've met everyone here except Special Agent in Charge Polichek. 'SAC' Polichek is with the US Department of the Treasury."

Polichek was studying me like I was some kind of exotic animal in a cage – no nod, no smile, no nothing. 'Mr. Personality'. He kept sizing me up with a deadpan gaze, like I wasn't even in the room. The guy was giving me the creeps. He was obviously Sarah's boss, and another American cop in the Yukon. How many more were out there? Was the U.S. planning some kind of invasion of Canada?

Polichek finally acknowledged me with a nod. I nodded back, folded my arms and looked out the window. This was too weird. Polichek was the man who'd been sitting beside Kurtz last night at the blackjack table in Gertie's. Both Kurtz and Polichek had witnessed one of the greatest kisses ever given by a Special Agent to a Yukon bush pilot, in the history of Special Agents kissing Yukon bush pilots. Now that I knew Sarah was a Special

Agent, and undoubtedly working with these guys, I wondered how she was dealing with the fallout. Or had her by now famous kiss, and subsequent seduction of me, all been planned, plotted and orchestrated. Was what I thought to be a budding love affair actually just part of some covert scheme to catch some bad guys? Or a Machiavellian plot by the Americans to annex the Yukon? Whatever, I decided the personal details of our tryst weren't for consumption by the cops. Robson spoke again.

"Mr. Brody, with your co-operation we should be able to wrap this meeting up in a very short time, and send at least one man to jail for a very long time. First though, I'm going to ask you for your statement. Are you prepared to recount to us all the events you witnessed this morning – everything you did, saw and heard – from approximately six thirty this morning until you left the Yukon water aerodrome at approximately eight thirty this morning? Are you willing to give us your personal account for that time period?"

"I'm ready to give my account of events starting at seven o'clock this morning, not before."

"Oh? And why's that?"

"Because nothing I was doing before seven had anything to do with what happened on the docks this morning." I was looking at Robson but could feel the eyes of everyone else on me. Did they really have to know that I was in a shower with Sarah Marsalis at six thirty, or did they just *want* to know. I looked around and caught a glare from Kurtz. Owen and Polichek were looking down.

"Alright, then please give us your account of events beginning at seven this morning. Mrs. Hanlon, are you ready?"

"Yes, sir," she said.

"Please proceed to make your statement, Mr. Brody."

"Well," I said, "I met Sarah Marsalis on the sidewalk in front of the Downtown Hotel at seven o'clock this morning."

I talked for ten minutes straight without being interrupted. I described in detail everything I did, saw, and heard, right up to my 'conversation' with Staff Sergeant Robson at the top of the jetty.

When I finished my account of what had happened, I said, "And that's what I heard and saw this morning. That's my statement."

I looked at Robson for approval, then around the table at the other three men. Polichek and Owen were nodding, apparently satisfied with what they'd heard. Kurtz looked unhappy. He always looked unhappy.

Robson said, "Thank you, Mr. Brody. Thank you, Mrs. Hanlon." She stood and carried her machine out the room. "Your statement will be typed and ready to sign in a couple of hours, sir. If you could return here at five o'clock to sign it, that would be much appreciated. Is that a convenient time for you?"

I wasn't sure why Robson was so being polite to me. Perhaps it was the presence of the three American cops, but regardless, I was beginning to feel that I might get along with him after all. Maybe.

"Five o'clock will be fine," I said.

"Good. And thank you again, Mr. Brody. You've been very helpful. We'll see you at five. Can you find your way out the building on your own?"

"Yes."

I stood and left the room feeling utterly baffled No questions, no pictures, no advice, no warnings? It didn't make sense. Maybe they were saving that stuff for five o'clock. That's when they were going to tie me to a chair, get out the pliers, and start pulling out my fingernails. I walked out the front door and took a big breath of fresh air.

I suddenly thought about going home. I'd had enough of cops and criminals in the last two days and was getting tired of surprises. I hate surprises. I just wanted to see my dogs, change my clothes, put up my feet and watch the river go by. There was a hockey game on TV tonight. Tomorrow I might even fix a car or build something.

First things first, though. I needed to check on my plane. See how the police had treated it. See if it was still airworthy. If it was, I could fly home after signing my statement. I headed down Queen Street toward the docks and decided to call Minnie, tell her I'd be home tonight and that Reggie could return my dogs. I pulled out my phone and flipped it open. The screen said 'low battery'. I'd never seen that message before.

I turned right on Third Street and made a detour to Deb's Soup Kitchen. I could use Deb's phone.

I hoped Sarah wouldn't be there.

TWENTY EIGHT

Wei Lee was frantic. He'd been pacing for an hour. He went to his desk and pressed the intercom button. He waited. No answer. Lynn must still be at lunch. He paced some more, wrung his hands, felt a knot tightening in his gut. Where was Lynn? Why hadn't Henry called? Why hadn't Tommy called? He looked at his opulent Rolex with all its dials and bezels and roman numerals. It took him a moment to decipher the time of day. Five minutes past one. Don't these people who work for me know what time it is? He jabbed the intercom button again.

"Yes, Mr. Lee."

"Lynn, you are late. Lunch is one hour. You are to be here at one."

"I know Mr. Lee. But it is just one o'clock now. I am here on time, sir."

"No, you are not, Lynn. My watch says it is six minutes past one o'clock. You are late."

"Mr. Lee, I am quite sure that the correct time is one o'clock. Perhaps I could help you adjust your watch."

Lee glanced at his big new watch. For a hundred thousand dollars a watch ought to keep the correct time. "Yes, Lynn, you can do that for me. But later. Now, why hasn't Henry called?"

"I don't know, Mr. Lee. His office says he went to lunch with clients. He has a message to call you when he returns."

Lee hung up and resumed his pacing. Things were falling apart in the Yukon. This morning Arturo had called from Las Vegas. Arturo said that Tommy and Arturo's man Ricky had been arrested on suspicion for murdering two men. The police had taken Tommy to jail. And this man named Ricky, the one who Tommy said was an idiot, he'd been beaten up by some woman and taken to a doctor. What kind of a man gets beaten up by a woman? The phone chimed. Lee pressed the intercom button.

"Henry on line one, Mr. Lee," announced Lynn.

Wei Lee pressed another button and said "Henry, we have problems."

"Yes, Mr. Lee. Our lawyer in Vancouver just called me. Tommy is in jail in Dawson. Our lawyer says Tommy is being held for questioning regarding the murder of our gold pilot, and another man too. Mr. Pistone's man was also arrested, a man named Constanzia. Our lawyer is now on his way to the Yukon. He will arrive in Dawson this evening. He will call me after he talks to the police."

"Henry, why did the police arrest Tommy? He did not murder our gold pilot. Maybe that idiot who works for Arturo, this man Ricky, maybe he would do such a thing. But not Tommy."

"Of course, Mr. Lee. But Tommy was with the man named Ricky when the police made their arrests. The police always arrest everyone. But we should not worry. We have an excellent lawyer. I am sure the police will let Tommy go."

"Where is our gold, Henry?"

"Our lawyer says the police took it."

"Why did the police take our gold? Can they do that?"

"The police always take everything, Mr. Lee."

"I want that gold back, Henry. It is our gold, not theirs. The bank in Vancouver called me today. They say that without more gold, there will be no more loans. They say construction of our new building may stop next week unless we ship them more gold."

"Yes, Mr. Lee. I also spoke with our bank today. The police will have to give us our gold back, but they may keep it for a long time. We must immediately replace the gold taken by the police this morning. We need to send gold to the bank in Vancouver this week. I have called our gold buyer. He is arranging for more gold. But we will need to pay for it. We must quickly ship more fish to the Yukon. No fish, no gold, no loans."

"This is not a problem, Henry. We have lots of fish in Haines. Call the cook in Whitehorse. Tell him to call the fish pilot. The fish pilot must pick up more fish in Haines. As soon as possible."

"I did that, Mr.Lee. The cook has been calling the fish pilot all morning. And yesterday too. But the fish pilot does not call back."

TWENTY NINE

The sign on the front door said 'closed' but I could see them through the front window. They were having an animated conversation, laughing together about something, waving their hands like women do, sitting at *my* table. I opened the unlocked door and they both looked at me when the bells jingled.

"Sorry, we're closed," Deb yelled. She and Sarah both thought that was very funny and laughed together. I walked over to them and could see why. They were drinking wine. Female bonding at its worst. This was terrible.

"Ladies," I said. "Getting an early start?"

"Just having a glass of wine after a long hard day," Deb said. "Not everyone had time for a nap this morning." They both giggled.

I looked at Sarah and said, "So Deb, anything about my day you haven't heard about?"

"Don't think so, Brody. We pretty much covered your day half an hour ago." They both giggled again. Sarah didn't seem the least bit embarrassed about having told Deb how I'd spent my morning.

"Alright, I'll leave you girls alone. Hey, Deb, I need to use your phone."

"Why don't you use your own phone?" she asked, pouring more wine.

"It needs charging."

"Well then, plug your phone into your charger and make your call."

"I don't have my charger."

"Where is it?"

"At home."

"You left your charger at home?"

"I never carry my charger," I said. "I charge my phone at home."

They looked at each other and shook their heads.

"What?" I said. "This has never happened before."

"You know where my phone is," Deb said with a sigh.

"Where's Bobby?" I asked on my way to the counter.

"At Larry's house."

"I thought you said he was tired."

"With all the sugar in that ice cream cone you bought him? He'll be revved up for hours."

I looked behind the counter and found Deb's telephone. The women were cackling and laughing loud enough to be a distraction, so I went down the hall and out the back door. I sat down on the back steps in the alley and called Minnie. She answered on the first ring.

"Minto Café."

"Hey Minnie, it's Brody, how are you?"

"Well, hello there Casanova."

"What? Minnie, it's me, Brody."

"Not around here you're not. From now on you're Casanova. That's what all the boys are calling you now, Casanova."

"Casanova? Look Minnie, I'm calling about Russ and Jack. Are they okay? Are they with Reggie?"

"Are they with Reggie? We had a busload of seniors come in last night and Reggie made off with a load of table scraps. Your dogs have been following him around like puppies ever since. I don't know if they'll want to go home with you when you get back. If you ever do get back. Are you ever coming back, Brody?"

"Yes, I'm coming back, I might even be back tonight."

"Say Brody, is it true she gave you a long wet one in Gerties last night?" I heard the phone hit the counter and she started into one of her long bouts of roaring laughter.

"Minnie," I yelled into the phone, but had to wait her out.

A minute later she asked, "You still there?"

"Yes, I'm still here."

"So is it true?"

"Is what true?"

"About the long wet one that S. Marsalis gave you last night in front of a big crowd at Gertie's."

"Who told you about that?"

"Every truck driver coming south this morning, that's who told me. It sounds like you two are getting pretty serious. You gonna run off with her? Start a family? Hey, want me to rent your place out?" The phone hit the counter again and she started another long bout of laughter. She was still laughing when someone else picked up the phone.

"Hi Brody."

"Hey, Reg. How are my boys?"

"Good. Hey, that Chinese guy named Charlie keeps calling for you. He says he's desperate to get fish. He says if you don't get him fish by tomorrow, he'll have to find someone else. He sounded pretty mad."

"Reggie, if he calls again, tell him I'll fly to Haines soon, maybe I can go tomorrow afternoon."

"Okay. And Mom says she wants fish too."

"How much does she want?"

"Don't know." I could still hear Minnie laughing and was about to hang up when she came back on the phone.

"Brody?"

"What?"

"Is it true that someone shot the pilot in that missing plane?"

"Yes."

"Someone really shot him? Like murdered him?"

"Yes."

"You be careful out there, Mister."

I hung up and went back into the restaurant. Sarah was walking down the hall toward me. She stopped and we looked at each other, waiting for someone to say something.

Finally I asked, "Are you looking for me?"

"Nope, just going to the ladies room."

"Oh," I said, and stepped aside. I walked out to the counter and put Deb's phone back, then headed for the front door. Deb got up to intercept me. She folded her arms and stood in my way.

"I think she's a keeper, Brody," she said with a very serious look.

"Oh, do you now?" I said, clearly aware she was blocking the door.

"Yes, I do. So don't mess this one up. She's beautiful, she likes you, and she's very nice."

"Nice? How would you know? Did she tell you to say that?"

"Of course not."

"Well, we'll see. But thanks for your opinion."

"Brody, don't be stupid your whole life. If she didn't like you, she wouldn't have kissed you in front of all those people."

"Did she tell you about that?"

"That she kissed you in Gertie's last night – in front of everyone? Are you kidding me? She didn't have to tell me. That's all over town. You two are famous." She paused and smiled, studying my face. "I just knew you had a crush on her. I just knew it". She smiled with smug satisfaction, looking terribly pleased with herself.

Women.

I shook my head and thought about leaving town right then, even if it meant missing my five o'clock meeting with Robson. This town was too damn small. I'd already given my statement to the cops and could sign it later. I could be in the air in half an hour, be home for dinner. I could be alone again. I reached around Deb and grabbed the door knob.

"Where are you going? Come on, have a glass of wine with us."

"No thanks. Got to go. Got to check on my plane. Thanks for the use of the phone. Bye."

I turned the door knob and she reluctantly stepped out of the way.

"Hey! Where are you going?"

It was Sarah this time, asking the same question.

"To my plane," I said.

"Why?"

"Because I'm going home tonight and want to make sure it's ready to fly. Make sure the cops didn't mess with it."

"Your plane's fine," she said, "No one has messed with your plane."

"How do you know?"

"Because I'm a cop. And I told the other cops no one was to mess with your plane."

She had her arms folded and was smiling at me. I wasn't sure what to think, or whether to believe her, but found myself breaking into a smile and shaking my head.

"Come on, sit down and chat with us for a while. We both have to be at the same place at five o'clock."

"We do? We both have to be at the same place at five o'clock? Are you sure about that?"

"Yes, I'm sure about that."

"Why both of us?"

"You'll see."

"Well I'm still going out. I'm not staying here."

"Where are you going?"

"I'm going to see a man about a horse, okay? Goodbye ladies."

The reality was I suddenly had an overwhelming urge to re-establish my independence. Buying a phone charger would be a good start. I knew they were watching when I walked past the window, but didn't look up at them.

* * *

It didn't take long to find one in the drugstore. Actually, it was a fifteen year old boy who found it. He'd asked me for my phone and judiciously selected one from an impressive selection of models hanging on a carousel. Obviously I wasn't the only one from out of town in the market for a charger. I paid him and asked him if he'd charge it for me. He told me to come back in half an hour.

I left the drug store and wondered what to do to kill a half hour. I sure didn't want to go back to the hen party at Deb's so decided on a brisk walk around town to get some air and exercise. When I started walking north toward the Duncan's house, I realized I was implicitly trusting Sarah that my plane would be left alone, that it would be airworthy for the flight home tonight. It was as good a time as any to drop in on Katy Duncan, to follow up on things, to see how she was holding up.

I struck out for the northeast section of town and recognized lots of people on the streets, though none who I really knew, other than to have seen them around town before. They'd all wave and smile at me from the other side of the street, and I'd wave and smile back from my side. Now and again I'd get a sense of what a celebrity has to put up with. People would wave at me, I'd wave back, then they'd whisper and giggle and turn their heads away. It had just a been kiss in a nightclub. I wondered why people are so fascinated with the innocuous things other people do.

When I turned onto Fourth Street, a block from Katy Duncan's house, I glimpsed a couple walking toward me on the other side of the street. I vaguely recognized the man as a miner who worked in the Dawson area. Didn't know much about him, only that he'd been working for several years at various mines south of town. Wasn't even sure of his name, it might have been 'Terry', but that was only a guess. He was with a tall skinny woman I'd never seen before. They each looked about forty, were wearing ball caps and sunglasses, dirty clothes and muddy boots. The impression conveyed was that they'd just arrived in town from out in the bush somewhere. People who look like they need a shower and a change of clothes aren't a remarkable sight in Dawson at this time of year, but what struck me as unusual were their halted movements and nervous gestures. They were looking around furtively, as though they were being followed, or looking for someone. I thought little of it, gave them a wave of my hand, and didn't get one back.

I turned left at the next corner and saw a police car parked in front of the Duncan's house. I stopped in the street to admire their property again. It was just as impressive in the bright afternoon sun as it had been yesterday – the fresh paint, the shiny red pickup in the driveway, the wet green lawn. I wasn't going to change my mind – it had taken a lot of money to make it so picture perfect.

Who knew what was going on inside today with an RCMP cruiser parked outside? It had to be official business and I decided it wasn't in my best interest to drop in again without an invitation. I'd had enough face to face time with cops in the last twenty four hours anyway, and was scheduled for more at five o'clock. I'd have to ask Deb later how Katy Duncan was holding up, how she was coping with the disaster in her life. I kept going and took the long route back to the drugstore.

When I walked in, the kid had my phone and new charger on the counter. I stowed them in my backpack. He told me the phone was almost charged and should be good for a couple of days on standby, a little less if I made a few phone calls. I felt much more independent and tipped him ten bucks. He was thrilled.

With half an hour to kill before my five o'clock meeting, I headed back to center town. It would take me past Deb's Soup Kitchen and provide a chance to sneak a peak in the window, to see if Sarah had left, or if the two were still hard at it. Hopefully they hadn't opened another bottle. If they had, Sarah was going to need help walking the three blocks to the RCMP building. I'd forgotten to ask her if she wanted a ride to Minto tonight. I was adamant on going home after my statement was signed. For some reason, I thought again about the man and woman I'd seen near Katy's house, and the state of their clothes. Mine were probably nearly as bad looking, and were getting as tired of me as I was of them. It would be nice to get cleaned up.

The front door of Deb's Soup Kitchen was still unlocked and I walked in. There was no one in sight and things were quiet. The place looked clean and ready to close, like it always does late in the afternoon. I dropped my backpack inside the door and called out, "Hello, anybody here?"

Deb came down the hall with her phone to her ear, holding a finger up at me. She seemed concerned about something. I sat down and watched her. She was pacing, biting her lip, talking quietly into the phone. She disappeared down the hall for a moment, then came back. She said something else into the phone, pushed a button and dropped it in her apron pocket. She looked at me with a hollow look in her eyes.

"Bobby's missing," she said.

"Call the police," I said.

THIRTY

Everyone was somber and silent.

There were six of us, sitting shoulder to shoulder at the round table in the same room where I'd given my statement only hours ago. We were waiting for Robson.

Sarah sat on my left, Kurtz and Owen sat to her left, Polichek was on my right, and to his right was Sergeant Arcand. The chair opposite me was vacant, assumedly assigned to Staff Sergeant Robson. I looked out the window and considered getting up to open it, but didn't. Polichek was tapping his fingers on the table and I had an urge to give him an elbow. Kurtz and Owen had their briefcases in their laps, sorting and organizing pictures and papers. A minute later the big man himself entered the room, carrying a stack of documents. He appeared stressed and sat down and spoke.

"The first piece of business is to tell you that every available officer and vehicle in this detachment is currently patrolling the streets and highways of Dawson, searching for a missing child." Robson pulled out a sheet of paper from the pile in front of him and read from it. "The missing child is one Robert Larabie, six years old, white, male, forty-two inches tall, weighs twenty kilograms or approximately forty-five pounds. He was last seen at approximately three thirty p.m. today, walking west on Queen Street toward his mother's business on Third Street. He was wearing a blue hooded sweatshirt with a hockey team logo, blue jeans and black sneakers. He was reported missing by his mother at four ten p.m. According to the boy's mother, he was at a friend's house this afternoon from two to three thirty p.m. He called his mother at three thirty p.m., told her he was about to leave his friend's house, that he was going to walk over to her restaurant on Third Street. It shouldn't have taken him more than ten minutes to get there. With the assistance of his mother and father, we're canvassing all his known friends, family and acquaintances for information as to his whereabouts. I have no other news to report at this time. I will let you know if and when there is any news." Robson put the sheet of paper down, breathed deeply, then looked around the table for a reaction. No one said a word.

I'd never experienced such anxiety. After the scolding Sarah had given me in the park, the notion of a possible tragic outcome was unbearable to think about. I was sick that I might somehow be responsible for Bobby's disappearance. The concept overwhelmed me. Bobby Larabie was officially missing and unaccounted for and I could barely stay seated in my chair, desperately wanting to jump up and run outside, do something – anything – to help find him. I could only imagine the range of emotions affecting Deborah Larabie. It was no consolation to think that Bobby may simply have run off with friends on an impromptu adventure. The specter that he was in grave danger – or worse – was the reality. Robson broke the silence.

"Mr. Brody, we all appreciate you coming in on time, in particular because I know you're closely associated with the missing boy. I'm sure you'd prefer to be out there helping to find him, not sitting in here with us. So we'll take as little of your time as possible. But I do want to assure you that as I speak, both the police and the community are doing everything possible to find this child. There is very little else that can be added to the current efforts to find him, even if you were to be out there helping. But right now we need to talk to you about something else, something possibly related and perhaps crucial to our locating the Larabie boy. First though, I'd like you to take a few moments to read the statement you provided us earlier today. If you approve it, please sign it in front of Mrs. Hanlon. She's a notary public and will witness your signature." Robson pushed a stapled document across the table to me. "Please read your statement in the front office, Mr. Brody. You'll find Mrs. Hanlon out there waiting for you. She'll accompany you back to this meeting room when you're done."

I picked the statement off the table and left the room. I was in a daze as I walked down the hall with my head down, my eyes glued on the official looking document in my hand, not seeing a single word, thinking only of where Bobby Larabie might be. At the end of the hall I looked up to see his mother standing in the reception area.

"Deb? What are you doing here? Why aren't you at the 'Kitchen'? What if Bobby calls or comes back?"

"His father's there, with friends. The police wanted pictures. I had to go home to get some."

She was clutching some photographs in her hand. She held them out to me, then fell into my chest and hugged me in despair.

When she let go she said, "God, Brody, where did he go? He's always been so responsible. He'd never run off without telling me where he's going, he's never let me down. Where could he be?"

She was near tears. Mrs. Hanlon was watching from behind a desk. She stood and approached us.

"Are these the pictures of your son, Mrs. Larabie?"

Deb wiped her eyes, nodded, and handed Mrs. Hanlon the photographs.

"Thank you, I'll return these to you in a moment". Mrs. Hanlon took the photos from Deb and walked over to a copy machine.

Deb's cell phone began ringing in her vest pocket. She grabbed it with urgency and put it to her ear.

"Yes?" she said. She listened for a moment. I held my breath. "Hello, is someone there? Hello?" She waited some more, then said, "Yes, but this isn't his phone number, so please be brief." She handed me the phone with a look of contempt. "Make it quick," she said, turning her back to me.

I took the phone from her and said, "Hello?" I waited. "Hello?" Dead silence. I was about to give the phone back to Deb when I heard a click and a humming sound.

"Mr. Brody?"

"Yes?"

"He's at the Gold Rush Gas Bar out on the highway." The voice was far away and electronically altered. It sounded like some alien creature from outer space. "Talk to the cops, talk to the lawyers, testify in court, next time you don't get him back."

The line went dead. I slapped the phone into Deb's hand, spun around and dashed down the hall to the meeting room.

I flung the door open and looked at Robson.

"I know where he is," I said.

* * *

Bobby Larabie was fine.

He'd been sitting for half an hour on a log curb, throwing stones at a sign post, waiting in the parking lot of a convenience store, ten miles south of Dawson on the highway. He'd been waiting patiently exactly where he'd been told to wait. A woman had dropped him off there. She was a tall woman who smelled of cigarettes. He'd never met her before, but she seemed nice when she picked him up in town in a white pickup truck. The woman said she knew his mother well, said she was doing his mother a favor by driving him down the highway to the convenience store, said his mother would be by soon to pick him up. She told him his mother had an important errand to do first, but she wouldn't be long. But instead of his mother, a policewoman had come by to pick him up. The policewoman's name was Constable LeMay. She had driven him home in a big shiny police car. When he got home his mother was waiting in the driveway. She'd cried and cried and wouldn't let him out of her arms for ten minutes. He wondered why she'd been crying and wouldn't let him go. He hoped she'd be happy again soon. He wondered why he'd had to spend so much time today walking and driving around town with three different women, none of whom he'd ever met before.

All he wanted to do now was eat dinner and play with his trucks in his room.

THIRTY ONE

A collective sense of relief filled the room after Sergeant Arcand announced that Bobby Larabie had been found safe and sound. He was currently in a police cruiser being driven home to his parents. That was the good news.

The bad news was that someone had just delivered a very clear warning meant to intimidate me. Someone who was clearly prepared to harm a child. I was seething over what had happened. In just one afternoon a premise of security had been stolen from Bobby's childhood, a freedom he might never enjoy again. What just happened could remarkably change the rest of his upbringing. I was enraged that someone had the audacity to do that to him.

This was personal now. I wasn't going to lead my life under the shadow of threats made against me or anyone else. It was time to fight back. The burning question was how.

My seething was interrupted when Staff Sergeant Robson spoke. "That's great news Sergeant Arcand. The best news possible, given the circumstances." He looked at me and nodded, clearly relieved. I nodded back.

"Mr. Brody, we now have your signed statement. Thank you for that. It will greatly aid our prosecution of the murders of the two men you found yesterday. But you must be wondering why you're still here." Robson paused and shuffled some papers, apparently unsure where to start.

Yes, I thought. *Why am I still here?*

He spoke slowly and deliberately. "Mr. Brody, as you are well aware, some very serious crimes have been committed around this town in the last two days. I thought I'd start by bringing you up to date on the most serious one, the murder of the two men you found on the river. We'd also like you to consider what we have to say about the possible motivations for these crimes, and how you might...contribute...to our investigations. Are you interested in listening to what we have to say?"

"Absolutely."

"Good," he said. "Let me start by telling you about the two men we arrested this morning at the docks. They are Mr. Tommy Kay of Los Angeles, California, and Mr. Richard Costanzia of Jersey City, New Jersey, though we believe Mr. Constanzia is currently a resident of Las Vegas. Both men are known to work for criminal organizations. Both men have long arrest records for everything from assault to weapon charges to racketeering. We were very surprised to learn that Mr. Kay has never been convicted of a crime, however, in spite of his many arrests, but this other fellow Costanzia, he's done a number of stints in jail on numerous convictions.

"Regardless, what's most important is that we think these were the two men seen boarding the NOCA Beaver yesterday morning. We therefore think one or both of them murdered Robert Duncan and David Marsalis, the two men you discovered on the river yesterday." Robson paused so I could digest what he'd said. "Are you with me so far, Mr. Brody?"

"I'm with you," I replied, mulling over that name, *David* Marsalis.

Sarah's brother.

"Good. Yesterday the bodies of the two deceased men you found in NOCA's plane on the river were transported to Whitehorse for autopsy. The official autopsy results are not expected until tomorrow, but we've just been informed by the medical examiner that two, twenty-two caliber bullets were removed from the body of Mr. Duncan, and another was removed from the body of Mr. Marsalis. A fourth twenty-two caliber bullet was removed from the plane's console on the passenger side. No shell casings were found, but we'll keep looking. The plane will undergo a comprehensive forensic examination after it's been towed back to Dawson. Perhaps we'll find a casing then, perhaps not. Nevertheless, the bullets taken from the bodies of Mr. Duncan and Mr. Marsalis are valuable and critical evidence. The four bullets will be sent to Vancouver for ballistic analysis.

"Also, this morning we seized two guns at the docks. You saw them both. A thirty-two caliber Colt revolver that Mr. Constanzia was waving around at you and Special Agent Marsalis – we don't know anything about that one yet, though we intend to find out – and a twenty-two caliber Ruger pistol which we believe was the murder weapon. Somehow Mr. Kay's fingerprints weren't found on either gun, even though the Ruger was at one time stowed in his luggage. However, Mr. Constanzia's fingerprints are all over the Ruger, and we think it was recently fired. That's critical, because this morning Mr. Constanzia referred to the Ruger as 'my gun', as witnessed by both you and Special Agent Marsalis. Also, we don't think it's a minor coincidence that the ten round magazine in the Ruger contained only six rounds when we seized it. Both guns will also be sent to the lab in Vancouver, with the four bullets. We're confident that ballistic tests will prove the three bullets removed from the bodies of the two murdered men, as well as the one recovered from the dash of the plane, were all fired from Mr. Constanzia's Ruger.

"If that's the case, then Mr. Constanzia is the prime and obvious suspect for the murders. And we're optimistic that we can charge him for those murders, hopefully sometime tomorrow. We're just waiting now for the Yukon crown prosecutor to arrive from Whitehorse to hear our case, and review the primary evidence.

"However, Mr. Kay's possible role in the murder of the two men is another matter. His attorney is expected to arrive in town later this evening. And we're assuming his attorney will point out the following facts to the crown prosecutor: that Mr. Kay did nothing illegal at the docks this morning – other than throw a camera into the river – that Mr. Kay's fingerprints aren't on either of the guns we seized, that if his fingerprints are found in the NOCA airplane it's only because he's been on that plane numerous times before yesterday, and that no one can positively identify Mr. Kay as having boarded the NOCA Beaver yesterday morning. So unfortunately, it looks like we really don't have any evidence to charge Mr. Kay with anything, and we're probably going to have to release him tonight."

"He beat me up yesterday," I said. "He threw me into a truck and beat me up."

"He did? Did you report that to us?"

"No, I didn't."

Robson gave me a look of disappointment.

"Mr. Brody, everything I've just told you will be soon be released to the local media for public consumption. But the big picture of what's really going on around here can best be explained by the people you're seated with. These law enforcement professionals think you might provide them with some valuable assistance with their own criminal investigation. Are you interested in what they have to say, and to consider the conversation as strictly confidential?"

"Yes," I said, pondering the words, 'their own criminal investigation'.

"Good. Now if you'll excuse Sergeant Arcand and I, we have the abduction of a child to investigate."

Robson and Arcand got up and left the room. I sensed they were more than happy not to stick around for the rest of the meeting. Special Agent Stanley Kurtz got up and pulled their vacated chairs away from the table. There was instantly a lot more elbow room.

"Mr. Brody," asked Kurtz, reseating himself, "why did Mr. Kay beat you up yesterday?"

"He wanted to know why I'd been talking to you guys. It was his way of encouraging me to answer his questions."

"You say he threw you into a truck. Can you describe the truck?"

"Yeah. It was an old blue Chevy pickup truck, a crew cab with blue vinyl seats."

Kurtz glanced at Owen, then asked, "Was Mr. Kay driving the truck?"

"No, another man was driving. I got to sit in the back, with Mr. Kay."

"Who was driving the truck?" Owen asked.

"I'm not sure, but he kind of looked like that white haired guy in one of those pictures you showed me yesterday."

"You mean this man?" Owen slid over the same photo he'd shown me yesterday. The bird watcher.

"Yeah, I think that was the guy driving."

"Think, or are you sure?"

"Think."

"Why didn't you report this assault to the police?" asked Kurtz.

"Don't know. Maybe because I was concussed. Maybe because I didn't have time. Maybe because I was hungry. Maybe because all that guy Kay wanted me to do was more or less what I was planning to do anyway."

"And that was?" asked Owen.

"Fly to Haines, pick up a load of fish, fly it to the Yukon. The only change was that he wanted me to fly the fish to Dawson, not to Whitehorse, like I usually do. Oh, and he wanted me to fly him down to Juneau this morning, first, before I went to Haines. That's why he was waiting for me at the docks. Otherwise it was just going to be business as usual."

"What kind of questions did Mr. Kay ask you?"

"Well, it's not all that clear because he almost knocked me out, but he definitely wanted to know why I'd been talking to you cops. I remember him asking about my meeting with you guys yesterday. I told him you'd shown me some photos of people. He seemed very interested to know who the people in the photos were. He wanted to know about Sarah…Marsalis, Special Agent Marsalis here, he wanted to know about her, who she was, and what she'd been doing in my plane."

"And you told him what?"

"I told him she was taking pictures of a mine on Thistle Creek."

"Jesus," said Polichek out of the blue. "Why'd you tell him that?"

"Well," I said, leaning forward so I could look directly into his eyes, "maybe if we put you in that gorilla's jail cell for ten minutes, you'd realize that when he asks you a question, you answer the question." I kept staring at Polichek, beckoning a response. He just shook his head.

"This is getting worse and worse," he said, clasping his hands behind his neck, looking up at the ceiling.

"SAC Polichek, sir?" said Kurtz.

"Yes, Agent Kurtz."

Kurtz stood and gestured at the door. "A word, sir?"

Polichek got out of his chair and the two men left the room. I looked at Owen and Sarah who were conspicuously quiet. Neither would look me in the eye. A minute later Kurtz re-entered the room, without Polichek. Who knows what Kurtz had said to him, but it looked like it was just going to be the four of us now. Owen spoke first.

"Mr. Brody, let me introduce myself formally. My name is David Owen. I'm an FBI Special Agent working with the RCMP on an international criminal investigation. The FBI and the RCMP are jointly investigating the smuggling and trafficking of undocumented Chinese immigrants by a particular crime syndicate based out of LA. Special Agents Sarah Marsalis and Stanley Kurtz are with the U.S. Department of the Treasury, IRS division, and are also working on the case."

"The IRS? Why the IRS?" I asked, looking at Sarah and Kurtz.

Owen raised his hand. "Allow me to explain."

I leaned back in my chair and folded my arms. "Okay, explain," I said.

"The case we're working on concerns the smuggling and illegal immigration of Chinese nationals into North America. These immigrants are being recruited from the lowest economic echelon of their country. They're poor, uneducated and naïve. Accordingly, they're easily convinced to believe the false promises made by so-called human traffickers, who are touting better opportunities for them in America. Once a trust is established by the traffickers, the first thing they do is con their victims out of every penny and possession they have. Then they put them on ships – usually stowing them in freight containers – and move them to North America like any other cargo. Entire families are shipped from Hong Kong to LA where they're broken up and separated on arrival. Each individual is then transported to a different city, and placed in a job most profitable for their traffickers – or as I prefer to call them – their 'masters'. And Mr. Brody, I'm not being sarcastic when I use that word, 'masters'. What I've just described to you is nothing short of a modern day slave trade, an age old business being conducted under a different name in a different century. What we used to call the slave trade is still a lucrative business, a very viable and robust industry that we regrettably dignify these days by calling it human trafficking. Every year people continue to be smuggled into North America by criminal organizations to fill the faceless occupations of society. There are now millions of immigrants who've been smuggled into North America to toil in our orchards and fields, slaughterhouses, textile factories, and the laundry rooms of our finest hotels. But the worst crime committed is what's done to their children, the children who are stolen and separated from their parents the minute they're unloaded from a shipping container. These children are immediately exploited in the most profitable business of all, the sex trade as it's commonly called these days, though I like to call it what it really is, child rape and pornography. The FBI currently estimates that world-wide, the human trafficking business currently generates a trillion dollars annually. That's trillion with a 'T', Mr. Brody."

Owen paused to take a breath. He had a hard look in his eyes.

I swallowed with a dry mouth and reached for my glass of water. Owen had just given me an enlightening insight into a sordid business. But surely human trafficking had no relevance to my life, let alone what I'd been through in the last two days. Surely there was no 'human trafficking' or prostitution going on up here. Not here in the Yukon.

"Why are you telling me about human trafficking and child pornography?" I asked.

"Because it's why we're here."

"It is?"

"I'm almost finished."

"I'm listening."

"Good. Prosecuting criminals who run international human trafficking organizations is problematic, let alone virtually impossible. For example, the man we're after runs a trading company that imports stuffed toys from China. Obviously that's not all he's importing, but suppose we were to witness the unloading of fifty undocumented immigrants from one of his containers at the Port of LA. And suppose we were to arrest him for smuggling them into America. He's simply going to lawyer up and deny the charge. He'll claim he had no idea of how or why fifty Chinese Nationals might have got into a container with his shipment of stuffed toys, a container he doesn't own, a container loaded on a ship three weeks ago and seven thousand miles away in Hong Kong. If we were to arrest and charge the men unloading the undocumented immigrants from his container, what would we have? A few men who said they were hired to unload boxes of stuffed toys? Men who've never met the boss? Who don't know even know his name? Who wouldn't say a word anyway for fear of ending up dead in a ditch at the end of the day?

"The owner of the container can't be held responsible, he doesn't know or control what gets loaded into his containers. The captain of the ship can't be held responsible, his ship left Hong Kong with three thousand containers and every one of them was duly processed by a customs broker. And the guy driving the bus to pick up these unfortunate people? He was just following company instructions. A company with a customer who walked in the office last week and chartered a bus with cash, a customer who's long since disappeared, never to be seen or heard from again."

I leaned forward and put my elbows on the table. "So how are you going to get this guy?" I asked. "And what are you doing up here if he's smuggling people into LA?"

"We're here because we're following his money."

"Following his money."

"That's right. We're following his money. A lot of money. Specifically, his cash. A whole lot of cash from a cash only business. Millions and millions of dollars he and his organization of human traffickers have earned illegally. It's all being sent up here. All the cash he's making by importing, selling and renting enslaved people, and all the cash he's making from a chain of massage parlors he operates in California, none of which, by the way, are actually providing massages. And just so you know, all that cash he's shipping here? He hasn't paid a dime of income tax on it."

Owen paused for another sip of water. I waited for him. "You see, Mr. Brody, the biggest challenge for any criminal organization isn't how to make money, it's how to convert it into a legitimate asset. So the focus of our investigation isn't on human trafficking, it's on the laundering of the cash earned from human trafficking."

"There's money laundering going on up here?" I asked.

"Yes," replied Owen. "Major league money laundering, by the man we're investigating."

"How does he launder his money up here?"

"He buys gold in Dawson with it, then accounts for the gold as though he produced it from a mine he just happens to own and operate on Thistle Creek. You might be interested to know that you loaded two briefcases of his gold into your plane this morning. Those briefcases each contained about fifty pounds of gold. Fifty pounds of gold is worth a million dollars at today's gold price. So you handled about two million dollars worth of gold."

"I thought those cases were a little heavy to be paper work," I said, thinking about the mine on Thistle Creek.

Owen nodded. "Actually, there *was* paper work in those briefcases. In each one we found legitimate receipts and export documents issued by the Dawson mining recorder. The gold in those briefcases was legally authorized for export, and the export royalties had been paid. So all that gold was a perfectly legal cargo approved for export from the Yukon. And right now, it looks like we'll probably have to give it back to him."

"So this man you're after, the owner of the gold in the briefcases, where did he buy the gold?"

"From a gold buyer here in Dawson."

"There's a gold buyer here with that much gold to sell?"

Owen nodded again. "Lots of them," he said. "You see, most mines around Dawson need to sell a large percentage of what they get out of the ground every month to pay operating expenses. So the gold buyers here do a very good business. They buy gold for cash, then sell it to people with cash who want to buy gold. Many of the gold traders and buyers up here are turning over millions of dollars annually. So finding gold to buy in the middle of gold mining country is never a problem. Thousands of ounces of gold are mined around Dawson every summer, and most of it gets bought and sold right here in town. It's a very robust but discreet business that's been a part of Dawson's economy since the gold rush."

I shook my head. "Never met a gold buyer," I said.

"Actually you probably have and didn't know it. You'll find lots of gold buyers here in Dawson, just like you'll find them in every other gold camp in the world. Walk into any bar in this town and ask where you can find a gold buyer. You'll be drinking beer with one in ten minutes."

"I had no idea." Then I asked Owen, "So why did those two guys in jail want to take those briefcases full of gold to Juneau? What would they do with them there?"

Owen took a deep breath and looked at Kurtz and Sarah. He exhaled and nodded at Kurtz. I had obviously asked a question he wasn't sure how to answer. Kurtz nodded at Owen. Sarah was looking down at the table.

"We don't think the gold was going to Juneau," Kurtz said. "If you'd taken off this morning, you'd probably have been told to land on the Yukon River, somewhere around the mouth of Thistle Creek. The gold would then have been unloaded on the river, handed off to someone in a boat, then you would have been told to take off and fly to Juneau."

"I don't get it," I said. "You're telling me that those guys on the dock this morning bought gold in Dawson, got export permits and paid royalties, then chartered a plane just to fly it eighty miles south to Thistle Creek?" Sarah raised her hand at Kurtz. She leaned forward and spoke.

"The export permits are only required to take the gold out of the Yukon. But it's not being taken out of Canada," she said. "It's being shipped to a bank in Vancouver."

"How do you know that?" I asked.

"Because with the co-operation of the Canadian tax authorities, and a Canadian bank, we've been auditing the mine's tax returns. For the last two years the Thistle Creek mine has been reporting copious amounts of gold production and shipping it all to a bank in Vancouver."

"You've lost me," I said. "What does your auditing of the mine's tax returns and their gold deliveries to a bank in Vancouver have to do with flying gold to Thistle Creek?"

"It's all about *optics*, Mr. Brody. It's the crux of the ruse. These criminals are trying to paint a picture for the authorities, creating a deception to legitimize their gold. They're trying to create the impression that their mine on Thistle Creek is the source of all that gold production they've been reporting. Of course we know that's not true, because they've been flying the gold they're buying in Dawson down to their mine, and adding it to its meager production. We've known for some time that their mine can't possibly produce anything close to what they're shipping to the bank in Vancouver. In fact, we think their mine is at best producing barely enough gold to break even. That assumption is based on the reported historical gold grades mined from Thistle Creek, and interviews with the mine's previous owner. So we've come to the obvious conclusion that most of the mine's reported production is actually just gold being purchased in Dawson. Simply put, we think the Thistle Creek mine is nothing more than a money laundering scam."

"Wow." I sat back. I knew precisely then why the beautiful stranger in the little green Corolla had chartered my plane to take pictures of a gold mine.

"So how do they get the gold from the mine to the bank in Vancouver?" I asked Sarah.

"Every two weeks or so an armored truck drives down to the Thistle Creek mine and picks up a load of gold. The truck drives the gold to the Dawson airport where it's put on a commercial flight to Whitehorse. The plane is a DC3, operated by NOCA, if you're wondering. Anyway, at the Whitehorse airport the gold is transferred from the DC3 to a commercial jet and flown south to Vancouver. The bank accepts the gold at the Vancouver airport. It's loaded into an armored truck, driven downtown, and delivered to a very secure underground bank vault. The whole process has all the appearances of a perfectly normal exercise, transporting gold from an operating Canadian gold mine to a major Canadian bank for deposit."

"How do you know all this?" I asked her.

Owen answered for her. "We've had this crime boss and his organization under surveillance for a couple of years," he said. "When we started to follow his money last summer, we began watching the people who worked for him. Some of them were making frequent trips to Dawson, including your 'friend', Mr. Kay. It took us a while to figure out what they were doing with all their cash, once they got it to Dawson. After we observed them buying gold with it, it took us a while to figure out what they were doing with the gold. They weren't driving away with it, so for a while we were stumped. But we kept watching them. It turns out what they were doing was taking the gold down to the docks in briefcases, getting on a plane – the same one every time, that float plane owned by NOCA Air you found – and flying it out of here. So we checked the NOCA plane's flight plans to see where it was going. The flight plans always stated that the NOCA Beaver flights were non-stop charters to Juneau. We contacted customs in Juneau and told them to start inspecting the luggage of all passengers arriving on NOCA charter flights. We asked U.S. customs to detain and interview any passengers carrying gold with them. But customs in Juneau told us none of NOCA's passengers ever had any gold with them when they arrived. They didn't even have briefcases. So we wondered what was happening to the briefcases on those flights going to Juneau. We interviewed the pilot several times to see if he was stopping anywhere on the way down. But he always denied making a stop. He told us he was taking off from Dawson and flying non-stop to Juneau every trip, just like his flight plans said. Of course we didn't believe him. We knew he was stopping and dropping off the gold somewhere on his way to Juneau. We just didn't know where."

I nodded with understanding. I thought about what Dale Morrow had said to me yesterday, about Robert Duncan and his mysterious charter flights to Juneau.

"So how did you figure out the scam?"

"We got a break last fall," Owen said. "An Indian in a bar told one of our undercover agents that he'd seen NOCA's float plane land on the Yukon River near the mouth of Thistle Creek. The Indian told our UC that he saw the plane land, then a passenger in the plane handed down a couple of briefcases to a man in a boat. Then the plane took off. The Indian said the plane wasn't on the water for two minutes. We did a little research and found out that this crime boss we're investigating just happens to own the mine on Thistle Creek. That's when we began to tie things together."

"He's a Native," I said.

"Pardon?" asked Owen.

"The man in the bar your agent was speaking to, he's not an Indian, he's a Native. Indians live in India. Here we call aboriginal people what they are, Natives or Aboriginals. You might even refer to them as men and women."

"Sorry," he said, looking genuinely embarrassed and contrite. "I appreciate you telling me that. Anyway, a couple of weeks ago we decided to start surveillance on the river near Thistle Creek, to see if there would be any more drop offs like the one the man on the river saw last fall. We also interviewed the pilot of the NOCA plane again. This time he talked, after we let him know that the alternative was to be implicated in a criminal conspiracy. Then we brought in an undercover agent to pose as a mining consultant. He was to be our eyes and ears at the mine, and on the river. Two days ago our UC left Dawson for the Thistle Creek mine to see if he might get hired on as a geological consultant. It's the last we saw or heard from him. We had no idea how he was making out until yesterday, when you found him with the pilot in that plane on the river. It's a tragedy that's affected everyone here. We don't know what happened, but indications are he was made."

The room went silent. Sarah got up abruptly and walked out. She closed the door behind her. No one said anything for almost a minute. I felt horrible for her.

"That undercover agent, his name was David Marsalis, right?"

Owen answered with his eyes. We were quiet again.

"So," I finally said, breaking a long silence, trying to get the conversation back on track, "you're trying try to bust this guy for some kind of cash or gold smuggling thing, like a financial crime, but not for human trafficking, which is how he's making his money."

"Exactly," said Owen.

The door opened and Sarah walked back into the room. She sat down beside me. No one looked at her.

Owen continued. "That's why we have two accountants from the IRS working with us. Special Agents Marsalis and Kurtz are with the U.S. Treasury Department. They're CPA's who've been working closely with the FBI, the RCMP, and the Canadian tax authorities and banks, helping to build a financial crime case against this human trafficker."

"So you're a real CPA, like a real accountant, like a real IRS auditor?" I blurted out at Sarah.

"Yes, *like* a real IRS auditor," she said, obviously still upset but nevertheless poised. "I'm a Certified Public Accountant, and, I'm also a US Treasury Special Agent. So is Special Agent Kurtz."

"Damn," I said, leaning forward and looking into her eyes. "You're a CPA from Virginia, doing an audit in the Yukon for the IRS, trying to bust a human trafficker from LA."

"That's right. It's a whole lot easier to bust a scum bag slave trader for income tax evasion and money laundering than for human trafficking."

"Wow," I said, unashamedly admiring her for a moment. I leaned back in my chair, thinking about what she'd just said, then asked, "Hey, isn't that how they got that Chicago bootlegger back in the thirties? They got him on income tax evasion, right?"

"I guess you saw the movie too," she said. "That's exactly how they put Capone away, and that's exactly how we're going to put this asshole away."

I sat back, folded my arms, looked at her some more, then at the two men. Owen drank more water. My glass was empty. Kurtz was reading something. The room was quiet. Now I knew what was going on. If 'loose lips sink ships', then I had a pretty good idea why Robert Duncan had been murdered. The stakes were high and the bad guys were ruthless. I knew what they did for a living, the scam they were working, and why there were a bunch of American cops in the Yukon trying to bust them. What I didn't know, though, was why three Special Agents who worked for Uncle Sam would want to explain any of it to me. How did I fit in the picture? How could I possibly help the FBI and the U.S Treasury Department bust a human trafficker for money laundering?

I leaned forward and put my elbows on the table.

"Mr. Owen, I have some questions."

"Go ahead," he said.

"How are these guys getting all that cash into the Yukon?"

"In the back of your plane."

THIRTY TWO

I didn't want to believe him but Special Agent David Owen seemed very sure of himself. He said that in the past year I'd been flying millions of dollars of U.S. cash from Alaska to the Yukon. Bundles and bundles of it – stacks of twenty, fifty, and one hundred dollar bills – shrink-wrapped in clear plastic, packed in styrofoam boxes, with salmon and crabs and ice.

It took him some time, but Owen eventually convinced me it was true. Then he convinced me to keep flying those styrofoam boxes from Alaska to the Yukon. He made me an offer I couldn't refuse. We made a deal. Special Agent David Owen of the FBI was a very convincing guy.

Owen explained how he knew there was more than just fish and crabs in those styrofoam boxes 'in the back of my plane'. For almost two years he and a team of FBI agents had been investigating a man named Wei Lee. Owen said that Lee was the boss of a major human trafficking organization based out of Los Angeles. Lee was sending the cash he made in California up to Alaska, and he'd been using me and my plane to then smuggle it into Canada.

Owen described the man the FBI was after. He showed me two photos of him, the same two photos he'd shown me yesterday. One was a telephoto shot of a short Asian man getting into a limousine, the other a driver's license photo. Lee looked like any other Asian business man, and other than his strange dark eyes, could have been anyone at all. But this particular business man was evil. Owen said Lee was a sociopath who treated the people he was importing in shipping containers as nothing more than a commodity, nothing more than commercial cargo to be sold to the highest bidder.

Owen said that based solely on their age and gender, Lee would sort, sell and exploit the people he was smuggling according to their economic utility. He'd send the adults and teenage boys to employers that needed 'temporary' labor. That made him some money. But most of the money he made was in prostitution. He used the adolescent girls he brought in to populate a large staff of prostitutes, putting them to work in one of the fifty or so massage parlors he owned in LA and San Francisco. Prostitution was an incredibly lucrative business for Lee. Not only did 'his girls' earn him a lot of money, but most of what they earned they had to give back to him, to pay for the heroin they were addicted to. The remainder of Lee's 'container cargo' – the pre-adolescent girls and boys – were simply disposed of as 'surplus goods', sold to a clandestine network of evil sickos who do whatever evil sickos do to kids in the depraved world of kiddy porn. My skin crawled when Owen told me that. I thought about what might have become of Bobby Larabie. It was easy to despise a man like Wei Lee.

Owen described how the cash generated in Lee's massage parlors was moved from California to Alaska. In both Los Angeles and San Francisco he had women driving mini-vans around the cities, making daily visits to every massage parlor he operated. The women would pick up the day's cash receipts from each parlor and dump it into shopping bags behind the driver's seat. Hidden from view behind tinted windows in the back of each mini-van was an armed guard. At the end of each day, the mini-vans would drive out to the suburbs and disappear into garages of middle class houses in middle class neighborhoods. Each night the cash was counted, and sorted and bundled by denomination. The next morning the women would deliver the bricks of bundled cash to the local office of a

CPA firm. The name of the firm was 'Henry Tai, CPA and Assoc., LLC'.

Henry Tai, Certified Public Accountant, was Wei Lee's partner.

Inside Tai's offices the cash was recounted, re-bundled, and sealed in shrink wrap. Owen gave me some insight as to how the FBI estimated the amount of cash being handled by Tai's people. He told me that a single bill of US currency weighs about a gram, and so a million dollars in one hundred dollar bills weighs approximately twenty two pounds. For ease of handling, a million dollars in one hundred dollar bills is usually divided into ten bundles of a hundred thousand dollars each. Each one hundred thousand dollar bundle is then a manageable four inches thick and weighs a little over two pounds. So a pound of hundred dollar bills is worth roughly forty five thousand dollars. And a pound of twenty dollar bills is worth roughly nine thousand dollars. Knowing that, I could understand how a styrofoam box purportedly containing eighty pounds of fish and crabs could easily contain hundreds of thousands of dollars of cash, simply by replacing fish with cash.

The cash that was sorted and bundled inside Tai's accounting offices in LA and San Fran was packed into file boxes. The boxes were sealed and labeled as 'confidential income tax records'. Once a week, a bonded courier company would pick up the file boxes from Henry Tai's offices in LA and San Francisco. The courier company took the boxes of 'tax records' to the airport where they were loaded onto a commercial cargo jet and flown to another accounting office, one that Tai operated in Juneau, Alaska.

Twice a month, a delivery van from the Panhandle Fish Company would drive into the rear parking lot of Tai's office in Juneau. The driver of the van was a man named Jack Kolinsky, a man I knew. Kolinsky would always enter Tai's office through a back door and emerge a few minutes later carrying a large duffle bag. He'd load the duffle bag into the back of his van, then drive his van down to the harbor and onto an Alaska State car ferry destined for Haines. Six hours later, and ninety miles north of Juneau, Kolinsky would drive his van off the ferry in Haines and over to his seafood warehouse.

Inside his warehouse, Kolinsky would pack the bundles of shrink wrapped cash into styrofoam boxes with fish, crabs, and ice. He'd adjust the contents of each box so its total weight was approximately eighty pounds. Then he'd securely seal the boxes with tape and fiberglass strapping. The styrofoam boxes were ready for export to Canada. He'd then store and lock the boxes of 'fish' in a walk-in commercial freezer.

Jack Kolinsky received his instructions to ship fish to Whitehorse from another man I knew, Charlie Woo, the cook who worked in the kitchen at the Fifty Below Hotel in Whitehorse. Woo would call me, I'd fly down to Haines, load up my plane with 'fish', and fly it up to Whitehorse.

According to Owen, the FBI had been watching the machinations of Wei Lee's cash handling system since May of last year. The shipments of cash from California to Juneau had stopped last fall, but had resumed again in early May this year. Over the past ten months, FBI undercover agents had taken thousands of photos and amassed hours and hours of surveillance. Owen said that almost everywhere Wei Lee's cash was handled – inside his massage parlors, the mini-vans, the houses in LA and San Fran, Tai's three accounting offices, even inside the cargo bays of jets – the FBI had installed cameras and recorded hundreds of hours of high resolution video evidence of all the action. I asked him if the FBI had installed any cameras in my plane. He told me no. I intended to verify that.

But in spite of all the video and undercover evidence gathered in the past twelve months on Lee's cash laundering machine, Owen said the FBI was still missing a critical piece of evidence. Owen said the FBI still didn't have forensic proof that the cash Wei Lee was smuggling into the Yukon was the same cash being used to buy his gold in Dawson. The FBI needed proof that the gold Wei Lee was shipping south from his Thistle Creek mine included gold bought in Dawson with cash he'd smuggled into the Yukon – '*in the back of my plane'*. That evidence would expose Wei Lee's scam. It was the crux of the FBI's case to prove a tax evasion case against Lee. The FBI needed that forensic evidence to 'seal the deal', as Owen put it.

Owen then told me why I'd been sitting around a table for over an hour with three U.S. Government Special Agents. He asked for my help to bust Wei Lee. He asked me if I was prepared to mark the cash inside the styrofoam boxes of fish with an ultra-violet dye. If I could inject a dye into the cash in the boxes of fish that I was flying up from Haines, and the dyed cash was ultimately discovered in the briefcase of a Dawson gold seller, then the FBI would have their case. They could charge Wei Lei and Henry Tai for numerous financial crimes including money laundering, a host of conspiracy charges, unregistered international cash transfers, and the big one: income tax evasion. Income tax evasion was the charge the FBI really needed to put Wei Lei and Henry Tai away for years and years.

So Owen made me an offer to help me make my decision. He said he couldn't deputize me, and he couldn't employ me, but he could charter my plane. If I was prepared to inject some special dye into some boxes of fish, the FBI was prepared to give me a six month contract for a hundred hours of flying time. I'd be paid for the hundred hours of flying time whether or not they used the hours. Owen told me if everything worked out, he doubted if the FBI would ever ask me to fly a single hour for them.

It sounded like a no-brainer. I could make sixty thousand dollars of easy money, paid out over six months. It would make my whole summer. The contract would be virtually all profit. What could go wrong? What could be easier? How could I lose? All I had to do was inject some kind of an invisible dye into a few boxes of fish in the back of my plane. I'm always alone when I fly fish from Haines to Whitehorse. I could land anywhere on the way up and inject the dye. No one would ever see me.

So I took the deal. I agreed to keep flying styrofoam boxes packed with fish and cash from Alaska to the Yukon, whenever I was asked, or until the FBI made their arrests. Owen and I shook hands on it. He said he'd send me the paperwork.

David Owen was a very convincing guy.

* * *

"So you're going to show me how to inject that dye into the boxes?" I asked as we walked out of the RCMP building.

"Shhh! Yes," she said, looking at me scornfully. "Don't talk about that out here. I'll show you when we get to Minto."

"Minto? Are you going to Minto? Hey, I'm going to Minto. How are you getting to Minto?"

"Brody, please don't mess with me right now. I know you're going to Minto and I'm coming with you."

"Are you now?"

"Yes, you and I are flying to Minto, right after I find a grocery store."

"Why do you need a grocery store?"

"Because we're doing Mexican tonight". She smiled and gave me a mischievous look.

"We are? But I thought you said…"

"Don't start," she said, "not if you want to have a very nice evening with me. Now let's find a grocery store, okay?" She took a quick look around, kissed me and patted my butt. "Come on, let's go."

She started off down the sidewalk. I stood where I was, watching her walk away in those lovely jeans of hers. I figured if she wanted to 'wear the pants' right now, and there was any chance those pants might come off later, then I ought to do exactly what I was told. But not quite yet.

"Hey Sarah," I called after her. She stopped and turned around. "The grocery store's this way," I said, pointing back over my shoulder with a thumb.

We headed the other way toward my favorite Dawson grocery store. A block from the grocery store we passed the liquor store. We were almost past it before she noticed.

"Oh, look," she said. "Wait". She shaded her eyes and peered in the window, then back-pedaled to the front door and disappeared inside.

I did what I was told and waited outside, soaking up some sunshine while she took her time inside. It was a warm evening and it felt like spring might have finally arrived in the Yukon. I was looking forward to all three weeks of it. I leaned against the warm building and decided to call Minnie with my almost fully charged cell phone. The phone rang four times before Minnie picked up.

"Café!" she yelled over the noise and clatter of a dinner crowd.

"Hi Minnie, it's Brody."

"Well, well, Casanova, how are you? Where are you?"

"I'm good, Minnie. I'm just leaving Dawson now, I'll be home in a couple of hours. Look, could you tell Reggie to take my dogs down to the shop and tie them up at the side door?"

"Okay. Reggie needs a favor from you so I'll send him down with your dogs in a couple of hours."

"No Minnie, just tell him to…"

"Feedin' a busload here, Brody! Gotta go!" She hung up. Great. Sarah was planning a romantic evening in my cabin on the river, and Reggie was going to drop by to ask for a favor.

I was closing my phone when she marched past me and said, "That was lucky. They were about to close. Come on, one more stop."

Lucky my ass. Here we go again with the drinking. I followed her down the block to the grocery store and watched her go inside. I walked halfway down the block to a spot in the sun and decided to call Deb. She didn't answer and I didn't leave a message. In a way, it was a relief she didn't pick up. I really had no idea what to say anyway. What do you say to someone whose kid just got abducted because of something you got yourself mixed up in? I'd have to think about that, but not tonight.

Sarah emerged from the grocery store with a bulging plastic bag in either hand. She stopped out front on the sidewalk, looked back and forth, smiled when she saw me, and walked over. Hot on her heels coming out of the store were three teenage boys, stalking her like fish on a lure. Sarah held the grocery bags out to me. I reached out my arms and embraced her. The boys made a ninety degree turn off the sidewalk and stepped onto the street. I took the bags from her.

"What was that for?" she asked, smiling, happy.

"Chivalry," I said, watching the boys cross to the other side, giving us fleeting looks as they retreated. I wondered if this was going to be *their* summer. They seemed ready for it.

"Well, thank you, that was nice, shall we go?"

I took the groceries from her and we walked the three blocks to the docks. Sarah had been right. No one had messed with my plane. An RCMP cruiser was parked near the top of the jetty. A cop was leaning on the fender with his arms crossed. He looked like a high school kid to me. My father used to say you knew you were getting old when the cops started to look like kids. The young constable was relieved to see us.

"You've had a long day," Sarah said to him.

"Yes, Mme.," he said, tipping his hat, standing up straight.

"Any visitors?"

"No one."

"Good. Thank you very much Constable. I think we're all set now. Please thank Staff Sergeant Robson for your time here today."

"Yes, Mme."

He tipped his hat again, got in his car, and drove off. We walked down the jetty to the dock. Sarah had a smug look.

"I know, I know," I said. "You told me no one was going to mess with my plane. So don't mention it."

"I didn't say anything. But you should know by now you can trust me."

"Really?" I said, more like a statement than a question.

"Yes."

"Then I trust you have my passport. And my wallet. And my knives."

"Your passport and wallet are in here," she said, patting her bulging backpack. "I'll give them to you later. But you can't have your knives back. They're evidence. Sorry."

"Evidence. Well then I'll have my wallet and passport right now, please. I'm not flying anywhere without *my* passport and *my* wallet in *my* backpack." I set the grocery bags down on the dock, stepped on the float, and started unlocking doors.

She huffed loud enough so I'd be sure to know she was being terribly inconvenienced, then lowered her bulging backpack to the dock with its bounty of bottles clinking and squeaking. She began unpacking bottles, lining them up in a neat and orderly row along one of the dock planks.

"Going to a party?" I asked, looking down at her from the cargo door ladder.

"A small one, but it could go all night," she replied in a matter of fact tone, still digging out bottles.

I was shocked when I looked inside my plane. There were patches of white powder everywhere, on every surface, every place the police had dusted for finger prints. Little squares in the powdered patches showed where a fingerprint had been lifted with a piece of tape. There must have been a hundred of them. Collectively they looked like some trendy motif for a modern wallpaper. You'd think the cops could have cleaned up after themselves. Slobs. I sighed, then climbed out the right cargo door, stepped down on the far float, and carefully inspected the airfoils and control cables. I took a quick look inside the right float to see if there was any water. It was dry. I got back in the plane, closed the right cargo door, and did a cursory scan of the console to make sure everything was in order. It looked fine except for a whole bunch more of those white powder patches with the little clear squares. I climbed down on the left float and repeated an inspection of the plane's left side. Sarah was carefully repacking bottles into her backpack. I checked inside the left float for water and it too was dry. I walked to the front of the plane to check the engine and oil cooler. I grabbed a prop blade and leaned out over the water to look in the engine cowl. As best as I could tell without a plank to stand on, the engine and oil cooler were clear of bird nests and debris. We were good to go. I looked around and saw Sarah sitting cross legged on the dock, studying my passport.

"Hey!" I yelled. "That's none of your business!"

She laughed. "Hey yourself there, Mr. C. Edward Brody, looks like you've done some travelling, you've really been around, haven't you?" she said with glee, flipping through the pages. "Is it okay if I call you Mr. C. Edward Brody? Born...um, let's see... you're thirty nine! You look much younger!" She laughed like I'd never heard her laugh before with her head thrown back, rocking on her butt. "This is a terrific picture of you, Edward! Could I get a copy?"

She was still laughing after I'd taken a few long strides and yanked the passport from her hands.

"Call me Edward again and you're on a bus to Minto," I growled.

"So what's the 'C' stand for?" she asked, grinning and holding up a hand.

I grabbed her hand and hauled her to her feet, then said, "Come on, we're going. Where's my wallet?"

She plucked it out of a jacket pocket and handed it to me.

I looked through it, counted the credit cards, made sure my drivers license was there.

"Thank you," I said.

"So Eddy, huh?" she said, laughing. "May I call you Eddy? Or do you prefer Ed?" She laughed some more. I ignored her.

Women.

Fifteen minutes later we were airborne and headed to Minto.

THIRTY THREE

I always enjoy flying from Dawson to Minto because I get a bird's eye view of one the world's great earth moving projects.

We took off from the Yukon River heading south, then climbed out to the east in a long left hand turn until the Klondike River was under the nose. Below and to our right were twenty square miles of mine tailings, a legacy to over half a century of gold dredging.

Millions of tons of earth were mined, and millions of ounces of gold were recovered from the Klondike River valley by enormous floating dredges. The steam powered behemoths that worked the river valley left long trails of washed rocks behind them, creating miles and miles of furrowed piles that wander back and forth, looking like giant caterpillars from the air. The mosaic of rock trails left by the dredges blankets the Klondike River valley, for ten miles east out of Dawson, and up the creek valleys to the south. But all the earth and rocks ever mined by man and his gigantic mining machines pales in comparison to what was moved to create the Tintina Trench.

The Tintina Trench is a spectacular manifestation of tectonic plate movement and the immense forces in the earth's mantle that move continents around. The 'Trench' overlays the Tintina Fault, the contact boundary between the Pacific plate and the North American plate, two separate tectonic land masses floating on a subterranean ocean of molten rock, miles below the earth's surface. Moving in opposite directions about the same speed as your fingernails grow, the two plates have been in a perpetual collision for two hundred and fifty million years, shearing and crushing each other, raising mountains and plateaus, reversing the flow of rivers, and shaking the earth. With a collision of that magnitude, something had to give, and about sixty million years ago the Pacific Plate was forced to move northward, sliding ever since for hundreds of miles along its contact boundary with the North American plate. After millions of years of weathering, and hundreds of cycles of glaciation, the crushed and weakened rock along the surface of the contact boundary eroded much faster than the surrounding land, and so a depression formed along the fault. Nature wasn't in a hurry to build the Tintina Trench, but in a quarter billion years, she never took a day off.

Although different names are assigned to each leg of its eighteen hundred mile length, the Tintina Trench is the surface expression of a single continuous fault line that starts at Woodchopper Creek in eastern Alaska, crosses the entire Yukon on a southeasterly track, then veers south into British Columbia, runs all the way down the west side of the Rocky Mountains, and finally terminates at Flathead Lake in northern Montana.

Today I was using the 'Trench' to navigate my way home. Ever since airplanes arrived here in the twenties, pilots crossing the Yukon have used the Tintina Trench as an aid to navigation. Varying between two and fifteen miles wide, and hundreds of feet deep, it's easily seen from the air and is one of the prime aviation corridors in the territory. Whenever I get lost, I need only locate the Trench or the Yukon River to get my bearings again.

I looked over at Sarah, thinking for a fleeting second that she might be interested in hearing a little about the remarkable landscaping project going on below us. But she was fast asleep with her headphones over her ears, her head propped against the window, her arms folded across her chest. It was hard to reconcile the image of the peaceful woman sleeping beside me with the one who'd beaten the crap out of a gun wielding bully this morning.

Twenty miles east of Dawson I looked down at the southern terminal of one of the world's great dirt highways. Turn north onto the Dempster Highway at its junction with the Klondike Highway, and you're on your way to the Arctic Ocean. The Dempster is a four hundred and fifty mile dirt road that crosses the Tintina Trench, winds its way north through the Ogilvie Mountains, then forges northeast through miles of arctic tundra and wide open wilderness until it ultimately reaches the town of Inuvik on the Beaufort Sea. If you think you've ever been stuck on a highway in the middle of nowhere, stop your car on the Dempster Highway where it crosses the Arctic Circle. Turn off your engine, get out of your car, look around and listen. You'll probably have a better appreciation of where 'the middle of nowhere' is actually located.

I flew straight down the Tintina Trench for another seventy miles, then turned south over the bridge at Stewart Crossing for the final fifty mile leg to Minto.

* * *

A strong northwest wind had given us a twenty mile an hour push down to Minto. A little over an hour after leaving the waterfront in Dawson, we landed with a couple of bounces on a rough Two Spirit Lake. With its engine idling, my rugged and reliable old plane was yawing and rocking over the lake's black choppy water, steadily plowing through the waves toward the dock on the south shore. I needed to head southwest to get to the dock, but the wind out of the northwest kept pushing the tail to my left, and the nose to my right. I was having to work the rudder and throttle constantly to keep the plane on course. It was seven thirty in the evening.

When the dock got close it occurred to me how much my life had changed in the past thirty-six hours. Thirty six hours ago my charter passenger had been mad as hell, wouldn't talk to me, and was adamant we were *definitely* not going to be doing Mexican 'anytime soon'. Now we were lovers and she was all set to cook

Mexican and stay the night at my place. And sometime soon she was supposed to show me how to inject some fluorescent ultraviolet dye into a bunch of cash hidden in a styrofoam box full of fish. The whole situation seemed bizarre. Two days ago we were strangers – today we were working together to bust a human trafficker for income tax evasion. And the FBI was going to pay me to help them – sixty thousand dollars worth of help. I guess one can never really know what tomorrow will bring. At least not in the Yukon.

"Is it Cody?"

"What?" I said, trying to focus on the task at hand.

"Cody, the initial 'C' in your name, does it stand for Cody? 'Cody Brody'. That has a nice rhyme to it." She chuckled and smiled at me.

"It's not Cody and quit guessing," I said. " Hey, where's your car?" I asked, hoping to change the subject as we closed within twenty feet of the dock.

"You know where it is, it got towed over to that cop buddy of yours."

"His name's Daryl Pageau and he's not my buddy. And how do you know I know?"

"I'm a cop. It's my job to know what you know."

I shook my head, opened my door, and stepped down on the left float with the engine still ticking over. The prop was spinning lazily in front of me, not five feet away. You're not supposed to stand on a float when the engine's running, but this is the Yukon. Up here we do whatever works and today I had a passenger with two perfectly good feet, and two rudder pedals on the floor in front of her. She was going to help me dock a beast of a floatplane in a crosswind.

"Hey, see those pedals at your feet?" I yelled through the prop wash and the noise of the engine. "I'm going to need your help so pay attention." I put my left hand on the wing strut for support, ready to jump on the dock. The first wave that rolled over the float thoroughly soaked my boots and pants The plane was rocking and drifting sideways in the wind and the waves, but steadily closing in on the dock. Then a big gust of wind pushed the tail around to the left, moving the nose out to the right, away from the dock.

"Push the left pedal all the way down," I shouted. She did and the plane straightened out. I took a big stride from the float to the dock and lassoed the rear cleat with the first rope I picked up. I let the rope pay out as the plane glided down the dock, then made another wrap around the cleat and held on. The rope tightened, the dock creaked, the Beaver stopped. The wind swung the plane into the dock and the left float hit the tires with a bump, a splash, and a few squeaks.

Docking a float plane in a crosswind is a *piece of cake*.

My boots and jeans were soaked when I climbed back into the cockpit. I pulled the mixture lever all the way back to full lean and the engine coughed and quit. I turned off the mags and the master switch, and lifted the rudders out of the water. On the dock again, I tied up the plane at the front, then opened the cargo door and leaned in.

"Good job, Sarah. I think you're ready to solo."

"Uh-huh," she said, undoing her seat belt.

She slid between the seats and handed down all the stuff we'd stowed behind the cargo net. Then she climbed down the ladder, stepped on the dock, and with a big yawn stretched her hands over her head. When she began ferrying our stuff over to my pickup truck, I got back in the plane and secured the yoke with bungee cords. Bottles were clinking when she picked up her second load. I looked around the cockpit and cargo bay for a hidden FBI surveillance camera, then shrugged off the notion that anyone could install a spy camera in my plane without me noticing, let alone hide it. Though I couldn't find a camera, I once again noticed all those powdery fingerprint patches. They bothered me. They bothered me a lot. They would have to go. I grabbed the engine cover, placed the wood plank across the front of the floats, stepped out, and put it on. I locked the doors, admired my plane for a moment, then headed over to join Sarah at my truck. She was leaning against the tailgate with her arms folded, studying me carefully as I approached her with my waterlogged boots making squishing sounds.

"What?" I said.

"Nothing," she said, shaking her head with the hint of a smile.

Ten minutes later we pulled up behind her car, parked well to one side in Constable Daryl Pageau's wide gravel driveway. The little green Corolla was dwarfed by a huge, blue and white RCMP four by four, parked slightly ahead in front of Daryl's well maintained little house. I didn't see his highway cruiser.

"See you in ten," she said.

She got out of the truck and headed to the front door. A big dog barked in the backyard.

"Hey," I shouted from the behind the wheel, "Why don't you start your car before I go? Make sure it starts."

"It'll start."

"What if it doesn't?"

"Then your buddy will help me start it," she said, climbing the stairs to the front door.

"What if he's not home?"

"He's home."

"How do you know he's home?"

"Brody, he's home, and I need to do some cop stuff right now, so please, go. I'll see you in ten minutes."

She rang the door bell. Maybe she knew that's all she had to do to get me to leave. It sure worked. I spun the tires and backed up as fast as I dared. I wanted to be gone before Daryl came to the door.

He was the last person I wanted to see tonight.

THIRTY FOUR

Reggie's tow truck wasn't in the cafe parking lot when I drove by. Maybe he was out picking up a vehicle on the highway. Or delivering my dogs.

I turned off the highway and drove slowly down the lane to my shop. If Reggie had already dropped off Russ and Jack, I didn't want to run them over. They usually come charging out of the woods at full speed when they hear my truck coming, and I'm always careful not to hit them. Today they came running up the road at full speed. They go everywhere at full speed.

I stopped and opened my door. They both made circus leaps into the cab, landed in my lap, then went into a competitive frenzy for my attention with wagging tails and slapping tongues that knocked my hat and sunglasses off. My two dusty little dogs were squealing with delight as they smothered me with saliva, frantically licking my face until I finally had to take a breath of air and pushed them over to the passenger seat. Is there a greater bond in the animal kingdom?

I put the truck in 'drive' and continued idling down the two rut lane. Russ put his front paws on the passenger door armrest and began drawing sloppy smears with his nose all over the side window, trying his best to see where we were headed. Jack jumped back into my lap, but before he could do any nose art on my side,

I hit the button and lowered my window. Russ immediately saw that Jack had an open window, jumped into my lap too, muscled his head under my left arm, and leaned against Jack. I turned into the parking lot in front of my shop, struggling to steer accurately with two dogs wedged between me and the steering wheel. They had their heads out the window with their paws hanging over the door, craning their necks to see where we were going, looking like train engineers pulling into a station. I had to open my door and let them jump out before putting the lever in 'park' and turning off the engine.

The lot in front of my shop was a hotbed of activity.

The front end of Daryl's police cruiser was hanging high in the air behind Reggie's tow truck. The hood on his tow truck was open. To the right of Reggie's tow truck was a small yellow pickup truck, a Ford Ranger. I knew the truck and knew who owned it. Reggie and Charlie Woo stepped out from the front of the tow truck.

"Hi, Reggie. Charlie, what brings you up here?" I asked with genuine surprise.

He walked up to me and said, "Hello Mr. Brody. I must talk to you, Mr. Brody. About something very important."

"Alright Charlie, can it wait a few minutes?"

"Yes, Mr. Brody."

"Call me Brody, Charlie. Something wrong with your truck, Reg?"

"Runs rough. Just quit. Won't start."

I walked to the front of Reggie's big old tow truck and looked at the engine. It was beyond me how an engine as filthy as it was could possibly run.

"Hey, thanks for looking after my boys, Reg, I appreciate it."

I surveyed the oil caked engine compartment for an obvious problem. The truck was so old it had a carburetor – definitely not as efficient as the electronic fuel injection systems used on newer vehicles – but easier and cheaper to fix when things go wrong.

"No problem." As usual, Reggie was always economical with words.

"Have they eaten?"

"Nope."

"What's wrong with Daryl's car?"

"Won't start." I instantly had a hunch why both vehicles were in front of my shop.

"When did you last fill up, Reg?"

"Noon."

"When did Daryl last fill up?"

"Don't know."

I walked back to Daryl's cruiser and opened the door. I turned the key to the first position and watched the fuel gauge move. It was full. I turned the key off.

"Reggie, when was the last time the café got a load of gas?"

"A while."

"Well, I'm guessing that lately the cafe's been selling water with gas."

He gave me a puzzled look.

"I think you've got water in the underground gas tank at the café," I said. "Water's heavier than gas, it sinks to the bottom of the tank. When that big underground tank is almost empty, the water at the bottom of the tank gets sucked up with the gas and pumped into customer's vehicles. That's bad for business, Reg. Engines run terrible if there's water in the gas. Hang on, okay?"

He nodded. I grabbed my keys and went into the shop. I came out a minute later with a gallon of gasoline anti-freeze. I poured a little into Reggie's truck, then a little into Daryl's cruiser.

"What's that?"

"Mostly methyl alcohol. It blends water with gasoline so everything burns. It's a way to burn off water in gas and get an engine running again, if water is the problem. We'll see. Easier than emptying two full tanks of gas to find out. Try starting your truck. Keep trying if it doesn't start right away. And give the pedal a few pumps."

He pumped the gas pedal and cranked the starter for ten seconds. The engine sputtered, then quit.

"Again," I said.

This time the truck started, sputtered and popped for ten seconds, and quit again.

"Again," I said.

This time the truck started and ran smoothly. We waited a minute. It didn't quit. It ran great.

"Let it run for a few minutes Reg, then drop Daryl's car. I think you better go into the shop and call your Mom right away. Tell her to stop selling gas until you've poured this whole jug into the underground tank at the café. The whole thing, okay?"

"Okay," he said. I picked up the jug of alcohol and put it beside the door of his truck. He closed the hood and went into the shop to call his mother.

I looked at Charlie and said, "Sorry to keep you waiting Let's talk over here."

We walked over to my truck and I leaned against the hood. The dogs were keeping a wary eye on me to see if we were going for a ride.

"So Charlie, you drove all the way from Whitehorse just to talk to me? What's up?"

"Big trouble, Mr. Brody," he said, rocking from foot to foot. "I am very afraid. We must talk. I call you and I call you and you don't call back. I drive up here to find you."

"Very sorry about that, Charlie. I know you called and should have called back, but I was really busy yesterday in Dawson. I couldn't get fish for you yesterday or today anyway. Thought you could wait until I got back. But I'll fly down to Haines tomorrow morning and deliver a load of fish to you in Whitehorse in the afternoon. How's that?"

"Maybe not to Whitehorse. Maybe not tomorrow," he said. Charlie looked around furtively with his hands in his pant pockets. He was wearing a short sleeved shirt, khaki cotton pants and brown leather shoes. Nothing expensive, but clean and neat. He was a small wiry Chinese man, nicely groomed, perhaps thirty years old. His English wasn't great but he always seemed to understand everything

I'd say when delivering fish to him. Other than what Owen had told me, I really didn't know much about him except that he worked in the kitchen at the Fifty Below Hotel in Whitehorse, and was always waiting at the lake on time with the guy from customs. He was the only person who'd ever called me with instructions to pick up fish in Haines. He'd always paid me the next day with a check, and he'd always tipped me with a couple of fresh salmon. I had no reason not to trust and like him.

"Not Whitehorse? Somewhere else?" I asked.

He shook his head and looked down when Reggie came around the corner. Charlie went silent. Reggie worked a few levers and lowered Daryl's RCMP cruiser to the ground. He got down on his knees, removed some chains, then got in his truck and pulled ahead a few feet. He got out, walked to the back of the truck, raised the tow yoke, then walked over to us.

"Call your Mom, Reg?"

"Yeah."

"Good. You're going to pour that whole jug in the underground tank, right?"

"Yeah. Hey Brody?"

"What?"

"Can you do the band a favor?"

"Sure. What?"

"Can you bring up four canoes from Whitehorse?"

"Four? Yeah, I guess so. Not all at once, though. Two at a time. Whose canoes?"

"Ours. We bought them from Chief Dan."

'Chief Dan' may or may not have been a 'chief', but that's what everyone in Whitehorse called him. Dan Belanger was a mover and a shaker who lived in Whitehorse and seemed to do very well for himself, networking with local businessmen and politicians, and negotiating deals with the Canadian Government on behalf of several native bands in the Yukon. I'd never been sure what qualified him to serve in that role. I wasn't even sure if he was actually a Canadian native. He didn't look like an aboriginal to me, though he certainly portrayed himself that way, overtly selling the image with his long gray hair tied in a pony tail, always wearing a suede moose skin jacket with frills on the sleeves and ornate beadwork adorning the lapels. He once told someone I know that he was a disenfranchised Mohawk, born and raised in Ontario. He claimed he'd received a message from the great Raven spirit to go to the Yukon to serve his brothers up there. No one seemed to know much more about him than that, except that he owned a nice house in Whitehorse, never missed a party, liked to talk, and drank a lot of beer.

"Why did you buy four canoes from Chief Dan?"

"For the regatta."

"What regatta's that?"

"Out at the lake. On Canada Day. We're having a canoe race. And a big party too."

"That's a month away," I said "Can't someone haul them up here with a truck and a trailer?"

"Chief Dan says it will cost four hundred dollars extra. Mom said that's too much. Arlo says we need the canoes here right away."

"Why right away?"

"We need to train."

I nodded. "Right. Train. Who's 'we', Reggie?"

"The Minto team. Me and Arlo and Andy and Daryl. Arlo is our captain. He says we need to train if we want to win the race. It's all the way out to the point and back. There's two other bands coming in for the race. We need to train."

It was all I could do not to roll my eyes. Arlo was fifty years old, definitely never an athlete let alone a canoeist, and definitely not a leader. I couldn't imagine either Arlo or his slightly younger sidekick, Andy, training for any athletic event, let alone a canoe race. For one thing, it would compromise their commitment to a lifetime of drinking beer and telling lies. But I didn't want to rain on anyone's parade, in particular Reggie's. He was a young native man who rarely got an opportunity to do something athletic or competitive. If there was going to be some fun for him preparing for a friendly canoe race, then I'd do everything possible to help him out.

"Okay, no problem, I'll fly them up. Maybe I can fly the first two up tomorrow afternoon. Maybe the other two next week. Call Chief Dan. Tell him he can deliver two canoes to my plane tomorrow."

"Okay. I'll tell Arlo. You need to get a check from Ma to pay Chief Dan."

"Good. Say Reg, how much are you paying for those canoes?"

"Four thousand."

I grimaced. "Are paddles and lifejackets included?"

He shrugged. "Don't know. Arlo knows. He made the deal with Chief Dan. Arlo said the canoes are really expensive because they're really fast. He says they're racing canoes. He said we need them to win."

Arlo wouldn't have a clue what a fast canoe looked like, let alone might cost. Advantage to Chief Dan, who as far as I knew hadn't been in the canoe business until he cooked up this deal with Arlo. I wondered if Chief Dan and Arlo were up to something. Reggie and Daryl each weighed well over two hundred and fifty pounds. Arlo and Andy weren't as heavy, but each was the proud owner of a fully paid beer belly and I wouldn't be surprised if they each weighed over two hundred pounds. A sleek, fast canoe wouldn't make any difference to any of the men on the 'Minto team', even if they could fit into one. Fast canoes, my ass. Hopefully no one drowned in whatever the band had bought.

"Well it all sounds pretty exciting, Reg. Say, before you go, I was wondering if you'd be interested in doing something for me tonight. Make an easy hundred bucks."

"What?"

"Go out to my plane with some paper towels and window cleaner and clean the inside of my plane. Wipe the whole thing down, sweep it out, clean the gauges, make it look new inside. Are you interested? You'd have to do it tonight."

"Okay. Leah's off at nine. She can help me."

"Great, thanks."

Reggie had a key to my plane so I could leave him to it. He was the only one around here that I'd ever trust with a key to my pride and joy. He trudged over to his tow truck and got in. Just as he put it in gear I heard a vehicle coming down the lane. It was Sarah. She stopped and waved at me. I walked over to her as Reggie drove around in a long half circle and rolled out behind us, headed for the highway. Sarah leaned over and rolled the passenger window down.

"Hi," I said, "Get all your cop stuff done?"

"Yes, everything okay here?"

"Yeah. So who's cooking tonight?"

"I am and I'm famished, so the sooner I get to it, the sooner I'll be in a better mood."

I decided to leave that one alone. "Sarah, would you mind if my friend Charlie here joins us for dinner?"

"No problem," she said, looking over at Charlie standing in front of his truck. He was nervously smoking a cigarette. "Hey," she whispered, "isn't that…?"

"Yeah, it is. I need to talk to him about something after dinner."

"So do I," she said.

She drove off with Russ and Jack in hot pursuit.

THIRTY FIVE

The shark fin soup had no equal in Chinatown. Wei Lee thought the Peking duck had also been exceptional, and he and Henry had enjoyed their feast with an excellent 2009 von Hovel Riesling. But Lee would pass on an after dinner coffee. He hadn't been sleeping well and the superb coffee at his favorite restaurant was something he would regrettably forego. Henry also declined coffee. But Lynn, who had sat quietly between the two men throughout the evening, would indulge. Wei Lee was envious. He wondered if she was letting both men know that whatever might be troubling them, wasn't bothering her at all.

Lee put his hand over hers and appraised his prized possession. She raised her chin and looked stoically at him. Lynn Chan had the face of a doll with a complexion as smooth as glazed porcelain. Her lips were full and lush, garnished tonight with a glossy red lipstick that made them look wet. Lee thought Lynn's lips were the most beautiful he had ever seen.

He'd first laid eyes on Lynn three years ago, the day she'd walked into his office behind Henry Tai. Lee had been looking for someone to run his office and asked Henry to help with the recruiting. Henry had found Lynn and made the introduction. Wei Lee's shy new executive assistant was the most beautiful gift he could ever have hoped to receive from his good friend Henry, and a woman he had come to trust. Ever since joining the Lucky Star Trading Company, Lynn had been Wei Lee's favorite.

He knew he could marry her tomorrow – if he wanted – but knew better. Why men do such foolish things he would never understand. Especially in California, he thought, where divorce laws are so unfair. It was only a matter of time before a married woman got fat and angry and bored and thought life would be better with someone else. And always they wanted so much money when they left. What had his lawyer in Los Angeles called a divorce settlement? A 'break-up fee for a bad contract gone bad'? Yes, a bad contract indeed. So no, not ever, not ever would he get married. Not even to Lynn. Even if she was both an American and a Canadian citizen, even if she had a law degree from Stanford, even if she spoke Mandarin and Cantonese, even if she called him *Mr. Lee* in bed, even if she was the only person he knew who was not afraid of Tommy, and more important, the only woman who Tommy feared. He planned to have his way with Lynn later that evening. That would be easy. It was falling asleep after that would pose the challenge.

Lee shook himself from his cynical musings and took a deep breath. He looked at his watch. Lynn had been right. There had been nothing wrong with his new watch. She had set it to the correct time and he knew with certainty it was now exactly nine thirty-two. Henry's phone chimed and he excused himself with a nod to Lynn, then one to Lee, rose and left their table for the bar. Lee watched Henry struggle to seat himself on a tall mahogany barstool, beautifully upholstered in dark red leather with bright brass rivets.

"Lynn, have you reviewed the partnership agreement for our new building in Vancouver?"

"Yes, Mr. Lee, I did this afternoon. The contract is very clear. In particular, the terms of the dilution clauses. Avoiding dilution of your position is all we need to be concerned with. Next week we must make our next to last construction phase payment, then a final construction phase payment has to be made in early July. If we make those two payments, Lucky Star will control the new condominium building when it is completed. Lucky Star will then manage all the maintenance and administration contracts, and will receive commissions on the sale of every unit. The new condominium building has turned out to be an excellent investment, Mr. Lee. The property's value has doubled since construction began three years ago. Congratulations are in order to you, sir."

Lee bowed his head and with a wan smile said, "The dilution clauses, Lynn. What do they say?"

"Well, Mr. Lee, as you well know, Lucky Star currently holds a fifty one percent interest in the new building. Your associate, Mr. Pistone in Las Vegas, he holds the other forty nine percent. So Lucky Star is presently in control of the building's construction, and most important, the building partnership. With control of the building partnership, Lucky Star will appoint the property manager when it is completed. That property management company will of course be wholly owned by you, Mr. Lee. So provided you make the final two construction payments on schedule, you will continue to manage the construction phase, and then all the building's maintenance after it is completed in September. Your management company will administer all those maintenance contracts, and those contracts will earn millions."

"Lynn, I know all this. But what do the dilution clauses say?"

"Yes, Mr. Lee, I shall explain now. The terms of the dilution clauses in the partnership agreement are very clear and should be of great concern to you. If Lucky Star were to default on a remaining construction payment, then Mr. Pistone has the right to make that missed payment to the credit of his own account. For each such payment he makes on your behalf, Mr. Pistone would gain a further five percent interest in the building. So should you fail to make just one of the two remaining payments, Mr. Pistone could increase his interest to fifty four percent of the building partnership, and take over the property's management. You would lose control of your building, Mr. Lee. But that can only happen if you default on a payment. And I'm sure you won't let that happen."

"Of course not, I will not let that happen. Now Lynn, how much money do we need for our two remaining payments?"

She paused as their waiter placed a perfectly brewed cup of dark coffee in front of her. Lynn was silent until the waiter left.

"Mr. Lee, you know very well how much money." Lynn dropped a cube of sugar in her coffee and added a little cream. She stirred the coffee slowly with a small silver spoon. Lee watched with lust as the cream merged with the coffee in long white swirls. The coffee's aroma was intoxicating. She took a delicate sip and continued. "The amount of the next payment, which is due next week, is one million dollars. The final payment to complete the construction phase is due in the first week of next month, in July. It is also one million dollars. If Lucky Star makes both scheduled payments on time, then the bank will finance the remaining construction and you will maintain your controlling position. So it is all very simple, Mr. Lee. Lucky Star must make two more construction phase payments, on time, and for that it needs two million dollars."

Lynn looked at Lee for a moment in case he might have another question. He didn't. He was quiet and brooding, fixated on her coffee. She drank again, then elegantly set her cup down and gazed around the room. They were quiet for a while, thinking about money.

Lee finally leaned back in his chair when he saw that Lynn's coffee cup was almost empty. He stared at the red lipstick on its rim, then looked over at Henry at the bar, still on his phone.

Given all the recent trouble in the Yukon, Lee wondered if Arturo Pistone had been setting him up for a fall. Could it be that Arturo was trying to take control of their building partnership? And those lucrative management contracts? Or had what just happened in the Yukon actually been bad luck for Arturo too? Had Arturo simply made a mistake in judgment? Had he simply sent the wrong man to Dawson to guard his gold? Or had he purposely sent a fool to the Yukon, knowing well the chances were good that a fool might sabotage Lee's business? What was his man's name? Ricky? Yes, Ricky. The man Tommy said was an idiot, the man who had murdered Lee's gold pilot, the man who was responsible for all this unnecessary police interference in Lee's gold mining business. Lee tried to ignore a nagging suspicion that Arturo might be trying to undermine his Yukon business, that he might be attempting to wrest control of his new condominium building. But he knew he need only focus on the task at hand to alleviate either of those threats. If Arturo Pistone was up to no good, he could deal with him later. Right now all he needed to do was buy and ship another two million dollars worth of gold – and the first million right away. Otherwise he faced losing those management contracts. He could not let that happen.

He mulled over the challenge. The police had seized two briefcases of gold this morning and were unlikely to return them anytime soon. One of those briefcases held a million dollars worth of his gold. *His gold.* Next week's construction payment was now as good as gone. What Lee needed to do immediately was buy another million dollars worth of gold and deliver it to the bank in Vancouver by the middle of next week. He watched Henry slip his phone into his pocket. Henry had finished his call and was sliding off the barstool.

"Lynn, now is a good time for you to freshen up. Then call Milton and have him bring the car around. I must speak with Henry now."

Henry arrived at the table but remained standing while Lynn calmly finished her coffee. Lee stood up. Lynn elegantly dabbed the corners of her mouth with her napkin, rose from her chair, and made her way slowly out of the dining room. Lee admired her hips swaying erotically under a shimmering skin tight dress. The two men sat down.

"Tell me, Henry."

"That was our lawyer, Mr. Lee. He is now in Dawson. He said the police have just released Tommy. But he told me they will not be releasing Mr. Pistone's man, this man Constanzia. Our lawyer says the police will charge Constanzia with the murder of our gold pilot, perhaps as early as tomorrow morning. And…"

"And?"

"Our lawyer says the police will be keeping our gold until the murder trial of Constanzia is over. Our lawyer says it will be months before we get our briefcase back."

Lee grimaced and took a deep breath. He was expecting this news, but now that it was official, the stakes were clearly defined. He put a hand to his chin and pulled down the corners of his mouth. "Henry, what does this man Constanzia know about our gold business in the Yukon?"

"I don't know Mr. Lee. We must ask Tommy. The police took Tommy's phone this morning and will not return it to him. Our lawyer says Tommy went to the drugstore to get a new phone. Tommy will call you when he has a new phone."

Wei Lee leaned over the table toward Henry. "Henry, we need to ship more fish right away. That is our only priority now. We need to buy more gold immediately and ship it to the bank in Vancouver. We have a construction payment due next week. We must not miss that payment."

"Of course not, Mr. Lee. I have already called the fisherman in Haines. I told him to prepare a shipment of fish and to call the fish pilot. But the fisherman says no one can find the fish pilot. He has disappeared. Perhaps he is afraid now. Perhaps he has flown away."

"Don't worry, Henry. Tommy will find the fish pilot. Tommy will find him and he will fly our fish to the Yukon."

THIRTY SIX

Dinner was excellent. We had beef tacos, refried beans, guacamole, chips and salsa. Just your standard, middle of the week TexMex meal which I'd thoroughly enjoyed because it was simple, delicious, and stuck to my ribs.

I was working on my second Corona, sitting on the deck with Charlie, enjoying the first balmy evening of the year, watching the swollen spring river hissing and rushing past us. Now and again a whole tree would float by. Sarah was inside, cleaning up the kitchen. What a perfect evening. And what a perfect place to spend it after two dangerous days in Dawson. I was happy to be home.

My dogs were happy too. While Sarah was making dinner I baked the rest of the salmon left over from the other night. If you ever want to know what it's like to be a real hero, mash up some sockeye salmon straight out of the oven in front of two hungry dogs, then give them all they can eat. Talk about earning true love and respect. But in spite of being served a gourmet meal, they weren't outside admiring me with the reverence I deserved. I knew where they were. They were inside my cabin, watching a beautiful woman wash dishes. I looked at their shiny bowls on the deck, then over at Charlie who was sitting a guarded distance to my right. He seemed a little more relaxed after a beer and a good meal.

"So Charlie, you say you have big trouble. What kind of trouble do you have?"

Charlie leaned forward in his chair, rested his forearms on his knees, and looked down at the deck. He didn't say anything. I didn't mind waiting for him to gather his thoughts. I took another sip of beer and watched a hawk soaring high over the hills on the other side of the river, searching the ground for an easy meal with eyesight so acute it's beyond human comprehension.

Finally Charlie spoke. "Mr. Brody, I am very afraid of all these men who want you to fly fish in your plane. They are… scaring me. I think they are having a fight."

"What men?" I asked. "Who's having a fight? Jack calls you, you call me, I go pick up the fish. What's to fight about? And who is 'they'?"

"Three men. They are all calling me about flying the fish."

"Three men?"

"Yes, three. Yesterday, Mr. Jack in Haines, he called me. He told me to call you. He said it was time for you to go to Haines and pick up more fish. He said you must fly the fish to the lake near Whitehorse. I said okay, that is always where we meet your plane when you fly fish to Whitehorse. So I call you to tell you this, but you don't call back. But also yesterday, Mr. Tommy, he called me too. He said you must fly the fish to Dawson, not to Whitehorse. Mr. Tommy said you must fly the fish to Dawson and deliver it to Mr. Ralph at a dock. Mr. Tommy says I must find you right away and tell you that. I said okay, Mr. Tommy, you are the boss. But I don't know where you are. I call you again and again, but you don't call back. Then this morning, a man named Mr. Terry called me. He said he is a mine manager in Dawson. He told me everything has changed. Mr. Terry told me you should pick up fish from Mr. Jack in Haines, but you must fly it to a mine on a creek, not to Mr. Ralph at the dock in Dawson, not to Whitehorse, to a mine on a creek. He said you know this creek and you know this mine. I told Mr. Terry that I do not know him, that Mr. Tommy is my boss, I told him I only listen to Mr. Tommy. I told him that Mr. Tommy should call me if the plans have changed. But this Mr. Terry, he said if the fish were not delivered to the mine he would…"

"Hold on a second, Charlie. Who are Mr. Ralph and Mr. Terry?"

"Mr. Ralph, he is the man who takes the fish from me in Whitehorse. Mr. Terry, he says he is a mine manager, but I do not know him."

"Mr. Ralph takes the fish from you in Whitehorse? I thought the fish was for the hotel, the Fifty Below Hotel."

Charlie bowed his head again. "Not the hotel. Mr. Ralph takes the fish from me and puts it in his truck, behind the hotel. He takes it away. The hotel does not know about the fish I get from you. Please do not tell the hotel, Mr. Brody, I will lose my job."

"Well, I didn't know that, Charlie, I thought the fish was for the hotel. But don't worry, that's our secret, okay? I will not tell anyone at the hotel where the fish goes. Now, this Mr. Ralph, who is he? What's his last name, do you know?"

"No, I do not know."

"What does Mr. Ralph look like?"

"Old. He has all white hair."

"Does he have a big blue truck?"

Charlie looked at me alertly. "Yes, a big blue truck. Do you know him?"

"Yeah, I know him," I said nodding, watching the hawk circling on the other side of the river. "I met him in Dawson yesterday. And this Mr. Terry, do you know his last name?"

"No."

"No? You've never met him, you don't know what he looks like?"

"No."

"You've never met him, you don't know him, but he's telling you where to fly the fish."

"That is right. I only talk to him once, on the phone, only this morning. Mr. Terry says he is a mine manager. He says he knows Mr. Tommy and Mr. Ralph. But he says he is now in charge of flying the fish. He said you must now fly all the fish from Haines to his mine on a creek, not to Dawson, not to Whitehorse. He told me never to meet with Mr. Ralph in Whitehorse again. He told me you will know where the creek runs into the river near his mine. He says you must always fly the fish there now. Never to Whitehorse. Never to Dawson. Only to his mine. He said Mr. Tommy will not call me anymore. Why does he say that? I don't know what to do Mr. Brody. What should I do? I do not know this Mr. Terry, but he said I must tell you to fly all the fish to his mine or he will…"

"Will what Charlie? What did he say he'd do?" Sarah asked from behind me. I hadn't heard her come out of the cabin and had no idea of how long she'd been listening to the conversation. Charlie looked up at her, shook his head, slumped forward with his elbows on his knees, wringing his hands. He was staring down at the deck again and didn't seem prepared to give her an answer. Sarah picked up a deck chair with one hand and put it down next to him. She had a Margarita in her other hand. "You can tell me, Charlie. I know all about the fish that Mr. Brody flies to Whitehorse. Mr. Brody and I can help you with your troubles. But I need you to tell me what Mr. Terry said he would do."

Charlie looked at Sarah with a look of bewilderment. "Who are you?" he asked her. "How do you know about the fish?"

Sarah leaned closer to him. She spoke barely loud enough for me to hear her. "Charlie," she said. "You're just going to have to trust me. I can't tell you who I am, but I know why you're here in the Yukon. I know that you were sent up here to work for Mr. Tommy. I know you have a young son in Whitehorse. I know you and your son are in Canada without papers. I know that you came here from China. And I know how to protect you and your boy."

Charlie stared at her in astonishment. He put his hands on the arms of his chair as though poised to jump up and run away. I looked at Sarah for a reaction. She didn't move, other than to take another sip of her drink. She held a steady gaze on him. How would she know Charlie had a son? Or how he'd got here and what he was doing? And that Tommy Kay was his boss? It might just be guessing on her part, but she sounded so sure of herself. How could she know those things? Were they true? What was she up to?

"Charlie," she said. "Did Mr. Terry say he would do something to your son if Mr. Brody didn't deliver the fish to his mine? Did he say he would take your boy away? Or hurt him?"

Charlie nodded almost imperceptibly, still poised to get up and dash off. He was clearly frightened, now having to deal with yet another total stranger vying for control of his life. He glanced at me, as if I might somehow make the confident woman sitting beside him go away. I shrugged my shoulders and looked across the river, just as the hawk folded its wings and fell into a steep dive, disappearing behind the trees.

Sarah put her hand on Charlie's shoulder.

"Don't worry, Charlie," she said. "Everything's going to be alright. I promise. Here's what we're going to do."

THIRTY SEVEN

I was sitting in my favorite deck chair with my head hanging over the back, holding an empty bottle of beer high above my open mouth, contemplating the distorted view of the bright blue sky through its glass bottom, watching the last foamy drops slide down its neck and drip onto my tongue. I heard Charlie's truck start and drive off. A moment later Sarah stepped onto the deck and walked up behind me. She wrapped her arms around my neck and planted a kiss on my cheek. Jack and Russ sat down in front of us with their tails wagging, staring up at the two of us. They seemed to be in a good mood. They certainly liked having an alpha female hanging around the place.

"You still have those red scratches on your face," she said, "do they hurt?"

"Nope, but my ear's pretty sore."

"Well I have just the thing for that," she said, plucking the empty bottle from my hand and disappearing into the cabin. The dogs followed her inside.

I scanned the sky across the river for my new friend the hawk, but couldn't locate him. Or maybe it was a her. Whatever it was, it would be nice if it took up residence here for the summer. I'd rather sit on my deck after dinner and spend an evening watching a hawk soaring around than turn on a television. With one exception, of course – when the Stanley Cup Playoffs are underway – and my Phoenix Coyotes are still playing hockey in the longest, roughest, toughest, most competitive sports tournament in the world. Like tonight, for example. If I hadn't been entertaining a house guest, I'd no doubt be inside watching the third period, hawk or no hawk. I think the game of hockey is the most compelling and spectacular contest of speed, strength and athleticism of all the professional team sports. And unlike professional football, the National Hockey League still hasn't let Madison Avenue ruin the natural pace of their game by saturating its television broadcasts with commercials. In fact, the NHL won't even allow television commercials during team time outs. So a thirty second time out doesn't turn out to be a five minute game stopper to pitch cheap cars and lousy beer. Good for the NHL.

Anyway, if I knew anything about playoff hockey, there was a pretty good chance tonight's game would go into overtime. And when there's overtime, there's no telling how long it will take for someone to score the winning goal. So even if I was 'entertaining' a house guest, maybe later on I'd get a chance to check in on my favorite hockey team.

I heard the cabin door open and felt footsteps behind me. A frosty Margarita appeared before my eyes.

"For your ear," she said. "Strictly for medicinal purposes. Drink up."

I sighed. "Alright, but just the one. I'm flying tomorrow. The twelve hour rule, you know?"

"But you're not flying until noon. And it's only nine o'clock now."

"How do you know what time I'm flying?" I asked. I took a sip of my Margarita. It was excellent. I raised my glass to her. We clinked glasses.

"Because Charlie's going to call you at your shop tomorrow morning and tell you when you're flying. He's going to call between nine and eleven, after he's heard from Tommy Kay. You'll have to wait until he calls before you'll know where and when you're flying your load of fish."

"How do you know that Kay will call Charlie?"

"He'll have to call Charlie. Kay will get out of jail tonight and the first thing on his agenda will be to replace that gold we took from him this morning."

"Don't you have to give it back, if you're not charging him with anything? "

"No. That gold is evidence in a murder investigation. We're going to hold it. Too bad for Tommy Kay and Wei Lee."

"So what will they do?"

"We're betting Lee will have to buy more gold from his gold buyer in Dawson. He didn't buy that gold we seized for a souvenir. He needs gold to secure more bank loans. He has to replace it. So Kay will have to call Charlie because he needs you to go get more cash in Haines to buy another million dollars worth of gold."

"You cops sure are conniving and mean," I said. "Expropriating an innocent man's gold like that."

"Yeah, we're really mean," she said, slapping a mosquito on her thigh. "But those guys are definitely not innocent. We cops play by the rules. We don't beat people up. And we don't kidnap kids." She drank to that.

I wasn't sure if she was entirely right about what she'd just said, but let it lie. Then I said, "Hey, what do you mean when you say Wei Lee needs gold to secure more bank loans? What bank loans?"

"Oh, it's complicated Brody, I'll explain some other time."

"Hey, why not now? This is a perfect time," I said, casting my free hand out at the scenery in front of us. "Come on, I've got time. Why not try giving a dumb pilot a simple explanation of why Lee needs gold to secure more bank loans."

She inhaled deeply, then said, "Alright, I'll try." She drank then continued. "Wei Lee flies his dirty money up here in the back of your plane. You know that already. It's perfectly good American money, but it's illegally earned income from prostitution and human trafficking. So he has to clean it up, and he doesn't want to pay any income tax when he does. Are you with me?"

"I'm with you."

"Good. So what he does is open a gold mine up here, then he buys gold in Dawson with the dirty money that you're flying in, then he reports that the gold he bought in Dawson came from his mine. Right?"

"I knew that. I'm still with you."

"Good. So here's what he does next. This is what he does to avoid paying income tax. And it's perfectly legal." She paused to drink again, then continued. "Suppose you found some gold in the ground. You found something of value. But until you sell the gold you found, you haven't earned any income for income tax purposes. Not until you sell the gold you found are you liable to pay income tax."

"Why's that?" I asked.

"Because when you found the gold, all you did was produce something, you created an inventory, in this case gold inventory. It's just like if you were growing apples or wheat, or manufacturing something in a factory. Whatever you grow or build or mine may be valuable, but it's still just something you have for sale. That's called inventory. And you don't pay income tax on inventory. You're only liable to pay income tax when you make a sale, when you sell your inventory, when you have *income*. Still with me?"

"I guess."

"Good. So here's why gold is special. Because unlike apples or wheat or something you manufacture, gold never spoils, never goes out of fashion, never goes out of date. So there's absolutely never any urgency to sell your gold inventory if you don't want to. Gold lasts forever, it's valuable, it's compact, you can move it around easily, you can divide it up, melt it, whatever, it's always going to be the same valuable thing no matter how long you keep it. Everyone knows what it is, and exactly what it's worth per ounce, every hour of every day, anywhere in the world. You can buy all you want and sell all you want, whenever you like, wherever you like, and you never even have to negotiate the price. Right?"

"Right".

"Okay. So when Lee needs to raise cash he doesn't sell the gold he claims to have produced at his mine. If he did sell that gold, he'd have income, and he'd have to pay income tax. Instead, what he does is he ships his gold to his bank in Vancouver, then borrows against it. He uses his gold as collateral to make bank loans. And his bank gladly accepts his gold as collateral for the loans he makes because there's no better collateral in the world. The bank is satisfied that he came by the gold honestly, because he operates a gold mine in the Yukon. So Wei Lee gets the clean cash he needs with bank loans, and because there's no income tax on money that's borrowed, he doesn't have to pay any income tax. Follow all that?"

"Yeah. That's not so complicated. But it's pretty sick that he can get away with not paying income tax by borrowing money he doesn't need to borrow."

"What he's getting away with is human trafficking, prostitution, money laundering, and lying about where his gold came from. But sick or not, borrowing against his gold inventory to beat the tax man is perfectly legal."

"What a world," I said.

"What a world, indeed," she said. "Whoever borrows the most, wins."

"Is that how it works?"

"Well sure, and I'm not the first one to say it. It's always been that way. Working doesn't make you rich. Money makes you rich. Rich people don't work to earn money, they work so they can pay interest on the money they borrow. They drive fancy cars and live in fancy houses with money they've borrowed, not money they've earned."

I dwelled on that concept for a moment. Now that she seemed in the mood for talking, I thought I'd try a different question. "So what did you just tell Charlie?" I asked.

"That he's in real danger. That his son's in real danger too. That we're going to have to find a safe place for him and his son to stay until this is over. That he should do whatever Tommy Kay tells him to do, and ignore those other guys like Terry Mcilhaney and that gold buyer named Ralph. Which is why we'll wait for Kay to call Charlie in the morning. Which is why you're not flying anywhere until Charlie calls with Kay's instructions."

"That guy Ralph, the man with all the white hair and the big blue truck. He's a gold buyer?"

"Yup. Big time. He sells Wei Lee most of his gold."

"And that guy Mcilhaney, is that what you said his name was? Is that this Terry guy's last name?" I asked.

"Yeah. Terry Mcilhaney, he's Wei Lee's mine manager at Thistle Creek."

I thought hard whether 'Mcilhaney' was the last name of the 'Terry' I'd seen today. I didn't know.

"So," I said. "You went ahead and made a decision for Charlie, decided he should only follow the instructions of Tommy Kay, and not Wei Lee's mine manager, this Terry Mcilhaney."

"Right. We need Tommy Kay to keep doing his thing if we're going to bust Wei Lee. We've got to keep Kay in the game until you can mark a bunch of Lee's cash. This guy Mcilhaney, he's just Wei Lee's mine manager, working some angle while Kay's stuck in jail. He's probably just trying to steal from Lee."

"So where are you going to put Charlie 'until this is over'?"

"Here would be a good place."

"Here?" I turned and looked at her.

"Not *here* in your cabin. But somewhere around here. Perhaps there's someone in the native village here that he could stay with. Tommy Kay or Terry Mcilhaney won't go looking for Charlie in a native village in the middle of nowhere. Do you think you could help us with that?"

I thought about what she had in mind for Charlie. I felt a tinge of resentment that she thought someone in my community ought to take on the risk of hiding a stranger from an organized crime thug.

"I'll see what I can do in the morning," I said, a little perturbed.

"Thanks." Then sensing my resentment, she said, "Look Brody, Charlie's in Canada illegally, and so is his son. If we were to move the two of them out of the Yukon, or surround them with cops in Whitehorse to protect them, then it will mean they'll get processed through the system, and they'll become exposed to the wrath of the Canadian immigration authorities. If we can quietly hide them here for a while, I'll do my best to grease the wheels so Charlie and his boy can get on a fast track to legal status."

"Alright, Sarah. Sounds like you just made a deal. I'll see what I can do in the morning. But I'll hold you to that commitment to help Charlie and his boy get legal here."

"Brody, I told you before. You can trust me."

"I know. Now tell me more about this guy Terry. Who is he? And what will he do to me or Charlie if I deliver fish to Tommy Kay, and not to him?"

Sarah sat back and took another good slug of her Margarita. She slapped at a few more mosquitoes who apparently found her as attractive as everyone else did.

"I don't know what he'll do," she said. "I do know Terry Mc-ilhaney's been managing the Thistle Creek mine for a couple of years. And we think he might have recently jumped ship and started working for Lee's partner, a drug dealer from Vegas named Arturo Pistone. Pistone and Lee are partners on a construction project in Vancouver."

"How would you know that?"

She sighed. "Look Brody, we're cops, okay? We've had twenty people working hard on this case for over a year. We watch, we listen, we investigate, we research, we spy, we snoop, we find things out about people. Like who they are, and what they're up to, it's what we do."

"Okay. So you think this guy Terry might have jumped ship and gone to work for Lee's partner from Vegas, who you think may be moving in on Wei Lee's action up here. That's why Charlie's been getting different instructions from different people. Like Terry

Mcilhaney and Jack Kolinsky and Ralph somebody with the big blue truck. So what else do you know about this guy, Mcilhaney?"

"Well, lots of stuff. Stuff I don't have time to tell you about right now. Look, all you have to know is what that punk Constanzia said to Kay in front of us on the dock this morning. Stuff like how 'he'd made a new friend', and 'from now on I'm calling the shots'. We think that kind of talk indicates that Pistone has started a run for control of Lee's money laundering machine. And maybe his assets too, like the Thistle Creek mine and a new condominium tower he's building in Vancouver. We think Constanzia probably met with Terry Mcilhaney yesterday and Mcilhaney somehow got him to change his allegiance from Lee to Pistone. Mcilhaney probably supplied Constanzia with that gun he was pointing at us today. And Constanzia was probably planning to throw Kay out of your plane somewhere over the ocean this morning – if we'd ever taken off – then made off with *both* briefcases full of gold. That would have royally screwed things up for Lee, and for our investigation too." She paused and sipped her drink. "Look, we're so close to wrapping up our case against Lee. All we need is for you to make one more fish shipment and mark some cash. That's it, that's all that's left to do now. Then we can make our arrests. Then it's over."

I nodded. "I guess it's a good thing you kicked the crap out of Constanzia this morning," I said.

She smiled at me. "I was very lucky that worked out. I was really scared."

"Lucky for me too, Sarah. We'd probably both be dead if you hadn't pulled that off. That was pretty impressive, what you did this morning on that dock. And you didn't look scared to me."

We clinked glasses and were quiet, lost in our own thoughts. Sarah finished her drink. Mine was about done too and I downed the last of it. Without a word Sarah stood and took my glass and went inside. She was doubtless off to make me another drink but I didn't stop her, though I hardly needed another. While waiting for her I thought about how convoluted everything had become. There seemed to be so many bad guys vying for control of Wei Lee's money laundering scam. All these criminals were floating around the Yukon, waving guns at people, kidnapping kids, making threats, buying gold with dirty money, and now they were at war with each other over a mine. I thought how ironic it was to have organized crime up here in the tranquil and pristine Yukon wilderness. Then something occurred to me while I was scanning the sky for my hawk.

"Hey Sarah?" I said quietly, after she'd handed me a fresh Margarita and sat down again. "Tell me about your brother. Was that man we found in the plane yesterday really your brother?" I looked intently at her. She stared into her drink.

"Later."

"When's *later*?"

"Just later, okay?" She swirled her drink and watched the ice spin, avoiding my eyes.

Clearly she didn't want to talk about him. I'd been wondering why something so shocking as finding your brother murdered had hardly seemed to have affected her. I decided to try another subject.

"Okay, then how about you tell me a little bit about your buddy, Special Agent Stanley Kurtz. He's always giving me a dirty look. What's with that guy anyway? He acts like he hates me."

"He's not my buddy. Next question," she said.

"You don't want to talk about him either?"

"Next question," she repeated, looking out at the river with a fierce look.

"Alright, then what about this guy, Terry Mcilhaney?"

"What about him?"

"What does he look like?"

"Why do you want to know what he looks like?"

"I don't know. Just wondering. This afternoon I saw this guy in Dawson walking down a street near Deb's restaurant. Hadn't seen him for awhile, but he's been hanging around Dawson for a couple of years. I think he's a miner and I think his name's Terry."

"What was he doing?" she asked, whirling abruptly in her chair to look at me.

"Just walking down the street."

"By himself?"

"No, he was with a woman."

"A tall, skinny woman?"

"Yeah," I said, sitting up too. "How did you…?"

"Shit," she exclaimed, jumping out of her seat. She plunked her glass down, leapt off the deck and ran toward her car.

I stood and yelled, "Hey, where are you going?"

"RCMP. I think you found our kidnapper!"

The dogs charged after her. I whistled and yelled, but they didn't come back.

* * *

I wasn't sure what had got Sarah so excited, other than my saying the man I'd seen this afternoon might have been named Terry, and he'd been walking down a Dawson sidewalk with a tall, skinny woman. Obviously she knew something about the two that I didn't. Maybe the man I knew as Terry was *the* Terry Mcilhaney, Wei Lee's mine manager on Thistle Creek. But so what? And why that tall, skinny woman he was walking with would motivate Sarah to charge off to Daryl's was beyond me. Did she really think either of those two people could possibly be a kidnapper? Did she really think they might be the ones who abducted Bobby Larabie? Why would they do that? I decided not to worry about it. Instead I decided to make the most of my free time and watch some hockey.

I went into the cabin with our Margarita glasses and set them down on the kitchen counter. It was already getting chilly inside. Even with a warm sunny evening, it would be cold tonight. I was too lazy to start a fire in the woodstove so went to the closet beside the bathroom and turned on the propane heater. I set the thermostat to seventy and heard the fan start. I hoped there was enough propane left in the little tank outside to run the heater all night. One of these days I was going to install a large permanent tank behind my cabin, one that could heat the place for a whole winter.

I turned on the television and tuned in the hockey game. Just as

I'd hoped, the score was tied after three periods. The first overtime period would start in fifteen minutes. This was excellent.

Take your time with the RCMP, Sarah. I'm going to watch some hockey.

I had one of my four minute showers and felt like a new man. I emerged from my bedroom appropriately dressed in my usual hockey watching garb: wool lined moccasins, sweatpants, and an official Phoenix Coyotes sweatshirt. I sat down on the couch with a big glass full of ice. I was all settled in to watch some Stanley Cup hockey in my Yukon man-cave.

THIRTY EIGHT

Wei Lee was thrashing and kicking.

He was wearing silk pajamas, standing alone in a long hallway, on the top floor of his new luxury condominium building. Somewhere below was a fire. Smoke was seeping out from under every door along the hallway. It was pitch black and he ran blindly to one end – to the exit door. It would open to a stairway and he could escape. But the exit door was locked. He ran to the other end, tried that exit door. It too was locked. He ran back to the other door, tried it again. Nothing had changed. Both doors were locked. Back and forth he ran, over and over again, from one door to the other, but the result was always the same. There was no way out. The smoke was building, getting thicker and thicker. He couldn't see, could barely breathe. He knew he would die if he couldn't escape. Then he heard a ringing, barely audible, but definitely a ringing. A fire alarm had been set off, somewhere far below him. Help would arrive soon. Hurry. Please hurry. The ringing stopped. He became frantic and panicked, dropped to the floor, pressed his face into the carpet, tried to breathe, thrashing and gasping for air.

Then someone grabbed him. Rolled him over. Someone had come.

"Mr. Lee, Mr. Lee, you are dreaming!"

Wei Lee fluttered his eyelids and looked up at Lynn's face. She was above him, straddled over his belly, her tiny hands on his shoulders. He hated that feeling, to be dominated by someone. He realized what had happened and was deeply embarrassed. He pushed Lynn off and got out of his enormous bed, walked to the window and stared out at the sparkling city, a sprawl of lights twenty floors below him. Breathing heavily with his heart pounding, he slowly grasped the new reality of where he was, safe and sound in his bedroom, in his luxury penthouse in Los Angeles. He wiped the sweat from his forehead, tried to control his shaking.

"You must go now, Lynn. Please go now," he said, not looking at her.

"Yes, Mr. Lee. Your phone was ringing, Mr. Lee. It is beside your bed, on the floor."

"Why is it on the floor?" he demanded.

"I don't know."

"Please, Lynn, just go."

"Yes, Mr. Lee."

When he heard the heavy front door close, Lee went out to the kitchen and had a glass of cold water from the refrigerator. He splashed water on his face at the kitchen sink, then dried himself with a dish towel. He used the phone in the kitchen to call the doorman in the lobby, gave instructions to call a taxi for Lynn. She was not to leave the building without an escort to her car. The doorman said he understood.

Wei Lee walked back into his bedroom. He was not about to get back into bed and try to fall asleep again. It would be a while before he could do that. He was still thinking about his dream when he saw his cell phone on the floor. He picked it up off the thick carpet and looked at the display. The call he'd missed was from a number he didn't recognize. It had an area code he'd seen before, but couldn't remember where or when. He was tempted to call the number, to see who had woken him up in the middle of the night.

The phone rang in his hand. The display said it was Henry. It was one o'clock in the morning.

"Yes?"

"Hello, Mr. Lee. I am very sorry to wake you. But it is very important that we talk. Tommy just called."

"Of course, Henry. What did Tommy say?"

"He said Arturo Pistone is trying to take over your gold business. He said Arturo is on his way to Haines with cash. Tommy wants to know what to do."

Wei Lee sat down on his bed. "Henry, how can Tommy know this?"

"Tommy was released from jail last night. Our gold buyer picked him up at the police station. Our gold buyer told Tommy he was visited by our mine manager – and a woman – yesterday afternoon when Tommy was in jail. Our mine manager told our gold buyer that he was now in charge because Tommy was in jail. Our mine manager told our gold buyer he wants to buy all the gold around Dawson. He told our gold buyer to bring all the gold he has to our mine tomorrow. He says the fish pilot is flying to Haines tomorrow, to meet with Arturo. He says Arturo will be bringing cash and that the fish pilot will fly his cash to our mine to pay for the gold. Our mine manager told our gold buyer not to talk to Tommy again."

"What do you think this means, Henry? Why would our mine manager say such things? And why would Arturo travel to Haines with cash?"

"I think it is obvious, Mr. Lee. Arturo wants to buy all the gold in Dawson. He is trying to destroy your gold business. To prevent you from financing your new building. He is trying to take control of your mine and your building. Maybe your fish business, too. There can be no other explanation."

Wei Lee pondered what Henry had just said. He knew Henry was right. With Tommy in jail, Arturo Pistone had decided to make his move. Arturo wanted to buy all the gold in Dawson so there would be none for Lee to buy. Lee knew if he couldn't get his hands on a million dollars of gold in the next few days, he'd lose control of his building. Arturo would be well aware of the dilution terms of their partnership agreement.

"Henry, next week, instead of a gold shipment, perhaps we should send cash directly to the bank in Vancouver, make our next construction payment that way."

"No, Mr. Lee. We must never do that. That would be very unwise. If there is ever an audit, we would have to show where you got so much cash, and so quickly. We would have no explanation. The bank in Vancouver would also ask questions. It would be a foolish risk for you to make a payment with cash. You must use a gold shipment from your mine."

"Of course, Henry. You are right". Wei Lee felt his stomach churning. Henry had been right all along. He should never have offered to help Arturo clean up his drug money using his own sources for gold. He should never have allowed Arturo to get anywhere near his business in the Yukon. In the last two days he'd lost a pilot, a million dollars of gold, and now his entire business was under siege. It was time to push back.

"Henry, do you think that Arturo knows what Tommy just told you? "

"I don't know, Mr. Lee. We only know what our mine manager told our gold buyer, and what our gold buyer told Tommy."

"Henry, what is the name of our mine manager?"

"His name is Terry."

"And who was the woman with this man Terry?"

"I don't know, Mr. Lee."

"And what is the name of our gold buyer?"

"His name is Ralph."

"Yes, I remember now, Ralph. Henry, do you think Arturo knows that Tommy has been released from jail?"

"I don't know, Mr. Lee."

"What about our mine manager, this man Terry, does he know Tommy is out of jail?"

"I don't know, Mr. Lee."

"Are you certain Arturo will be in Haines tomorrow?"

"That is what our mine manager told our gold buyer."

Wei Lee looked down at the lights below him. It was as if all the stars had fallen from the sky. They were scattered everywhere, all the way to the horizon.

"Tell me something, Henry. How will Arturo travel to Haines?"

"Probably like most people. He will fly to Juneau on a commercial flight, then he will take the ferry to Haines."

Wei Lee nodded, scanned the horizon, then made his decision.

"Henry, arrange a trip for me. In the morning I shall fly to Juneau. Also, arrange a plane to pick up Tommy in Dawson. And call the fisherman in Haines. Tell him to meet me and Tommy at your office in Juneau. Tomorrow we shall *all* travel together on the ferry to Haines. Me, Tommy, the fisherman, *and* Arturo."

"Yes, Mr. Lee."

THIRTY NINE

The game was tied with a minute to play in the first overtime period. Each team had hit at least one goal post, but no one could score. The goaltenders had been amazing. If no one scored in the first overtime period, there'd be an intermission to resurface the ice, and they'd start a second overtime period. The first team to score a goal would win the game. No matter how long it took, they'd play until someone scored.

I find the stress of watching sudden death overtime hockey almost unbearable. I'd been chewing crushed ice for the last forty five minutes and had almost emptied my fourth glass. I was about to get up for a refill when Sarah walked across the deck. She came into the cabin with my dogs at her heels and plunked herself down on the couch beside me. She gave me a big smile, kissed me on the cheek, and dropped some papers face down on the coffee table. She seemed to be in a good mood. The dogs sat down at her feet, staring at us attentively with their tails wagging, anticipating the next exciting event in their lives.

"Those are for you," she said, pointing at the papers. "What are you watching?"

"Hockey."

"Hockey. I like hockey. I went to a hockey game once."

"Good."

"It's amazing you can watch a hockey game on television up here. You live in the middle of nowhere."

"Everyone lives in the middle of nowhere."

"Who's playing?"

"Phoenix and Vancouver."

"Is it a good game?"

"Very."

"What's the score?"

"It's a tie."

"How much longer until it's over?"

"Don't know."

"You don't know?"

"Nope."

"Well then I think I'll have a shower. Okay?"

"Yeah. Have a shower."

"Want to wash my back?"

"It's too small. Damn!"

"Damn what? My back's too small?"

"No. Almost scored."

"What's too small?"

"The shower. Oh!"

"The shower's too small to wash my back?"

"Yeah. Too small. Shoot, shoot," I cried out, furiously chewing my last piece of ice.

Sarah watched the television for a moment, then stood and walked out in front of me, intentionally blocking my view of the game. I leaned over to my right and could barely see half the screen. She pulled her fleece jacket over her head and tossed it at me. I yanked it off my head and looked up at her in surprise. She grabbed her T-shirt at the waist and pulled it up to her neck, exposing her breasts.

"Is the shower too small for you to wash these?" she asked.

The siren sounded to end the first overtime period. I stared at her bosom with my mouth open, still full of crushed ice.

"There might be enough room," I managed to mumble without drooling too much.

She smiled and walked away.

I got up and followed her into the bathroom.

Damn woman.

* * *

While Sarah was washing her hair, I did a thorough job of washing her breasts and everything else I could get my hands on in the tiny shower. When things began to heat up we moved out of the shower, onto the bathroom floor, then onto some towels we'd thrown on the bedroom floor, then finally into my little bed. Twenty minutes later I was lying on my back with her on top of me. She was straddling my hips with her hands on my chest, her thick wet hair dripping on my face. We were both gasping for air.

"Wow," she said.

"Wow, yourself," I said.

"Hey. They just let Tommy Kay out of jail. Thought you should know." Her chest was heaving, she was breathing in gulps, it was outstanding to watch.

"Is that all you have to say after that?" I asked. "You're not going to tell me a few lies first, like 'that was incredible', or 'you're amazing', or 'I've never felt like this before'?"

"Sorry," she said with a chuckle. "I've never felt like this before."

We smiled at each other. Truth be told, now that her breasts had been thoroughly cleaned, I was wondering if the hockey game was still on, whether I might dare extricate myself and go out to the living room to see what was happening. I decided the game could wait. I liked where I was.

"So Tommy Kay is out of jail and walking around a free man," I said.

"Yeah. Now we wait for him to call Charlie. And for Charlie to call you."

"Hey Sarah, why did you take off like the place was on fire?

Was it because of that skinny woman who was walking with that guy Terry? Is that *the* Terry who works for Wei Lee?"

She fell forward onto the bed beside me, propped her head up with an elbow, and dropped her other arm over my chest. "Yeah. That was Terry Mcilhaney you saw today, the guy who manages the mine on Thistle Creek, and someone we've been looking for. And the tall skinny woman he was with is from Las Vegas. Her name's Rose Rivera."

"Rose Rivera. Sounds like a movie star."

"Hardly. This Rose Rivera is a drug dealer. She's been working for Arturo Pistone about eight years. She used to be a show girl, dancing in various revues up and down the strip. Then she turned thirty, which is like retirement age in that kind of work, lost her job, and met Pistone. Rivera was a heavy cocaine user when she was dancing, and still is. She'll do anything for it. And Pistone is a major Vegas drug dealer. He retails every drug known to man through a network of high class escorts he's got working the strip. So Rivera went to work for Pistone as an escort because it was the best way she knew how to pay for her nose candy. She went from a show girl in the bright lights to pushing Pistone's product in hotel rooms.

"Anyway, about three years ago some guy beat Rivera out of a lot of cash on some big coke deal that Pistone put together. Pistone tracked the guy down somewhere in California. He sent Rivera and one of his heavies out there to collect his dough. Rivera and Pistone's heavy kidnapped the guy's son from his mother, right in a Wal-Mart parking lot in the middle of the day. They got caught red handed, though. They were pulled over by the cops driving a rental van, two miles away. They had the kid in the back of the van, inside a cardboard box. Rivera was driving the van but neither she nor Pistone's heavy could be clearly identified on the Walmart surveillance tape, or by the three year old kid or his mother. But Rivera squealed and walked out of jail in return for fingering Pistone's heavy as the kidnapper. Of course she didn't dare mention Pistone's role to the police, so she got to live. And she still works for him. All we know is that if she's kidnapped one child, she'd do it again. Bobby Larabie's description of the woman who picked him up off the street today was Rose Rivera to a 'T'. And his description of the white truck she was driving was as good as a picture of Mcilhaney's pickup truck. We also know that kidnapping has always been part of Pistone's MO. Whenever he wants something badly enough, he just grabs someone's kid. We weren't sure why Rivera came up here to hang around with Terry Mcilhaney, not until today. We were watching the two of them all last week, trying to figure out the connection. When Bobby Larabie was taken today, it was easy to connect the dots. But the RCMP lost their tail on Rivera and Mcilhaney a couple of days ago. So when you told me you saw them together in town this afternoon, that was a really big break for us. The RCMP has really stepped up their search for them now."

I was looking at the ceiling, slowly shaking my head. "Some people and their lives," I said.

"Yeah, some people," she said. She gave me a long kiss, then rolled off me and got out of bed. She looked spectacular, now standing beside me naked, her smooth skin damp and glistening in the midnight sun sifting through the blinds. I grabbed her by the wrist to keep her from walking away, wanting a little more time to take it all in. I marveled at her sinewy body, her sculpted legs and buttocks, the muscle tone in her abdomen and upper arms. She had the figure of a professional athlete. I could just make out the subtle change of shade from her back to her buttocks, last summer's tan almost gone. She looked down at me expectantly.

"What?" she asked.

"How do you do it? How do you stay in such great shape?"

"Running, and Pilates."

"Is that a fish?"

"No, Brody. Pilates is not a fish. It's an exercise regimen. Now, I need to shower again." I let go of her wrist and she walked to the door.

"It sounds like a South American fish," I called after her as she was leaving the room.

She back peddled to the bedroom door, gave me a long sardonic look over her shoulder, then disappeared into the bathroom. I clasped my hands behind my head and stared up at the ceiling, thinking about how lucky I was. Then I thought about Bobby Larabie and listened to the shower running.

* * *

The aroma of percolated coffee was wafting in from the kitchen when I opened my eyes and stretched out my arms. I was alone in my bed. I pulled out the drawer on the bedside table and looked at my old alarm clock, something I rarely use. It was seven o'clock in the morning. I closed my eyes again, feeling no compulsion to get up. I like my sleep, mostly because I hate being tired. It's not the body that sleeps, it's the brain. Let alone poor concentration and compromising your immune system, nothing will make you look older and uglier faster than missing a good night's sleep. On that latter item, I need all the help I can get. I buried my face in a pillow and went back to sleep.

Half an hour later there were footsteps on the deck and the front door opened and closed. I rolled over on my back and stretched without opening my eyes. When the shower started running, I thought about Sarah's breasts, then for some reason about Pavlov's dogs. Coincidentally, I heard my two dogs pattering over the wood floor in the living room. Russ and Jack came trotting into the bedroom covered in road dust, jumped up on the bed, and attacked me with their tongues. I eventually had to pull the covers over my head to get some air. They took the hint and jumped down. When they left the room, I got out of bed and put on a pair of sweatpants and a T-shirt. I had to step over both dogs on my way out to the kitchen. They were lying in front of the bathroom door, soaking up the steam escaping underneath it, waiting for Sarah.

I poured myself a cup of coffee and noticed her sneakers on the front doormat. She actually is a runner, I thought.

"Good morning," she said effervescently, emerging refreshed and beautiful from the bathroom, planting a long wet kiss on my mouth that instantly put me in the mood again. Sadly, she turned her back to me, poured herself a cup of coffee, and walked over to the couch. Oh well.

"Good morning to you too, Sarah. Go for a run?"

"I did. The three of us ran all the way up to the highway and back. Four times. How far do you think that is?" The dogs sat down in front of her, apparently thrilled to be on her running team.

"About four miles."

"Good. Haven't run for a week. It felt great."

"You look great. See any bears?"

"No. Are there bears around here?"

"Well yeah, of course there are bears around here. They live in the woods, didn't you know?"

"Shit," she said. "Why didn't you tell me? You should have told me. Are they dangerous?"

"Depends on what kind of mood they're in."

"Brody, I'm serious."

I laughed. "With those two dogs, you had zero chance of a bear encounter this morning."

"Your little dogs could protect me from a bear?"

"Damn right they could. They may be little, but they're fast, fierce and fearless. They'd run any bear off that comes anywhere near you. No sane bear wants to deal with two crazy little snarling dogs running circles around it, even if it desperately wanted to take a bite out of that great ass of yours."

She put her coffee down and asked, "Is that true?"

"About the bear or your great ass?"

She shook her head with disgust. "The bear, Brody. Your dogs could protect me from a bear?"

"Yes. They'd die for you."

She looked at me for a second, then looked down at Russ and Jack, and gave a gentle mussing to each one of her greatest admirers. It was the first time I'd seen her touch either one. They were as good as hers now.

"I have a question for you."

"What?" I said on my way to the couch, sitting down beside her. I noticed the papers she'd brought me last night. I turned them over.

"Why do you have a salt shaker in your bathroom?"

I picked up the papers off the coffee table. They were stapled together. It was my new contract with the FBI. David Owen must have faxed it to Daryl from Dawson. Owen had signed it. I wondered if everyone at the café knew about it already.

"Brody?" she repeated, leaning against my shoulder.

"What?" I said, starting to read the first page.

"Why do you have a salt shaker in your bathroom?"

"French fries," I said, flipping the first page over to read the second one.

"Brody!"

"Oh. For mosquito bites. Wet your fingers with water, shake a bunch of salt on them, and rub your itchy mosquito bites really hard. No more itch."

"Really?"

"Really."

"I didn't know that. Never heard of that."

"Yeah, well you know kung fu, and I know mosquitoes."

"And you know how to fly," she said.

"And I know how to fly," I said, turning to the last page.

FORTY

Charlie Woo called me at nine o'clock sharp. We talked for ten minutes to make sure we got everything straight, everything we were going to do if things went according to plan, and everything we were going to do if they didn't.

I hung up the phone and wondered if my next flight to Haines would be business as usual. I wandered around the shop for a minute, then went outside and thought about my life. How much I liked my dogs, my shop, my cabin, my plane. How I didn't want anything or anyone to take any of it away. And how much I was going to miss Sarah Marsalis who hadn't even been a part of the picture three days ago. Half an hour ago she'd packed most of her things into her little car and driven over to Daryl's, 'to do some more cop stuff'. Then she was going to leave.

This morning I'd signed the contract that Owen faxed me last night. Sarah said she'd fax it back to him when she got to Daryl's. My contract with the FBI was now a done deal. The only thing I didn't like about the contract was that my fee for flying Sarah out to Thistle Creek was implicitly included in the first month's installment. That didn't seem right to me – I'd flown Sarah out to Thistle Creek before I'd even met David Owen – but it certainly wasn't a deal breaker. With potentially just one more shipment of fish to be picked up in Haines, I felt fortunate to have a reliable source of income for the summer.

But there *was* someone who owed me money. On the bench in front of me I made out an invoice for two hours flying time in my DeHavilland Beaver, *'per agreement made on the river'*. I put the invoice in an envelope and wrote on the outside, 'attention Staff Sergeant Robson'. I slid the envelope into a side pocket on my backpack. I planned to personally deliver it to Robson this afternoon in Whitehorse. I needed to talk to him about something else anyway.

I heard Sarah's car rolling over the gravel outside the shop. That was a surprise, she'd barely been gone an hour. I hustled over to the washing machine and transferred a small load of laundry into the dryer. I was nervous and under a lot of pressure. This was the first really big test of whether Sarah and I might ever have a shot at a meaningful relationship. This was the first true test of trust between us. She'd asked me to wash and dry her clothes.

As far as I'm concerned, clothes aren't worth owning if they don't come out of the dryer the same size and color as when you put them in the washing machine – regardless of what combination of chemicals, water temperature, or machine settings you may happen to use. Apparently that's not the case with a woman's wardrobe, especially a Special Agent's wardrobe.

She'd insisted that her laundry be washed on the gentle cycle using a cold water wash. She'd been pleased when I told her that I had scent-free detergent, *'but don't use too much',* she'd said. She was dismayed to learn that I didn't have dryer sheets to eliminate static electricity. Static electricity? Does that harm clothes? I looked at the console on the dryer and all the dials and programs to choose from. I selected 'delicates' with one little dial and turned the pointer on the big dial to a section I'd never used before. It had a lot of esoteric technical jargon printed all around it, things like 'intellidry', 'extended tumble', 'wrinkle release', and 'cool down'. Drying her clothes was more complicated than landing in a crosswind. I pushed the big dial and the dryer started, though with all the settings she'd told me to use, there probably wasn't going to be much actual drying. I didn't see the sense of using a perfectly good clothes dryer to tumble a ball of wet laundry for a very long time with barely any heat. It would have been a better idea to have hung her stuff up outside on my old clothes line. It would probably take less time and they'd smell fresher. But orders are orders. Anyway, I figured if she wanted her laundry dry when she left, she was going to have wait a while. That was okay with me, I was in no hurry to see her leave.

The side door opened and she strode in with the dogs in tow. She got right to the point and said, "Did he call?"

"Yup."

"Told you," she said, tiptoeing over exhaust parts and the lift on her way to the bench.

"You're so smart," I said.

She gave me a long kiss and nice hug, as though it was the natural thing to do now. I liked the concept. She walked over to the dryer to 'audit' the settings I'd selected, apparently approved of them, and came back to the bench.

"Did you catch those kidnappers yet?" I asked, leaning against the bench.

"Nope. No sign of them anywhere. We sent a helicopter out to the Thistle Creek mine this morning, but there was no sign of Mcilhaney's truck. No one's seen it on the mining roads or highways or anywhere else around Dawson. Which is really strange. And something else that's strange is that the mine looked abandoned this morning. The pilot said when he landed at the camp there wasn't a machine operating or a soul in sight. But we'll get them, Brody. Mcilhaney and Rivera are somewhere in the Yukon. Every cop in the Yukon and Alaska is on the lookout for those lowlifes. Every border station and airport has been alerted. They can't go anywhere, they won't get far. We're going to get them, count on it. Now tell me what Charlie said."

I told her what Charlie said. Tommy Kay had called Charlie at six o'clock this morning. Kay told Charlie that he was looking for me. Kay wanted a load of fish flown from Haines to Whitehorse, tomorrow. Charlie told Kay he knew how to contact me and that I was waiting for instructions. Charlie said Kay was pleased to hear that. Kay told Charlie that I should be in Haines tomorrow afternoon at four o'clock. I was to pick up a load of fish from Jack at the usual spot and fly it directly from Haines to Whitehorse, just like I always have, not to Dawson as Kay had 'instructed' me when we were in that big blue truck a couple of days ago. Why had Kay all of a sudden changed the delivery spot? Charlie said he didn't know. Charlie said he'd been told to call the customs officer in Whitehorse to clear the shipment of fish when I landed. Charlie said he would be waiting at the lake when I arrived, and we'd load the fish into his truck. It all sounded like we were back to the usual routine. Fly a load of fish from Haines to Whitehorse.

"Did Kay tell Charlie what to do if Terry Mcilhaney calls him?" she asked.

"No. We didn't talk about that. But I asked Charlie if anyone else had called him since he left here last evening and he said no."

"That's good," she said. "Have you found a place yet for Charlie and his boy to stay?"

"Hey, a little time, okay? You've only been gone an hour. I'll find him a place. And you're going to help Charlie and his son with their immigration, right?"

"Yes. I said I would, and I will."

"Good, thank you."

"You're welcome," she said.

I was irritable because she was leaving and it showed. "Sarah, look, I'm sorry…"

"Me too. Forget it. How about I show you how to mark the cash in those boxes of fish now."

"Let's do it," I said.

With the sweep of her forearm she cleared some space on her end of the bench, then put her backpack down. She reached inside and pulled out a long, slender plastic box. She opened it. Inside were two small metal canisters, three long needles, and what looked like a very thin ice pick.

"This is your kit. Very simple to use," she said.

"Simpler than doing your laundry?"

"Much simpler," she said with a wry smile. She held out the tool that looked like an ice pick. "Use this to identify what's inside the box. It's basically just a very high quality probe. It's super thin, incredibly sharp, and made of very hard steel. It will pierce any soft material with ease, and because it's so thin, will barely leave a trace of a hole when you pull it out. Don't bend it or try to pry anything with it because it's brittle. But you can push it straight into just about anything as hard as you want. If you're not sure where to inject the dye, poke a few holes in the box with the probe and locate your target. The fish will feel soft, even if they're frozen. The cash will feel different, depending on the angle that the probe contacts the bills. You'll definitely notice a lot more resistance if you poke into the top of a stack of bills than from the side, and the probe slides between them. Which is how you want to inject the dye: into the side of a stack, between the bills. Keep the plastic sleeve on the probe until you need to use it. Got all that?"

"Yup."

"Good. Injecting the ultra violet dye into the cash is easy. The dye's inside these two canisters. I doubt if you'll need to use them both, but we're giving you two just in case." She held up a canister in one hand, and a needle in the other. At one end of the needle was a threaded bushing protected by a plastic cap.

"Watch," she said. "You have a choice of these three needles. The needles are hollow, just like the ones a doctor uses. Each needle is a different length, use the shortest one you think will reach your target. When you're ready to inject the dye, take the plastic cap off the end of the needle and screw it on the canister. That perforates the canister, then you're locked and loaded. Push the needle through the side of the box, push it into the cash, and press the button on the end of the canister. The dye will flow out of the canister under pressure, travel down the needle, and into the cash. Just a short shot is all you need for each injection. Do two or three shots into each box if you can, but you really only need to do one box. In fact we only need to find one bill marked with that dye and we've got our evidence."

"Just one?"

"Just one. More than one would be nice, but one is all we really need to seal the deal."

"Owen says that a lot, 'seal the deal'," I said.

"It's a good way of describing our objective," she said.

"Right. Hey, I have a question."

"What?"

"Suppose you find this ultra violet fluorescent dye of yours on some cash in a gold buyers briefcase in Dawson. And you go out and charge Wei Lee with money laundering. Won't his lawyer argue that the dye on the cash you seized could have come from anywhere, that it could have come from somewhere else besides out of this canister?"

She studied me carefully with a knowing smile, then said, "You know Brody, you are not just a pretty face."

"Let's not discuss my face."

She chuckled. "You're better looking than you think big guy," she said, and patted me on the butt. She was in a great mood. After years of trying to figure out how to make a woman happy, I think I'd finally learned the secret this morning. Do their laundry.

"Thanks," I said. "Now, are you going to answer my question?"

"Yes. The dye in those canisters isn't the same glow in the dark stuff you can buy at a party supply shop. We got this stuff from the guys wearing the white coats in the labs at Quantico. This dye will only fluoresce under an extremely narrow spectrum of ultra violet light. The boys in the lab call it tailored fluorescence, which means it was custom formulated for this particular case. It will only glow under a very specific and very narrow band of the UV spectrum. Only a very sophisticated and expensive spectrometer can detect that dye, and we just happen to have brought one up with us."

"You sound like a scientist, Sarah. I think you're actually the one who's not just a pretty face."

She smiled at that. "There's more," she said. "The dye in these canisters has very distinct physical properties and specific molecular characteristics. It was formulated for our case with a unique recipe of ingredients that can be precisely identified using micro spectrophotometry and mass spectrometry analysis, whatever those are. All I know is that if we present the boys in the lab with one of Wei Lee's twenty dollar bills, they can positively verify whether or not it has this particular dye on it. They told me that the chances of the exact same dye coming from another source is as likely as finding two twenty dollar bills with the same serial number. So that dye's as good as a fingerprint to us."

"That's amazing," I said. "And so are all those fancy words you're throwing around." She gave me another one of her radiant smiles. "So is it poisonous?" I asked. "What if I get it on my hands?"

"It's perfectly safe. It's made entirely from organic compounds."

"And you believe that because that's what the boys in the lab at Quantico told you."

"Yes, and I trust them."

"Okay, then I guess I'll trust you."

We were both quiet for a moment. "Well, here goes nothing," I muttered. I put the canisters, the needles and the probe back into the plastic box, put the top on it, and dropped it into my backpack.

"Now what?" I said, leaning back on the bench beside her. She had her arms folded and was looking at the car lift and the assortment of junk on the floor that I needed to clean up. Russ and Jack were sitting on the floor in front of us, staring at Sarah in awe, wagging their tails. They were apparently as impressed with her technical acumen as I was.

"I wait for my laundry to dry," she said. "Then I leave." She shrugged her shoulders, bit her lip, and looked down at the floor.

"Do you really have to go? I don't need to fly to Haines until tomorrow. We could do Italian tonight." We looked at each other for a long time.

"I'd really love to stay another day, but I do have to go. I have things to do elsewhere and my job here is done. Besides, I've been made. I doubt if Tommy Kay thinks I work for a Juneau newspaper, not after what went down yesterday morning in Dawson at your plane. I can't risk being seen hanging around with you."

"Understand," I said, nodding, thinking about Tommy Kay. "So what *things* do you have to do?"

She took a deep breath. "Well, first I need to bury my brother. I called the coroner's office in Whitehorse this morning. They've completed his autopsy. I'm taking his body back to Juneau this afternoon. My plane leaves Whitehorse at three. So I need to be out of here by noon."

"Sure going to miss you, Sarah."

"Going to miss you too, Brody."

"Do you think we'll ever get to do Mexican again?" I asked.

"Hope so. Maybe next time we can do Mexican in Mexico. Go to a quiet place with warm turquoise water, a white sandy beach, palm trees and real Margaritas. Just hang out together for a week, do Mexican every night, spend our days in flip flops."

I had an instant vision of her scantily clad under a white hot sun beside a turquoise sea, tanned from head to toe, flip-flops on her feet, walking beside me on a long white beach. "Sounds like a plan," I said. "Let's do it. Have you got my phone number?"

"I have your phone number."

"Will you call me?"

"I'll call you."

"Promise?"

"Promise."

She grabbed my hand and pulled me toward the stairs.

"Where are we going?" I asked.

"Upstairs."

Halfway up I stole a glance at my dogs. They were watching us from the foot of the stairs, furiously wagging their tails. I guess they approved.

"Stay," I said.

FORTY ONE

Ralph Braun was thinking about gold nuggets. He'd never seen anything like what he'd seen this morning. He'd heard of it of course, he'd lived in Dawson for almost thirty years. But such events were rare these days. Most of the Klondike's ancient creek channels have long been discovered and mined out. But it could still happen. Because it had just happened on Thistle Creek.

Because gold is where you find it.

Millions of years ago, the gold eroding out of lode deposits around Dawson was washing down the hills into the valleys below. When the gold reached the creeks, it sunk down to the bedrock and began migrating downstream, pushed along slowly and erratically by the forces of flowing water and shifting gravel. But gold is heavy – incredibly heavy – eighteen times heavier than water for a given volume, and it doesn't like to move.

Gold just wants to stop and hide.

The path for most of the gold sliding along the bottom of the ancient creeks was over broken and weathered bedrock, riddled with cracks and crevices. It would fall into those cracks and crevices, settle to the bottom, and stop.

For millions of years, the cracks and crevices in the ancient creek bottoms around Dawson served as traps for gold nuggets. The nuggets would fall into the cracks and crevices, one at a time, one after the other, year after year for millions of years, until the cracks were full.

If you're mining for gold around Dawson these days, perhaps there's still one left on your claim. Perhaps there's one of those chunks of ancient bedrock from an ancient creek bottom that had lots of cracks and crevices, still buried in the ground below you, still packed full of gold nuggets. And perhaps today's the day you just happen to dig up that particular piece of ancient bedrock and feed it into your sluice box. And when you turn off your water pump and machines at the end of the day, you'll do what every miner does. You'll look in your sluice box to see what you found. Perhaps today's the day you'll be looking at what they call 'a thousand ounce cleanup'.

Eureka.

* * *

Dense misty clouds hovered over the hill tops, and here and there were sliding down the dark green valleys like thick fluffy avalanches. Ralph Braun was driving his big pickup truck through the mist and the drizzle, carefully navigating his way through the twists and turns on the muddy road running up the side of the Thistle Creek valley. The road was slick, it had rained hard last night, but with a dozen pails full of mud and gravel in the back of his truck there was no need to use four wheel drive. Each pail weighed at least a hundred and fifty pounds and the heavy load over the rear wheels gave his truck tremendous traction.

The pails were full of what Ralph had just shoveled out of a sluice box, the same sluice box he'd been gawking at a little over an hour ago. The gold in the pails behind Ralph Braun was easily worth a million dollars. It was a great day to be a miner on Thistle Creek. Unless your name was Terry Mcilhaney.

Ralph had heard a rumor in Dawson last night and told Tommy about it when he picked him up at the police station. Early this morning the two had set out for the Lucky Star mine. They'd started the sixty mile trip heading southeast on the Bonanza Creek road, then turned southwest onto a rough road that took them to the west end of King Solomon's Dome, then they'd turned west onto the Thistle Creek valley road and driven almost all the way down to the Yukon River. The hour and a half drive to the Lucky Star mine had been rough and wet and slippery. When they arrived at the mine site, Ralph was disappointed to see the camp apparently abandoned.

But Tommy wasn't deterred. Not after what Ralph had told him about the phone call Terry Mcilhaney made to Charlie Woo. Not after what Ralph had told him about his conversation with Terry Mcilhaney. Not after Ralph told him about the rumor going around town, the rumor about the Thistle Creek sluice box.

Tommy got out of Ralph's truck and barged into a long yellow trailer, the crew's sleeping quarters. A minute later he emerged with a tall skinny woman wearing pajamas and a ski jacket, leading her by the ear out into the middle of the muddy yard. The woman was screaming and cursing and hitting him, but he wouldn't let her go. After a few good slaps and squeezes in the right places, she apparently told him what he wanted to know. Tommy hauled her by the ear over to the repair shop and they entered through a side door. Ralph heard two rifle shots cannonade inside the big metal building. He'd been terrified that Tommy may have been shot, that he might be next. But a moment later the enormous overhead door opened and Tommy walked out unscathed, holding the woman's ear in one hand, and Terry Mcilhaney's pant cuffs in the other. He dragged the limp man over to Ralph's truck with his head bouncing over the rough ground the whole way. Mcilhaney's face was covered in bright red blood. It was badly bruised and cut, and his nose terribly broken. He must have made Tommy angry when he shot at him. Tommy let go of Mcilhaney's pant leg and kicked him in the ribs. Twice.

A white pickup truck was parked inside the shop. Tommy told Ralph to drive it outside and close the shop door. Ralph did what he was told while Tommy kept an eye on his prisoners. Then Tommy told Ralph to clean out the sluice box with Terry. Ralph and Terry loaded two stacks of five gallon pails and a couple of shovels into the back of Ralph's truck, then drove it over to the wash plant. Terry was groaning and whining during the short drive and Ralph told him not to drip any blood in his truck. Tommy tossed the tall skinny woman into the white truck and followed them.

Ralph had never seen so many gold nuggets in a sluice box. He could see places between the riffles where someone had already been digging with their fingers, no doubt helping themselves to some nice pieces. Terry told Ralph that after he'd looked in the sluice box last evening, he'd sent his whole crew off to town. He said he'd wanted to clean up the sluice box this morning – by himself. Terry said he'd been concerned about theft. He said that Tommy didn't believe him. Ralph didn't believe him either.

Tommy watched Ralph and Terry take the good part of an hour to shovel all the gravel and gold out of the sluice box into the pails. Terry was now bleeding badly. He was slurring through missing teeth and a broken jaw, kept complaining that he couldn't see because his eyes were swollen shut. Tommy kept telling him to shut up. Terry handed the pails from the sluice box down to Ralph, who loaded them into the back of his truck. Now and again Ralph looked over at the tall, skinny woman beside Terry's white truck.

Tommy had zipped her ski jacket up to the collar and tied its hood tightly over her head, then holding her arms behind her back, had yanked the sleeves down over her hands. Then he'd slammed the front door of Terry's truck over the ends of the sleeves, and locked the doors. She'd been screaming and cursing and kicking the door of the truck with her heels ever since, struggling to escape. Whenever Tommy got tired of her screaming and cursing, he'd walk over to the truck and slap her on the head. After Tommy hit her the fourth time, she'd sunk to her knees, kneeled down in the mud, and started to cry.

* * *

Ralph squinted through his wet, muddy windshield at the white pickup truck ahead. Terry Mcilhaney was at the wheel, the tall skinny woman sat in the center, and Tommy – even with his massive shoulders and torso – had managed to squeeze in on the passenger side. When the slow moving truck crested the ridge at the top of the Thistle Creek valley, it stopped for a moment, then turned right and disappeared into the fog. Ralph had his instructions. He turned left. He climbed up and over a short hill that overlooked the steep valley on the other side, then drove two hundred feet along the top of the ridge to the first corner. He pulled over, turned the engine off, and waited. He thought he heard a noise from somewhere behind him. It sounded like a 'boom' but he couldn't be sure, not with all the windows up.

Five minutes later Ralph saw Tommy appear in his rear view mirror. Tommy rose over the top of the hill with his great bulk ominously silhouetted against the mist, his massive arms splayed out at his sides, swinging his thick legs around one another as he lumbered down the road toward Ralph's truck. Tommy stopped once to brush some mud off his track pants, then resumed his casual pace down the hill. Tommy cast an aura of immense power and presence when he walked. He reminded Ralph of a big male grizzly bear in the fall, overfed and content, sauntering along, going nowhere in particular, not in a hurry, not a care in the world. Like a big alpha grizzly bear, Tommy was king of his physical domain. And like a big alpha grizzly bear, he knew it.

Tommy got into Ralph's truck without a word. He was breathing normally and absolutely calm. It was nine o'clock in the morning.

Ralph pulled back on the road and they headed toward town. A few moments later Ralph thought he heard a helicopter, but couldn't see anything with all the fog and mist surrounding them. When they reached the Klondike Highway, Ralph turned left and headed west to Dawson. The drizzle had stopped and the ceiling was lifting. Ralph thought that it might turn out to be a nice day, in spite of its somber start.

"What should I do with what's in those pails?" Ralph asked Tommy.

"Clean it, melt it, pay the royalties, put it in briefcases. Tomorrow it gets shipped. Get it done."

"You know, Mr. Kay, all those nuggets in those pails can be sold for jewelry. You could get twice their gold value by weight if you sold them individually to collectors and jewelers, just so you know."

"I said melt it," Tommy said, staring straight ahead.

"Okay. You're the boss," Ralph said, sighing with resignation, trying hard to suppress his disappointment.

Tommy looked at Ralph like a lizard would look at a bug. Ralph regretted having stated the obvious.

Twenty minutes later they were driving down a muddy street in Dawson. Ralph pulled over and stopped in front of Tommy's hotel. Tommy got out of the truck and looked at Ralph.

"Buy all the gold you can find around here. Put it in briefcases. We'll take it all. It ships out tomorrow with what's in the back of the truck. Pick me up here in an hour. I need a ride to the airport."

Tommy slammed the door.

FORTY TWO

We were lying in the narrow bed in the apartment over my shop, holding onto each other lest we fall out, panting like we'd just reached the summit of some Himalayan mountain and were out of oxygen.

"You know I can't do this every ten hours," I said, breathing in gulps with my heart pounding.

"Why not. Don't you like it?"

"Of course I like it. My point is I'm not twenty anymore."

"Could have fooled me."

"Well don't be fooled."

She looked into my eyes. What eyes she had. She owned me with those eyes.

"So is it Cameron?" she asked.

"What?"

"Your name. The 'C'. Does it stand for Cameron?"

"No, it doesn't stand for Cameron. And I told you already, I'm not telling you what the 'C' stands for. So stop asking. Brody is my name. Call me Brody and I'll know who you're talking to."

"Wait, I know, it's Charles, isn't it? Charles Brody. That's a very nice name. Is it Charles?" She smiled at me with her eyebrows raised, beckoning a confirmation. Evidently she enjoyed teasing me.

"It is *not* Charles," I said. "Now quit with your guessing."

"Okay, then how about Carey?" This time she laughed.

I was too uncomfortable in the little bed anyway, so on that cue rolled out and went into the bathroom. Hopefully that would end the interrogation. Cops and their questions. I guess being nosy is in their DNA. I had a one minute shower without closing the door.

"It's all yours," I said, wandering around the little room, being careful not to hit my head on a rafter, trying to locate the clean clothes I'd been wearing when she dragged me upstairs.

"Hey, how about Cedric? Is it Cedric?" She was sitting up in the bed, cross legged without a stitch on, smiling and studying me as I got dressed. I suppose if I had her body, I wouldn't be modest either.

"Hey yourself," I said, trying to keep my eyes from wandering while zipping up my blue jeans. "And stop with the personal questions. You told me in Dawson you'd tell me everything I wanted to know about you as soon as we got to Minto. But every time I ask you a question, you just clam up. So why should I answer any of yours?"

"Wait a minute," she said. "Let's get our facts straight. What I said to you in Dawson was that I'd tell you everything you wanted to know as soon as we got to Juneau. Not to Minto. This is Minto."

"Sarah, please. What's the difference?" Though I knew she was kidding me, I was still frustrated with her reticence. I thought I'd better get out of there before saying something stupid. She was suddenly quiet and brooding. I buttoned my shirt, pulled on my socks, and walked over to my boots. I could feel her eyes but kept my back to her and opened the door.

"I'll be downstairs," was all I said when I stepped out on the landing and looked down the stairs. Russ and Jack were at the bottom, wagging their tails like they hadn't seen me for two days.

"Brody, wait."

I turned and looked back.

"Come here and I'll tell you something about myself," she said.

I walked to the end of the bed. Her countenance had completely changed. She looked scared, like a kid about to dive off a ten meter platform for the first time. She'd pulled up a sheet and had it wrapped around her shoulders, as if suddenly needing protection. I waited her out and said nothing. She took a deep breath and exhaled, staring at the end of the bed.

"Okay. I'll tell you something about myself. Here goes." After a long pause she said, "I hate commuting so I live right downtown in D.C. I walk to work every day, rain or shine. I'm thirty seven years old, single, never been married. I have an eighteen year old daughter who I raised myself. She starts university in the fall. I got drunk at the Christmas party last year and went to bed with Stanley Kurtz. Just the once. I hadn't had a drink since then, not until I had that glass of wine on your deck two nights ago. My brother was an FBI agent, he was working undercover for us when he was murdered in that plane we found. I hadn't spoken to him for almost twenty years when I called him three weeks ago. I went to Juneau last week to visit him even though I knew he might not be there, but I got to meet his wife and kids for the first time. I hated my brother forever because of something he did a long time ago, now I hate him for dying on me like that, before we had a chance to make amends." She paused and took a breath. "So how's that for a start Brody? How's that for a couple of issues? There are more if you have time. Do you want to hear some more?"

I stood on wobbly legs, trying to process everything she'd just said, admiring her courage, realizing she actually must trust me and appreciating her frustration. She really hadn't owed me any of the ignoble details about her life. I suddenly felt guilty about what had just occurred. I walked around to the side of the bed, sat down and put my arm around her.

"Actually I do have a question."

"What?" she asked, with misty eyes.

"Are you hungry?"

"Famished," she said, now with tears running down her cheeks. She punched me in the chest with the side of her fist, then put her head against my shoulder. "Damn you, Brody, or whatever your name is."

* * *

While Sarah was in the shower I rummaged around downstairs for a knife to replace the one the cops had confiscated, for *evidence*. I guess they thought that without my favorite knife to wave around in court, their case against Ricky Constanzia would be weak. I found a suitable replacement in my tool box, sharpened it on the bench grinder, and put it in my holster. You can't fly a float plane without a sharp knife.

As long as the shower was running there was an opportunity to do a little work. I picked up a tire gauge off the bench and dragged the compressed air hose out to Sarah's car. I checked her tire pressures, cleaned her windshield and filled up the windshield washer reservoir with the water hose outside. It had all been a good idea. One of her tires had needed a little air and her washer reservoir took a lot of water. I repeated the same service on my truck. I've always felt that doing even the little things to maintain your equipment pays big dividends. It's also a great way to kill time and I've always preferred puttering to drinking and talking, though there are people out there who accuse me of simply being anti-social. Whatever, I suppose it's a question of perspective.

I walked over to Daryl's cruiser and got in. It started but ran rough. I turned it off, then turned the key back to the ignition position so the electric fuel pump would run. I lifted the hood and grabbed a rag, unscrewed the cap off the fuel injector rail, and with the rag held over the end, pressed the valve. I held the valve open until the rag was soaked with fuel, then released the valve. I got back in the car and waited for the fuel pump to pressurize the fuel rail again, then started the engine. It still ran rough. I revved the engine a few times and left it idling. If water in the fuel had been why it was running poorly, then it should run better in a few minutes, after the gas anti-freeze worked its magic. I checked the car's tire pressures while waiting. One needed a shot of air. All of a sudden Daryl's car began idling smoothly. I threw the gas soaked rag in a barrel I use to burn trash. I walked back into the shop dragging the air hose behind me, coiled it up, and hung it on the wall. There was still no sign of Sarah, so I washed my hands in the sink and got into Daryl's car. I drove it down the road to my cabin, turned around, and put my foot to the floor a few times on the way back. The car ran great again. I could spin the tires and spit out long plumes of gravel, just like the cops in the movies. Daryl could catch speeding tourists again in his powerful highway cruiser. I put his keys in the usual place, under the drivers mat, and locked his car. With my finger I scrawled 'Ready' in the layer of dust on the driver's window.

There was still no sign of Sarah but I could hear my hair dryer running, so decided to do a bit of cleaning around the shop. I knew as soon as I got my hands dirty again she'd come downstairs. I was right. I'd just picked up her old brake rotors when I heard her feet on the stairs. I carried the rotors outside and dropped them in the scrap metal bin, then went back inside to wash my hands again. She was emptying the dryer beside me and seemed to be enjoying the process of revisiting with her clothes. She was removing them one at a time, holding each one out at arm's length for a judicious inspection before a careful folding. I stood at the sink, watching the exercise with great apprehension, waiting for the verdict.

After an interminable period of silence I decided to take the initiative. With a towel in my hands I asked, "Well, how did I do?"

"Oh, you did an excellent job. Thank you very much," she said. I hadn't felt such a welling of pride since I was a boy, not since my mother and I won the three-legged race at the county fair.

"Are they dry?" I asked.

"Yeah, they're dry."

Amazing. I made a mental note of how long her clothes had been in the dryer. I'd have to remember to turn the dials back to where they belonged. The little dial had to go back to 'regular', and the big dial had to go back to 'timed dry'. Otherwise the dryer would run for two days the next time I used it.

"Ready to eat? I know this great little place up the road with food that really sticks to your ribs."

"I'm ready. Let's go," she said, carrying a neat little pile of laundry out to her car. I was relieved that she didn't seem to be concerned with the idea of going to the café for breakfast. She opened the trunk and stowed her clothes carefully in her big backpack.

"I'll drive," I said.

"Oh. I'm taking my car," she said. "You take yours. I'm going to hit the road after I eat."

"Are you sure? We're both coming back this way."

"Look, it's nothing personal Brody, it's about *optics*. I need to be seen arriving at the café alone, in my own car, and leaving the café alone, in my own car."

I nodded. "Okay. Understand. I'll be right behind you. Just got to tie up the dogs."

On my way back into the shop, I tried not to reveal how depressed I was.

FORTY THREE

Twenty minutes later we walked into the café. As usual Minnie was sitting on her stool behind the counter. She generally greets me the same way every time I walk in, and today wasn't going to be any different. Things were about to get loud.

Minnie looked up from some paper work. It took her a second to recognize who I was standing beside. Then her eyes got huge.

"Brody!"

"Minnie!" I reciprocated.

"You're alright!"

"I'm fine!"

That was typically all the bellowing it took for Minnie to greet me in her own special way. My arrival had been duly announced to everyone in the place. Now we could sit down.

Seating was rarely at a premium in the Minto café at eleven o'clock on a Thursday morning. Three of the boys from the highway department were drinking coffee at a table along the left wall. On the other side of the room an elderly couple was eating breakfast. They probably owned the camper with Iowa plates I'd parked beside. I was surprised to see no one seated at the front window.

"Over here," I said to Sarah, nudging her with a bump of my elbow, steering her toward my favorite table, a table for two on the right wall, just this side of the couple from Iowa. A table for two was what I'd really wanted, but Sarah had her own idea of where she wanted to sit.

"Let's sit here in the sun," she said. "How about this one?"

She wanted to sit on the fifty yard line. She wanted to sit at the most coveted table in the Minto cafe, the one situated dead center beside the biggest front window. It was only an old mica-top chrome legged table with four chrome chairs, but it had an expansive view of the parking lot, and the gas pumps. Was today our lucky day or what? I shrugged.

"Okay," I said. "We can sit here."

"Which side do you want?" she asked.

"Well," I said, "that's a decision you really ought to make. See, if you sit on that side, you'll have to constantly stare down those three guys sitting at that table over there against the wall, but if you sit on this side, then you'll be undergoing a thorough appraisal of your rear end for the next half hour. So you decide."

"I think I'll let them appraise my rear end," she said with a chuckle. "You can field their questions at the press conference after I'm gone."

I had to smile. She followed my lead and tossed her backpack and jacket on the chair next to the window. We sat down on the outside chairs. Hopefully that would discourage any one from joining us. I just wanted to eat and have another half hour alone with Sarah Marsalis. Fat chance.

Minnie predictably arrived at our table seconds after we'd gotten comfortable. With one hand she effortlessly swung a chair out from a table behind her and plunked it down between us.

"My word, you *are* S. Marsalis," she said. "You own that car that Daryl crashed into the pole out there last Sunday, don't you?" Sarah nodded and smiled. Minnie sat her enormous bulk down and put her hand over Sarah's.

"You're even prettier up close, honey. Is everything alright now? I'm so sorry about what happened to your car. Is Brody treating you well? He can be very charming but he's very strong minded, you know. You have to be very careful with independent men like him, but I'm sure you know that. You be sure to tell me if he starts giving you any trouble, okay?" Minnie gave Sarah's hand a pat.

I shook my head and rolled my eyes. Sarah smiled at Minnie with genuine warmth and nodded in agreement.

"Minnie, meet Sarah. Sarah, meet Minnie." I stood up.

"Brody, sit down," Minnie said without looking at me. I obeyed and sat down. "Do you want something to eat, hon? You look like you could use a proper meal."

"I think we both want breakfast," Sarah said, smiling at me.

"Leah!" Minnie bellowed over her shoulder in the direction of the kitchen.

"Hey, Minnie," I said. "I brought you something from Dawson."

"Fish?"

"No. Tomorrow I'll have fish. But today I brought you this." I reached into my pack and pulled out the loaf of Deb's soda bread.

"Well thank you, that's so very sweet of you. Would you like some of *my* toasted soda bread with *your* breakfast?" she asked with blatant sarcasm.

"Gee, that would be great, Minnie, thanks."

Leah arrived at the table with a pen and an order pad in her hand, looking as unenthusiastic about life as any eighteen year old could possibly be. I think Leah's fantasy is to elope with a tall dark stranger driving a fancy new sports car and leave the Minto café behind with the wheels spinning. I stood again and told Leah to make my usual breakfast. Minnie didn't try to stop me from leaving the table this time. I walked behind the counter at the back of the dining room and grabbed a couple of printed forms from a stack beside the radios. Leah walked past me on her way to the kitchen with my loaf of soda bread. On my way back to the table I stopped and had a brief chat with the boys from the highway department. I asked them nicely if they would stop staring at Sarah's rear end. They denied they had been. Then I asked them about the weather forecast. Highway guys are always up to date on the weather. I went and sat down with the women again. They seemed to have lots to talk about and were chuckling away. They ignored me and I ignored them. I was suddenly in a better mood anyway. I filled out two flight advisories – one for today and one for tomorrow – and slid them over to Minnie. She picked them up and scanned them both.

"You're going to Whitehorse? Right now, today?"

"I am, need anything in town?"

"This says only one soul is on board to Whitehorse today," Minnie said, giving me a suspicious look, then one for Sarah who was gazing out the window at the gas pumps.

"That's right. Sarah's driving her car to Whitehorse."

"I see," said Minnie, looking at Sarah again, hoping for an explanation. None was offered. "Is that little car of yours safe to drive now, Miss Sarah? Did Brody here fix it for you?"

"Minnie, my car's never been safer, it has brand new brakes," she said, smiling warmly.

"Well that's good, hon. By the way, Daryl left for town about an hour ago, so you can speed halfway to Carmacks if you want."

Sarah looked puzzled.

"Carmacks is the next town down the road," I said. "It's about forty miles south of here. They've got their own cop. But without Daryl patrolling his section of the highway today, you can drive as fast as you want down to Five Finger Rapids, that's about twenty miles from here. That's where Daryl's territory ends and the Carmacks cop takes over."

"I see," she said. "Well, I think I'll be taking my time and obeying the speed limit all the way to Whitehorse, but thanks for the tip."

Minnie stood up and grabbed my two completed flight advisories. "I'll get you my grocery list, Brody."

"Hey, Minnie?"

"What hon?"

"Could you give me a check for those canoes? I'm going to try to pick up a couple of them today in Whitehorse. Oh, and could you leave the check blank?"

"Blank? Why blank? What are you up to?"

"Minnie, trust me, okay?"

She gave me a long dead pan stare that any cop would be proud of, then said, "Trust you?" After another long stern look she said, "Okay, but I want a receipt from Chief Dan. And you and me have some catching up to do when you get back, *Mister*." Minnie turned and marched back to the counter.

Leah arrived with our breakfast plates and a stack of heavily buttered soda bread toast on a separate plate.

"Thanks, Leah."

"Okay," she said. "Hey Brody? We cleaned your plane last night, just so you know."

"Oh, great. Thanks for doing that, Leah. I'll pay Reggie when I see him in the village. If you're talking to him, tell him I'll be over there in half an hour."

She hesitated, then said, "Well, actually, Reggie didn't help clean the plane. He was watching the hockey game in the bar. I got a friend to help me."

"Oh, is that right? Then I guess I should pay you, Leah. How much do I owe you and your friend?"

"Reggie said eighty."

"Eighty, huh? Tell you what, let's make it a hundred. Because I really appreciate you and your friend going out to the lake and doing that for me on such short notice."

"Thanks," she said, suppressing a smile when I put the cash in her hand. I could swear Leah had a bounce in her step when she left our table.

"That was generous of you," Sarah whispered.

"Not really. The deal I made with Reggie last night was for *him* to clean my plane for a hundred dollars. But I guess he contracted the job out to his little sister for eighty dollars, then went to the bar to drink his profit and watch the hockey game."

"Oh."

"Is that the kind of thing your brother did to make you so mad at him for all those years?"

"No, not even close. What my brother did was somewhat more egregious." She glared at me for a second, then to emphasize her point gave me a good kick in the shin. I winced, but resisted the urge to rub it. She glared at me some more. I broke down and rubbed my shin.

"Sorry."

"Me too."

We were hungry. We ate our breakfasts. In ten minutes we'd cleaned our plates and the toasted soda bread was history. We were feeling better.

"Hey, Brody? Why were you high-fiving one of those guys at that table behind me?"

"Oh. Coyotes won last night. Series is tied."

"What coyotes?"

"The *Phoenix* Coyotes. They're my hockey team."

"Oh. That's the game you were watching last night. But then you turned it off."

"Yeah. Something came up." I grinned at her.

She grinned back. "You are so corny," she said, shaking her head. She looked around, then said, "About Charlie and his boy, when will you…"

"Sarah, everything's under control, okay? Trust me. And you're going to look after…"

"Yes. I said I would, and I will. Trust me."

We gazed at each other for awhile. I guess we were both contemplating that concept. *Trust.*

After a while she said, "Hey, know what?"

"What?"

"That thing you told me about rubbing salt on a mosquito bite?"

"Yeah?"

"It works."

"I know it works."

"Where did you learn that? Is that local knowledge?"

"Nope. Just knowledge."

She nodded. I finished my coffee. We looked at each other for a long time. All of a sudden there wasn't anything to talk about.

She slid her chair back, stood and said, "Breakfast is on me. I'll be back in a moment, excuse me."

She walked past the meeting of the Minto Highway Department, still in progress, and headed down the hall leading to the pay phone. She was wearing those tight blue jeans from the day I'd met her, and a snug fitting white T – shirt. Every man in the place had his eyes locked on those jeans, even the old fellow driving the camper with Iowa plates. I wondered why her jeans never seemed to wrinkle or sag. Mine always loosen up after a couple of hours. Maybe hers were made out of some high tech material. Maybe she'd been fitted by the boys in the white coats who worked in the labs at Quantico. My thoughts drifted to what I was supposed to do in Haines tomorrow.

When Sarah came out of the hall five minutes later she stopped in front of Minnie and they chatted for a minute. Sarah pulled some cash out of her front pocket and paid for our breakfasts. I was a little surprised when Minnie got off her stool and walked around the counter. The two women embraced as if they'd known each other for years. Then Sarah walked back to our table. She didn't sit down, though.

"Here's Minnie's shopping list," she said, dropping a folded piece of paper in front of me. She reached over and grabbed her jacket and backpack off the chair. She slung them both over her shoulder. She stood in front of the table, looking down at me with her back to the room, and took a deep breath.

"Please do not get up. I'm going now. Don't leave here for at least ten minutes. Optics. Remember?"

"Right. Optics." I looked up at her from my chair for a long time. "So you're really going?"

"Yes. I'm really going. Thank you for everything you did for me." She paused a second, swallowed, then said, "I'm going to miss listening to the river when I go to sleep tonight. And your dogs too."

Her eyes were moist. She extended her hand out to me. We shook hands.

"Good luck tomorrow, *Mr. Brody*," was the last thing she said to me.

Then she turned and walked out of the café. I watched her walk across the parking lot. When she got to her little green Corolla, she opened the door, threw her stuff on the passenger seat, and got in. She closed the door, started the engine, backed up, and rolled out to the highway. She stopped, looked left and right, and drove away.

From the time she'd left the table to the time she turned onto the Klondike Highway, she never looked back. Not once.

Optics.

She was gone.

FORTY FOUR

My plane thumped and skipped over the choppy waves until I pulled the yoke back. Then it leapt off the lake like it was running up a ramp. Taking off in an empty Beaver is always fun because it can climb so fast.

DeHavilland's objective when it conceived the Beaver was to build a *short take off and landing* bush plane, or as it's called in the acronym rich vernacular of aviation, a 'STOL' plane. With four hundred and fifty horsepower, the Beaver is a powerful plane that can take off and land at low speeds, and fly in and out of confined spaces on steep angles. In other words, it can take off and land in places where others can't.

But there's a price to pay with the thick high-lift wings employed on STOL aircraft: high aerodynamic drag and low straight line speed. So the disadvantage of every STOL aircraft is that once they're in the air, they can't fly very fast. The irony of wilderness aviation has always been that even with long distances to cover, you need to use a slow airplane so you can land at your destination.

Even so, the DeHavilland Beaver revolutionized the speed and ease at which people and cargo could be transported in and out of remote places. As one old bush pilot told a DeHavilland engineer during the Beaver's design phase, "it only has to be faster than a dog sled."

In three minutes I climbed three thousand feet, then retracted the flaps, eased the throttle back, adjusted the fuel mixture and the prop pitch, reduced my climb angle, and continued heading straight into a brisk southwest wind.

I scanned my gauges. Not only was every indicator where it ought to be, but the whole console was clean and shiny. So was the rest of the interior. Gone were all those white powdery fingerprint patches that I'd found so irritating. Leah and her friend had done an outstanding job of cleaning the interior of my pride and joy. I'd have to congratulate them.

It was a little before one o'clock in the afternoon and turning out to be a beautiful day. Visibility was unlimited, as they say in weather speak, which means the air was crystal clear and there wasn't a cloud in the sky. The boys from the highway department had been right. A high pressure system was building over the Yukon and should dominate the weather for the next several days. What a day for flying.

I know my way to Whitehorse – I've flown there from Minto hundreds of times – but ignored the compass and my usual heading today. Whitehorse is almost due south of Minto, but with a strong wind blowing out of the southwest, my plane would be drifting east, so I was in no hurry to turn south yet. Instead, I kept the nose pointed straight at Klaza mountain, elevation six thousand feet, forty miles southwest of me on the eastern end of the Dawson Mountain Range. A few minutes later, and a hundred miles beyond Klaza Mountain, the snow capped peaks of the St. Elias Mountain Range began to rise out of Kluane National Park. Now there's a mountain range. In a word, they're *high*. The St. Elias Mountains are young, rugged, steep and still rising, still getting pushed up another couple of inches every year by the Pacific Plate. I climbed for another five minutes, still heading southwest, until the star of the show appeared through the prop.

Mount Logan.

Logan is Canada's highest mountain at over twenty thousand feet, yet it's just forty miles from the Pacific Ocean. Instead of

Kluane National Park, I think they should have called it 'Tectonics' National Park.

When I reached an altitude of seven thousand feet, I leveled out, trimmed the elevator for level flight, and set a cruising airspeed of a hundred and ten miles an hour. I took one last opportunity to admire Mount Logan – cloaked in brilliant new snow and sparkling in the sun – then started a shallow left turn toward Carmacks, thirty miles south.

Carmacks is the only place in the Yukon where the Klondike Highway crosses the Yukon River. Remarkably, the vehicle bridge at Carmacks is one of only four bridges on the entire two thousand mile Yukon River. In comparison, the only slightly longer Mississippi River has two hundred and twenty bridges.

Other than having a good steel bridge for cars and trucks to cross the Yukon River, Carmacks is just one of those sleepy little Yukon towns where not much happens. It has a cop, a dirt airstrip, a hotel and a bar, a campground, a variety store, and a gas station. Otherwise it's like any other non-descript community on the Klondike Highway, just a place with a name that merits a dot on a Yukon road map.

About fifteen miles north of Carmacks I looked down to my left at four rock columns sticking out of the Yukon River. They looked like little islands from the air, splitting the river into five fast flowing channels, hence the name of the infamous river mark, Five Finger Rapids.

The rapids are the only real challenge to navigation on the Yukon River between Whitehorse and Dawson. In the bygone era of steam powered travel on the river, the big paddle wheelers used giant winches mounted on their foredecks to pull themselves up through the rapids. Many ships were badly damaged on the short trip through the fingers, and one scuttled steamer still sits exactly where it met it's fate years ago, now lying semi-submerged downstream, its hull torn apart, rotting away in the shallows.

Friends of mine who are avid kayakers tell me that any novice canoeist can safely negotiate Five Finger Rapids, provided they use the far right channel on the east bank. My friends also tell me that the far left channel on the west side of the river is almost impossible to navigate by anyone who's not an expert white water kayaker. I looked straight down at the rapids as I headed toward Carmacks. My kayaking friends were right. I could clearly make out white water on the finger closest to me, the west channel, and darker water on the far side, the east channel. White and dangerous or dark and calm, it's all cold water to me. So no thanks, not interested.

My thoughts drifted back to Sarah Marsalis. I wondered if she'd broken the speed limit driving her little car down to Five Finger Rapids. I wondered if she'd pulled over to look down at them from the highway lookout. It depressed me to think she'd actually left. I missed her more than I wanted to admit. I wondered if she'd ever call me. She promised she would. But talk is cheap. Emotions and the best of intentions fade with time.

Time would tell.

FORTY FIVE

It was a quarter after two when I landed on Schwatka Lake, the flooded section of the Yukon River above the Whitehorse power dam. Schwatka Lake is the float plane aerodrome for the city of Whitehorse. It's also the very place where over the past year I'd been delivering hundreds of pounds of fish, and million dollars of cash, to Charlie Woo. Today I had no fish or cash on board, but as agreed on the phone, Charlie was waiting at the wharf. I docked my plane and we got in his truck and headed to town.

With a population of over thirty thousand people, Whitehorse is the biggest little government town in Canada. Politicians have never liked living in places where people work hard and produce things, so in 1953 they moved the capital of the Yukon from Dawson to Whitehorse. Since then, the evolution and growth of Whitehorse is a bit about history, a bit about politics, but mostly about sovereignty.

Americans comprised the majority of gold seekers who came to the Yukon in 1898. They built and operated most of the steam powered paddle wheelers that plied the Yukon River and opened up the Klondike. They built and operated the enormous dredges that mined the Klondike River valley for over sixty years. In 1901, the Americans completed the White Pass Railroad, a remarkable feat of engineering, built to carry men and machines from the town of

Skagway on the Pacific coast, inland to the Yukon and Whitehorse. In 1942, the US Army blazed a seventeen hundred mile trail from British Columbia, across the Yukon, and into Alaska. They named their rudimentary dirt road the Alaska Highway. It too was a remarkable achievement, built in less than a year to provide an alternate supply route for the defense of Alaska against a potential Japanese invasion. Although three quarters of the Alaska Highway is in Canada, and runs straight through the city of Whitehorse, the US government wouldn't hand over control of *their* highway until years after the Second World War ended. Ever since, there's been an overt yet undeclared mandate of the Canadian government to re-establish and maintain sovereignty over its Yukon Territory. These days, Canada's federal government continues to pour millions of dollars annually into the Yukon and the City of Whitehorse, for no other reason than to ensure that Canadians occupy their territory.

Money. Population. Occupation.

Optics.

With all that money flowing in, Whitehorse has grown into a vibrant little city with a buoyant economy, dependent almost solely on three well funded governments for its livelihood. If you happen to be in Whitehorse today, and you're not employed by the city government, the territorial government or the federal government, then you're probably just passing through town, or still in school.

"First stop is Main Street, Charlie." I handed him Minnie's shopping list and a couple of hundred dollars. "See you at the Kayak Store around four, okay?"

Charlie nodded. He drove slowly but competently down Fourth Avenue. Most of the streets in Whitehorse are paved and quiet to drive on. Its sidewalks are concrete or brick. I kind of missed Dawson.

Charlie stopped at the traffic light at the corner of Fourth and Main and let me out. I watched him drive off, then walked back to the Whitehorse detachment of the RCMP. It was a much, *much* bigger building than the one in Dawson, a long three story box with cop cars parked all around it. Behind the building a tall steel radio tower rose into the sky like a steeple. The tower was littered with satellite dishes and all kinds of weird looking antennae. The cop business must be good in Whitehorse.

I walked in the front door and asked a bored looking woman at a reception desk where I might find Staff Sergeant Robson. The woman made me fill out a visitor register, then pointed at a walk-through metal detector at the end of a hall to her left. She put me through the regular airport routine – the 'remove your belt and all loose change and metallic objects from your pockets' deal – then asked me to walk through the scanner. She swept a beeping wand up and down and all over me a few times. She took my knife and searched my backpack.

"Please don't forget to pick up your knife on your way out, sir. Go to the end of the hall and take the elevator to the third floor."

Elevator. Third Floor. Big city.

I pressed the button on the elevator. While I was waiting, two giant cops packing handguns on their hips tried to stare me down as they walked past me. They disappeared into an office. There'd be no stealing staplers in this place.

I got out of the elevator and walked out into an open reception area and over to a long counter. A short barrel-shaped woman in a black and white polka dot dress was standing with her back to me. She was shuffling stacks of papers on a long table. She turned around and looked directly at me, then turned her back and continued with her paper shuffling.

I gave her thirty seconds then cleared my throat and said, "Good afternoon Mme., perhaps you could help me? I'm here to see Staff Sergeant Robson."

"I saw you, sir, I'll be with you in a moment," the woman replied in a bored tone without looking at me. She worked on her paperwork for another full minute before stomping up to her side of the counter, stopping opposite me. "May I tell the Staff Sergeant who you are and what this concerns, sir?" she asked impatiently, breathing hard, brushing invisible dirt off her hands on the hips of her polka dot dress. I could picture her wearing a hard hat.

"My name is Brody," I said. "He'll know what this concerns."

"I'm afraid Staff Sergeant Robson is a very busy man, Mr. Brody. Perhaps you could tell me precisely what the nature of your business is, and I'll see if he's available."

I leaned over the counter, got in close to her face and whispered, "Well, this morning when I went out to my pickup truck, I saw this cardboard box sitting in the back. Well I sure didn't put it there, it sure as heck wasn't mine, so I opened it up and looked inside. Guess what was inside the box?"

"What was in the box, sir?"

I looked around, then back at her. "A human head," I whispered.

"A human head," she said with a deadpan stare she must have learned by hanging around cops.

"That's right, a human head," I whispered again, nodding.

She inhaled deeply and looked at me with disdain, then said, "Wait here."

She walked all the way down the hall and disappeared around the corner at the far end. I was fiddling with my cell phone when she returned five minutes later.

"Follow me, sir," she said curtly, breathing really hard now. She turned and headed back down the hall. I followed at a safe distance, not wanting to get clubbed by one of her wildly swinging arms. When we got to the end of the hall, we turned right and continued all the way to the end of the building. She stopped at the last door on the left, knocked twice, opened the door, and motioned for me to enter. I did. She stomped off without a word.

Robson was on the phone when I walked in. He glared up at me from behind his adequate dark wood desk and pointed to a chair in front of him. Instead of sitting down I walked over to a big window with a great view of the city and the mountains to the east.

"Tell Ottawa to keep us posted," he growled into the phone and hung up.

"Nice office you got here, Staff Sergeant."

"What do you want, Mr. Brody? And I said sit down."

"Thought I'd hand deliver my invoice to the man who hired my plane on the river a couple of days ago." I ceremoniously placed the envelope containing my invoice on the corner of his desk, then tapped it with a finger. I sat down.

He grabbed and opened the envelope, pulled out my invoice, scanned it for a second, then dropped it in his 'out' basket.

"I asked you what you wanted."

"Oh, I was wondering if you know a man named Dan Belanger. He lives here in Whitehorse, walks around town with a frilly moose hide jacket, works with…"

"I know who he is, what's your interest in him?"

"You know who he is?"

"I asked you a question."

"Right," I said. "Well, I'm just wondering about him because I think he's trying to rip off the Minto band on some canoes they want to buy. Thought you might give me some…insight on how I might deal with that situation."

"How about I tell you all about Mr. Belanger after I ask you a few questions?"

"Okay. Like what?"

"Like where do you think Terry Mcilhaney is hiding?"

"I have no idea. How would I know that?"

"Because you know him."

"Not really. I saw him yesterday on a street in Dawson. I might have met him once a couple of years ago. But you can hardly say I know him, didn't even know his last name until last night."

"Is that so?"

"Yes. That's so."

"And how about that woman he was with. Do you know where she might be hiding?"

"That woman named Rose Rivera? No. Don't know her and don't have a clue where she might be hiding. Why would I?"

"You know her name," Robson said.

"Yeah, I was told her name last night."

Robson briefly pondered my answer, then said, "You and your

new lady friend, that Special Agent Marsalis, you're quite the couple now, aren't you?"

"What's that supposed to mean?"

"It means you two seem to be sharing everything lately."

"What's your point Robson, I mean Staff Sergeant Robson, sir?"

"My point is that you probably know too much right now for your own good. Now, you're sure you don't know where this woman, this Rose Rivera, or this man Terry McIhaney, where either of them might be hiding?"

"I already told you. No. Haven't got a clue."

Robson nodded. "You know, Mr. Brody, we have a very serious situation developing in the Yukon right now. And it can't be allowed to continue or it could get out of control."

"What's *the* situation?" I asked.

He leaned back and folded his arms. "We think there are two organized crime syndicates up here going hard at each other for control of something, at least that's the way it looks to us. And we don't want things to escalate. That's *the* situation."

"Escalate?"

"Yes. Escalate. Meaning more murders, more missing people, more kidnappings. We're not dealing with a bunch of street punks here. It's never pretty when two criminal syndicates decide to go to war, and it's often the beginning of the end for a nice community. Everyone, and I mean everyone loses something in an organized crime fight, even when they're not directly affected or involved." He let me consider that concept for a moment, then said, "Do you have any idea what a surge in violent crime does to the price of real estate? The public trust that's taken out of communities and neighborhoods? How it changes the way people behave and go about their daily business? Especially in a nice place to live like we have up here? So no, we definitely don't want any more murders or kidnappings around here, now do we?"

"Well, no."

"*No* is the right answer," he said, leaning forward and putting his hands on the desk, giving me his cop stare again.

"Bobby Larabie," I said to him.

"What about him?"

"Is he safe, are you protecting him?"

"He's safe. We've got someone watching him twenty four hours a day. At great expense to taxpayers, I might add. He won't be abducted again though, that's for sure. And…"

"And?"

Robson paused and appraised my clothes and weathered ball cap. "And from now on, you're going to be sharing everything with me – and I mean everything – everything that you see, hear or even think might help us nip this little crime spree in the bud, got that?" Robson leaned over his desk and slid his personal business card over to me. He tapped it with a thick finger.

I picked up the card and looked at it. "Yeah," I said. "Sure."

"Good," he said. "And by the way, the dumbest thing you did this week, and you've done some pretty dumb things, was walk into this building today."

"How's that?"

"Because if you're being watched you're as good as made now, and I would sincerely hope you have a fully paid life insurance policy for your loved ones."

"No one's watching me."

"I hope not. But in case you're wrong about that, I'll have you escorted out the back of the building when we're done here." A wry grin spread over his face. "Now then, what are you doing tomorrow?"

"Flying to Haines."

"Picking up fish?"

"Picking up fish."

"From anyone special?"

"Nope. As far as I know I'll be meeting the same man I always deal with, a man named Jack Kolinsky."

Robson nodded and leaned back, pausing this time to appraise the sunglasses in my shirt pocket. It was impossible to tell if he believed anything I said. Or what he was thinking.

"I understand you've been asked to inject some kind of UV dye into those boxes of fish you'll be picking up," he said in a matter-of-fact tone. "Am I right?"

I nodded, wondering who might have told him that, though I wasn't going to ask. "That's right," I said.

Robson looked out his big window for a while. "May I give you a piece of advice, Mr. Brody?"

"Go ahead."

He leaned forward again.

"Tomorrow. In Haines. Do exactly as you're told. *Exactly*. Keep your head down and don't look anyone in the eyes. And don't even think about injecting that dye into any boxes of fish unless you're out in the middle of nowhere, miles and miles from anyone who might be trying to keep an eye on you, okay?"

"Okay."

He gave me his best cop stare ever to reinforce the message. All I could manage to do was stare back. I suppressed the urges to swallow or blink. This time when he leaned back in his chair he put his hands on the armrests.

"Good," he said. "I'm glad we had this little chat. And I'm glad we have a very clear understanding that you're going to provide the RCMP with any and all new information you come upon that might help us catch a couple of kidnappers. Right?"

I nodded. "Right."

"Good. Now then, you wanted to know something about a Mr. Belanger?"

FORTY SIX

Staff Sergeant Robson told me to take the elevator down to the main floor and wait for him at the back of the building. I stood leaning against the wall beside the back door for ten minutes, watching people getting on and off the elevator. I was starting to get worried about the time of day because I had things to do. I was also looking forward to leaving the confines of another hermetically sealed building.

Robson and a woman finally appeared, walking around the corner at the end of the long hall I'd come down earlier. It was the woman who'd put me through my security scan. They stopped in front of me. The woman handed me a large unsealed envelope, nodded without a word, then turned and walked away.

"What's this?" I asked Robson.

"Look inside."

I did. It was my knife. And a check.

"Hey, thanks," I said, "That was fast." I put the knife in its holster and the check in my pack.

"We aim to please around here," Robson said with another one of his wry grins. "By the way, we did a little search around the building. We didn't see anyone who might have been watching you. You can never be sure, but it looks your visit here today might stay a secret. Lucky for you. But you won't be paying us any more unannounced visits, right?"

"Right. Thanks for the check."

Robson nodded and opened the back door. There was a muddy unmarked police car idling ten feet in front of us. The man behind the wheel was wearing blue coveralls with the collar buttoned tightly around his neck. He was staring straight ahead. Robson leaned his face in close to mine.

"You stay in touch, Mr. Brody. There's your ride. Everything's arranged. The man in that car will take you where you want to go."

I got in the car.

* * *

The man driving the unmarked police car was a young native, maybe twenty five, probably right out of cop school. He was strong and healthy and had a buzz cut just like his boss. He looked professional and competent and 'cop' was written all over him, even with the tight-fitting coveralls that hid his uniform. Robson had come up with the plan and arranged my limo ride to the Kayak Store. My driver would be at my disposal for the rest of the afternoon. I confirmed my destination with him and we didn't say a word during the short drive to the river.

"Ten minutes," I said when we pulled into the parking lot. I got out and he drove off.

Though only five blocks from the RCMP building, I was standing in a different world. Thirty or so pale skinny people dressed in tight athletic clothing were wandering around a large assortment of kayaks and canoes spread haphazardly along the bank of the Yukon River. They were packing and unpacking things, fussing with paddles and camping equipment, communicating with each other in every language but English. They were preparing to launch. They were in the perfect spot to start a river trip down the Yukon River.

At an elevation of two thousand feet above sea level, Whitehorse is the highest city in the world that can be reached by river from tide water. Of course with a current averaging five miles an hour, the only way to see the Yukon River if you're paddling a kayak or canoe is to travel downstream. Which means that Whitehorse is a great place to be selling and renting canoes and kayaks. I walked over to the Kayak Store, a small log building surrounded with wood scaffolds holding hundreds of new and used kayaks and canoes of every description.

I walked through the open front doors and saw a bony looking woman about thirty five standing behind a cash register. She was ringing up a sale for a young couple. The three of them looked like they'd just come from a Greenpeace convention. They were speaking German. I waited. The couple left with two bulging plastic bags full of plastic clothes. The woman behind the counter looked at me inquisitively, then recognition filled her face.

I knew who she was. She was a friend of Deb's. We'd been introduced at Katy Duncan's wedding two years ago. We hadn't exactly hit it off.

"Hello there, Brody. Long time no see. What brings you in here? Still flying hunters into our wilderness to murder our wildlife?"

"That's not until August, Ingrid. These days I'm just raising money for the Save the Lycra Tree Foundation. Care to donate?"

She folded her arms and gave me a stern look. "What can I do for you?" she asked.

"Actually, I'm looking for some used canoes. Need four of them. Got any for sale?"

"Don't think so. We usually sell our old rental stock in the early spring, but I'll get Johann for you. You can talk to him about canoes." Ingrid went over to the phone on the wall and paged Johann over a loudspeaker that blared outside. A minute later a tall and lean bearded man walked into the store. Johann was Ingrid's husband, and easily twenty years her senior. Ingrid spoke to him in German. She talked, he nodded, she talked, he nodded, she talked some more, he nodded some more. I was sunk. Who knows what she'd just told him about me aiding and abetting those monsters who come up every year to murder Yukon wildlife? Or my campaign to save the Lycra tree?

"Hello," he said with a strong German accent and generous smile. "You are looking for used canoes?"

"Yeah, got any for sale?"

"I might. Let me show you."

I followed him out to a tall scaffold with four very heavily scratched canoes stacked on one side.

"These four are all I have left. But I have already taken a one hundred dollar deposit on them," Johann said. "They were supposed to have been paid for and picked up two weeks ago, but the buyer hasn't come back. I wish he'd come and get them. I could use the rack space for new stock. If they're still here at the end of the week, then I will sell them to you. If you are interested."

"I might be. What am I looking at?"

"These are two year old rentals. Fifteen footers. They've been paddled down to Dawson on the river and trucked back here about thirty times. They're still good canoes but not shiny enough for the kind of customer we have these days. We replace our rental stock every two years."

"Are they fast?"

Johann chuckled. "No, no," he said. "Not fast at all. They have flexible polyethylene hulls, very wide and stable, very tough. But not fast at all. They're good canoes for novices and river tourists, very safe you know? You can't put a hole in them unless you use an axe. But fast?" He chuckled again, shaking his head in amusement.

"What are they worth to you, Johann?"

"I sold them with eight new paddles for fifteen hundred dollars. But I have not been paid and they are still here, right?"

"Right, still here," I said. "Look, I'll leave you my card. Would you call me if they become available?"

"Sure, I will do that." He took my card and handed me one of his.

"Thanks. Say, Johann, did you happen to sell a man named Chief Dan Belanger any canoes this spring?"

He perked up. "Yah! He is the man who gave me the deposit on these canoes right here. How do you know this?"

"I didn't. I was supposed to pick up some canoes that Chief Dan sold to my friends. I was wondering if this is where they might be. Now I know." I looked over the canoes for a minute. Not much to analyze. They were green, scratched up, but otherwise looked to be in good condition. "Johann, do you know how to get in touch with Chief Dan? Do you have his phone number?"

"No need to phone him. He's always in the same place at this time of day." Johann pointed across the street at the Fifty Below Hotel. "Check in the bar," he said.

* * *

I was about to cross the quiet street when my driver rolled up from out of nowhere and stopped in front of me. I pointed at the hotel and he gave me a subtle nod, then drove away. I crossed the street and walked into the hotel lobby, then followed a well worn path on a tired red carpet down a long dark hallway. In less than a minute I'd left a bright sunny day outside for the confines of a dreary bar. It felt like walking into a cave. The stale stench of beer dominated the atmosphere in the almost empty room. I waited for my eyes to adjust to the darkness and surveyed the room for Chief Dan Belanger. I didn't see him. A couple of native men were seated together at a table in the middle of the room. They both looked like they were down on their luck, each nursing a bottle of beer in silence. They didn't look up when I walked past them.

I spotted the moose hide jacket at a table in a dark corner. Chief Dan was wearing it. I went over to the table.

"Mind if I join you?" I asked, placing a hand on the back of a chair.

"And who might you be?", he asked, his hand firmly gripping a bottle of beer.

"Name's Brody. I'm from Minto. I understand you sold my friends there some canoes. I'm here to pick them up." He nodded at the chair in my hand and tilted his bottle of beer back until it was empty.

"You buying?" he asked, setting his bottle down.

"Nope. Not drinking either." He looked me over and shrugged.

"Are you going to sit down or not?" he asked. I did. He leaned back and held his bottle up and caught the eye of the woman behind the bar. He lifted his index finger off the bottle, then turned his attention back to me. "Those canoes need to be paid for before I release them to you. You bring a check?"

"Yeah, I brought a check."

"Four thousand, right?"

"Actually, it's blank, but it's signed and dated. I haven't filled it in yet, wasn't sure about the amount, or the payee."

"The amount's four thousand and I'm the payee," he said. "Dan Belanger's my name. Need a pen?"

The woman came over and dropped another bottle of beer in front of him. She looked at me and I waved her off. Belanger gave her a handful of coins and his empty. She left, not looking pleased. He tilted the bottle back and downed half of it.

"I have a pen," I said. "But I have a problem with the amount."

"I don't give a rat's ass what your problem is, whatever your name is. If you want the canoes, you pay me four thousand dollars. If you don't want to pay the four thousand dollars, then leave."

"Look, I don't mind paying you for the canoes, but I can't see giving you a check for something you don't own, and I'm not going to pay you four thousand dollars for something I can buy across the street for fifteen hundred. See my problem?"

His eyes narrowed and he leaned forward, now glaring at me. He had the leathery face of a heavy drinker and looked like he could use some sleep. "What'd you say your name was?" he asked.

"I said my name's Brody."

"Well you listen good, *Brody*. I made a deal with those dumb ass Indians up in Minto, and a deal's a deal. And it seems to me you're sticking your nose into someone else's business, like you're some kind of big agent or something. But if I was you, I'd quit while I was ahead, while you can still walk out of here. Now you go back to Minto and tell those dumb ass Indians up there that they can come get their canoes when they pay me four thousand dollars. Tell them that's the deal they made, they can take it or leave it. Now pay up or leave."

"Okay, but before I leave, I'll need your jacket."

"What?"

"Your jacket. Sorry. Forgot to tell you. You're out of business, Chief Dan. You won't be needing your jacket any more."

"My jacket? Who the hell do you think you are asking for my jacket? And who the hell do you think you are telling me I'm out of business? You wise-ass son of a bitch! Do you know who I am?"

"Yeah, I know exactly who you are. You're Dan Belanger. And I know exactly what you are too. And if I don't go out that back door in the next five minutes with your jacket in my hand, then the police will come in here and arrest you. So give me your jacket."

Dan Belanger flexed the muscles in his neck and pumped out his chest. He downed the rest of his beer and slammed the empty bottle down hard on the table. I hoped he didn't have a weapon. He clearly had a bad temper and was about to lose it. He put his hands on the table and leaned forward, like he was about to pounce.

"Are you a cop?" he hissed.

"Nope."

"Then what's this shit about police arresting me? For what? I've done nothing wrong."

"Yes you have. Statutory rape, for starters."

"What?"

"You heard me. You've been partying with little girls from the local village here in Whitehorse, you've been getting them drunk, and you've been having sex with them. And you've been doing it for a long time. You're what, pushing fifty? The girls are fifteen and sixteen. That's statutory rape."

"You're full of shit," he said. "And who I have sex with is no one's business but mine. Now screw off."

"You're wrong about that," I said. "If they're fifteen or sixteen, and you're getting them drunk and having sex with them, then it's everyone's business. That's why there's a law."

Belanger was ready to explode. "Well it's my word against whatever those little half-breed drunken sluts have to say in court, now isn't it? If those girls want to get drunk and have some fun, why not? They're not virgins. Besides, I never asked them how old they were, and they didn't tell me. So I'll take my chances in court. Go ahead and arrest me. But you can't have my jacket. Now get the hell out of here, asshole. Get out!" he yelled.

Heads turned. We had an audience now, albeit a small one. The woman at the bar seemed wary that something violent was about to happen. She stepped toward a phone on the bar. I leaned over the table and gave Dan Belanger my best version of a cop stare.

"Okay, *Chief* Dan. I'll get out. I'll walk out that door back there without your jacket and then a cop will come in and arrest you. You'll be in jail in an hour. Then you're in for what you deserve. Because your 'brothers' up at the jail will be laying a beating on you tonight. They'll be told what you did to those girls, they'll be told who you are, what you are, and what you're not."

"What I'm not? What's that supposed to mean?"

"Well, for starters, you're not a First Nations Canadian. You're just a con-man from Quebec whose last permanent residence was a federal penitentiary in Ontario. You were inside for three years for insurance fraud before you came up here, am I right about that? Now there's a good headline for the papers in town. *'Chief Dan's no Chief'*."

I stood up and realized I was shaking. This kind of confrontation was hardly my specialty. I needed to get out of the bar. For one thing the air was stifling and I craved fresh air. For another, I wasn't sure what Belanger was going to do. He stood and faced me but said nothing. I could tell he was weighing his options. He was breathing heavily, looking around furtively as though he was considering making a run for it. Then I watched the life go out of him. He knew his gig was up. His whole world had just disintegrated. He sagged and dropped the bravado. The woman at the bar was watching us.

"What if I give you my jacket?" he whispered. "Then what?"

"Then you get the deal of the century," I said. "You get to leave the Yukon and never come back. You walk out the back door with me, you go to the nearest real estate office, you sign a contract to sell your house. Then you go to your bank and close your accounts. You go home, pack a few things, get in your truck and drive south. You leave tonight and you never come back. Not ever. Understand? You just disappear. Do all that and you don't go to jail, you don't get beaten up, you don't face charges. Like I said, the deal of the century."

He took a long time to weigh what I'd just told him.

"Okay," he said, "but we go out the back door together. And I don't take off my jacket until we're outside."

"That'll work."

"Another thing," he said, glaring at me.

"What?"

"I'll be seeing you again, *Brody*. I'll get you for this."

"Hey. Don't blame me. I'm just the messenger. You've got no beef with me."

"Messenger, my ass. You'll pay."

"You know," I said, "maybe I should be scared of you. Maybe I ought to take the offer off the table. Let your brothers at the jail deal with you while you wait for your trial. The police have a lot more on you now than when I walked in here ten minutes ago. You've just said a lot of things that will put you away for a long time."

He leaned back and smiled. "Bullshit," he said calmly, regaining some of his composure. "It's your word against mine on what was just said in here. You got nothing."

"Wrong," I said. I pulled my cell phone out of my shirt pocket and held it up to his face. He looked at the screen.

It said '*Recording*'.

* * *

The sunshine was blinding. It took a moment for my eyes

to adjust when I pushed open the door at the back of the bar. I stepped out into a small gravel parking lot and squinted at my driver. He was leaning against his blue unmarked car with his arms folded, staring at the door behind me. His car was dripping wet and sparkling clean. He'd obviously gone somewhere to get it washed for the special occasion. He'd also lost his coveralls and had metamorphosed into a poster boy for the RCMP. He was now a striking figure of authority, a tall, young, fit and handsome native RCMP constable, wearing his crisp starched uniform and polished leather shoes with pride. His mirror sunglasses and the gun on his hip enhanced the image. Dan Belanger stepped out behind me. He looked at the imposing native man standing twenty feet in front of us. The cop stared back at Belanger with a look that could kill.

'Go ahead. Make my day'.

"Your jacket," I said.

The exit door slammed shut behind Belanger with a loud 'clank'. He stared for a moment at the intimidating lawman in front of him. If there was any doubt about what Dan Belanger might do when he left the bar, the icon of authority and confidence standing before him made all his options moot. Belanger let his moose hide jacket slide off his shoulders and handed it to me.

"Remember," I said. "You're going to disappear now or face the alternative. Jail. And a few good beatings. Now go do what I told you to do. You're leaving. Tonight."

I walked over to the young Constable and handed him the jacket. "Thanks for the ride," I said.

The cop nodded with his teeth clenched and threw Belanger's jacket into his car. He got in behind the wheel. We both watched Dan Belanger walk down the alley and disappear around the corner.

* * *

Robson's plan had worked. Dan Belanger, a predator and a con man, was about to leave the Yukon. But I can't say I was feeling particularly pleased about what had just transpired. Justice had hardly been served as it should have been.

Robson had told me that for some time there'd been rumors circulating around town that Belanger was partying in his house with young native girls. As they say up here, 'the Yukon's a small town', and some of the native members of the local RCMP detachment had heard enough from their wives and friends to know that Belanger had been up to no good with certain adolescent girls. The problem was that none of the girls would file an official complaint, and the crown prosecutor was adamant that unless they came forward and filed charges, he couldn't prosecute Belanger. It was just another one of those deals that everyone knew about, but where justice would never get served in the courts.

So Robson had done the next best thing. He'd used intimidation and bluffing to run Belanger out of town. It wasn't lost on me that he'd sent one of his young native officers to help me work the ruse. That had been very astute of him, and as it turned out, very effective.

In the end, Robson had served his constituency well by getting rid of a problem. Whitehorse and the Yukon would be a better place to live now. But Belanger was still a free man and would soon be someone else's problem. He'd soon be committing the same transgressions elsewhere and I didn't feel great about that.

I took a few deep breaths of the cleanest air in the world and looked up at the pale blue sky over the river. I had things to do.

The first thing was to buy some canoes.

FORTY SEVEN

It took a few minutes to convince Johann that Dan Belanger wouldn't be coming back to pay for his canoes. Then Johann sold me the four used canoes and eight adult paddles for the same price he'd charged Belanger. Johann said he'd be keeping Belanger's deposit in case he came back. That was fine with me.

I also bought eight adult lifejackets, four children's life jackets, four children's paddles, some rope, a lock and chain, and four bailers. Johann didn't have any children's paddles in the store but said he'd get them from his warehouse tomorrow. I told him that was not a problem because I'd be back tomorrow anyway. He agreed to deliver the four canoes and the equipment he had in stock to my plane by six o'clock. I told him I'd be waiting. When Johann handed me his invoice, I filled out Minnie's check for an amount less than half of Belanger's original deal with the band. I was feeling a lot better about my day.

Charlie had been waiting patiently in the parking lot. I walked over to his truck and he rolled down his window.

"Okay, Charlie, I'm done here. Could you pick up four kid's paddles here tomorrow morning and bring them with you when we meet me at the lake?"

He nodded.

"Great, thanks. I've got to make a couple of phone calls and do a few more errands. You should go get your boy, now. We'll all go up to the plane together. About an hour from now."

"Will I see him tomorrow?"

"Yes. Tomorrow when I get back from Haines and drop off the load of fish, we'll all fly up to Minto. You can stay with him there until it's safe to come back. But you need to stay here tonight, Charlie, you need to be in cell phone range in case Mr. Tommy calls. And you have to be here to meet the plane tomorrow when I fly in from Haines. Did you call the customs guy?" He was despondent but nodded his head.

"Good. Look, Charlie. It's just for one night. Your boy will be fine. But you know these people who are calling you are dangerous, you know what they said they might do, so your boy can't stay here tonight. You'll be with him again tomorrow, in a place where you'll both be safe. I promise."

Charlie nodded again. "I have lost his mother. I don't want to lose my son."

"Charlie," I said. "You will not lose your son. It's just one night, that's all."

"One night," he said.

I put my hand on his shoulder and looked at him. He stared straight out the windshield.

"What's your son's name?"

"Charlie."

"Charlie Junior. That's a great name."

He nodded.

"I'll meet you behind the Pagoda in an hour, Charlie."

* * *

On my way over to the post office I called one of the fuel companies in Whitehorse. Yesterday I'd flown from Dawson to Minto, today from Minto to Whitehorse, this evening I'd be flying back to Minto with a couple of canoes on the floats, and tomorrow I had to fly back to Whitehorse in the morning. That totaled more than five hundred and fifty miles with four take offs, well over the four hundred and fifty mile range of my plane. I asked for a fill up before six o'clock and the guy who took my call said he'd get it done. I also wanted full tanks when I took off for Haines and asked for another fill up at one o'clock tomorrow afternoon. The guy who took my call said he'd get that done too.

I went into the post office and opened my mail box. It was stuffed full. I carried the pile of mail over to a counter for some quick sorting. Most of it was junk, but there was a bill from the 'Mahoney Bros. Fuel Company' for a very expensive fill up two nights ago in Dawson. That had arrived fast. I wondered why bills always move through the mail system faster than checks. I also wondered, if I asked nicely, whether Tommy Kay would reimburse me for the after hours surcharge.

The monthly bill from my favorite parts supplier had also arrived, and so had the usual assortment of aviation notices, warnings, bulletins and requests for statistical information from the Canadian Government. I don't know if there's ever been an aircraft built that needs more than one pilot to take off, fly and land it, yet the number of people working in office buildings who want to help me fly my airplane keeps growing every year. What really irks me is that most of them make more than I do. Go figure.

I dropped the junk and flyers into a recycling bin, shoved the important stuff into my backpack, and headed for the bank.

There was a poster in the front window that said I'm richer than I think. Everyone in the poster was smiling. I guess the bank was lending them money. Apparently I was in the right place to borrow myself into prosperity, just like Sarah had explained. But today I only wanted to deposit a check and get a little cash. I joined a long line of people shuffling through a maze of red velvet ropes hanging from chrome posts. Five minutes later I was at the front of the line. A nice young woman waved at me from the end of the long counter. After serving me she said I could have avoided the wait in line by depositing my check and getting cash using the ATM in the lobby. I asked her what an ATM was. She told me. I told her I'd never used one. She said a customer representative would be happy to show me how, if I didn't mind taking a seat and waiting a few minutes. I thanked her and told her I'd done enough waiting for a day.

I went outside and sat down on a bench on one of the wide brick sidewalks that run up and down both sides of Main Street. It was warm in the sun and everyone seemed to be in a good mood. The young girls were all dressed for summer, even if the temperature wasn't quite warm enough for tight shorts and T-shirts. I pulled out my cell phone and dialed my favorite parts store. I asked for my favorite parts guy.

"This is Christine, how may I help you?"

"Hey, Christine. Brody here."

"Brody! Are you in town?" It was a good guess. She knew my cell phone didn't work in Minto.

"I am," I said. "And I need a favor. How about dinner for five?"

"No salmon?"

"Sorry. Maybe tomorrow. It'll have to be Chinese today."

"Alright then. Make it dinner for five. So what's the favor?"

I told her what I needed.

"Make it dinner for six," she said.

*   *   *

Charlie and Charlie Junior were parked in the alley behind the Pagoda Chinese restaurant. I was holding three bags of Chinese food. I had to set down the two biggest ones on the ground to open the passenger door, then got in. I put the bags on the floor between my feet and looked at Charlie Junior.

He was standing on the bench seat with a hand on his father's shoulder. Each time I looked at him he'd turn his head away. He might be three or four years old, very slim but healthy, and very shy. He was dressed neatly in a long sleeved yellow top and jean coveralls. He wore sneakers. There was a small backpack decorated with Disney characters on the seat.

"How old is he, Charlie?"

"Almost four."

"How's his English?"

"He speaks very little. But he will understand everything you say."

"Good," I said, watching Charlie Junior sneak another peak at me. "Let's go to the lake, Charlie."

"Why do you buy Chinese food at the Pagoda?" he asked, driving carefully.

"Why not? It's good," I said.

"Much better at my hotel. No MSG. Fresher ingredients," he said.

"Didn't know they had Chinese food where you work, I'll have to try it next time."

"Come when I am cooking. I cook for you."

"You cook Chinese food?"

"Yes. For one year and more," he said.

"Then I'll be sure to come by. "

When we got to my plane there was no sign of Johann or the canoes. I got out of the truck and walked around to Charlie's side.

"You've got to say goodbye now, Charlie. You need to leave. You can't stay here. Sorry. Tell Junior you'll see him tomorrow."

I walked to the back of the truck and unloaded Minnie's groceries. I closed the tailgate and looked through the rear window at Charlie talking to his son. Charlie Junior was upset that his father was leaving. His father was trying to console him but it wasn't helping much. The door finally opened and Charlie got out with his boy in his arms. He spoke rapidly to him in Chinese, lowered him to the ground, knelt down, and gave him a hug. He stood, said something, then gave him a pat on his bottom. The boy didn't move. Charlie handed me the boy's backpack, then got back in his truck. I took the boy by the hand and led him to the rear of the truck. He was looking back at his father the whole time, whimpering, tears running down his cheeks. It was gut wrenching.

"Call me in the morning, Charlie. Ten o'clock," I said.

Charlie nodded, got back in his truck, and drove away. Charlie Junior began to wail. Damn. This was an utterly absurd and outrageous situation. Taking a boy from his father to hide him from the world, *just in case*. I thought about what Robson had said about crime, what it can do to people and communities. I was developing a real hate for criminals.

I held Charlie Junior's hand and pulled my cell phone out of my jeans with the other. I called Christine.

"We're here," was all I said, and closed my phone. Charlie Junior wasn't finished with the crying. I picked him up in my arms and looked at him. He calmed down a bit, wiped his eyes, and looked at me.

"Charlie," I said. "Have you ever been in a DeHavilland Beaver?"

* * *

I heard a car. I'd just finished stowing Minnie's groceries and the small bag of Chinese food in the back of my plane. I looked at Charlie who was sitting on his knees in the pilot's seat. He was quiet now, fascinated with all the dials and gauges on the console. Now and again he'd grab the yoke and move it back and forth.

"Look Charlie, Christine's here," I said, pointing at the road. He slid between the seats and looked out the cargo door, curious. I swung him out of the plane down to the wharf. With his backpack and two bags of Chinese food balanced in one arm, I took his hand with the other and we crossed the road to Christine's old car. It had a few new dents since I'd seen it last fall. Two teen age boys were sitting in the back seat with their heads hanging down, ignoring us, concentrating on their cell phones. There was a child seat mounted between them. Christine smiled at Charlie Junior.

"Hi, Brody," she said, looking at Charlie. "Hello Charlie. I'm glad to meet you." She got out of the car and ordered one of her boys into the front seat. She picked up Charlie in her arms as though he was hers. "We're going to have so much fun tonight, Charlie," she said. "Just wait until you meet Andrew and Barnie". Charlie looked baffled but his eyes never left Christine's. He was mesmerized by her.

Andrew was Christine's youngest son and Barnie was a good

natured but very goofy mutt that Christine had inherited from an elderly neighbor who'd died a few years ago.

Christine was about forty, getting wider every time I saw her, and never stopped smiling. She was wearing blue jeans and a working man's collared shirt with 'Chris' stitched on a pocket. Christine lived south of Whitehorse on a lake with a live-in boyfriend who never seemed to have a real job, but was always busy improving their rustic property. Last I heard he was putting an addition on an addition. If he wasn't hammering or sawing he was tending to the biggest private greenhouse I've ever seen. The two of them seemed to live well enough on one income. Christine never talked about the father of her two older boys, he was apparently long gone, and I'd never asked her about him. Andrew had been born ten years after the two boys sitting in the car. He was obviously by the boyfriend. Andrew was about Charlie's age, not yet in school, still at home, and probably already pretty good with a hammer and a saw, would be my guess. I didn't know much more than that about Christine and her family, but trusted her and knew she was an excellent mother.

Christine said, "So what's the deal here, is he yours?"

"Hardly. His father is single and hasn't been in town very long. Doesn't have much of a support group yet, you know? We've both got to go somewhere on business for a couple of days. He was kind of in a jam so I called you. We'll be back to get him in a couple of days. I'll introduce you to his dad then. He's a great guy and a very good father. I really appreciate you doing this, Christine."

"Brody, why do I have the feeling you haven't told me a damn thing about what's really going on here?"

She coaxed Charlie into the car's child seat and strapped him in. He looked uncertain about what was going on but was apparently resigned to another transfer of custody. He looked up at the teenager beside him who hardly noticed him, still busy working his cell phone. I knew then that Charlie would be just fine with Christine and her family.

"It's a little complicated, Christine. Let's just say you're doing a great thing and I'll tell you everything when I come back."

"Which is when?"

"Soon, a day or so."

"This better not be anything illegal."

"It's definitely nothing illegal."

"I'm not working tomorrow," she said. "I'll be out at the lake for three days, then I go back to work. You call every day. You keep me posted."

"I'll keep you posted, Christine. See you later, Charlie." I gave him a wave and he didn't wave back. I handed Christine the two bags of Chinese food.

She smiled at me, though not with her eyes, and drove off.

* * *

At six thirty I was taxing over Schwatka Lake with full tanks and a canoe strapped to each float. Johann had turned up just before six and helped me load a pile of paddles and life jackets and other stuff into the cargo bay behind me. I gave him a bunch of my business cards and offered him my standard ten percent finder's fee for any customers he might send my way. He was impressed that my plane could carry 'boats on the floats'.

I left the other two canoes locked to the wharf and planned to fly them to Minto tomorrow evening. I was looking forward to that. I'd be done with the canoe delivery business, would have injected that top secret dye into my last load of fish from Haines, and hopefully could stay in Minto for a while. Work in my shop, putter around the house, live a normal life again.

I felt guilty about misleading Charlie as to where his boy would be staying the night. But the reality was there was really no one in Minto that I felt comfortable leaving him with, especially if I wasn't going to be around. I also didn't have the proper sized ear protection for a child, and my plane was simply too loud for a four year old to endure for any length of time. But the main reason I'd sent Charlie Junior off with Christine, instead of taking him to

Minto with me, was because I really didn't want his father to know where he was. If the bad guys ever got a hold of Charlie Senior, they would break him as easily as anyone else. They'd drive up to Minto to grab Charlie Junior, but he wouldn't be there. That was my thinking and it made sense to me. Then I thought about my grandfather. He used to say that you could tell how well you were living by the number of lies you told everyday. If he was right, then today had been a bad one.

I got clearance from Whitehorse air traffic control and took off with full flaps into a strong south wind. A Beaver can easily carry two canoes, but it's a handful to fly. I was using fifteen degrees of flaps and a lot of throttle to maintain a cruising airspeed of barely ninety miles an hour. My plane was fluttering around like a leaf in the wind, the floats swinging under me like a pendulum. It felt like plowing snow with two flat tires and pulling a trailer at the same time. Even with a tailwind, it was going to take an hour and a half of hard work to fly home.

I was looking forward to sitting on my couch, eating some Chinese food, and watching a hockey game.

FORTY EIGHT

The next day at noon, Whitehorse Air Traffic Control cleared me to fly a straight-in approach down the city's east side. I flew right over the power dam and made a pretty good landing into a south wind on Schwatka Lake. It was the first thing that had gone smoothly since I left Whitehorse yesterday evening.

After landing in Minto last night, I'd waited an hour at the lake for Reggie to arrive and take delivery of his 'new' canoes. He'd had a flat tire on the drive out and had to hitchhike back to the café for help. He'd found a friend in the bar to give him a ride out to the lake, but the 'friend' didn't have time to deal with canoes when there was a hockey game on TV. The 'friend' dropped Reggie off in front of the dock without stopping his truck, then did a U-turn with the wheels spinning, heading back to the bar for the rest of his game. Canadians and their addiction to hockey.

We left Reggie's canoes on the dock but loaded all his new paddling equipment into my pickup. He was as excited as I'd ever seen him and had questions about every item. We stopped beside his truck on the highway and checked out his flat tire. It was destroyed. His truck would have to stay where it was until a new one came in from Whitehorse. I drove him to his house in the village and we unloaded his paddling equipment. He talked me into having a beer with him. Then another one. I didn't get home until eleven.

When I got back to my cabin, Russ and Jack greeted me with subdued enthusiasm. They were both hanging their heads and whimpering, each with a nose sprouting a full bouquet of porcupine quills. I was pulling quills and they were yelping and whining until well past one o'clock in the morning. Russ would eventually need a trip to the vet in Whitehorse to get two stubborn ones removed. I ate a little Chinese food around one thirty. Russ and Jack wouldn't eat. I went to bed at two and tossed and turned all night, worrying about my dogs and my trip to Haines. I slept late and just made it up to the shop in time to answer Charlie's phone call. As agreed, he'd called me at ten, but only to report that Tommy Kay had not called yet.

I hung up and searched everywhere for my spare flare gun to replace the one Ricky Constanzia had dropped in the river. No luck there, then I remembered lending it to some hunters last summer and forgetting to get it back. I'd have to buy another one in Whitehorse. When I left the shop, the dogs' noses were swollen and they wouldn't eat. I felt badly about leaving them alone. Reggie would pick them up later.

Then, on my way out to the lake, I stopped at the café to fill my truck with gas, eat a hot breakfast, and get what I really needed, coffee. But to complete the streak, the power had inexplicably gone out at the café early that morning. The gas pumps weren't working so I couldn't fill up, the grill wasn't working so I couldn't have breakfast, and the coffee was long gone. I settled for two tuna sandwiches and two bottles of water to go. How I hate some mornings. I took off for Whitehorse at ten thirty, grumpy and hungry.

When the floats settled into the water on Schwatka Lake, I lowered the rudders, turned around, and taxied back to the wharf. I was surprised to see Charlie waiting for me, pacing up and down, half an hour early. I hadn't expected to see him until after one o'clock, after the fuel truck had been out to fill my plane. I opened the cockpit door, killed the engine, and coasted up to the dock. Charlie lassoed the rear float cleat with a dock rope. The rope tightened and the plane stopped with a bump against the tires. He tied the rope expertly, just like I'd shown him last summer.

"You're early, Charlie," I said, stepping off the float onto the wharf and grabbing a rope to tie up the front.

"Tommy Kay just called," he said. "He says you must leave right away. He says you must fly the fish to Dawson now. He was yelling at me."

"Dawson? You're sure? And he was yelling?" I checked Charlie's knot and noticed four small paddles lying on the dock. Kid's paddles. Johann had come through.

"Yes. Yelling. Mr. Kay always yells when he is in a hurry. He says you must leave for Haines right away. You must now take the fish to Dawson. Not to Whitehorse. He says the fish must be in Dawson by six o'clock."

I sighed. What were those scoundrels up to now? Could they not stick to a plan? It looked like it was going to be one of those days when I simply couldn't expect the expected. I looked at the two canoes chained to the wharf – the two canoes I'd intended to fly up to Minto tonight – *after* I'd delivered a load of fish to Whitehorse. Whitehorse – not Dawson – Whitehorse. Now what do I do?

I didn't want to make another special trip tomorrow, from Minto to Whitehorse, just to pick up two canoes. For one thing, the fuel cost alone would be well over two hundred dollars. And I sure didn't want to fly today down to Haines, then all the way up to Dawson, then back down to Minto – a trip of almost six hundred miles – with two canoes tied to the floats. Then I had an epiphany. If one's whole day is going to be nothing but surprises, why not be impulsive? I knew what I'd do.

"How is my boy?" Charlie asked.

"He's fine, just fine," I said, without actually knowing with certainty that Charlie Junior was indeed safe and sound with Christine, though I had no reason to believe it wasn't the truth.

"I can go see him now, yes? If you must now fly to Dawson, then I will now drive my truck to Minto to see him, okay?"

I was stymied and didn't know what to say. If Charlie drove up to Minto now he wouldn't find his son there. And I really didn't want his truck anywhere around Minto, not if the bad guys might be out looking for it. I had no idea how to deal with the situation. I was about to get busted for having mislead him. But all I knew and cared about was that his boy was safe at the moment, even if he was being cared for miles south of Minto.

"Hey," I said, without answering his questions. "Let's call Charlie Junior right now."

Charlie perked up. I dialed Christine but there was no answer. I left a message for her to call back with Charlie Junior at her side. He could say hello to his father then. I closed my phone.

"No one's home, Charlie. But the woman looking after him will call back. In the mean time, could you do me a favor?"

"What?" he asked, with disappointment etched in his face.

"Could you go to the safety supply store and buy a flare gun and a box of flares?" I handed him a piece of paper, pointed at a street address in Whitehorse, and the model number of the flare gun and flares I wanted. He nodded.

"Thanks. Here's the money," I said. "And if you have time, pick me up a sandwich and a large coffee. But be back here by one o'clock. Okay?"

I handed him the cash for the flare gun. Charlie ran to his pickup, and by his driving standards, roared off to do my errands. I was in a real jam now. I really hoped Christine would get my message and call back. I looked at the canoes tied to the wharf.

Time to get going.

FORTY NINE

At one fifteen I took off for Haines with three full fuel tanks, two canoes strapped to the floats, four kid's paddles stowed in the back, and Charlie standing on the wharf scratching his head. And oh yeah, there was a brand new flare gun and a box of flares in a shopping bag behind me.

I don't know how many favors I'd called in this week, and couldn't count how many times I'd said 'trust me'. It had to stop soon. The next time Daryl told me to 'stay away' from someone, I might be inclined to take him seriously. Of course I was thinking about Sarah Marsalis. A lot. It seemed as though we'd met a long time ago, but I just couldn't stop thinking about her.

Christine had called me back and Charlie had had a brief chat with his son. Junior was doing fine and Charlie was rejuvenated. Christine was planning a shopping trip to Whitehorse in the afternoon and would meet Charlie in town to return his boy. Charlie was confused why his son would be returned to him in Whitehorse that afternoon. And as if that wasn't confusing enough for him, I dodged the rest of his questions and told him to drive to Minto with Charlie Junior as soon as he'd hooked up with Christine. I gave him a spare set of keys for my shop and my truck, and told him what to do when he got there. Then I called Minnie and asked her to get Reggie to give Charlie and his boy a hand when they arrived.

I also told Minnie about the changes to my flight plan today. I asked her to tell Reggie that his other two canoes would be arriving a little later than expected, that he should expect me at the lake about seven o'clock. I told Minnie what I wanted Reggie to do if I hadn't turned up by eight. Minnie had a lot of questions and I did a lot of talking without answering any of them. Minnie growled at me and bid me a safe flight.

Besides putting off a lot of explaining that would have to wait, I promised Christine a box of salmon for taking care of Charlie Junior. Fortunately, I was heading to the right place to get a good deal on an eighty pound box of sockeye salmon.

As for the canoes tied to the floats, my brilliant albeit impulsive plan was to drop them off in Minto on my way up to Dawson. There would be a compromise in fuel efficiency today, but it would save me a trip back to Whitehorse tomorrow. I'd have to put Christine's box of salmon on the bus in Minto tomorrow. *Then*, I could relax.

* * *

Haines is almost straight south of Whitehorse, a short one hundred mile flight. The easiest way to navigate there is simply to fly down the southern section of the Klondike Highway, which intersects the Alaska Highway ten miles south of Whitehorse. From there the Klondike Highway runs south to the town of Carcross, then along Bennett Lake, through the White Pass, and finally descends the Coastal Mountains to the deep sea port of Skagway on the Pacific.

The southern section of the Klondike Highway was completed in 1978. It roughly traces the overland route to the Klondike taken by thousands of gold seekers, who in 1898, began their trek inland to Dawson from Skagway – on foot. With a police enforced ton of supplies mandated for each man, their adventure began with a dozen or so arduous and dangerous twenty eight hundred foot climbs, straight out of the town of Skagway, up into the Coastal Mountains, up and over the legendary Chilkoot Pass. Once they got all their supplies to the top of the pass, they pressed on with their cargo to the southern end of Bennett Lake. At Bennett Lake the 98er's stopped to cut down trees and build rudimentary rafts and barges for their next challenge: navigating the uncharted Yukon River to Dawson, another four hundred river miles north.

I still marvel at the resolve of those men, how they undertook such an incredible challenge against all odds, simply to pursue a dream of finding a fortune in the Yukon. It wasn't two lifetimes ago when they got off a ship in a tough little town called Skagway to embark on a four hundred and fifty mile expedition, inland to Dawson and the Klondike goldfields. The journey would prove to be an adventure in itself, heading into an unknown wilderness and environment few had ever experienced, let alone seen or understood. Their mission would take them into a frontier where there were no towns, no roads, no cars, no planes, no trains, no stores, no doctors, no phones, no mail – and they would do it without a map. All they had was their will and a dream, a faith in their own resourcefulness that they could survive and overcome whatever challenges befell them.

I often lament how real adventure is no longer available to humans. Today every square inch of the world has been mapped by satellites. Just about anyone with money can hire a team of Sherpas to drag them to the top of Everest, then call their friends on a satellite phone to brag about it. We're flushing toilets at the south pole. We've walked on the moon. Some might argue otherwise, but I say the last of the real adventurers – the authentic pioneers and explorers of our planet – are long gone now, leaving behind just a few grainy photographs to document their feats, their silent stares all that remain to ponder their courage.

* * *

It was another beautiful day for flying with clear blue skies and a few puffy clouds. My old plane was chugging along at a hundred miles an hour, swaying and yawing in the winds swirling around the mountains, working hard against the drag of the two canoes strapped to its floats. When I crested the top of the White Pass, the ground fell away abruptly. I eased the throttle back and pushed the nose down, letting gravity propel the plane as it descended into a narrow mountain valley, heading toward Skagway and the Pacific Ocean. Boiling creeks and tall frothy waterfalls adorned the near vertical cliffs on either side of the steep valley, purging the spring's snow melt from the jagged peaks above. The White Pass Railway occasionally appeared on my left, its tracks snaking in and out along a craggy mountain side, its rail bed impossibly carved out of sheer rock faces. A few miles from the ocean the landscape instantly morphed into a lush paradise of leafy green trees and thick vegetation.

Five minutes after entering the valley, I'd descended four thousand feet and the little town of Skagway appeared through the prop. Stretching out to the south beyond Skagway was Taiya Inlet, shimmering like silver in the afternoon sun. Taiya Inlet is the northernmost tip of the Lynn canal and the deepest fiord in North America. The Lynn Canal comprises the northern end of the inland passage which skirts the west coast of lower Alaska. I thought about Sarah and what she must have felt when seeing such awesome scenery for the first time. If she was like me, and most everyone else, it would have taken her breath away.

I flew over Skagway and headed out over the ocean, passing low over a cruise ship and an Alaska State Ferry heading the other way. People out on the decks looked up and took pictures of me. Haines was now less than fifteen miles south, but I kept a wary eye out for a quick change in the weather. Taiya Inlet is long and narrow, squeezed between high, steep, snow capped mountains, and at any time a wall of fog or rain or snow can form at its south end, instantly fill the valley, then roar north like a locomotive. When you see something like that coming at you, you turn around and run.

Ten minutes later I was descending into Haines, a quiet little fishing town sprawled across a narrow peninsula that bisects the north end of the Lynn Canal. Haines has no air traffic control so I dialed in the local air traffic frequency and broadcast my location, altitude, heading, and intention to land. I touched down beside the Haines Seaplane Base on the east side of the Chilkat peninsula, taxied in, and tied up at the public dock. I got out, breathed in the salt air, and took a moment to savor the vistas – the boats in the harbor, the tall blue mountains with their snow capped peaks, the thick green forests that run into the sea. Haines is a jewel to behold, a beautiful and tranquil place.

An elderly couple were leaning against a railing on the breakwater above me, taking in the scenery, watching me walk up the jetty toward the restaurant perched on top. When I got to the top of the jetty, the couple smiled and I managed a perfunctory nod while scanning the parking lot, confused and distracted why neither Jack or his van were there. Jack always waits for me inside the restaurant – 'The Captain's something or another' – and comes down to greet me when I land.

Where was he?

There must be a law that every seafood restaurant has to have a two fluke ship anchor lying outside its entrance. The anchor in front of this one needed a coat of paint. I went inside and looked around. No sign of Jack. I sat down at a glossy dark table beside a big picture window with a view of my plane, the harbor, and the sea beyond. The décor was predictable for a seafood joint. Fishing nets were strung all over the ceiling and the grey clapboard walls were littered with ship pictures, ship wheels, plastic fish, plastic crabs, lanterns and ropes and floats, and old brass compasses. So what's for dinner in here?

A pretty young woman emerged from behind the bar, sporting a smile to melt hearts, carrying a plasticized menu in her hand. We were the only people in the whole place. When she got close, I beat her to the punch and said, "Hi, just coffee please. I'm waiting for someone."

"Okay. Can you wait five? I'm brewing fresh. Is that your plane down there?"

"Yes and yes," I said with a smile.

She smiled back. "Where y'all coming from?" she asked with

that seductive drawl they proudly cultivate in the south. Love that drawl. I liked everything about her already. She seemed like a genuinely friendly person and maybe, just maybe, semi-interested in getting to know a lonely pilot from out of town, or for that matter, probably anybody from out of town. I couldn't blame her for wanting some conversation, she looked like she could use some on a dead quiet afternoon in a dead quiet restaurant in a dead quiet town. But I was pre-occupied. Where was Jack?

"Flew down from Whitehorse today," I said. "Hey, seen Jack around?"

"Jack Kolinsky?"

Small town. I nodded and said, "Yeah."

"Haven't seen Jack for a couple of days. Someone said he went to Juneau."

I nodded again and said, "Guess I'd better call him then." She smiled expectantly, then left when I buried my face in my backpack. I took out my cell phone and called Jack. No answer. I left a message and told him I was waiting at the usual spot. Then I called U.S. Customs, told them I'd just landed, told them where I'd be waiting for them. They said they'd send someone down.

Ten minutes later I was nursing my second cup of coffee and getting grilled by a fierce looking woman with a moustache from U.S. Customs. Every document I carry was spread out on the table for her judicious inspection, and I was answering every question she could come up with. But she just wouldn't quit with the questions, kept going on and on with her own particular version of a fishing expedition. I guess it wasn't a busy day for her, so lucky me, it was my turn to get the third degree. My experience with customs officers is that if you remain calm, keep handing them documents and answering their questions, sooner or later they'll tire, and will let you go on your way. Today was no exception. When the fierce looking woman finally stood and stomped out of the restaurant, I had the distinct impression she was disappointed to have had to stamp my passport. I called Jack again. Still no answer.

I went outside and looked around again for his van. No sign

of it. It was utterly perplexing to me that he wasn't around. It seemed to be yet just another unexpected event in my day, another justification to do something impulsive. I walked back into the restaurant.

"Amy," I said. I knew her name now. "When was the last ferry from Juneau?"

"I think one came in last night."

"Well if Jack comes in, would you tell him I flew over to his warehouse? I'll be waiting for him there."

"Okay, Brody". She knew my name now too. I love small towns.

I left Amy a big tip and she thanked me with a smile worth twice as much. I went outside again. If I'd had a vehicle, I could have driven across to the west side of the peninsula and been at Jack's warehouse in ten minutes. But all I had was my plane, so I took off from the harbor and flew across. I landed in front of Jack's place on the east shore of Chilkat Inlet. His boat was there. His van was there. Great. Maybe I'd just arrived in town earlier than expected. Maybe he was still inside his building, preparing my load of fish. I was definitely in the right place to pick up my cargo and that box of salmon I'd promised Christine.

I tied up at the end of the long dock that extends from Jack's warehouse out into a sheltered bay. I wasn't sure whether the tide was coming in, or going out, but I could see it was either halfway in, or halfway out, judging by the algae and barnacles on the pilings. I wasn't expecting to be around long enough to worry about the tide, all I had to do was pick up some boxes of fish. I left the ropes securing my plane a little loose to accommodate any change in sea level. I slung my backpack over my shoulder and strode up the long wide dock, past Jack's fifty foot crab boat – 'Jack's Folly' was painted on its stern – toward a large steel building. I stepped off the dock and looked up at the tall overhead door that serves the loading and unloading of his boat. Above the door, just under the roof line, was a faded white plywood sign that said 'Panhandle Fish Co., Haines, AK'. On the ground at the right end of the building were row after row of rusty crab pots, stacked five and six high. A huge bundle of round orange floats lay behind the traps, tethered together and secured by a chain that ran into a thicket of trees. The floats reminded me of kid's balloons. I thought about Bobby Larabie and Charlie Junior.

I walked across the muddy ground to the man door in the centre of the building. It wasn't locked. I wiped my feet on the mat and entered. Even with the lights off, it was brighter inside than might have been expected, with two large skylights flooding the concrete floor with sunlight. I flicked a few switches on the wall anyway. The fluorescent lights high above me buzzed and flickered for a second, then came on. It was downright bright inside now. But there was no one around.

"Hello! Jack! You in here?" I waited a moment, heard nothing, then went outside and circled the building. No sign of him anywhere. I walked a hundred feet up the two rut driveway to the highway, looked up and down, but neither heard or saw a thing, not a soul or vehicle was around. All was quiet, quiet enough to be unsettling. Where could Jack be if his van and boat were here? Even if he'd gone to Juneau, surely he would have returned in time to load my cargo of fish. I assumed if something had come up, he'd have called Charlie to change the pickup time. He had to be around somewhere, his boat and vehicle were both here. I walked back down the driveway to his van. There was no heat radiating from the engine. I walked back down the dock to his boat. I stood beside it and listened.

Silence.

"Hello! Jack!" I yelled. "You on board?" I waited. No response. The only sounds were the wind rattling the mast wires, the waves slapping the hull, and me, standing alone on the dock, breathing heavier than I ought to be.

I went back to the building and went inside again. I stood in front of a small desk smothered in papers and shipping documents, and looked around. At the right end of the building were two, long stainless steel tables for gutting and cleaning fish and crabs. Hoses with shower nozzles dangled over the tables, hanging from pipes mounted high above on the ceiling. A couple of steel carts loaded with large plastic tubs were parked beside the tables. Next to the overhead door were two rubber tired wagons and a propane powered forklift that Jack uses to ferry his catch from his boat to his building. On the end wall, tall stacks of grey plastic tubs rose halfway up to the ceiling. Folded cardboard and empty styrofoam boxes of every size were stacked on long shelves along the left wall. Beside them were three enormous rolls of plastic bags, each mounted on a long steel rod, and next to those, an industrial shelving unit filled with supplies. An ice making machine purred away in the corner. Jack had quite the seafood processing facility. The place definitely smelled of fish, but everything was clean and organized.

I turned and looked at the other end of the building. Of course. Jack would be working in his freezer.

I zipped up my jacket and prepared to enter a world where the temperature is always zero degrees – all day, every day, all year long. I walked past his desk toward the other end of the building, and stopped in front of the walk-in freezer. It occupied a whole corner, was easily twenty feet square, and well over ten feet high. A heat exchanger with large pipes running out to the exterior wall sat on top of its flat roof. The freezer had two wide and tall opposing doors that could be swung wide open to allow a forklift to drive in and out. I thumped twice on one of the heavy doors with my fist.

"Hey Jack, you in there?" I hollered.

Nothing. I looked around, then down at the big chrome handles on the doors. A large steel padlock was hanging on a hook, unclasped. I pulled hard on one of the handles until the latch released with a resounding 'ker-clunk'. I pulled the heavy thick door out a few feet and a cloud of icy fog billowed past my feet.

"Jack, you in here?" I hollered again, poking my head in the freezer.

I let the fog dissipate then leaned inside. The cold hit me like an avalanche. I gasped, crossed my arms and clutched my sides, then stepped all the way inside. I stood and scanned the freezer for Jack.

There was no sign of him. I rubbed my hands up and down my ribs, then tucked them under my armpits.

Boxes of fish and crabs with 'Panhandle Fish Co.' printed on their sides were stacked to the ceiling on three walls, and in two rows down the center. Directly in front of me, pushed up against the boxes in the center row, was a steel table on wheels. On top of the steel table were four long styrofoam boxes. They lay side by side, their ends facing me. They were sealed shut with tape. On the ends of each box someone had scribbled 'PPAG', the call letters for my plane. At least my cargo was here, and it looked ready to go. But only four boxes. Not much of a load, usually there were more, sometimes as many as a dozen, but that was okay with me. It would be an easy trip. I could load the four boxes myself and be gone in ten minutes – if I wanted – but knew I should wait for Jack. Where was he? I had to find him. He had to be close. He had to be around somewhere.

The big freezer door closed behind me with a slow 'ker-clunk'. It shouldn't have closed on its own. I panicked and spun around, slammed my open hand on the round chrome pad that pushes a rod through the door, operating the handle on the outside. It worked. The latch released and the heavy door opened, moving out a few inches. My panic attack had been for nothing, but my heart was pounding. You don't ever want to get stuck in a commercial freezer wearing only a windbreaker and a ball cap. I pushed the heavy door wide open, this time well past center. I didn't need any more surprises today, especially like that one. I looked back in the freezer at the four styrofoam boxes on the table. It would have been easy to inject the dye into them right then and there. The dye kit was in my backpack, hanging from my shoulder. I heard the compressor start outside and the fan above me began to turn. Mist started pouring out from the two vents in the ceiling. I shivered and decided to wait, find out where Jack was instead of acting on an impulse. Injecting dye into those boxes here and now would be risky. I remembered what Robson had told me about taking chances. I'd do the injections later, like he'd advised. I'd land somewhere on my way back to the

Yukon, far away and miles from Haines, somewhere in the middle of nowhere, and inject the dye there.

Then for some reason, instead of walking out, I stepped to the right of the table and walked to the back of the freezer.

They were lying on the floor against the back wall, behind the center row of boxes. My heart skipped a beat when I saw them. Two men, wearing dress pants and shirts, shiny shoes, but no jackets. They were curled up, lying on their sides in the fetal position, their knees pulled up to their chests, the fingers on their hands grotesquely knurled together in front of their faces, as though they were contemplating them in some strange religious ritual. Their faces were blue, their lips, ears and fingers black. Frozen mucous ran out of their noses and down their chins. Their eyes were opaque, half closed and unfocussed, staring straight ahead through frosty eyelashes, seeing nothing at all. I took two quick steps, dropped to my knees, and grabbed the first man's arm to shake him. It felt like a cold steel railing. He was frozen solid. So was the other man. They were both very dead. And neither one was Jack Kolinsky. Who were they?

The man whose arm I'd grabbed was thin and balding. He was clutching a gold crucifix in his hands, still on a chain around his neck. His hair was jet black but his icy moustache looked grey. It was hard to tell his height, but he certainly wasn't tall. He might have been in his sixties. The other man looked much younger, much bigger and stronger, taller and thicker, clean shaven. He also had jet black hair, combed straight back. He had rings on the fingers of both his large hands. He had a large bruise on the back of his neck and a frozen trail of blood ran out his ear and down the inside of his shirt collar. I stood up in shock and stared at them in disbelief. My legs were weak and beginning to shake, and not because of the frigid cold. I had to get out of there. Call the police. What on earth had happened to these men?

"A terrible tragedy, don't you think?"

I spun around to face the voice.

I felt as good as dead when he looked in my eyes.

FIFTY

He was the most sinister looking man I've ever laid eyes on. He was no taller than a boy and probably weighed about the same. His paper thin skin was so smooth and white it was almost translucent, and his age impossible to judge. But the palpable spell he cast over me with his lifeless black eyes was paralyzing. There was something entirely unrealistic about them, something altogether missing, like death warmed over. He stared blankly at me, like a mannequin stares out from behind a store window. When he walked toward me, it seemed almost surreal that he was alive and could actually move. I could do no more than wait for him, paralyzed by his gaze. He stopped beside me and looked down at the men on the floor.

"What happened to these men was very unfortunate," the strange looking little man said. "Evidently they were trying to steal fish. Perhaps they heard the owner enter the building and hid back here. The owner must have locked them inside when he went home last night. How tragic, to freeze to death like that, just for a few boxes of fish. Of course the owner is not to blame. He was merely protecting his property. How was he to know there were men in his freezer when he padlocked the doors? He always locks his freezer when he leaves his building, to prevent people from stealing his fish. You can't be too careful these days, there is so much crime now, so many people are out to steal what is rightfully yours. Of course sometimes a box of fish can be a very valuable thing, but you know that already, don't you Mr. Brody?" I felt his eyes on me again.

I nodded because I didn't know what to say and wanted to live. I didn't look at him and wondered how he knew my name.

"Come," he said. "It is too cold for you to stay in here any longer, look at the way you are dressed." He walked out of the freezer. I followed him. Tommy Kay brushed my shoulder as he closed the door behind me. *Tommy Kay.* I didn't look him in the eyes, just like Robson had advised. *Do exactly as you're told.* Now I was scared. Tommy Kay and his boss. The man named Wei Lee. The sociopath. Now what?

It felt almost balmy outside the freezer. I dropped my backpack on the floor and unzipped my jacket, rubbed my hands together, then sensed Kay step up behind me. His hand came down hard on my shoulder.

"Don't move," was all he said. I didn't. He yanked off my jacket and wrung it in his hands like a dish cloth, then dropped it on the floor. He picked up my backpack and squeezed it for a while. When he was satisfied I wasn't carrying a gun, he dropped it on top of my jacket. He frisked me, pulled the knife from my holster, then stepped around me and stood beside his boss.

"My name is Wei Lee," the little man said. "You will call me Mr. Lee. Every one addresses me this way." I watched him remove his wool hat and puffy insulated ski jacket. He held them out to Kay without taking his eyes from mine. Kay took them from him. Lee smoothed his straight black hair and brushed the lapels of his checked flannel shirt. Kay was staring daggers at me, holding Lee's folded jacket over one of his thick forearms, like a butler in waiting. Kay's wide shoulders and thick neck made Lee seem all the more smaller. "Tommy," he said. "Go get our fisherman. It is time to put our fish in the plane. We are leaving for Dawson now."

'We' are leaving for Dawson now? What does he mean by *'we'*?

Tommy looked at his boss, then at me. He was hesitant to leave.

Without breaking his gaze on me, Lee said, "It's alright Tommy. You may go. I'm sure Mr. Brody will be a perfect gentleman. We are only going to be discussing a little business. There is no need to be concerned, isn't that right, Mr. Brody?"

Tommy gave me a menacing look from under those drooping eyelids of his. I managed to meet his eyes and nod. Tommy turned and dropped Wei Lee's coat and hat on the desk, then lumbered toward the man door, his enormous arms and legs swinging about in great wide arcs. After the door closed behind Kay, Lee began pacing back and forth with his hands behind his back. He finally stopped, put a finger to his lips, then pointed it at me.

"You, Mr. Brody, have not been a reliable pilot. You are a very difficult man to locate when I require your services. So I have decided to purchase your airplane. Of course I will need a pilot. You will be my pilot. You will fly my airplane for me. And I will pay you well to do that. But you will only fly for me. You will always be available, always on time, always punctual. If you are unreliable, you will be terminated. Do you understand?"

My airplane? Terminated? The man was diabolical. His attitude was beyond arrogant or hubristic. David Owen's description had been spot on. Lee was indeed a sociopath. I was beginning to get my bearings again. Never mind Robson's advice. My plane wasn't for sale. And neither was I. Now was the time to let him know it.

"Mr. Lee, if and when I decide to sell my plane, I'll be sure to let you know. But right now, it's not for sale. I'm very sorry."

He nodded at me with the hint of a sardonic smile. "I respect a man with an independent spirit such as yours, Mr. Brody. And you obviously have a strong one. I consider that an admirable quality in a man. But I do not have time to deal with fools. Are you a fool?" Lee glanced back at the door that Kay had just exited. Message sent and received.

I took a deep breath and shook my head. "No," I said, trying to appear confident, though failing miserably, I'm sure.

He reached in his shirt pocket and handed me a folded piece of paper. "Good, I didn't think so," he said. "My accountant has prepared a bill of sale for your plane. As you will see, I have already signed it. He tells me you are getting a very fair price. You will sign the bill of sale when we arrive in Dawson. There you will be paid your selling price, in cash."

I quickly unfolded the piece of paper and scanned it for the price. Four hundred thousand dollars. Not bad, but not nearly enough. Not with new floats and a three blade prop. Not with less than three hundred hours since a complete overhaul. Not in this economy. Besides, no amount was enough. My plane wasn't ever going to be for sale.

"Mr. Lee, your offer is very generous, but as I said, my plane is not for sale. And I think right now we should be more concerned with dealing with the *tragedy* that occurred in that freezer behind me. We need to call the police."

Lee stiffened. "No! We shall not be calling the police. One calls the police when one needs protection. The police can no longer protect the men in the freezer. And the men in the freezer are not a threat to anyone, are they? So there is no need to call the police. Do you agree? Do you understand?"

I nodded at him once and looked down at the floor. I folded the bill of sale and put it in my shirt pocket. What was going on here?

Wei Lee was obviously culpable for the demise of the two dead men in the freezer. He wanted to buy my plane so he could control me. And he was used to getting his own way. But if he bought my plane, he wouldn't need me anymore. I'd be like any other pilot for hire – disposable. As he'd just said, I could be *terminated*.

I looked up when the door opened, just in time to watch Jack Kolinsky come hurtling into the building and fall hard to the concrete floor on his hands and knees. Kay casually walked in after him, dusting off his hands. Jack had barely managed to get back on his feet, bent over with his hands on his knees, when Kay snapped a hard kick at the back of his legs. Jack fell hard to his knees again, but once more managed to stand up. Kay shoved him toward us. Jack had apparently been in a recent conversation with Kay and it hadn't gone well. His eyes were swollen almost completely shut and his nose was broken. There were bruises and blood all over his face. His jaw was askew and his lower lip was split. He was hunched over, clutching the right side of his ribcage with his left hand. I could relate to how he was feeling. Wei Lee turned and looked at Jack Kolinsky.

"Ah, Jack! You are back. Very good. You will please help Mr. Brody load our boxes of fish in the plane. And please, hurry, both of you, we are ready to leave now."

'We'. He'd said it again. *'We'* are ready to leave now? Charlie hadn't mentioned that I'd be taking on passengers in Haines. I couldn't let that happen. There'd be no opportunity for me to mark the cash. Besides, where were these two lowlifes going to sit with only one passenger seat?

Jack looked at me as though he was ready to break down. He'd been severely beaten and was a vanquished man. I wondered what he'd said or done to bring out the ire of Tommy Kay. He turned and took a step toward the other end of the building. Kay grabbed his arm and stopped him. "Forklift," Jack slurred through missing teeth, pointing at the machine near the overhead door. Kay let him go.

* * *

All four of us were at the end of the dock in front of my plane. Kay was standing beside me, staring at the canoes on the floats. Behind us stood Lee. Jack was behind us all, sitting in his little forklift with the motor idling. The four long styrofoam boxes were straddled across its forks, ready to be loaded into the plane. Lying on top of the styrofoam boxes was a brown cardboard box that said 'Wild Alaska Sockeye Salmon'.

That extra box had been a tough one to negotiate but Lee had conceded it to me after some smooth talking on my part. At least I thought it had been some smooth talking. I'd explained to Lee that I always receive a free box of salmon for delivering his fish. Hey, why not try? I was just a dumb working stiff pilot working for the upper class and appreciated a tip as much as the next guy. Had Lee extended an olive branch to me when he approved my taking a box of salmon from Jack's freezer? I somehow doubted it. More likely he thought there were benefits in tipping those who might serve him well later, that he could buy dedication and allegiance with money and favors.

Wei Lee walked behind the forklift to watch us load the boxes. Tommy Kay spoke.

"What are these?" he asked in an angry voice.

"Canoes," I said.

"Take them off."

"I can't. I have to deliver them this afternoon to my friends in Minto. I said I'd deliver them and I'm going to deliver them. On the way to Dawson."

"Take them off ," he said again, louder this time, wagging his finger in my face and glaring at me.

Lee stepped between us. "Mr. Brody," he said. "You will obey Mr. Kay. You must take these canoes off at once. We must leave now. Please do as you are told."

"But, Mr. Lee," I said, "these canoes must be delivered to Minto today. This morning I filed a flight a plan with the government. My flight plan says I will land in Minto and deliver them. If I don't land in Minto on schedule, then my friends will think something has happened. They will call the police. The police will start a search and every plane in the Yukon will be sent out to look for me. Do you want that attention?"

Talk about taking a long shot and telling a blatant lie, but what else could I do? Maybe he'd buy it, maybe he wouldn't. It was worth a try. I didn't want to return to Haines tomorrow just to pick up two canoes, and knew they'd never get delivered to Minto if Lee 'terminated' me later today. I thought about Reggie and his regatta while Lee thought long and hard about what I'd just said, staring at me, analyzing me, but saying nothing.

"Look, Mr. Lee," I continued, "this morning I didn't know I was supposed to fly you men to Dawson. I loaded these canoes on my plane in Whitehorse because my friends in Minto want them delivered today. Minto's right on the way to Dawson. We have to stop there anyway, to fuel the plane. It will take only ten minutes to land in Minto, drop them off, fuel the plane, then continue to Dawson. My friends won't even be there when we land. But if they don't find those canoes on the dock at Minto at five o'clock, they'll think something has gone wrong. They *will* notify the police. It is senseless to take that risk. It is just so much easier to let me deliver them as planned, and avoid a needless air search by the police."

I hadn't held my breath for so long since I was a kid in a swimming pool. My argument was pathetic and weak and full of holes, but it was worth the shot. Lee kept staring at me, then finally said, "Okay, Mr. Brody. You may deliver your canoes. But let me be clear. You will pay a high price if I find you are lying. Do you believe me?"

"Yes, Mr. Lee. Thank you."

Lee nodded at Kay. "Tommy, the canoes can stay on the plane. Check everything else. Then load the fish. We need to go."

"Open the door," Kay snapped at me. He wasn't pleased about just having been overruled by his boss. I leaned over a canoe and opened the cargo door, threw my pack and jacket on the passenger seat, and stepped back to the dock. Kay stepped on the float, swung a leg over a canoe, and put a foot on the top rung of the ladder. The ladder creaked and the plane rocked when he stepped up and entered the plane. He rummaged around the back. There was very little to analyze and it didn't take him long to find the plastic bag Charlie had given me in Whitehorse.

"What is this?" he asked, looking in the bag.

"A brand new flare gun and flares, for emergencies," I said.

He held the bag out the door, grabbed the bottom, and shook its contents into the ocean.

"Damn," I said. "I just bought those."

He glared at me again, then took another look around and saw my pack sitting on the passenger seat. He'd already checked it once, but he grabbed it anyway, turned it upside down and shook out its contents on the floor. He knelt over the pile of papers, maps, and everything else that had just fallen out. He honed in on the plastic case that contained the dye kit. He picked up the case and opened it. My heart rose to my throat.

"What is this?" he asked, squinting at the odd looking steel canisters and injection needles.

"They're for the plane's fuel system. I need that equipment to check the fuel. It's important safety equipment."

That was the best I could come up with. I could have kicked myself for not having stored the kit under a seat. I should have taken Robson's advice – land in a remote place – then inject the dye.

Kay studied the open box in his hand, handled each piece, then reached out and shook it over the water. Splash. Splash. Splash. Every piece in the kit was in the water, sinking to the bottom of the Pacific Ocean. Then he dropped the box in the water too. Splash. It floated like a toy boat. My heart sunk. My chance to be a hero was dashed. There would be no arrests for money laundering, no convictions for income tax evasion. It would be back to the drawing board for David Owen and his team at the FBI, and business as usual for the bad guys. I was devastated.

"Load the fish," he barked.

He got out of the plane and I got in. I scooped up everything on the floor and stuffed it all back into my pack, except the two bottles of water I'd bought this morning at the café. I put those on the pilot's seat, then stowed my jacket and pack behind the cargo net. I motioned to Jack and he expertly drove the forklift forward at an angle toward the plane, stopping with the front wheels at the edge of the dock. He pulled a lever that raised the forks up – being careful not to hit the wing – then worked another lever that extended the forks forward until the tips were just over the edge of the cargo bay floor. He got down from his seat and pushed while I pulled, and we slid all the boxes off the forks into the plane. I shoved the boxes to the back of the plane and began arranging them. Jack got back on his machine and backed up a few feet. With the forklift idling between us and our adversaries, Jack stepped back on the float and leaned into the plane. I was on my knees, strapping the boxes to the floor, when he hissed at me. I turned and looked back at him. In a hushed voice he said, "Brody, if you don't kill them today, they'll kill you today."

He disappeared and I heard the forklift drive up the dock toward the warehouse. When I stepped back on the dock, Wei Lee and Tommy Kay were talking to Jack Kolinsky, a hundred feet away. The three of them were standing in front of the warehouse, having a heated exchange. Kay was leaning into Jack's face, poking him in the chest, yelling at him. I was fixated on them. What was going on now? Were they about to kill Jack? Kay must have felt my stare and looked down the dock at me.

"You! You start the plane!" he shouted, jabbing a finger at me. He turned back to Jack and used the same finger to poke him in the chest some more.

I stepped down to the float and opened the pilot's door. I was sick about losing the injection kit – deflated, humiliated and embarrassed – and certainly didn't feel like flying. I just wanted to run away and hide somewhere. I was about to lose my plane, and according to Jack, maybe my life too. But I had no other choice, no other choice other than to do what I'd just been told to do. 'Start the plane'. When I put a foot up on the pilot door ladder, I saw the two bottles of water sitting on the pilot's seat.

It was then that I had another epiphany. It wasn't a plan, not yet, just an impulse to do something crazy, something that might provide me with an option later on, and maybe a chance to save my life. I made a desperate decision in a desperate situation and opened the fuel door in front of me. I unscrewed the front tank's filler cap.

With my back to the three men at the other end of the dock, I poured both bottles of water into the front fuel tank.

FIFTY ONE

With six hundred pounds of fuel, six hundred pounds of people, four hundred pounds of cargo, a hundred pounds of luggage, and a couple of canoes tied to the floats, my DeHavilland Beaver easily took off from Chilkat Inlet into a south wind. It had been making takeoffs like that for sixty years and will probably be making them for another sixty years. The Beaver will likely be the first aircraft to still be in daily commercial service a hundred years after it was built. What a plane. And I owned one. And it wasn't for sale.

I climbed off the ocean with a slow right turn to the west and continued the turn until we were heading northwest, up the Chilkat Inlet toward Mount Seltat. Ten minutes later we were five thousand feet over the sea, still climbing, and I made another shallow turn to the right. The nose was now pointed directly at Minto, two hundred and twenty miles north. With a strong south wind pushing us from behind, we'd be there in a little over two hours. It was time to come up with a plan. But what?

I glanced at Wei Lee. He looked ridiculous wearing headphones over his wool hat and bug-eyed sunglasses. With his puffy gold ski jacket he reminded me of an insect missing its antennae. He seemed content and confident, watching the scenery creep by his window. I couldn't tell what Kay was doing. He was sitting behind me in an aluminum deck chair that he'd taken from Jack. The plane would rock every time he slid the chair from one side of the cargo bay to the other. He didn't have headphones, there were only two in the plane, and I hoped he was miserable with the noise from the big radial engine. I kept climbing, knowing well that a good way to calm down aggressive passengers, and even put them to sleep, is to deprive them of oxygen. At eight thousand feet I leveled out. At that altitude we were breathing thirty five percent less oxygen than at sea level. If nothing else, I hoped the diminished oxygen supply would keep the two men calm. With a little luck, the thin air might even give them both whopping headaches.

We left the Chilkat River valley and headed inland. Mount Seltat crept by us on the left and brilliant white glaciers rose under the plane as we flew into the Coastal Mountains. I watched Mount Skukum appear at one o'clock off the nose, smothered in ice and snow, over seven thousand feet high, thirty five miles north. I watched the altimeter as I trimmed the elevator to hold our altitude, eight thousand feet, plenty high to fly over anything on the flight path to Minto.

There's a saying that flying is hours of boredom punctuated by moments of sheer terror. But today wasn't going to be boring because there was lots to think about, in particular how to deal with the two criminals in my plane. First things first, though – fuel. There are three fuel tanks in the belly of a Beaver – the front and middle tanks each hold thirty five gallons – the rear holds twenty three. Today I'd flown from Whitehorse down to Haines on the front tank and in a little over an hour had burned two thirds of it, pushing two canoes at a hundred miles an hour into a strong south wind. Of course I'd switched tanks before taking off from Haines, having poured two quarts of drinking water into the front one. I was now flying on the rear tank, the objective being to lighten the rear of the plane with Kay and four hundred pounds of 'fish' and cargo back there. Climbing takes lots of power and uses lots of fuel. Canoes are obviously not aerodynamic, and adding their drag to a one ton load had turned my plane into a gas guzzler. So even with the wind behind us, the rear tank was going down fast.

It wouldn't be long before I had to switch over to the middle tank. Now finished with climbing, my plane was burning twenty two gallons an hour at an airspeed of ninety miles an hour.

Halfway up Kusawa Lake we were a hundred and sixty miles from Minto and the rear tank was virtually empty. I switched over to the middle tank and was now down to the final thirty five gallons of useable fuel left in the plane, barely enough to reach Minto. *Barely.* Of course the front tank was entirely useless now, with two bottles of drinking water sloshing around inside it.

Or was it? It was then and there that I came up with a couple of ideas that might save my life.

* * *

A few miles north of Carmacks the Yukon River begins to snake and weave, flowing back and forth, from east to west, then west to east, changing direction in one hundred and eighty degree hairpin turns, one turn after another, for about twenty miles. It was this section of the river that I thought was as good a place as any to hatch 'Plan A'. I also had another idea, 'Plan B' – it might work too – but it would clearly be my second choice. It was now or never to try either one.

I took a deep breath, slowly reached my left hand out to a spot low on the left side of the console, and turned the fuel selector lever to the front tank. What I expected to happen should be just a matter of time. If I was right, it wouldn't take long.

Wei Lee was dozing beside me. I had no idea what Tommy Kay was doing. I hadn't looked back at him once for the whole time since we'd left Haines. Not once had I heard either man say a word since we'd taken off. I guess flying at eight thousand feet for an hour had calmed them down.

I heard the first back fire from the engine a minute later. It was just a 'pop'. But a few seconds later there was another pop, followed shortly by another, and an other. Pop, pop, pop. The water in the front tank was in the carburetor now. Excellent.

"What is wrong?" exclaimed Lee, sitting up ramrod straight in his seat, trying to look over the console at the propeller.

"I don't know," I said with mock panic in my voice, pulling the throttle lever back and pushing the nose down. I pretended to get very busy with the controls, trying to solve the problem. I turned on the carb heat, pumped the flaps down ten degrees, and pushed the prop lever ahead to keep the revs up.

Pop, pop, pow – splutter, splutter – pop, pop, pow! The big engine was really struggling now, backfiring frequently, quickly losing power. I didn't want to damage it so backed the throttle off even more and richened the mixture.

"What is wrong?" he shouted again. "What is wrong with the plane?"

"I don't know!" I shouted back, doing my best to appear desperate and frantic. I pushed the yoke forward and adjusted the trim to hold the nose down and maintain airspeed, then started playing with various levers and switches that didn't have anything to do with engine, trying to impress my agitated passenger. I turned the plane a little to the left and pointed it exactly where I wanted to go. I kept pushing and pulling levers that had nothing to do with the engine or the flight surfaces. I must have turned the cabin heat on and off three times. I hoped Lee was sold on my efforts to save his life. The engine was really spluttering and missing now. It would almost stop, then start again, then almost stop, then start again. When I knew I could make it to my intended landing spot, I pumped the flaps down another ten degrees, pulled the mixture lever back to full lean, closed the throttle, feathered the prop, turned off the mags, and turned off the master switch.

The lights and gauges went dark. The radios quit. The engine stopped. The propeller stopped. The plane was dead in the air.

The only sound in the cockpit now was the wind rushing past the wings, the floats, and the canoes. It's an eerie experience to be high above the ground in an airplane when the sound of an engine dies, especially when it's the only engine you have. Wei Lee and Tommy Kay were about to experience their first dead stick landing.

"I have to make an emergency landing!" I yelled, though it was hardly noisy in the cabin. "Fasten your seatbelts!"

I felt a hand grab my seatback and looked to my right. Kay was on his knees with a hand on each seat. "What is wrong with the plane? What are you doing?" he screamed in my ear.

I turned to my right and looked straight into his enormous wide face and menacing eyes, now only inches from mine. It was terrifying to be that close to him. A tiger would have backed off. I turned away, yanked off my headphones, and yelled back, "The engine has stopped! I have to make an emergency landing! That's what I'm doing! Now let me concentrate!"

His hand came off my seat and the cabin went quiet. There was a job to do now and I was in charge. I hoped to keep it that way.

'Learning to fly' is five percent learning how to fly and ninety five percent learning how to stop flying, commonly referred to as *landing*. It had been a long time since I'd practiced landing without power, though it's not a particularly difficult thing to do in a small plane with big wings. The challenge is that you don't have an engine to adjust your speed and altitude on approach, so there's no changing your mind and 'going around' for another try if you make a mistake with your angle of descent. But as long as you have decent terrain to land on, pick the right landing spot – and make a perfect approach – it's a 'piece of cake'.

At two thousand feet over a dense spruce forest I surveyed the Yukon River. It was like a mountain road, winding back and forth in a series of short lateral stretches, each stretch terminating in a tight hairpin switchback. It looked like a compressed spring, coiled all the way to the horizon. The river was meandering steadily northward, but would flow east for a while, then turn north and double back to flow west, then turn north again and head back east, repeating the sequence over and over. We were heading north with a strong south wind behind us and would need to turn around, land in the other direction, into the wind. I planned to land on one of those north-south hairpin bends to give us a good long 'runway'.

We were flying without power, gliding and descending eight

hundred feet a minute, heading down the east side of the river's wide corridor. At a thousand feet above the trees I pumped the flaps down another five degrees, turned the wheel hard over to the left, and began a steep turn toward the river valley's west side. The cabin was dead quiet except for the wind whistling past us, though I'm certain my passengers were both wide-eyed and alert. I was a little high over the forest so stood on the right rudder and turned the wheel even farther left, side slipping the plane to lose altitude, sliding sideways through the air in a long descending left hand turn that was taking us ever lower. I finished the turn and straightened out when I was heading due south. My target was now dead ahead, a hairpin in the river. We were going a hundred miles an hour, skimming over the tree tops, a blur of green rushing under us just feet below the floats. The trees vanished in a flash when we crossed a strip of brown sandy beach, then the river was under us. I flattened the wings and let the plane sink slowly, bleeding off speed, keeping it pointed straight into the wind, holding the nose as high as I dared. Ten feet off the water I was still holding a little back pressure on the yoke, still bleeding off speed, letting the wings mush over a cushion of air just over the water. The plane was barely going sixty miles an hour when the floats kissed the river. They skipped once, settled down, planed for a hundred yards, and began to settle. I eased the yoke forward and let them plow into the water. Seconds later we came to a virtual stop against the wind and the current. We'd landed on the Yukon River.

'Piece of cake'.

It wasn't long before the current and the wind were combining to accelerate the plane backwards. In no time we were moving downstream at a good clip. Now for the real challenge. Secure the plane to land without damaging a wing, or the tail, or worse: snag a float or a wing on something, flip over, and sink the plane to the floats.

"What are you doing? Fix the plane!" Tommy Kay, my tyrannical tour guide, was animated again. Back to reality.

"I can't fix the engine on the river! We need to tie the plane to the shore! I need some rope!"

It felt good to yell at him though I didn't dare look at him when I did. As long as he needed a pilot, I could probably get away it. I opened my door and swung it forward against the fuselage. We were moving fast. The plane was like a weathervane with its nose pointed south into the wind, drifting north down the river, going backwards. It was difficult to tell where the current might take us. The south wind was pushing us toward the north shore as the river turned east. I could only hope that the current and back eddies would provide enough interference to keep us off the shore for a little while longer, out of harms way from rocks and trees. Three things had to go right for me to beach the plane safely. The first thing was to find a good strong tree on a wide open beach to tie a rope. The second thing was to figure out how to get the rope to the tree. The third thing was to get the first two things done in a hurry. The easiest way was obvious. I looked back at Kay.

"I need you to hand me that big bag of rope from the back of the plane," I said.

He looked at me with a combination of disdain and outrage. He only took orders from one man. Kay looked at Lee. Lee looked at Kay, then at me, then nodded. Kay crawled on his knees to the back of the plane and dug around. He picked up a duffle bag as easily as I'd pick up a grocery bag.

"Not that one, the other one," I said. He slid the other duffle bag up to me. I leaned back between the seats, unzipped it and quickly found what I wanted. The longest, strongest rope in the bag.

"I need my knife," I said, looking directly into his face.

"No. No knife."

"Then hand me a paddle."

"No. No paddle."

I looked at Lee. "Mr. Lee, do you want to drown? If we don't tie up the plane it may hit something and tip over. I can't tie up the plane unless I get a rope to the shore using a canoe. I need a knife and a paddle."

Lee looked at me for what seemed like a long time. We were moving fast, probably five miles an hour, drifting ever closer to the shore. The plane was starting a lazy spin to the left as we began drifting east. We were out of control and I was anxious.

"Tommy. Give Mr. Brody a paddle. And his knife." Kay didn't look pleased but did what he was told. I'd just challenged him again on a matter of his authority and could feel the tension building. At the first hint I was no longer needed, Kay would just as soon kill me as argue again.

He turned around and pulled out a paddle. He reached in his jacket and pulled out my knife. He handed me the paddle, then with a long cold stare held out the knife. Blade end first. I had no choice but to hold out my hand, palm up and open. He laid the blade in my hand and held on to the handle a little longer than he had to. 'I'll get you' was written all over his face. He let go of the knife.

I stepped out on the top rung of the pilot's ladder, and with one end of the coil of rope in my hand, leaned down and tied it to the bow of the canoe below me. Then I cut the straps holding the canoe to the float struts, hooked a foot under the gunwale, and flipped it over. The canoe fell off the float with a bounce and a bump and splashed in the water. When the canoe settled alongside the float I made a wrap with the rope around a strut and tied a loose knot. I grabbed the paddle and threw it into the canoe. Now I had a boat ready to go.

I stepped down to the float, crouched and peered under the fuselage at the river bank, looking for a place to tie up. We were moving around the bend and beginning to drift east, now just a hundred feet from the shoreline. As I'd hoped, at least for the moment, the current was keeping the plane out in the river. I grabbed the coil of rope off my seat, found the end, and threw the rest into the canoe. With the end of the rope in my hand I shuffled up to the front of the float and tied it to the front cleat. The canoe and the plane were now connected by a two hundred foot rope.

I was all set now and scanned the bank again for a landing spot. Five hundred feet downstream there was a stubby gravel spit protruding fifty feet out into the river. A few stubborn old spruce trees were still growing on it, leaning heavily over the water. If the shoreline downstream of the spit was open, then a tree on the spit would be a great place to tie the rope and secure the plane. I couldn't see the shore below the spit, but there were no tree tops in sight, and decided to gamble it was open beach. I untied the loose knot on the strut, jumped into the canoe, and paddled hard toward the shore with the rope paying off the bottom into the water behind me. I scraped bottom at the gravel beach fifteen seconds later, leapt out and dragged the canoe onto the shore. I untied the knot from the bow, and to my surprise, saw that the rope was about to go taut as the plane drifted past me. With the end of the rope wrapped around my wrist, I ran as fast as I could down the beach toward the spit, a couple of hundred feet downstream. I was barely keeping up with the plane drifting along beside me, trying to keep the rope tight and skipping it across the water so I could run with it. The shoreline was a mix of sand, gravel and small round rocks, wet and soft and slippery, and running on it was exhausting. I wasn't sure if I'd make it to the trees before the plane passed me, or before I passed out. I was losing the race with the plane but then, with everything I had left, made a final mad dash out to the end of the spit.

There was only ten feet of loose rope in my hand when I made the first wrap around a big spruce tree at the end of the spit. I made one more wrap, tied a knot with barely enough rope left, and watched. Seconds later the rope tightened as the plane drifted past the point. It jerked up like a fish that had just been hooked, spun toward me, then settled down. Waves built up at the front of floats as it braked against the current and began to swing around in a long arc toward the shore. It eventually stopped below me in a back eddy, fifty feet from the shore, now tethered to a single tree by a single rope almost two hundred feet long.

I walked back up the beach to the canoe and pushed off. I paddled down to the plane and pulled alongside the left float. Tommy Kay was standing on it, looking down at me as if I was crazy.

"What are you doing? Fix the plane. We must leave." Kay was yelling again.

"First we get the plane closer to shore. Then we'll see if I can 'fix the plane'. Now hold this canoe while I get another rope."

Lee looked down at me from the passenger seat, then nodded at Kay. Kay knelt down and held the canoe against the float while I climbed into the cargo bay and retrieved another rope. I got back in the canoe, paddled around the rear of the plane, and over to the right float. I tied one end of the new rope to its front cleat, then paddled to shore with it. I beached the canoe and walked toward the forest with the rope paying out behind me. I made a single wrap around the first tree I reached and tied a temporary knot. Now I could haul the plane in closer to shore. I pulled on the rope. The plane didn't move. I pulled harder. My feet slipped out from under me and my rump made a soft landing in the sand. I'd might as well have been trying to pull a truck out of a ditch. This wasn't going to work. Now what?

Then the rope went tight. I looked up at the plane and was flabbergasted. Tommy Kay was sitting on the float with his feet dangling in the water, pulling on the rope tied to the tree behind me. The plane was moving toward me. He kept hauling the rope in, hand over hand in an effortless rhythm, until the right float brushed the river bottom. The plane was now twenty feet from shore, thanks to the human winch. He was that strong.

I sloshed through the bitter cold water out to the plane.

"Loop the rope around that cleat," I said, pointing. He glared, then made the loop.

"Thank you," I said. He didn't say 'you're welcome'. I took it from him and tied a good knot. Kay slid off the float into two feet of water. He waded over to the canoe on the beach, and walked it back out to the plane. He held it while his boss got in, then walked the canoe and Lee back to the shore.

"You! You fix the plane," Kay shouted from the beach, jabbing a finger in my direction.

Lee stepped out of the canoe and looked up and down the beach with his hands on his hips, surveying his surroundings like he'd just discovered a new continent. I thought if I wanted to live a little longer, I'd better try to 'fix the plane'. I climbed into the cargo bay and found my bag of tools. It was time to put on a show for my passengers.

I walked to the front of the float, flipped a few latches, and raised the cowl on the right side of the engine. I hadn't done that for a couple of weeks and was pleased to see that everything was clean, oil free, and in perfect working order. But the scumbags on the beach didn't know that. I spent the next two minutes making a lot of noise with various tools, rattling them around in the engine bay, knocking them against things, frequently reaching down to the bag at my feet and switching them around, doing everything I could think of to present the appearance of a competent mechanic, trying in earnest to 'fix the plane'. I only burned myself once on the exhaust pipe. When I was tired of hitting my plane with tools, I wiped my hands on a rag, got back inside, and pushed the starter button. The prop turned a few revolutions and quit when I released the button. Of course the engine wasn't going to start, not with the mags off and the throttle closed. But the men on the beach didn't know that. I went back to the engine again and clinked and clanked some more with my head buried deep under the cowl. I had my back to the beach but knew the two men standing twenty feet behind me were watching my every move. I got back in the plane again, and without looking at them, pushed the starter button again. This time I let the prop turn for a good ten seconds. Of course the engine still wasn't going to start without ignition or fuel. I released the starter button, got down on the float, went back to the engine, stuck my head under the cowl one last time, then stepped back and threw my rag into the water with an overt display of apparent disgust. I kicked the front float strut and wondered if they were going to buy into my pantomime. I closed the cowl and threw the bag of tools back into the cargo bay. I sloshed through the water to the two men on shoreand said, "Looks like it needs a new magneto. Sorry gentlemen, we're going to have to wait for help."

"What is that? A 'mag-nee-tow ,'" asked Kay.

"It's the thing that makes the spark for the engine. It's cracked. It's finished. No spark, no engine, no flying. We need a new one."

He glared the curse of death at me.

"*Who* are we waiting to help us, Mr. Brody? *Who* will come?" It was Wei Lee speaking now. I wondered then if he believed anything I'd ever said to him. He was analyzing me with his dead dark eyes. It was impossible to read them, but perhaps they belied a hint of anxiety.

"Well," I said, slowly. "It must be five o'clock by now." I paused and looked at the enormous gaudy watch on his delicate wrist.

He raised it to his face. "It is exactly five fifteen. Why do you want to know the time?"

"Because we are now officially overdue in Minto. Like I told you in Haines, my friends were expecting their canoes at five o'clock. They will now report to the police that I am overdue. The police will soon start searching for us. But we'll be easy to find. We're on the direct path for the flight plan I filed. They'll know where to look for us. The plane will be easy to see from the air. We shouldn't have to wait more than a couple of hours."

"I asked w*ho* will be coming to help us!" shouted Lee.

"Oh. Like I said, the police, they'll probably come in a helicopter. It's too difficult to land a plane where we are right now. But the police have a helicopter."

He looked dark and intense and agitated. "Tommy!"

Kay stepped up beside Lee, poised to rip my arms off. *Please, no.* I looked at the canoe on the beach and was ready to make a run for it. Lee flicked his chin sideways without dropping his eyes from mine. Tommy turned and retreated down the beach about twenty feet, then stopped and turned around, watching us.

"Mr. Brody. Do you think I am a fool?"

"No, Mr. Lee, I don't."

"Good. Then listen to me carefully." He paused for a moment, looked me up and down, then locked his eyes on mine. "I am a business man, Mr. Brody. A very successful businessman. But I only stay successful because I do not allow anyone to steal from me, and I do not allow anyone to tell me lies. When people steal from me, when people tell me lies...they are making *fatal* mistakes. Do you believe me?"

I cleared my throat and nodded. "Yes, Mr. Lee."

He stared at me for a long time, then said, "Good. I am pleased that you believe me. That will be best for both of us. It will make everything much easier. Now, I have a problem. I am very good at solving problems. But perhaps today you can help me solve a problem." He paused for a moment. "In the plane I have some boxes of fish that must be delivered to Dawson. They must be there today. But the police do not deliver fish, do they?"

"No, Mr. Lee, but..."

"Stop," he said, raising his hand. "We do not need the help of the police because the police do not deliver fish, do they?"

"No."

"Good. I am glad you understand. Now, what else can you do to fix the plane?"

"Nothing. It has a broken part in the engine. The part can't be repaired. We need a replacement, a new part." I was still lying to him. If I wasn't wearing blue jeans he would have heard my knees knocking. He nodded, mulling over my answer, staring straight through me with his strange eyes.

Then something moved over his shoulder. It was a long way down the shore, almost too far to discern. But I knew what it was. Nothing else in this world moves like that. It was clearly coming toward us. Slowly but surely, and definitely toward us. I kept my eyes on it.

"Do not look at Tommy when I am speaking to you, Mr. Brody."

"I am not looking at Tommy, Mr. Lee."

"Then what are you looking at?"

"A bear."

FIFTY TWO

He was big, probably a male, tall at the shoulders, and thin after spending a long Yukon winter hibernating in a cave, eating almost nothing in the last five months. Bears are grumpy and hungry in the spring and I knew exactly why he was headed our way. With a sense of smell ten thousand times keener than ours, he'd picked up a whiff of something. Something called salmon. Just a few molecules from a box of fish in my plane had carried north to him on the south wind. He was following his nose.

"Where is a bear?" asked Lee.

"Down there, on the shore, at the very end," I said, pointing at a dark brown shape about a thousand feet downstream, clearly moving toward us. "He just came around the point. See him? Right beside the river."

"I do not see a bear."

You've got to be kidding.

"You will soon," I said. "As long as he keeps walking this way, he'll be here in a few minutes. I strongly suggest, Mr. Lee, that we leave right away."

"How can we leave? The plane does not work."

"In the canoes."

"I am not travelling in a canoe, Mr. Brody."

You may soon change your mind, you arrogant bastard.

I took a step to my left to get a better look at the bear. Definitely a grizzly. Definitely a male. I stood with my hands on my hips and watched him for a moment. He stopped and raised his nose to analyze the air, then lowered his head and resumed plodding toward us. He had no incentive to go any faster. No sense in wasting energy when you don't have to. He knew he'd get to where he wanted to go, just by walking. Don't we all?

We still had a couple of minutes provided he didn't pick up his pace. Or start running. Few people are aware of how fast a lazy looking grizzly bear can run. They can sprint thirty miles an hour. They can catch a horse out of the gate.

I wasn't sure what to do next. It had been a hell of a day. No breakfast or coffee this morning, an ornery customs officer, two dead men in a freezer, and here I was stranded on a river bank in the Yukon wilderness with two criminals, who according to Jack Kolinsky, planned to kill me today. And now there was a hungry grizzly bear approaching and Wei Lee was refusing to get in a canoe. It was time to try some more lies on him.

"Mr. Lee, may I be perfectly honest?"

"Of course, Mr. Brody."

"Well sir, I'm guessing that whatever's in those boxes in the back of the plane is a lot more valuable to you than fish. If that's true, you don't want to be around when the police come to rescue us. We're in Canada now and the first thing they'll want to see is your passport. And when they discover that you didn't clear Canadian customs, they'll want to look inside those boxes. And I'm guessing you don't want that to happen."

Lee cocked his head and looked at me quizzically.

"Continue, Mr. Brody."

"Well," I said, taking off my ball cap and scratching my head, trying to appear like I really wasn't in a hurry. "You could avoid that situation. Dawson isn't very far from here. The river current is fast and the paddling would be easy. We'd make good time, we could be in Dawson with your boxes in five or six hours. If we leave now, we'll be there before midnight. Better late than never,

Mr. Lee. And you won't have to deal with the police. And we won't have to deal with that bear over there. Which will be here in a minute or so. Just a suggestion. Sir."

I pointed at the bear again. "Look, Mr. Lee. He's getting closer." He *was* getting closer, close enough for me to see his eyes. Tommy was still glaring at me with hatred, apparently with no idea what was behind him. He'd hadn't turned around once, not even with all my pointing. But when Wei Lee pointed at the bear, Tommy Kay finally turned around and saw it himself for the first time. He didn't turn back to us.

Lee was squinting his eyes. "Yes. I think I see it. It is coming this way. You were not lying, were you?"

"No, I was not lying."

Not about that, you lowlife.

It dawned on me then that Wei Lee must have weak eyesight. He hadn't recognized the bear until it was only a couple of hundred feet away. I took a deep breath and waited for what seemed like a long time.

Come on, make up your mind. We have to go!

"You are a very logical man, aren't you Mr. Brody?"

"I try to be," I said.

He was mulling over his two choices: stay where we were and deal with a hungry grizzly bear, or leave in a canoe. He looked me over, analyzing me with clinical interest. Kay was watching the bear, then turned around and glared at me, as though he couldn't wait to kill me. As though the bear was somehow my fault. The bear that was getting ever closer.

"Mr. Lee…"

"Stop". Wei Lee raised his hand. He could see the bear walking toward us, now less than a hundred feet from Tommy. Tommy was watching it too. At that instant Lee must have finally appreciated its size and strength and power. Perhaps a primeval sense of fear had finally stirred inside him, something to instill a sense of urgency, a desire for survival.

"Alright, Mr. Brody. We shall canoe to Dawson. Tommy!"

* * *

We were on the plane when the bear arrived. Lee was sitting in the passenger seat. Kay was sitting on the cargo bay floor with his feet hanging over the other canoe. I was standing at the front of the float. He stopped in front of us.

He was big for a Yukon grizzly, over four feet at the shoulders, probably four hundred pounds, and like all bears his size at this time of year, looking forward to gaining another two hundred pounds over the summer. He was standing on all fours at the water's edge, calmly appraising us from twenty feet away, sniffing the air with the end of the wing directly over his head.

Please don't stand up. You might hit your head. And damage my plane.

'So where's the fish?', he must have been thinking, watching three strange creatures staring back at him from an odd-looking contraption floating on the river.

I pulled my knife out, knelt down over the cleat at my feet, and cut the rope that had been holding us to shore. It snapped and whipped through the air past his nose. He jumped, walked over to the rope, gave it a sniff, then moved toward us, stopping when all four of his island-sized paws were in the water.

The plane slowly drifted away from the shore, swinging out into the river. It stopped at the same spot where Kay had begun hauling us in toward the beach, about fifty feet from the beach, resting stationary in the eddy, once again tethered by a single rope to the tree on the spit, two hundred feet upstream. We'd gained a little breathing room. A little.

The bear lifted his head and drew circles in the air with his nose, then casually walked back on the beach and began investigating the scent of our shoes. He circled the spot where we'd been standing only a few minutes ago. No fish there. It was time for us to get going, before he figured out the plane was where he ought to be looking.

I retrieved the short piece of cut rope hanging from the cleat and tied it to the bow of the other canoe, then cut the straps holding it to the float, and flipped it over. It fell in the water with a bump and a splash. We had two boats in the water now, one on either side of the plane. I looked at the bear for a reaction. He was staring at me with his head tilted, apparently curious about what I'd just done.

Kay held the canoe against the right float. Lee climbed in and sat down on the front seat. I climbed into the plane and slid two paddles, the four styrofoam boxes, and the cardboard box with Christine's sockeye salmon out to Kay. With ease Tommy lifted the first three styrofoam boxes out of the plane and placed them on the floor of their canoe. There was a pregnant moment as we both stared at the three long white boxes in *their* canoe. There simply wasn't room for another one. The fourth styrofoam box would have to go in my canoe. So would my cardboard box full of salmon. Kay stood on the float and stared at me. I knew that stare. It was intended to intimidate and terrify, and it was working. I'd better take good care of that styrofoam box.

I handed Kay their luggage – two small soft bags – and he stuffed them under Wei Lee's seat. I held their canoe while Kay stepped in. It almost tipped over but I managed to save it. I handed him the two kids paddles and crouched down on the float.

"Hey, Mr. Kay," I whispered in deference to our new friend on shore. "Always keep your weight low and near the center of a canoe, and kneel on the floor when you paddle. Lay your paddle across the top of the canoe to balance yourself when you move around or it may tip over." He glared at me but took my advice. The bow of their overloaded canoe was high in the water when Kay got himself situated at the back. "Mr. Kay," I whispered again, "let's push those boxes and your bags forward a little, for balance." He gave me another one of his 'you're a dead man' looks but helped me shove the three styrofoam boxes a foot forward toward Lee. Lee was sitting on the front seat with his hands on the gunnels. It didn't look to me like he had any intention of doing any paddling, so I spared him any advice. The bow had gone down a little, but only 'a little'. I untied their canoe at the bow.

"Okay, Mr. Kay," I said. "You can let go now". I gave their canoe a mighty push backwards to send the two men on their way, out of the eddy, into the current, down the river. But Kay didn't let go, maintaining a firm grip on the float. Their canoe didn't budge. They weren't going anywhere.

"No," said Kay. "First *you* leave. Then *we* leave. Get in *your* canoe."

It had almost worked. It would have been that easy. Give their canoe a push, watch them drift away in the current, get back in my plane, switch back to the middle tank, start the engine, cut the rope, release the other canoe, and fly away. I could have taken off alone. I could have escaped. I would have had all the time in the world. Kay couldn't possibly paddle back to the plane to stop me, not against the current. And he wouldn't have had time to paddle to shore, run back up the beach, and swim out to the plane. Especially not with a big grizzly hanging around. No chance he could have got past the bear. All that the two men could have done was paddle down the Yukon River while I took off, watched them from the air, radioed the RCMP in Carmacks, and waited for the cops to come out and pick them up. But that scenario was moot now. Tommy Kay may have been 'dumb', but he was 'dumb like a fox'. He wasn't going to let go of the plane until I left in my canoe first.

So much for 'Plan A'.

I looked at the bear on the beach. He hadn't moved but was bobbing his head up and down. Not a good sign. He shuffled a few more feet out into the river to see what we'd do. He was giving us fair warning and getting way too close for comfort. He began swaying his head back and forth, huffing and snorting, bouncing up and down on his front legs. He was out of patience and letting us know it.

What's wrong with these two-legged creatures? Every time I approach two-legged creatures, they run away. Why don't these ones run away?

The big grizzly took another step out into the river. Then another. The current was now boiling around his front legs. Both cargo doors were open and the wind was blowing through the plane, straight into his face. I knew he could smell the fish inside. He knew exactly where the scent he'd picked up miles away was coming from. But could he possibly know that just forty feet in front of him was a veritable feast, a cardboard box full of sockeye salmon?

Evidently so, because now he was swimming out to the plane. *Shit!*

In twenty seconds – it felt like five minutes – and without once looking at the bear, I pulled out the two remaining boxes, the last paddle, my backpack, and threw them all into the canoe on the other side of the plane. I'd never moved so fast in my whole life. I was good to go.

I cut the rope on the bow and jumped in, grabbed a paddle with one hand, a float strut with the other, and ducked down to look under the fuselage. Where was he?

Kay was still holding on to the float on the other side and his canoe was blocking my view. Then he let go and his canoe moved back along the float. The instant its bow glided past the cargo door ladder, a big wet paw came out of the water and flopped down on the far float. Wei Lee must have felt the bear's breath in his face when he glided past him. That was close.

A second paw flopped down on the float, then an enormous wet head rose up between the paws. The float went down and the plane tilted when the big bear tried to pull himself up. He lost his grip and slipped back into the water. The plane rocked violently. I knew he wouldn't quit, though. He'd keep trying and it wouldn't take him long to figure out how to get up on the float and climb into my plane.

I couldn't let him do that. Somehow I had to stop him. If he got inside, he'd ravage the whole thing. He'd rip and tear things apart for an hour before he gave up looking for fish that weren't there, fish that were now in my canoe. He'd destroy my plane.

My only chance to save my pride and joy was to break a cardinal rule of wilderness living. I had to feed a bear.

I reached forward with my knife and slit open the cardboard box full of salmon, peeled open the flaps, and slashed the thick plastic bag inside. I looked back at Kay and Lee who were behind the tail of the plane, floating stationary in the eddy, looking back and forth at me and the bear. I knew that Kay could paddle up to me in a heartbeat. But that didn't matter. Bear or no bear, there was no longer an opportunity for me to escape by flying away. I could never hope to get back inside the plane and start it before Kay grabbed and killed me. He started paddling up to me but I ignored him. The bear was still trying to climb up on the other float and the plane was rocking wildly.

"Let go of the plane!" he shouted. I wasn't sure if Kay meant me or the bear.

The bear didn't let go and neither did I. I wasn't going to let go, not yet anyway. Instead, I reached inside the plastic bag, pulled out an ice cold salmon, and threw it under the plane to the other side. It hit the water with a splash. The bear looked to his left at the frozen fish floating beside him, his paws still draped over the float, his four inch claws shining through his wet fur. He was thinking – thinking about the fish beside him – the fish drifting ever so slowly away from him. He made the decision I was hoping for. He slipped off the float, and with a few powerful strokes, caught up to the fish, chomped down on it with his powerful jaws, and headed to shore with his prize.

"Let go of the plane! We must leave!" I looked to my left. Kay was so close he could have grabbed me. I did what I was told and let go of the plane. My canoe glided down the float and I stopped behind the tail.

Instead of following me though, Kay grabbed the cargo ladder and pulled himself in to the float. He turned his head and looked back at me.

"Go!" he yelled at me again. "Go!"

I didn't. I sat motionless in my canoe, watching the beach to see what the bear would do with his salmon. There was no salmon. He was looking at me, licking his chops.

'*More sir*'.

Okay, Mr. Bear. I'll give you more. Lots more.

I paddled toward the shore and heaved another salmon at him. It landed with a splash ten feet in front of him. He sloshed out into the water, picked it up with his mouth, and returned to the beach. He was a fast learner. I watched him eat his second fish. He put a paw on its tail, sunk his big teeth into its midsection, then lifted his head up and ripped it in two. He gulped down the piece in his mouth. The sand and pebbles he'd swallowed with it didn't seem to bother him. Just an average four pound bite of frozen fish for a four hundred pound bear, garnished nicely with a little sand and gravel. He gulped down the other half.

Good boy.

"Follow me, there's more!" I yelled at him, back paddling out of the eddy and letting the current carry me a hundred feet down the shore. I knew that once I'd left the eddy there'd be no going back, no way I could paddle against that current to return to my plane. But all I cared about was moving that bear down the beach. I let the wind blow my canoe toward the shore and used my paddle to push it in the last couple of feet until it grounded on the gravel bottom. I waited until the bear started walking toward me for his third installment. When he was close, I threw another fish on the beach, then pushed off and let the current carry me downstream. I watched him eat his third fish. Another hundred feet down the shore I grounded my canoe again and threw another fish on the beach. I waited for him to walk down and eat that one. He did. That was four. He followed me down the beach for another one.

Good Bear.

When he got close again, I threw him another one, pushed off and drifted down the shore once more. He ate the fifth fish in thirty seconds. Five down, five to go, though I was hoping he might say 'uncle' before they were all gone.

Sorry about your fish, Christine. I might have to feed them all to my new friend.

Turns out I did. I fed him the whole box, a total of ten sockeye salmon, more or less eighty pounds in total, in less than ten minutes. He followed me every time I'd moved down the beach, and every time he followed, I'd thrown him another fish. Quite the game we'd played.

He ate the last salmon just above the point where I'd first laid eyes on him, about a thousand feet downstream of my plane. I had nothing left to give him. But surely ten fish had been enough, surely he wouldn't have an urge to return to my plane to look for more. Hopefully I could return soon and find my plane still in one piece, fly it out of there before he got hungry again.

The last thing I did before paddling out into the river was watch him watch me for a while. He was sitting on the beach, squatted on his haunches. I was in my canoe, twenty feet in front of him, holding myself stationary in the current with my paddle shoved into the sandy river bottom. He was looking at me stoically.

"You leave that plane alone, you hear me?" I shouted at him, pointing at my plane. He stared at me without any reaction. Go figure. Then he settled down on his rear end and dropped his paws to his knees, studying me with a blank expression, proudly displaying his swollen belly with all the arrogance of an English earl. I hurled the empty cardboard box at him. It landed in the water between us, then slowly drifted toward him in the wind. He ignored it. He was done. He was full.

Uncle.

He fell over on his side, rolled onto his back, and with all four paws in the air, began squirming in the sand.

Time for 'Plan B'.

* * *

I looked up the shore at my plane while back paddling out into the river. Tommy Kay had let go of the ladder and was headed toward me. His paddling technique was hardly textbook, he was making short violent strokes, paddling as fast as he could, as though I was attempting to escape. He relaxed a bit when he saw I had my paddle resting on the gunnels, calmly waiting for him.

"What were you doing?" he yelled when the two men pulled up beside me.

"Feeding the bear," I said. "I was trying to get him to move down the beach, get him away from the plane. Hopefully he doesn't go back and tear it up."

"You are a fool!" Maybe you're right, I thought.

Lee raised his hand. Kay glared and looked like he couldn't wait for the signal to kill me. Lee spoke.

"Mr. Brody, you shall lead us. We shall follow. Please do not try to escape with my box of fish."

"I will not try to escape with your box of fish, Mr. Lee."

I looked down at the sealed styrofoam box on the floor of my canoe. I would have loved to open it up, though I had a pretty good idea of what was inside.

I watched the unlikely pair as I dug my undersized paddle into the river and accelerated past them, 'to lead us'. They looked ridiculous. Lee was sitting high on the front seat with his hands on the gunnels. He was all ready for a big river trip, wearing his wool hat, his puffy gold ski jacket, and those ostentatious bug-eye sunglasses with some designer's name scrawled on the arms in big gold letters. He reminded me of some boy king in a royal gondola, though without any white lilies being cast before him by adoring subjects. Of course Lee's 'gondola' was actually just an old, heavily scratched, green plastic canoe riding way too high in the front, and way too low in the rear. There was less than six inches of free board above the water line where Tommy Kay sat. Kay was wearing his blue track suit and it was straining to contain his mass. His wide hips were wedged between the gunnels, threatening to burst the hull apart. The child's paddle in his hands looked like a fly swatter. The two of them were entirely incongruous with the notion of elegance that a canoe ought to lend to a wilderness scene.

They were an accident waiting to happen.

FIFTY THREE

We paddled almost three hours before the river stopped weaving back and forth. It had seemed like a lot longer.

Throughout the last hour, every time I entered yet another hairpin bend, I would pray it was the last, that just around the next corner the river would open up, begin to flow north again, and release me from a claustrophobic water world cloaked in the cold dark shadows of a dense spruce forest.

It was just before nine o'clock when the river finally straightened out, broke out of the trees, and yielded another world. I looked over the bow with exhilaration. The Yukon River was once again wide and flat and open, glittering under the bright western sun like a carpet of diamonds. I laid my paddle across the gunnels and took a moment to rest my sore hands and arms. The evening air was cool but the sun's radiation burned into my face and hands, and through my clothes to my core. It felt good to be warm again. Although active, I'd been cold for hours, and my knees had stiffened up from kneeling on the bottom of the canoe. I sat up on the seat and stretched out my legs, leaned back and absorbed my new surroundings.

In the distance, at the top of an escarpment along the east side of the river, I caught a glimpse of a short stretch of guardrail. The Klondike Highway was up there somewhere. We were close.

"Why do you stop?"

Without looking over at Kay I said, "I haven't stopped, I'm resting."

"There is no time for resting. Paddle!"

They were only ten feet to my right. Wei Lee had gloves on his hands. Where did he get the gloves? I picked up my paddle and re-positioned myself on the floor for some more paddling.

"We're making good time," I said with as much authority as I could muster, calmly scanning the horizon like some seasoned river guide. "We don't have to hurry. Dawson isn't far now. Another three hours."

Another three hours, my ass. By bus, maybe. I'd just told the two of them another blatant lie. Dawson was actually another *three days* by canoe, almost two hundred and fifty river miles north. But neither Wei Lee or Tommy Kay knew that. It was the one and only advantage I had over them, and one that might help me escape. Without a clue where we were, how far we'd travelled from Haines, how far it was to Dawson, and like most people who never look at a map, who never concern themselves with where they happen to be standing on the planet, who have no idea where their destination is located – let alone the route to get there – Lee and Kay had no choice but to trust me. After all, I was their pilot. And as their pilot, I knew exactly where we were.

Exactly.

I started making long smooth strokes again but wasn't going to work hard. The wind was at our backs, blowing hard out of the south, and with a five mile an hour current under us we were moving along at a good clip. The river was still opening up, getting ever wider, perhaps now a thousand feet from one side to the other, beginning to curve to the right, taking us toward a rising gravel bluff on the east side that ran northward as far as I could see. In contrast, the terrain to the west – the land on my left side – was relatively flat and low and heavily treed. A tall spruce forest ran all the way down to the waterline and I could glimpse only an occasional patch of open shore where one might land a canoe. That was a concern to me.

I kept paddling for another half mile, heading toward the sandy colored bluff to the northeast, all the while veering as slowly as I dared over to the west side of the river, moving ever closer to the left bank. When I was within a hundred feet of the left shoreline, I could see that the trees were tall and green and healthy, towering over the river's edge and casting long dark shadows over the water. Eventually I left the bright sunshine in the middle of the river for the shadow of the forest, and the air was suddenly cold again. Five hundred feet ahead of us was a point sticking out, beyond which the river would begin to curve back to the left and bear northward again. From my vantage point close to the trees, it was impossible to see what lay around the corner ahead. But I had a pretty good idea.

I needed to speak to Wei Lee. I needed to give him a piece of advice about our itinerary. I did my best for the next several minutes to look like I was paddling hard, though I certainly wasn't. I waited for the two men to catch me. It didn't take them long.

"Why do you paddle over here? It's cold!" Kay hollered.

I turned my head. They were thirty feet to my right and closing in on me. I stopped paddling and waited for them to pull alongside. I knew they couldn't be happy about leaving the radiant warmth of the sun out in the river. It felt twenty degrees colder in the shadow of the trees. But Kay was always going to be wary and suspicious about what I was doing and where I was going. He was never going to let me gain any degree of separation from him, even if it meant that he and his boss had to get cold to stay close. I figured that as long as I stayed near the left side of the river, he would too.

I pointed over the bow. "Up around that point are some islands. Just past the islands the river splits into a fork. We want to go down the left fork, it will take us to Dawson. If we take the right fork, we'll be headed to Minto. So stay left. Okay?"

Wei Lee spoke. "How far is Minto? I am very hungry and very cold."

"Minto is two hours, Dawson is three hours. We can go to Minto if you want, but it's a very small town and there are no restaurants or hotels. We'd have to wait there overnight for a bus to Dawson in the morning." I paused a moment to let that sink in, then said, "Look, as soon as we get past that point ahead of us, the sun will come out and you'll be warm again. Then it's only another three hours to Dawson. Dawson has good hotels and good food."

What lies I was telling. There was no fork in the Yukon River anywhere around here. Minto was another thirty miles downriver and Dawson was well over two hundred miles beyond Minto. I'd never realized how good at lying I could be when I put my mind to it. Maybe I should have been a lawyer. I thought about my mother. She'd hired a lawyer once. He'd been a really good liar. He'd made out like a bandit.

As usual it took a while for Lee to respond. He studied me for a long time, perhaps looking for a twitch of the mouth, a blink of an eye, a clearing of the throat, a scratch of the face, any hint of nervous behavior, any hint that I might be lying to him. But the fact was I couldn't have been any calmer at that particular moment. I was resigned to my one and only remaining opportunity to escape. It would decide my fate. It was better than any other plan I could come up with. I knew what lay ahead and could only prepare myself for the challenge – and hopefully survive it. Besides, Wei Lee had no reason not to trust me. Everything I'd told him since we'd left the plane had panned out exactly as promised. Here we were, still safe and sound, and I'd just told him that Dawson was now three hours away. It was nine o'clock. Three hours ago at the plane I'd told him we'd get to Dawson by midnight. We were right on schedule. And so far I hadn't tried to escape with his damn styrofoam box.

So trust me, Mr. Lee. Trust me one last time.

Lee finally spoke. "Alright. We will go to Dawson. Tommy! Follow Mr. Brody!"

I paddled. Kay paddled. Perfect.

* * *

They looked high, even from a mile away: four pillars of solid vertical rock towering over the water, standing tall and majestic against a pale blue sky, glowing like bronze in the western sun, scattered across the river like abandoned bridge pilings. Five Finger Rapids, one of the Yukon River's few but infamous barriers to navigation, was dead ahead.

Two hundred feet above the rapids, a three foot drop in the bedrock under the river creates a shelf on the surface. The river cascades over the shelf and accelerates, then gets choked into a steep-sided canyon littered with rocks and boulders, then is forced through five narrow channels created by the four rock pillars. Five Finger Rapids. Five Fingers. Five channels. And only one, according to my friends, is a viable route for a novice in a canoe. I had no intention of confirming that.

I made a furtive glance over my right shoulder and saw that Lee and Kay were fifty feet behind me. They were just coming around the point. I thought Lee might not have the eyesight to appreciate the change of scenery, but Tommy Kay was another matter. He could see perfectly well and was cynical and suspicious to boot. He was also 'dumb like a fox'.

But my sole objective hadn't changed. I needed to escape and this was the place to try.

First, though, I needed a plan. I looked downstream at the river in front of me, then over to my right at the east shoreline, then to my left at the west shoreline. How could I get over to the east side of the river without those scoundrels following and catching me? The answer was pure intuition. I hoped it would turn out to be common sense.

It was 'Plan B'.

About four thousand feet downstream from where I sat, the river surface disappeared where it flowed over the bedrock shelf. The shelf stretched all the way across the river in a straight line, from one bank to the other. The shelf would be my benchmark because that's where the trouble would start. Once you've gone over the shelf, which is really just a short smooth waterfall, you've entered the rapids. From that point forward you're just along for the ride. And at the mercy of the river.

The spring river was high and fast and swollen, a million gallons per second of ice cold water rushing north at five miles an hour, carrying me and my canoe with it. The Yukon River's source is Atlin Lake – British Columbia's largest – two hundred river miles upstream from Five Finger Rapids. The enormous lake is the repository for the Llewellyn Glacier which anchors the northeast quadrant of the Juneau Ice Field, the fifth largest ice field in the Western Hemisphere. Atlin Lake is only forty miles east of the Pacific Ocean, yet in an irony of nature, its glacier source water has no short and easy path to the sea. Instead, bordered on all sides by mountains, ice melt from the Llewellyn Glacier flows north into the Yukon River system, a remarkable diversion of two thousand miles. Atlin Lake's frigid water is then carried to the sea by the Yukon River, all the way through the Yukon, all the way across Alaska, all the way to the Bering Sea before finally reaching tide water. So the Yukon River is truly a glacier source river, a cold, cold river flowing through cold, cold country that never warms up. I dipped my hand over the side for confirmation and yanked it out like I'd just touched a hot stove. It couldn't have been more than forty degrees.

I rubbed the feeling back into my hand and cursed because I didn't have a lifejacket. I cursed the bear who was the reason why. If it hadn't been for him, I could have grabbed one out of my plane. Now my chances of survival if I went overboard were slim and none. Falling into forty degree water is virtually paralyzing. It will pull the heat out of a healthy human body so fast that hypothermia begins in two minutes. Your dexterity is the first thing to go. In three minutes you'll lose the use of your hands and fingers. In fifteen minutes you'll lose consciousness. In half an hour you'll stop breathing and your heart will stop. So whatever my plan to get away from Wei Lee and Tommy Kay might be, falling out of a canoe into the Yukon River could not be a part of it.

But 'Plan B' was actually pretty simple: escape from Lee and

Kay by paddling to the other side of the river without getting caught – and without going into the rapids. Cross the river, beach my canoe, jump out, climb up the bluff to the Klondike Highway. Run away. Hitch hike to Minto. Call the cops.

Simple.

I really didn't care what happened to Kay or Lee, and certainly didn't care about their damn styrofoam boxes of 'fish'. I just wanted to get away with my life. If they decided to chase me across the river, and went into the rapids trying to catch me, so be it. Let them fend for themselves. This was a 'me or them' deal. It was survival of the fittest. Or the luckiest. Or the fastest. I had no other options, no other plans, no other choices. It was a life or death situation and I needed to save mine. It was time to do some dead reckoning.

I was now about three thousand feet above the shelf and the start of the rapids. The river current was five miles an hour. Five miles per hour is seven feet a second. Four hundred and twenty eight seconds to drift downstream to the shelf, and the start of the rapids. Seven minutes or so to trouble.

It was about a thousand feet to the other side of the river. I could paddle five miles an hour. I could paddle seven feet a second. A hundred and forty three seconds to paddle a thousand feet to the east bank. About two and a half minutes to cross the river.

Seven minutes less two and a half minutes before I needed to start paddling toward the east side of the river. Four and a half minutes from now.

Four and a half minutes drifting downstream at seven feet a second would take me nineteen hundred feet closer to the shelf, about two thirds of the way there. I scanned the river bank on my left and looked for a spot two thirds of the way to the shelf, a spot for me to stop and beach my canoe. I was in luck. There was a place – but only one – exactly two thirds of the way to the shelf. It would be cutting things close, the spot was barely a thousand feet upstream from the shelf, but definitely the last place on the bank where one could beach a canoe before entering the rapids. It would have to do.

I started slacking off. It didn't take long for Kay to react.

"Why do you stop paddling?"

"I feel sick."

"Paddle!"

"I can't. I feel sick. Its my stomach. I think I need to go to shore."

"No. You are not going to shore. Paddle."

Tommy Kay. Mr. 'Empathy'. I really hadn't expected to get his co-operation or patience, but I'd planted the seed. I was fifty feet from the heavily treed shoreline, doing my best to appear like I was paddling hard, keeping my eye on the river bank to my left, and the spot where I intended to beach my canoe. The current was strong and the water high and fast along the shoreline, skirting the trees, eroding the topsoil, exposing roots, knawing away at the forest floor. Kay and Lee were twenty feet out to my right. I kept paddling, putting little effort into my strokes, trying to look miserable, hoping Kay might pass me. I wanted him to be well downstream of me before I started out for the other side. The more time I spent paddling to the other side before he realized what I was doing, the greater would be my head start, and the better my chances to escape. But no such luck. He was too wary. He always wanted me ahead of him. He always wanted to be following.

"Paddle!" he yelled.

"I'm trying but I'm going to be sick. I need to go to shore. I've really got to go! I think I'm going to have diarrhea!"

'Diarrhea'. For some reason that word seemed to stun Kay. For once he didn't bark back at me. Perhaps he found it repulsive that a man would consider defecating outdoors. Or maybe the concept of diarrhea simply conjured up an image so vile he couldn't deal with it. He glared at me in silence. I began to slowly angle away from him, toward the spot I'd picked out. Even though I was still abreast of the two men, our separation had now increased to thirty feet. I knew I had them then.

I surveyed the shoreline below my landing spot. The river was speeding past the flooded forest. There was nothing you could call a river bank below 'my spot'. No beach, no shore, nothing but trees and roots and branches sticking out over the river. Nowhere to land. If I could beach my canoe on the one spot of gravel I'd picked out, then Kay and Lee would have no place to stop and wait below me. Not unless Kay was prepared to grab a tree branch and see if he could hold their canoe stationary against the fierce current. I was betting he was smart enough to not even try.

My 'spot' was no more than a small patch of washed gravel that had spilled out between some trees. It might have been the residue of a small mudslide, or maybe something created by an ice dam during the spring breakup. It didn't matter to me. I felt lucky to have found it. It was time to make my move.

"I've really got to go!" I yelled again. I abruptly turned left and paddled hard toward the shore. Kay started to chase me. I ran my canoe into the pile of gravel, stumbled a few steps forward over the floor of the canoe, and leapt out onto the ground. I grabbed the canoe by the bow and let the current swing the stern downstream. I let it swing until it stopped, then with my heels slipping on the rocks, pulled and heaved as hard as I could until it was high and dry, perched on top of the gravel pile. I'd done it. I was stopped on dry land.

I looked at Kay who'd stopped paddling. He was twenty feet away from me when he gave up his chase. He was still out in the river and we both knew he couldn't join me. He was too far from the bank and drifting downstream too fast to do that. He really had the menacing glare going now, realizing his only option was to beach his canoe somewhere below me and wait. I watched him drift past me, then paddle toward the shore, and disappear from sight. I had no idea of what he was doing, or where he had gone. All I knew was that I had gained all the advantage I needed. There was simply nowhere below me for Kay to beach his canoe. It was time to get ready.

I planned for a quick getaway when I landed on the other side of the river. I slid the styrofoam box all the way forward and wedged it under the front seat. I put my backpack on and adjusted the straps, then laid the extra paddle in front of me so I could grab it if I lost or broke the other one. I stretched and touched my toes, flexed my knees, and readied myself for the sprint of a lifetime. I almost laughed at myself. I was a pilot, not an Olympian. Stretching? Knee bends? Who was I kidding?

I shoved the canoe back in the water, put a foot inside, and pushed off. I walked to the stern as it drifted out, turned myself around, knelt down on the floor, pressed my butt against the seat, took a deep breath, grabbed my little paddle, looked across the river, and started paddling. Like my life depended on it. Because it did.

Klondike Highway, here I come.

FIFTY FOUR

I knew I wasn't going to make it when I was three hundred feet from the other side. I knew because I was only two hundred feet above the shelf.

Something in my dead reckoning had been terribly wrong. Maybe the current was more than five miles an hour, maybe I couldn't paddle five miles per hour, maybe the river was more than a thousand feet wide. Maybe, maybe, maybe. What was certain was that 'Plan B' wasn't going to work. I wasn't going to escape as planned. I wasn't going to reach the east side of the river. I was about to go through Five Finger Rapids. So were the two men in the canoe behind me.

I looked back at Kay and Lee. They were two hundred feet behind and a hundred feet below me. I'd gotten off to a hundred foot head start before Kay realized I was attempting an escape. He'd pursued me with a fury, paddling after me like a madman possessed. The big man had displayed more power and endurance than I ever could have imagined. All the way across, even though I'd been paddling a far lighter canoe, I'd barely gained a hundred feet on him. He'd been barking orders and shouting threats at me the whole way, all of which I'd naturally ignored. I'd left the west side of the river knowing well that trying to escape from Kay was going to be a life or death proposition. It still was.

It struck me then that Kay had somehow managed to stop his canoe shortly after I'd managed to beach mine on the gravel pile. He was now only a hundred feet downstream of me, yet I'd waited on the west bank for over a minute before taking off. He should have drifted much farther downstream than that. I knew he had nowhere to land on the west shore anywhere below the gravel pile. He must have grabbed a tree or branch to stop and wait for me. He was that strong. And that crazy.

Kay had gone quiet, his yelling and threats over with. He probably knew as well as I did that neither of us was going to make it to the east bank, knew that we were both about to enter the rapids. With the roar of the river in the canyon growing ever louder, Kay and Lee would have both known for some time that I'd set them up for a white water adventure. They both must have been pleased to realize that I was about to join them. Kay in particular would be pleased with that scenario, looking forward to ringing my neck when he caught up with me below the rapids.

I looked back at them again. They were almost at the shelf and about to enter the rapids, probably the center channel, behind the largest pillar. If nothing else, I still had a chance to make it to the far right channel, the one farthest to the east and next to the river bank, the one my friends had told me about.

My arms were aching and I was out of breath but I kept putting everything I had into paddling toward the bank. I knew there was a reasonable chance for survival if I could at least make it to the right channel. It was depressing to realize how close I was going to get to dry land when the current would sweep me over the shelf and into white water. But that was the reality. It was vividly clear how fast the current had been moving my canoe downstream, judging by how fast the bank was rushing past the bow. I'd simply started my crossing too late, too far downstream, too close to the shelf.

It dawned on me then why my dead reckoning had been so flawed. The wind! I'd been paddling abeam of the wind, the side of my canoe had been like a sail, and I'd been pushed downstream much faster than my estimate. How could I have been so stupid to miss that simple aerodynamic parameter? Maybe I really was just a 'dumb' pilot. Stupid. Stupid. Stupid.

I was twenty feet above the shelf and fifty feet from the river bank when I accepted defeat. But for another lousy fifty feet, I was going for a ride through Five Finger Rapids. I could have thrown my paddle to shore, I was that close, and that furious with myself. But I accepted my fate, admitted defeat, turned the bow of my canoe downstream, and prepared to go over the shelf.

I took a quick glance back for Kay and Lee. They'd vanished. They'd now be on the other side of the biggest pillar, which looked more like a fairly long island from my new vantage point. They'd be well into the rapids by now.

See you guys on the other side.

The bow stayed in the air for what seemed like forever, then dropped like a rock over the shelf and my canoe accelerated down a sheet of water, plunging into the frothy white water below with a great splash that thoroughly soaked my clothes. All of a sudden the river was roaring and boiling all around me, rushing into the canyon with currents and eddies swirling and colliding, waves knocking and buffeting my canoe back and forth, making it almost impossible to hold a straight line. The sensation was like skiing on ball bearings. I had no idea of what I was doing and simply picked out a spot downstream, trying my best to keep the bow pointed there, all the while trying to avoid the roughest water. A long line of standing waves to my right was the main obstacle, there was no way to go through those, so I stayed left of them, working my paddle on both sides of the canoe whenever the currents tried to spin me around, keeping my target more or less over the bow, and somehow managing to stay upright. There were some exciting moments when the bow began to porpoise up and down through a long section of upwellings, troughs, and whirlpools, and I could feel and hear submerged rocks and boulders pounding and scraping the hull. Every time the bow went down I took on a little more water, but it would always come up again, and in less than a minute – it had seemed like a lot longer – I was through.

Five Finger Rapids was behind me and the river was flat and calm again. I'd done it! Where do I pick up my T-shirt?

Piece of cake.

Though the roaring in the canyon was waning behind me, the river had picked up speed, moving even faster than before, veering left toward the northwest, away from the steep cliffs on my right, away from the Klondike Highway that ran above them. I was soaked from head to toe and there was a good four inches of water sloshing around the floor of the canoe, the reason why my knees and feet suddenly felt so cold. I was glad my backpack was where it should be – on my back. The styrofoam box hadn't moved, still wedged under the front seat. My extra paddle was floating in front of me.

I surveyed the right side of the river for a place to land. I needed to stop, empty the canoe and get out of my soaking wet clothes. But there was nowhere to do that here. Where the river met the land on my right, the steep rock cliffs rose straight out of the water, and continued for thousands of feet. It would be a while before I would have an opportunity to go ashore. The river continued to turn west, flowing out into the wilderness, taking me farther and farther away from the highway. I knew well that Five Finger Rapids is the last spot for miles that the Yukon River comes anywhere close to the Klondike Highway. The next place would be Minto, in front of my cabin, thirty miles north. I sighed with resignation. I'd have to paddle all night to get home.

Almost as an afterthought it occurred to me that getting through the rapids had hardly changed my biggest challenge, escaping from Tommy Kay and Wei Lee, two men who – if not before – would now certainly want to kill me. Had they made it through the rapids? Or had they found a place to land and stopped on the other side of the island? I thought about that, then doubted it possible, the water in the canyon was simply too fast and rough. They'd entered the rapids first, and if they'd made it through safely, should be well downstream of me. I scanned the river ahead, squinting into the low sun, the water still sparkling like diamonds. I couldn't see them. Where were they? I looked back, more out of paranoia than expectation. Of course I saw nothing, they couldn't be behind me, surely they had to be below me. I started paddling again, my water laden canoe sluggish and unresponsive, keeping my eyes peeled for their canoe. The water's reflections played havoc with my vision, the strength of the sun too bright to look up for very long. But they had to be close. Had they tipped over? Were they now in the frigid water? They wouldn't survive long if they were. I looked around and wondered what I'd do if I saw them in the water. Save them? How? And why?

I'd just lowered my head to rest my eyes when I thought I saw something.

* * *

He was silhouetted against the sun, floating in the middle of the river, his legs dangling behind him, clutching one of his precious white styrofoam boxes. I knew immediately it was Wei Lee. The man lying on the box was too small to be Tommy Kay. He was drifting in the current a couple of hundred feet ahead and just off to my left. I paddled over and pulled up beside him.

I realized my dilemma immediately. Here was a man who had threatened to kill me, yet now he was helpless, completely at my mercy. I had no idea why I'd even paddled over to him. To do what? And say what? It was the strangest feeling. I was frozen in time and space, and try as I might, couldn't say or do a thing. It was as if I had stage fright and had forgotten my lines, hoping desperately that the audience would disappear. I watched him for a moment and tried to gather my wits.

He was so still I wasn't even sure if he was alive. He was prone, lying on top of the box lengthwise with his arms wrapped around it, his chin hanging over the end, staring down at the water only inches below his face. Then a shudder rippled through him. He clearly had no idea I was beside him. I dug down deep and forced myself to speak.

"Mr. Lee."

He didn't stir but I heard him mumble, "Help me."

"Help you? Why should I help you? You're an evil man, Mr. Lee. A murderer and a thief. If I save you, you'll only kill me and steal my plane. "

"No, Mr. Brody. I do not kill. I do not steal. I said I would pay for your plane. I will double the price if you help me. Please, I need your help."

I looked away from him, at the clear blue sky to the east, at the horizon's shadow rising up the mountains, trying to focus my thoughts. This was a grade 'A' conundrum. Wei Lee was a killer. He would continue to kill. In his business, he had to kill to succeed. He'd threatened to harm me several times today, and tried to extort me into selling my plane. He was a parasite. He made a living off the misery of others. Certainly not a man to trust or respect. Who needs people like that? I looked down at him again, just a few feet to my left, semi-submerged in the ice cold water. He shuddered again. He was fading. I looked away again, then felt a tug on my paddle. He'd wrapped his feeble right arm around the blade, clutching it to his side. I didn't let go.

"Yes, you do," I said. "You do kill, Mr. Lee. You pay people to kill for you. It's the same thing. And you do steal. You steal people."

"I do not steal people. I free people. I give them new lives. Better lives."

"No. No you don't. You don't give them better lives. You give them nothing but misery. You addict them to drugs. You destroy their families. You steal their money. You take away their dignity and freedom. You take away their hopes and dreams. You're an evil man, Mr. Lee."

"Please, Mr. Brody, help me. I am so cold. I will make you a rich man if you help me."

"I'm already a rich man, Mr. Lee. I have my freedom and my dignity and my independence. Your money means nothing to me."

There. At least I'd got it off my chest. Wei Lee knew exactly where he stood with me. He knew that I knew who he was, what he was, and how he made his money. He knew I thought he was evil. So now what? Save him anyway? Could I ever trust him to leave me alone if I pulled him from his purgatory? I didn't think so.

Yet he was still a human being, totally helpless, desperate to live another day. He'd die soon if I didn't get him out of the water. And I was the only one around who could help him.

I took a deep breath. A myriad of emotions welled up and whirled around inside me, pulling on every string, playing on every innate sense and moral principal I'd ever held precious, principals that had guided me through my whole life, about what was right and wrong, about what was good and bad, about what was honorable and what was not. But in the end, I knew I had no choice. I had to do the right thing. I had to help him.

"Mr. Lee," I said.

He managed to raise his head off the box, trying but failing to look at me, still clutching the blade of my paddle under his arm.

"Yes, Mr. Brody?"

"You need a paddle. You can have this one. I've got a spare."

I let go.

* * *

The other two styrofoam boxes were floating together like little boats, drifting down the middle of the river in the wind and the current, a thousand feet from where I'd left Wei Lee with my paddle. I could have picked up another box right then and there, or at least *tried* to pick one up, load it into my canoe, double my take for the day. But I thought that the one box in the front of my canoe would be plenty for what I had in mind. The police deserved their fair share of the flotsam, and maybe there'd be enough evidence in those three boxes still floating in the river to help David Owen 'seal the deal', with or without any dye on the cash inside. I pictured Robson and his buddies at a press conference, standing proudly in front of three open styrofoam boxes full of cash. Cops and their props and their photo opps.

For as long and as hard as I'd been looking around, I hadn't seen Tommy Kay or his canoe. That made me nervous. Could he have possibly fallen out like Lee, then somehow managed to climb back in? Had he paddled off down the river alone, or gone ashore to recover somewhere? Neither scenario seemed likely. Surely if he'd been able to get back in his canoe he wouldn't have abandoned his boss, let alone three boxes full of cash. But his whereabouts would have to remain a mystery right now. I just wanted to go home and there were twenty five miles of river to navigate before I could pull up in front of my cabin. All I could do now was keep a wary eye out for Kay, who doubtless wouldn't be seeking permission to kill me now, not after what had just happened.

The air was dry and the skies were clear but the sun was getting lower and the temperature would soon be falling fast. I was cold and soaking wet, hungry and thirsty, and needed to get ashore to prepare for my journey home. The paddling was slow going with so much water in the canoe and it was a good half hour before a decent place to land presented itself on the west side of the river. I beached the canoe and got out, stripped off my clothes, and dumped the contents of my backpack on a sandy beach. I found my nylon windbreaker and the plastic bag with my clean dry T-shirt and boxers. They were all the dry clothes I had, but they'd make a world of difference for a night on the river. I lit a small fire and stood over it for a while – naked, shivering and shaking – trying to dry my skin, trying to warm up, thankful that at least the smoke was keeping the mosquitoes away. I rolled the canoe over, and while waiting for it to drain, used my knife to cut some branches off a tree. I rolled the canoe back on its keel and used the only rope I had – the short piece left on the bow – to tie some branches to the spars and fashion a rudimentary drying rack on top of the gunnels. I laid my wet clothes over the branches. When it got really cold later on, perhaps they'd be dry enough to wear again.

Then I ate two of the most gooey and mashed up tuna sandwiches I'd ever seen, though it should be said, none that had ever tasted so good. I'd completely forgotten about them. I'd been looking for a bottle of water when I spotted the odd shaped objects wrapped in cellophane, sitting in the sand beside some maps. I remembered buying them that morning at the café and felt lucky to have something to eat. Unfortunately I'd only bought two bottles of water with the sandwiches, thought it might have been three but no such luck, and knew they'd been poured into the front fuel tank of my plane. Win some, lose some. There was plenty of drinking water in the river.

When I was ready to go, I took a good long look for a large man in a green canoe on the Yukon River. It was close to midnight but there was still plenty of sunlight, and it would have been easy to spot him. But there was nothing out there. Not a sole was in sight. The river was empty.

I pushed off and set out for Minto.

FIFTY FIVE

Just before six o'clock in the morning, I ran my canoe aground on the rocky shore in front of my cabin. I was home – cold, hungry, thirsty, and tired – but home.

My knees and back were so stiff I could barely get out of the canoe. I stood hunched over for a long time before trusting my legs and back to work properly, then finally dared to stand up straight. Only then could I drag the canoe up on the shore.

I looked at my wet clothes spread over the branches. My drying rack hadn't worked very well, the clothes on it were still soggy, but they were doing a good job of covering up the styrofoam box under the front seat. I decided to deal with the box later. I grabbed my wet socks and put them on. They'd be better than nothing for the short walk up to my cabin. I didn't even consider putting on my soaking wet boots.

Charlie and Reggie had come through. As we'd planned yesterday, if I hadn't turned up by nine o'clock last night, he and Reggie were to go out to the lake to fetch my truck and drive it back to my cabin. Reggie would then have fed my dogs and taken them over to his place.

I walked into my cabin and was naked by the time I opened the closet door to turn on the electric power and propane heater. The temperature outside was forty degrees. The temperature inside was forty five degrees. I stood under a hot shower for ten minutes, got out and drank a quart of water, and decided eating could wait. I was feeling a lot better. My cabin was warm, I was warm, and all I really wanted to do was fall into bed and sleep for ten hours. But there were two things that needed to be done first.

I drove up to the shop and peered in a window. Charlie's little pickup truck was parked inside. He'd done as we'd planned. I walked around the corner and looked at the power meter on the side of the building. The dial was spinning. The electric heater in the apartment upstairs was on. Charlie would be up there sleeping with Charlie Junior. I unlocked the side door and tip-toed over to the phone.

Daryl picked up on the fourth ring. In a hushed voice I told him everything he needed to know about what had happened yesterday in Haines – and at Five Finger Rapids. Then I told him I needed to sleep and to not even think about calling or visiting me before noon. I drove back down to my cabin, walked down to the river, took the styrofoam box out of the canoe, and carried it up to my cabin. I slid it under my bed and went to sleep.

* * *

Three hundred and ninety-nine thousand, nine hundred and eighty dollars. That's how much cash was in the styrofoam box. I counted it three times.

For five nights after getting off the river, I was counting cash in my living room, watching hockey on TV, and coming up with the same result every time. I still wonder to this day why the total was twenty dollars short of four hundred thousand dollars. Perhaps someone along the way had sticky fingers, perhaps someone was sending someone else a message, or perhaps it was simply an honest mistake. I suppose I'll never know.

Regardless, I've always preferred to work with round numbers so dug into my personal supply of American dollars and slipped another twenty dollar bill into the stack that was short. I sorted the whole lot into eighty stacks, two hundred and fifty bills to a stack, each one worth five thousand dollars, and wrapped them up in elastic bands. I dropped them all into a garbage bag and weighed it on my bathroom scale. The bag weighed forty six pounds. That made sense to me because when I'd opened the box there'd been four sockeye salmon lying on top of the cash. Each salmon weighed about eight pounds, so the total weight of the styrofoam box had been approximately eighty pounds. Jack Kolinsky was obviously pretty good at packing fish and cash by the pound.

I assumed the box in my canoe had been the one Wei Lee intended to use to pay for my plane. The bill of sale he'd handed me in Haines said the purchase price was to be four hundred thousand dollars, and that was more or less what had been in the box. Wei Lee had told me in Haines that he'd pay cash for my plane when we got to Dawson. Of course neither the box or my plane had ever made it to Dawson. Wei Lee was probably dead, I still had my plane, and was now holding a garbage bag in my hand with four hundred grand of cash inside. I thought I'd better do something to cover my ass.

I signed the bill of sale Lee had given me and dropped it into the bag with the cash. If the cops ever found the bag and asked me where I got all that money, well, I got it from this guy named Wei Lee. He bought my plane, see, here's the bill of sale, signed by both of us. He paid me for my plane with the cash in this bag. Four hundred thousand dollars. But then he died before he could take delivery of the plane. I've been waiting ever since for someone from his estate to come around and pick it up, but no one ever has. Still have the plane, still have the cash, still waiting.

As for the actual styrofoam box – the incriminating 'evidence' as it were – well, I did a little magic trick using gasoline. I cut up the box and dropped the pieces into a fifty four gallon drum, then poured a gallon of gasoline over them. The styrofoam pieces melted and morphed into a sticky sludge on the bottom of the barrel. Magic. Then I tossed some shop garbage into the drum and burned it all.

The styrofoam box was no more.

OCTOBER

FIFTY SIX

Within five hours of calling Daryl that morning back in June, every available helicopter, plane, and boat within a hundred miles of Carmacks was headed to Five Finger Rapids. It was only supposed to be a search and rescue mission for two missing men in a canoe, but then Staff Sergeant Robson got wind of who was missing. He called Special Agent David Owen at the FBI and in no time the search and rescue turned into an international cop convention.

Later that same day I drove down to Carmacks with Reggie and a friend of his who had a motor boat. We launched the boat at Carmacks and ran down the river to fetch my plane. I couldn't believe what was there when we arrived.

On the beach in front of my plane were two helicopters, two large motor boats, and a crowd of heavily armed cops doing what cops do best, standing around. As usual, the cops had brought in civilians to do their heavy lifting. Three men and a woman were setting up a tent city complete with tables and chairs, a cooking facility, communication equipment, and even an outdoor privy.

Naturally they wouldn't let me fly my plane out of there. Staff Sergeant Robson had greeted me with his thumbs shoved under his gun belt, glared his usual glare, and informed me that for the second time in a week my plane was being treated as a 'crime scene'. My plane would have to stay 'right where it was', until either the rope holding it to the point gave way, or the cops got tired of camping.

As well as Robson and his charges, Daryl was there too, and so were Special Agents David Owen and Stanley Kurtz. We all sat down at a big round table under a big yellow umbrella, right there on a beach in the middle of nowhere, with my airplane floating on the river in front of us. For the next three hours we swatted at mosquitoes while I recounted what had happened the day before. The cops peppered me with all kinds of questions and I answered them all. A woman tending a smoky barbeque kept coming over to the table, asking if we wanted something to eat or drink. I kept ordering coke and hamburgers and must have eaten four of them over the course of the evening, still hungry from my long paddle down the river the night before. The cops declined to eat, preferring to ask me questions. Reggie and his friend spent the evening walking up and down the beach, studying the bear's paw prints in the sand, trying to estimate its weight, and eating lots of hamburgers too. The woman cooking hamburgers could have sold them a lot of beer while they were waiting for me – if she'd had any.

Robson kept pressing me with two questions, each of which he asked me ten different times, ten different ways, and every time I gave him the same two answers. First, Robson wanted to know why I hadn't called a Mayday when the engine in my plane had quit, and second, after I'd landed on the river, he wanted to know why I hadn't turned on the plane's ELT – the Emergency Locator Transmitter – an emergency radio with its own battery that emits an SOS signal. My only answer to the first question was that when the engine quit, so did all the electrics, and so did the radio. My only answer to the second question was, 'what emergency?' When Robson realized my answers were never going to vary, he announced to everyone around the table that Wei Lee had been found.

Lee was dead.

He was found tangled up in the branches of a floating tree, drifting down the west side of the river, six miles below the rapids. He was in rigor mortis when they discovered him, clutching a styrofoam box with a paddle wedged under one of his arms. They didn't yet know the cause of death but thought it was likely hypothermia. They'd found two more styrofoam boxes floating side by side in a small cove, three miles downstream from Lee's body. They'd also found an empty canoe, still upright but semi-submerged, flooded to the gunnels, floating near the boxes. They hadn't yet found any other paddles, any luggage, or any sign of Tommy Kay.

It was close to midnight when I left to go back to Minto with Reggie and his friend. Robson intercepted me when I was about to get in the boat, for a 'word'. With his chest puffed out he said he wanted to make two things perfectly clear to me. One, I was not to leave the Yukon without his permission, and two, that until I heard from him directly, I was not to return to my plane. Then he gave me his best cop stare ever. I gave him my best pilot stare back and told him to watch out for a big hungry grizzly bear.

That was the first of many days that summer I spent talking to cops and the authorities. Throughout the month of June, it seemed that almost every day there was a phone message left at the café for me to call either Special Agent David Owen or Staff Sergeant Alan Robson, on some 'urgent' matter.

A week after leaving my plane on the river with Robson, I was wondering what was going on. I wanted my plane back. Then one evening Daryl came by the shop and said that he'd been ordered to drive me to Whitehorse for a meeting with Robson and Owen. That was okay with me because I needed to go to Whitehorse anyway. The next morning, with Jack in my arms, I climbed into Daryl's car for an all expense car ride to the vet. When we got to Whitehorse, I dropped Jack off to get the last of the quills removed from his infected nose, then Daryl took me over to the RCMP building. I spent the best part of the morning with Robson and Owen, sitting around a table in Robson's office. I learned a lot.

First, though, Robson asked me to provide an official statement describing all the events on that fateful day when Wei Lee, Tommy

Kay and I had gone white water canoeing through Five Finger Rapids. The stern looking woman I'd met on my previous visit to Robson's office recorded my statement. She glared at me the whole time I was speaking with her fingers furiously pounding the keys of her machine. She must have learned her cop stare from Robson. It was probably worth an extra pay grade to her. After she left to type my statement, Owen brought me up to date on recent events in the FBI's investigation of Wei Lee's money laundering scam.

Owen said the three styrofoam boxes they'd recovered on the river each contained one million dollars of U.S. cash. When he told me that, I remembered foregoing the opportunity to load another box into my canoe to take home to Minto. If I'd picked up just one of those boxes floating in the river, I could have been sipping Mai Tai's on a beach in Tahiti, instead of talking to two cops in a sterile building in Whitehorse. Then I thought about the dangers of getting too much sun, and my pal Jack at the vet. I decided I was happy with what I had.

Owen went on to say that a couple of days after they'd recovered the styrofoam boxes from the river, the RCMP and FBI had raided the house of a Dawson gold buyer named Ralph Braun. Owen had told Braun he knew that Kay had assaulted me in the back of his truck, and that he knew Braun had been the driver. Owen also told Braun he'd been under FBI surveillance for over a year, and was suspected of aiding and abetting a criminal organization conspiring to launder illicit cash. When Braun heard those two things, he'd sung like a bird.

Ralph Braun told Owen and Robson all about what he'd been up to in the last two years. He told them he'd been selling millions of dollars of gold to a man named Tommy Kay. He'd been getting paid for the gold with cash delivered to him in styrofoam boxes by a man named Charlie. He'd been picking up the boxes behind a hotel in Whitehorse. Braun told Owen that the gold he'd been selling to Kay was always delivered in briefcases. Braun said Kay was taking the briefcases to a mine on Thistle Creek, in a plane flown by Robert Duncan.

When the police raided Braun's house, they'd found four briefcases in a safe. Inside each briefcase was a million dollars worth of gold, and a gold export permit issued to the Lucky Star Mine on Thistle Creek. Braun said he'd been waiting two days for Tommy Kay to show up with three million dollars in cash, and to pick up the four briefcases full of gold. When Owen asked Braun why Kay hadn't shown up, he said didn't know. When asked why he was expecting Kay to turn up with only three million dollars of cash – and not four million dollars – Braun said the gold in three of the briefcases had to be paid for, but that the gold in the fourth briefcase had come from the Thistle Creek mine.

Robson then asked Braun why gold belonging to the Thistle Creek mine was in a briefcase in his house. Braun said he'd picked up the gold at the mine a few days ago, and that Kay had told him to melt and refine it. When asked why the people at the mine would trust him to drive away with a million dollars of their gold, Braun said he'd been accompanied by Tommy Kay on the trip from the mine to Dawson. When asked who had been at the mine the day he'd picked up the gold with Kay, Braun told them there'd only been two people there – the mine manager, a man named Terry Mcilhaney – and a tall skinny woman, who he didn't know. When Robson asked Braun if he knew where Mcilhaney and the tall skinny woman were, he said he wanted to speak to a lawyer. The RCMP then arrested Braun on several conspiracy charges and seized the four briefcases.

Robson took over the meeting then. He said it was pretty likely that Kay, perhaps with the help of Braun, had killed and disposed of Terry Mcilhaney and Rose Rivera when they'd visited the mine. He doubted that Mcilhaney and Rivera, who were the prime suspects in the kidnapping of Bobby Larabie, would have been able to leave the territory with all the surveillance in place, that they were probably buried in a tailings pile somewhere, and were accordingly no longer a perceived threat to kidnap any more kids. Robson said that was only his hunch, but that the RCMP currently had 'boots on the ground', searching the hills south of Dawson for the missing pair. He warned me that until the two were found, I should continue to keep my guard up to protect Charlie Woo and his son in Minto. When I asked Robson why he thought Charlie and his son might be in Minto, he just stared at me.

After we broke for lunch I called the vet who said he'd had to put Jack under anesthesia to patch up his nose. He said that Jack would be fine, that he may not want to eat for awhile, that I could pick him up later in the day. I went to the post office to get my mail and there wasn't a check from the FBI for my flying contract. I went down to the river and bought three more kids paddles at the Kayak Store. I wasn't counting on getting back the ones I'd given to Kay and Lee on the Yukon River, and the kids in the band wanted to go canoeing. I called the propane store and made some inquiries, then called the local purveyor of airplane batteries up at the airport. The last thing I did was walk down to the local fish store that specializes in 'Wild Caught Alaska Seafood'. I paid full retail for an eighty pound box of sockeye salmon and asked that it be delivered to a woman named Christine at my favorite auto parts store. I couldn't believe how much they wanted for Alaska sockeye salmon in Whitehorse, but a deal's a deal, and Christine had earned the fish promised to her. I grabbed a sub and a coke on my way back to the RCMP building.

The woman at the x-ray machine said not to forget my knife and paddles when I left the building later that day. Robson and Owen weren't around when I got back, so I sat in Robson's office, ate my sub, and reviewed my official statement which had been left on the table for my signature. The two cops kept me waiting until two thirty. When they walked in together, Robson didn't say a word, but Owen apologized profusely. He said he was 'up to his ears' managing two 'situations', one in Haines, another in Los Angeles.

Owen told me that after hearing my account of what had happened on the river with Lee and Kay, the FBI had raided Jack Kolinsky's warehouse in Haines. Kolinsky denied there'd ever been two dead men lying in his freezer. He said he knew nothing about any cash ever being packed into any styrofoam boxes at his warehouse. He said he'd never heard of a man named Wei Lee. When asked about the injuries to his face, he told the FBI he'd fallen off his forklift. When threatened with a search warrant, he called a lawyer and drove home. The FBI then cordoned off his warehouse and declared it a crime scene. The FBI were still snooping around his warehouse two days later. Kolinsky had locked himself in his house and was refusing to speak to the police. Stalemate.

I asked Owen who the two dead men were that I'd seen in Kolinsky's freezer. Owen shrugged and said that without the bodies, they had no way of knowing. Robson just stared at me. Whatever.

Owen wrapped things up by telling me that not all had been lost when Tommy Kay had dropped the dye kit into the Pacific Ocean. Owen said that with Ralph Braun admitting he'd been picking up styrofoam boxes full of cash behind a Whitehorse hotel, admitting that the cash in the boxes had been used to pay for millions of dollars of gold he'd sold to Kay, admitting that Kay had been taking the gold to the Thistle Creek mine in an airplane, and with my account of what had happened at Kolinsky's warehouse in Haines, the FBI probably had sufficient evidence for an indictment against Wei Lee's partner, an accountant from LA named Henry Tai. The FBI were planning on charging Tai with several financial crimes, including money laundering and conspiracy to commit tax evasion. The FBI were only waiting for search warrants before they could raid Tai's offices in LA, San Francisco, and Juneau. Owen said they were also waiting for warrants to search Wei Lee's office and home in LA.

When he'd finished bringing me up to date, Owen asked me if I had any questions. I asked him where my check was. He said he'd find out. Then, as an afterthought, he said if I gave him a voided check, he'd arrange to wire the rest of the FBI's contract payments directly to my bank account. He shook my hand, thanked me for my co-operation, and said he needed to get back to work. He walked out of Robson's office and I never saw him again. My first check arrived in the mail a week later and I've been receiving a wire deposit on the first day of every month ever since. Even though he was a cop, I couldn't help but like Special Agent David Owen.

After Owen left Robson's office, I signed my official statement describing the events of the day that Wei Lee died. Robson said a copy of my statement would be sent to the Yukon coroner, who would be conducting an official inquiry into the death of Lee. Robson told me there was no hard evidence – 'as yet' he'd emphasized – that a crime had been committed the day Lee died. What he meant was a crime committed by me. He also let me know I could go pick up my plane any time I wanted. When I left his office, he growled that he'd be 'in touch'. I didn't forget to pick up my knife and paddles from the x-ray lady.

Daryl drove me over to the vet to pick up Jack. He was still mopey from the anesthesia, but glad to see me all the same. On the way out of town Daryl stopped at the airport so I could pick up two brand new batteries for my plane. I didn't really need them, but wanted it look that way. I wanted to lend credence to my claim that when the engine had 'quit' over the river, my plane had lost all its electric power. No power, no electrics, no radios.

Must have been a problem with the batteries.

I made sure that Daryl got a good long look at my two new batteries before loading them into his trunk. What better witness than a cop to have watched me buy two new batteries for my plane? What was that word Sarah Marsalis had used?

Optics.

The next morning, for the second time that week, Reggie's friend with the motor boat took me down the river from Carmacks to my plane. I brought the two new batteries with me. This time when we arrived at my plane, the cops were gone, the tents were gone, and the beach was empty. Reggie's friend pulled his boat up to my plane and I climbed in with the batteries. My friend the bear hadn't come back – at least he hadn't been inside my plane – but the cops sure had. The whole interior was once again plastered with those white powder patches with the little clear squares where they'd lifted more fingerprints. Cops.

I flew back to Minto on the middle tank and landed at the lake with almost no useful fuel left in any of the three tanks. That afternoon Reggie and I laid some logs on the beach and we winched my plane a few feet out of the water with his tow truck. While we were draining the front fuel tank, Leah and her 'friend' did another thorough job of cleaning the interior. It turned out that Leah's cleaning partner was a good looking young guy she'd met going to high school in Whitehorse. Leah was glowing all over and the two of them couldn't keep their hands off each other.

I installed the new batteries and wondered what to do with the old ones, which were still in great condition. I decided to use them for my cabin's power supply. Reggie and I rolled my plane back into the lake and refueled it from barrels. It was ready to fly again.

* * *

Charlie and Charlie Junior stayed in the apartment over my shop for three weeks in June – that was fine – but Charlie had been driving me crazy during the day. He was like me, he needed to be doing something all the time, and whether I liked it or not, had insisted on helping me around the shop. Unfortunately he didn't know anything about fixing cars or trucks, and I didn't have the time or the inclination to teach him how. It wasn't long before I asked Minnie if she could find something for Charlie to do at the café. It was a busy time of year and she agreed to give him a try in the kitchen. The rest, as they say, is history. Charlie started cooking for Minnie and soon after convinced her to add a few Chinese dishes to her list of daily dinner specials. He assured her that Chinese food was his specialty, that he knew what he was doing, and as it turned out, it was true. Charlie's dinner specials quickly became a hit with the locals and in no time he was cooking a full menu of Chinese food. Minnie was so excited she got Reggie to nail a sign up on one of the posts in the parking lot – the sign simply said 'Chinese Food' – but she said it increased her fuel and food sales by twenty percent overnight. She was so thrilled to have Charlie working for her, she had Reggie modernize one of the cabins behind the café. Charlie and Charlie Junior then had their own place to live.

The big canoe race was held out at the lake on July first, Canada's national birthday bash. Over a hundred people attended the party, including band members of all ages from native communities up and down the highway. The temperature got close to eighty degrees under a bright afternoon sun, and there'd been just enough wind to keep the mosquitoes away.

Only three canoes were available for the race, the police were still holding the one that Wei Lee and Tommy Kay had used for their white water adventure. But that was okay, there were only three two-man teams entered anyway. Arlo and Andy had withdrawn their entry two weeks before the big race, citing training injuries. Both men reconfirmed their team's withdrawal on the day of the big race, then opened their first free beer at ten o'clock in the morning.

The race was won by a couple of athletic teenage boys from the Carmacks band. Second place went to Reggie and Daryl. Free beer has a downside, and the third team entered was disqualified just minutes before the start for excessive blood alcohol levels. It didn't seem to bother them.

Determining the winner of the canoe race had been controversial, decided only after a formal protest had been lodged by the Carmacks team. Well before the race started, Leah and her boyfriend had been dropped off down the lake with clear instructions to sound an air horn each time a canoe reached the point, signaling to the paddlers that they could turn around for the return leg back to the beach. However Leah and her boyfriend were apparently otherwise disposed when the first place canoe went past the point, and they didn't sound the air horn until the second place canoe of Reggie and Daryl arrived, by then hundreds of feet behind the leaders. Although both teams turned around at the sound of the horn, Reggie and Daryl all of a sudden enjoyed a huge lead, and made it back to the beach first, welcomed in victorious with loud cheers from the boisterous and back slapping home crowd. Hours later, though, it was determined by the grand marshal that the kids from

Carmacks were the rightful winners. After a long and judicious inquiry, which included interviewing Leah and her boyfriend in a private hearing, it was determined that the Carmacks team had unnecessarily paddled an extra two hundred feet out into the lake before hearing the one and only horn blast, only then reversing their course, yet still managing to arrive back at the beach just feet behind Reggie and Daryl.

Ironically, that morning the local race organizers had appointed me as the grand marshal for the race, only to have their esteemed appointee discharge his duties on an impartial basis, and snatch away Minto's apparent victory later that afternoon. My official declaration of the actual race winner was poorly received by the hometown crowd, and a chorus of boos, sneers and snickers followed me up and down the beach for the rest of the day. But by the time the party broke up, after everyone had stuffed themselves with barbequed salmon and burgers, enough beer to flood a small town, and all the ice cream they could eat, the matter was soon forgotten. Most important to me, Reggie had been thrilled with his performance.

Last summer in the shop was my busiest ever but I still found time to fly my usual number of charters, catering to the niche market of people who will always need a float plane to fly them into the wilderness. My charter customers included all types. There were the modern day 'wannabe' adventurers, the ones who wanted to be dropped off in the middle of nowhere for a few weeks of camping with the bugs and bears, a little tree hugging, and lots of picture taking. Then there were the hunters, the ones who liked to kill animals, cut off their heads, and take them home to make their friends jealous. Of course there were lots of mineral exploration guys too, prospectors who wanted to fly into the back-country to stake new claims and find the next mega-mine ore deposit. And finally, there were the government officials and the 'save the planet' heroes, the people whose self-imposed social duty is to study the impact that everyone else is having on *their* environment. I charged every customer the same hourly rate.

In the shop I replaced three transmissions, one a month in July, August and September. After wrenching for twenty five years, I've never seen clean oil come out of a broken transmission. Nothing lasts forever, but you can always try by using clean oil. I've always believed that oil – not love – 'makes the world go round', and the cleaner the oil, the longer it will turn.

The coroner's formal hearing into the death of Wei Lee convened in Whitehorse in the middle of August. Robson was in attendance with a few other cops, as were some people from the local radio station, and a reporter I know who works for a Yukon newspaper. Surprisingly, it was a pretty low key affair and only a small representation from the public at large turned up. One person I didn't know, but definitely noticed, was a chiquely dressed and very attractive young Chinese woman seated at the back of the public gallery. She never took her eyes off me the whole time I was on the stand. She left before my testimony was over and I never saw her again. My guess was she might have been a relative of Wei Lee.

When the coroner called me to testify, I tried to answer all his questions more or less according to my description of events given in my official statement to the RCMP. One thing the coroner had been particularly interested to know was why no one had been wearing a life jacket. I explained that the two canoes had only been cargo and were never intended to be a part of any service being provided to my two 'charter' passengers. Had I intended to provide the use of the canoes to my clients, I testified that I would have also supplied proper sized paddles, bailers, first aid kits, survival food and water, cushions, and of course, lifejackets. I also explained that Wei Lee, Tommy Kay and I had only employed the canoes as a last resort, being the only viable means to return to civilization from my crippled plane. On that cue, the coroner asked me what exactly the three of us had in mind when we'd abandoned my airplane and ventured down the river in a couple of old canoes. I testified that our objective had been simple. Other than escaping from an aggressive grizzly bear, we'd *all* agreed to canoe down to the next place where the Klondike Highway met the Yukon River – just above Five Finger Rapids. I said it was only a three hour paddle from my plane, and the plan had been to land on the east bank above the rapids, climb up to the highway, and seek a ride back to civilization. Our *plan* had only failed because we hadn't been precisely sure where we were when we'd started to cross the river – we'd obviously started to cross far too late – and we'd *all* been swept into the rapids by the wind and current before we could reach the east bank. On hearing that explanation the coroner nodded, thanked me for my testimony, and excused me. I caught Robson rolling his eyes several times.

Two weeks later the coroner released his report and it was published in the local newspapers. The coroner concluded that Wei Lee's death had been accidental, the result of poor judgment on the part of *all* three canoeists on the river that day, and their failure to have worn 'personal flotation devices'. Life jackets. The official cause of Lee's accidental death was heart failure, a direct consequence of hypothermia. The coroner declared the current status of Tommy Kay as 'missing and presumed drowned'.

On a cold and dreary day in the middle of September, Daryl dropped by the shop to deliver some big news. Gilbert Mahoney had been delivering fuel to a mine south of Dawson when he'd spotted a white pick up truck lying upside down at the bottom of a ravine. The RCMP had investigated and discovered two badly decomposed bodies inside the truck. They were subsequently identified as Rose Marie Rivera of Las Vegas, Nevada, and Terry Ian Mcilhaney of Dawson, Yukon. Daryl told me that upon identifying the truck's deceased occupants, the RCMP had closed their file on the kidnapping of Bobby Larabie. Needless to say, the news was of great relief to me and everyone else concerned, and Bobby Larabie and Charlie Junior could feel safe again.

Daryl told me that upon the discovery of the deceased couple near the Thistle Creek mine, Ralph Braun's lawyer had negotiated a deal for immunity in return for his client's account of what might have happened to Rivera and Mcilhaney. Braun then told the cops in Dawson how the couple had probably met their fate at the hands of Tommy Kay. He described how Kay had beaten up the deceased pair at the Thistle Creek mine when the two men had driven out there to pick up gold one day last June. According to Daryl, with Braun's account of events that day at the mine, there wasn't going to be much of an investigation into the apparent double homicide, not unless Kay miraculously turned up alive. Daryl also told me that as part of his deal for immunity, Braun had agreed to co-operate fully with the FBI in their efforts to indict Henry Tai for money laundering. I was pleased for David Owen.

Later that same day I called Deborah Larabie to tell her how relieved I was that Bobby's kidnappers were no longer for this earth. She'd heard the good news too, so I was dismayed at how formal and reserved she seemed to be on the phone. I knew then that things between us had changed. On some hazy emotional basis, Deb was still holding me accountable and culpable for Bobby's abduction that day back in June. I know that when it comes to certain emotional matters, none the least those concerning mother and child, the facts aren't always necessarily relevant. The message I got was loud and clear, and I was sorry to hear it.

With some trepidation I told Charlie the same 'good' news – that his son was no longer in danger of being abducted by any of the criminals that had been circulating around the Yukon last summer – that he was free to return to Whitehorse whenever he wanted. I was relieved when he expressed no desire to leave Minto, saying that he'd never enjoyed life in Canada so much as he was right then, cooking at the café for Minnie and having his very own cabin for him and his boy to live in. The Yukon's a small town and I knew Charlie was well aware that Wei Lee was dead, and in all probability so was his former boss, Tommy Kay. With the kidnappers of Bobby Larabie out of the picture, Charlie's life was now as free and secure as it had ever been since he came to Canada, even though he and his son were still undocumented residents.

On that item, I thought often about the promise that Sarah Marsalis had made to me back in June, that she would endeavor to get Charlie and his son legal status in Canada. Of course there wasn't a day that went by I didn't think about her for all kinds of other reasons. I'd only known her for four days, she'd been gone over four months, yet somehow she was now a bigger part of me than the day she'd left. I suppose she would always be one of those people who, once they get under your skin, just never leave you for the rest of your life. It's one of life's mysteries not worth analyzing and the best you can hope for is to get used to it.

Still, there were plenty of days when I'd pick up the phone to call Sarah, then wonder what I was going to say, realize she probably hadn't called me for good reason, and I'd always hung up without bothering to dial. But I still intended to hold her accountable to help Charlie and his son get their papers, and would soon have to start thinking about how best to approach her on the subject.

On a more pressing issue closer to home, it was beginning to get damn cold around here, especially at night. The temperature was often in the twenties when I got up in the morning. It had already snowed a couple of times and ice skirted the lake whenever I went out to my plane before noon. My little propane heater was doing a great job of keeping my cabin warm at night, but I was getting fed up with changing the small fuel tanks it was going through at the rate of one every four days. I needed to do something about that. I was also getting tired of sleeping with four hundred grand stuffed in a garbage bag under my bed.

I needed to do something about that too.

FIFTY SEVEN

I've often been accused of admiring my work just a little too long, but today couldn't be blamed. This particular project had turned out perfect. In fact to my eyes, it was a thing of beauty. I stood looking at it with a foot on the blade of my shovel, my chin resting on a fist on its handle, taking it all in. It was time to call it a day while there was still some light left, but I took one last moment to admire my brand new propane tank.

It was clean and white and shiny and big, with a two hundred and fifty gallon capacity. It sat perfectly level with its four legs resting on two square timbers over a bed of crushed gravel, twenty feet behind my cabin. When the truck from Whitehorse came out to fill it on Monday, I'd have enough fuel to heat my cabin for a year. No more five gallon tanks that lasted less than a week. No more transporting little tanks back and forth to the cafe. This was going to be a real improvement to my standard of living on the river. But there was more.

Because what I'd buried under the tank was equally impressive. A few feet under the bed of gravel was a five gallon pail full of cash. Four hundred grand worth of cash, to be precise. I'd dug a hole for the pail two days ago, then put the cash in the pail, sealed it up, and buried it under a foot of dirt. Arnie had come down yesterday in a highway department loader with a bucket full of crushed gravel.

He'd dumped the gravel on the area over the pail, watched me spread it around, then he hoisted up the new tank with the loader and lowered it into place on the timbers. Of course Arnie never saw the pail, I'd covered it with dirt before he arrived. No one will ever see the pail but me. Correction. No one but me and my dogs.

"Well boys, time for hot chocolate," I said.

Russ and Jack were at my feet, staring at the new tank with their heads tilted, doubtless wondering why something that never moved could be so fascinating to me. They followed me into the cabin and watched me pour a cup of milk into a pot on the stove. I dropped a big piece of dark chocolate into the milk and left the pot to simmer over low heat. Then I took some baked salmon out of the fridge and mixed it with dog food in their bowls. I headed outside and they followed me in a frenzy, stepping all over my toes the whole way. I put their bowls down on the deck and they dug in. I went back inside and had a hot shower.

* * *

It was cold outside but I was warm from my shower when I sat down on the deck. I wrapped myself up in an old sleeping bag to stay that way. I squeezed the mug of hot chocolate in my hands to keep them warm, then thought about my new propane tank some more. The sun had set, it was almost four o'clock, and I squinted through the dusk at the trees across the river, searching for my two favorite hawks. There'd only been one at the beginning of June, then all of a sudden there'd been two. A male and a female probably, judging by the way they worked together. I hadn't seen them for a few days and was thinking they might have already gone south for the winter. It wouldn't surprise me if they had, it was plenty cold enough now, and getting colder every day. The snow on the mountain tops was up there to stay for another eight months, and tonight the temperature on the river would drop into the twenties. Next week I'd be pulling my plane out of the lake for the season. Reggie would help me winch it out of the lake onto a crib of logs, then we'd change the oil, drain the carb, take out the batteries, and cover it up for its sixtieth winter of hibernation. It was definitely that time of year again. Time to leave. Russ and Jack and I would be driving south soon.

I can usually tell who's coming down the road to my cabin by the sound of their vehicle's engine and the rattles in the chassis. Of course if it's Daryl, regardless if he's driving his big SUV or his highway cruiser, the dogs always bark. I thought it was probably Daryl who'd just stopped below my cabin because the dogs were barking like crazy, and I recognized the sound of a police car's big engine. It was still running when I heard a door open and close, then a trunk lid open and close. It wouldn't be a long visit if Daryl had left his engine running, and anyway, I was too warm and comfortable under my sleeping bag to get up to greet a cop. I just sat where I was, sipping my hot chocolate, looking in vain for my hawks. My guess was confirmed when I felt heavy footsteps plodding up the stairs to the deck. It would have to be Daryl in his cruiser who'd parked behind my truck, making another one of his unannounced visits. There are times I wish we had cell phone service in Minto, for no other reason than Daryl could call me instead of dropping by announced. Like today just before dinner time. I waited for him, sitting in my chair, all bundled up, staring across the river at the hazy profile of a dark and serene landscape.

It felt like a train rumbling over an old wooden bridge, the way the deck planks sagged and rebounded under each of his heavy steps as the big cop approached me from behind. His boat-sized shoes appeared in my peripheral vision. He sat down with a grunt in the chair beside me. Jack and Russ hadn't followed him up to the deck, though I thought nothing of it.

"Constable," I said, still staring across the river at the mountains.

"That's Staff Sergeant, not Constable."

I jumped, almost spilled my hot chocolate, and looked over at Staff Sergeant Alan Robson.

"Damn," I said, "you scared the crap out of me."

"Really? Any particular reason I scare you, Mr. Brody?"

"Hardly," I said. I sat back and thought about my new propane tank, then took another sip from my mug.

"Been doing a little digging around here?"

I almost choked on my drink. *Damn again.* He'd seen the shovel leaning against my pickup.

"Just installed a new propane tank, spreading some gravel around, if you call that digging. So what brings you to my home, Staff Sergeant?"

"Oh, just passing through town, thought I'd drop these off while I was in the neighborhood. I think they belong to you. Say, nice place you've got here," he said, looking out at the river, then back at my cabin.

He leaned over to his right and picked something up. It was a cloth bag. He dropped it on the deck between us. I stood up and let my sleeping bag fall to the deck. I opened the bag. Inside was my favorite hunting knife, my Swiss Army pocket knife, and two flare guns. I'd bought yet another flare gun after Tommy Kay dumped the last one into the ocean at the end of Jack Kolinsky's dock. Now I had three, enough for a garage sale.

"Thanks," I said. "Thought you needed these for evidence." I sat down again but left the sleeping bag at my feet.

"Not anymore."

"Oh?"

"Don't know if you've been reading the papers, but two weeks ago Richard Constanzia's lawyer made a deal with the crown prosecutor in Whitehorse. We already had plenty of evidence on Constanzia for a murder rap – we knew he killed those two guys in that plane last spring – then we finally got the ballistic report on his gun and the bullets. The ballistic results were cut and dry. It was a no-brainer that Constanzia was about to go down for a life sentence without parole. So he made a deal, took a twenty year sentence in return for squealing on his buddies. Told us everything we wanted to know, including who his boss was – some drug dealer named Pistone out of Las Vegas – but more important, Constanzia told us he'd arranged the abduction of Bobby Larabie with those scumbags,

Rivera and Mcilhaney. That information wrapped everything up for us very nicely. So there's not going to be a murder trial, and you get your flare guns back. Better check them out before you use them again. They were underwater for quite a while."

I digested that news but said nothing. It was almost pitch black but I didn't feel like asking Robson to come inside. Hopefully his business with me was done and he was about to leave. He couldn't be staying much longer, he'd left his car running. I was getting cold without the sleeping bag but wasn't going to put it on again, even though I was only wearing a sweatshirt. I looked over at him. He was wearing a parka and a fur hat.

"There's something else you should know about Richard Constanzia ," he said, finally breaking an eerie silence. "Something you won't be reading about in the papers."

"Oh yeah? What's that?"

"He's dead."

"Dead?"

"Yeah, dead. We flew him down south on Monday to begin his sentence at a maximum security facility on the lower mainland. Yesterday they found him hanging from a shower head. He was dead as a door nail."

"And somehow you don't think it was suicide," I said.

"We definitely don't think it was suicide. But it's unlikely we'll ever find out who killed him. The guests in penitentiaries like he was in aren't known for talking to the police about what happens inside. They know that organized crime has a long reach, and if you want to stay alive, you keep your mouth shut. So obviously we think Constanzia got whacked, and that the hit was probably ordered out of Vegas."

I nodded and wondered when he was going to leave. The guy was giving me the creeps. He didn't say anything for a moment.

"You know, crab season opened in Haines last week," Robson said.

"No kidding, crab season again already, huh?"

"Yup, crab season. You know apparently it's quite something

to see, all those boats circling around the harbor, then a horn goes off and they all charge off to sea in a mad dash to set their traps."

"Sounds amazing," I said. "I'll have to go see that some day. I'll put it on my bucket list."

I could feel his eyes on me. I was still staring across the river, even though it was impossible to see anything. I looked down again at the sleeping bag at my feet, thought about how cold I was, and wished he'd leave.

"Anyway," he continued, "when all those boats head out to sea, so do the State fishery guys. They're right on the sterns of those guys the whole way out, making sure everyone plays by the rules. And wouldn't you know it? The first boat they stopped and boarded belonged to your buddy, Jack Kolinsky."

"He's not my buddy and so what?" I asked, turning my head and looking at him.

"Well," he said slowly, "when the fishery guys inspected Kolinsky's crab traps, they found he was using a pretty unusual kind of bait."

"Staff Sergeant," I said, "could you get to the point? Please? I've got to make dinner." And I was really getting cold.

Robson nodded but took his time.

"Well, apparently what the fishery guys found in Kolinsky's traps were pieces of frozen meat wearing clothes. An arm in a sleeve, a thigh in a pair of pants, a foot with a sock on it, some fingers and ears too, well you get the picture. Turns out Mr. Kolinsky was using the two dead men you found in his freezer last June for crab bait."

I sat up straight. "Do you know who they were?"

"We do now. We know everything now. Kolinsky squealed like a greased pig after the fisheries guys arrested him and took him back to Haines. Your buddies Owen and Kurtz had a long chat with him the next day. Would you believe that Kolinsky didn't even know Wei Lee was dead, or that Tommy Kay is missing?" Robson smiled and shook his head at that. I think it was the first time I'd ever seen him smile. "Anyway," he said, rubbing his hands together, "Kolinsky said he was feeding those dead guys to the crabs because Kay told him he'd kill his family if he didn't."

"That doesn't surprise me," I said. "Kay's a monster. So who were the men?"

"Oh. Right. One of them was Constanzia's boss, a drug dealer from Vegas named Arturo Pistone, an enemy of Wei Lee and the guy who ordered the kidnapping of Bobby Larabie. The other guy was his hired muscle. And get this, the muscle's name was Tony Constanzia, Ricky Constanzia's little brother."

"No kidding," I said.

Robson nodded. "No kidding is right. Anyway, your buddy David Owen is real happy now. He said Kolinsky gave him everything he needed to bust Wei Lee's accountant. Kolinsky said that Kay beat up Pistone and Constanzia on a ferry coming up from Juneau, then locked them in his freezer in Haines. Kolinsky also told Owen he'd been packing Wei Lee's cash into those styrofoam boxes for a couple of years and had been shipping them to the Yukon in your plane. He promised Owen his full co-operation in the FBI's case against Lee's accountant if they gave him a break on jail time. Looks like Owen can 'seal the deal' on his case now, as he likes to put it."

I nodded. That was great for David Owen. It dawned on me then that all the bad guys were dead, if you included Tommy Kay.

"Did you find Kay's body?" I asked.

"His body? Who says there's a body?"

"Come on, Staff Sergeant, you really don't think Kay's alive and well and walking around somewhere."

"You never know," he said in a wry tone, "we never found him." He got up and rubbed his hands together, then put them in the pockets of his warm coat.

"Oh, one more thing," he said, towering over me.

"And what's that?" Robson reminded me of that TV detective who I used to watch when I was a kid. He was always saying 'one more thing'.

"Jack Kolinsky told Special Agent Owen that he loaded four

styrofoam boxes into your plane that day back in June. He even said you helped load them. But the thing is, we only found three boxes on the river. That means we must be missing a box. You wouldn't know where we might look for that missing styrofoam box, do you Mr. Brody?"

"Maybe Tommy Kay has it," I said. "Ask him." Robson gave me a long look and a nod, then started walking back to the deck stairs behind me.

"Yeah, we'll be sure to ask him. Hey, is that your old truck down there?"

"Yes. Why?"

"Oh, nothing, I suppose. But you know how it is, where there's smoke there's fire, right? Like when people come into a lot of money in a hurry, how they start spending it in a hurry. Know what I mean?"

"Yeah, I know what you mean," I said sarcastically, thinking about Robert Duncan and his fancy new red truck.

"By the way, speaking of trucks," Robson said from the top of the stairs, "I just filled up at that place up on the highway. When I went inside to pay for my gas, some big kid sold me a lottery ticket. He said the local band's raising money to build a new hockey arena in the village. First prize is a brand new pickup truck. The drawing's next summer. Thought you should know, I mean if you were thinking about getting a new truck."

"Thanks for that info, Staff Sergeant, but I like my truck."

"You be careful out there, Mr. Brody."

"I'll try."

"And Mr. Brody?"

"Yes!"

"You have yourself a very nice weekend."

"Thank you. You too, Staff Sergeant."

I listened to Robson walk down the stairs. I wasn't going to get up and go inside in case he came back with one of his 'Oh, one more thing' questions. I didn't want him coming into my cabin. I'd have to tough it out a few more minutes until he was gone. I reached down and picked up my sleeping bag, bundled myself up again, shivered and waited. His car was still running. I heard a door open and slam shut. Good. It opened and slammed shut again. Shit. Here we go again with another 'Oh, one more thing' question.

I waited for his footsteps on the stairs but there were none. Maybe he'd just freed a seatbelt stuck in a door. I heard the transmission go into gear and listened to his car turn car around. He roared off. Good riddance. Finally. He was gone. At last, I could go inside and warm up.

The dogs appeared in front of me, panting with their tails wagging. I hadn't heard them come up the stairs when Robson drove off. I leaned forward to get up.

"So what's for dinner?"

My heart skipped a beat. I fell back in my chair, staying perfectly still, staring out into the darkness, listening to the river, trying to comprehend what I'd just heard behind me. I took a deep breath and swallowed.

"Chinese," I finally managed to say.

"You cook Chinese?"

"Nope. But there's a new Chinese restaurant in town."

"Is it close?"

"Real close."

"Is it good?"

"Really good."

"Are you hungry?"

"Very."

"Me too."

She put her arms around my neck and slid a warm soft cheek up against mine. I could smell her hair.

"I missed you, Brody."

"Missed you too, Sarah."

FIFTY EIGHT

She was in the shower and I was on the couch, flipping through channel after channel of news hour drivel and car commercials. She said she'd been travelling all day and wanted to 'clean up'. I told her she could take her time to 'clean up' while I went out to pick up dinner. 'No', she'd said. 'I need to go with you'.

Need?

When we entered my cabin she walked straight into the bedroom, dropped her bags on the bed, dusted off her hands and emerged smiling. Some people are born with an innate self-confidence. I wasn't. I wouldn't dare do that at her place, but then again, I was as nervous as a nerd on prom night.

The dogs were lying in front of the bathroom door, basking in a layer of steamy air flowing out across the floor, waiting for her grand exit. Sarah Marsalis was back in town, they had her cornered, and this time they weren't going to let her get away.

"Hey," I yelled. "Leave her alone! Come here boys!"

They ignored me. I found the channel with the television schedule. Tomorrow was opening night in a new NHL season and there was a double header starting at four o'clock. My Coyotes were playing in the second game at seven o'clock. I'd have to plot and plan to keep that time slot open. I think I was paddling through Five Finger Rapids when the Coyotes were eliminated in the seventh game of the conference final. I was still really ticked about that, they'd lost their first chance ever to play in the Stanley Cup final. I needed a new season to start to get over it.

The bathroom door opened and closed, there was a pattering of dog feet, then the bedroom door closed. I heard a hairdryer start. She'd brought her own this time. The one I kept in my tool box was 'no good', or so she'd just told me. I watched the cabin lights to see if there was going to be a brown out. But there wasn't a flicker. Those two extra batteries from my plane made all the difference to my cabin's power supply. Five minutes later the bedroom door opened. I'd been waiting to go out and pick up dinner for half an hour. I was really hungry and thought all the waiting had better have been worthwhile.

"Ready?" she asked, standing in front of me.

I stared up at her in awe. The wait had definitely been worthwhile. She looked spectacular, glowing all over, wearing those tight blue jeans with a white turtle neck under a red sweater. Just a hint of make up and two tiny diamond stud earrings 'sealed the deal'. It all added up to that look that said, 'I can have all your worldly possessions just by going to bed with you'.

That look.

"Yeah," I said, suddenly feeling totally inadequate, my mouth instantly dry.

"Brody, do you have a warm jacket I could borrow?"

"Yeah. Hang on."

I went into the bedroom and grabbed a brand new ball cap off a shelf. If she was going to dress up for the café crowd, then so was I. I pulled a ski jacket out of a closet and walked out to the living room.

"Ready?" I asked, handing her the jacket.

"Ready," she said, putting it on. It was a little big, but looked a lot better on her than on me.

The dogs whimpered and whined when I closed the door on them.

"We'll be back soon," I said. They whined some more.

On the way down to the truck I noticed Sarah was carrying a slim leather attaché.

"What's in that?" I asked her.

"Tell you later."

"You look great, by the way."

"Thanks. So do you."

I nodded.

I know I look great. I'm wearing a new ball cap.

I opened the passenger door for her. It creaked and squeaked. I shoved some tools over to make room and pounded the seat. A cloud of dust billowed up. We waited for it to settle.

"You need a new truck."

"Maybe next year," I said.

* * *

We pulled off the Klondike Highway and parked in front of the café's main door. A crowd of men were milling about at the far end of the parking lot. We got out and Sarah walked around the back of the truck to take a look. She stopped beside me and we watched them for a moment.

"What's going on?" she asked.

About a dozen men were congregated around the lone light pole at the north end of the lot. Most of them had a bottle of beer in their hand, shuffling around and talking, watching two men under the light pole. A pickup truck was idling nearby, a steamy cloud of vapor pouring out of its exhaust pipe, hanging motionless in the cold still air, lending a surreal aura to the scene.

"Brody?"

"What?"

"I asked you what's going on down there."

I sighed. I hardly felt like telling her. Not right before dinner.

"It looks like a pulling," I said with a sigh.

"A what?"

"A pulling. They're going to pull out someone's tooth."

"What? A tooth? How?"

"See those two guys under the light pole?"

She pressed herself against my back for warmth and looked over my shoulder. "Yes, I see them," she said.

"Okay, look carefully at the guy with his mouth open. He's tying a piece of fishing line around a bad tooth. The other guy's going to tie the other end of the line to the pickup truck. Then the guy with the bad tooth is going to put his arms around the pole and someone will hold his face against it. Someone else will give a signal, and the truck will take off. When the line tightens, out comes the tooth. A pulling."

"My God! That's disgusting! That's barbaric!"

"Yeah, well it works."

"Can you stop them? That man needs a dentist. Think about his pain."

"I wouldn't worry about his pain. He's probably had seven or eight beers."

"Come on," she said. "I can't watch this."

We walked inside.

* * *

"Brody!"

"Minnie!"

Good. That was over with. I'd been duly announced. It was the dinner hour but there was nobody in the restaurant. I guess news of the pulling had emptied the building. Minnie's eyes got huge when she saw Sarah. She slid off her stool and trundled around the counter. They met halfway and Minnie threw her arms around Sarah. I left them there, embracing each other like long lost friends.

Women.

I headed to the counter to look at the menu and gave a wave to Charlie through the kitchen window. He acknowledged me with a nod. When I decided on dinner, I walked around the counter and leaned my head in the kitchen window. Charlie was flipping a wok full of stir fry vegetables with one hand while lifting a basket out of a fryer with the other. I gave him my order and he nodded again, not looking at me. Now there was a man who could multi-task.

I sat down on a stool at the counter and Sarah joined me. Minnie sat down behind her cash register, still flustered and red in the face.

"Say Brody, is that a new hat you got there?"

"Yeah. Big night."

"I'll say it's a big night. I just can't believe you came back, Miss Sarah. Surely you didn't come all the way up here just to see this guy!"

Sarah and Minnie laughed like old friends. I rolled my eyes and shook my head. We heard a roar from the parking lot. It was done.

"What was that?" asked Sarah.

"I guess the tooth came out," I said.

"Oh, God," she said, dropping her head into her hands and looking down at the counter. "I can't believe anyone would do that."

"That Arnie should just get it all over with and have every damn tooth pulled out of his dumb head," Minnie said. "That man wouldn't know what end of a toothbrush to hold if he took a course. Damn fool."

Sarah smiled at Minnie, then at me. I shrugged. Life in the Yukon.

"Minnie?"

"Yes, Miss Sarah?"

"Do you think I could have a minute with Charlie?"

I looked at Sarah quizzically. Minnie did too, then said, "Sure thing, hon."

Sarah got up and disappeared down the hall toward the bar. I watched Charlie through the kitchen window. He turned and looked behind him, raised a finger and went back to his cooking. A minute later I watched him walk out of my line of sight.

"Now what would she want with Charlie?" Minnie murmured at me.

I shrugged again. "Don't know."

The front door of the café opened to a cacophony of hoots

and hollers and a dozen men came walking in, one after the other, laughing and jostling each other.

"Reggie McCormack! You come here!" Minnie bellowed. Reggie pulled out of line and walked up to Minnie as the men dropped their heads and walked silently past us with sullen faces. As soon as they were well down the hall they picked up where they'd left off.

"What, Ma?"

"I told you to bring those men in through the side door when you were finished out there! I don't need a bunch of drunks walking into my restaurant at dinner time! Got that?" Minnie was as angry as I'd ever seen her.

"Sorry, Mom. Hi, Brody," he said. He sat down beside me, hanging his head like a scolded puppy.

"Hey, Reg."

Minnie was still steaming when Sarah appeared beside me. She was looking pleased with herself. I looked at her expectantly.

"What?" she asked.

"Nothing," I said, shrugging my shoulders.

"Hi, Miss Sarah," Reggie said, moving over to the next stool so Sarah could sit beside me.

"Hello, Reggie. How are you?"

"Fine. Hey, Miss Sarah, do you want to buy a lottery ticket?"

"A lottery ticket? What lottery is that?"

"You can win a truck. It's to build a hockey arena in the village."

"A hockey arena, huh? How much is a ticket?"

"Ten dollars. The drawing is next Canada Day, out at the lake."

"Well, I just happen to know someone who needs a new truck," she said, smiling knowingly at me. "Sure, I'll buy a ticket."

I was waving my hands and making big eyes at Reggie from behind Sarah's back when he pulled a crumpled book of tickets out of his pocket and handed her a pen. I couldn't get his attention though, he was concentrating on making a sale.

"You fill out this stub here, and this here's your ticket," he said, tapping the ticket with a finger. He handed her the open booklet. She started to fill out the stub.

"So Reggie, how much are you trying to raise with your lottery?" Sarah asked. She deftly completed the stub and handed the booklet back to him. He tore off the ticket and handed it to her.

"Four hundred thousand dollars," he said.

* * *

When we stopped below my cabin, the headlights lit up a few gigantic snowflakes that had just begun to fall from a pitch black sky. They were descending as slowly as parachutes, looking like miniature flying saucers, touching down so softly they must have had passengers on board. When we got up to the deck, the dogs were watching us from inside, sitting on the kitchen chairs with their noses pressed against the cold glass, trying to glimpse Sarah Marsalis, making sure she was still with me. They wagged their tails. We went inside. I threw another log on the fire. We ate our meal.

Then we went to bed. We couldn't wait to go to bed. Everything before had been mere protocol, a civilized prelim before launching our carnal attempts to ravish each other in a maelstrom of tangled sheets and blankets. All in itself that was great. But it seemed we were now a lot more than lovers. She'd come back. All the way back to the Yukon. To the 'middle of nowhere'. To see me.

I happened to really like Sarah Marsalis. I liked being around her. I wanted to be around her. I liked the way she talked to me, how she teased me, how natural and genuine and comfortable she seemed to be in every situation we shared. But to be perfectly honest, what I probably liked most about her was that she liked me. Maybe that was the crux, maybe that was the bond, the real reason why she'd come back. We simply liked each other. We were best friends. I realized then why I'd missed her so much after she'd left in June. And why I desperately wanted to trust her.

Is that love?

Don't know about that one. I think love is what you do, not how you feel. Simply liking someone is all that matters. Getting along and enjoying each other between episodes in the bedroom is what it's all about. It should all feel as natural and easy as falling off a log. You either get along or you don't. It's either fun or it's not. It either works or it doesn't. Anything else is just trying to pound square pegs into round holes, and fodder for the psychiatrists and psychologists and marriage counselors.

One thing I did know for sure, she was leaving on Monday. That was going to be depressing because Sarah Marsalis was a keeper.

"Four hundred thousand dollars, huh?"

"What? Four hundred thousand dollars, what?" I asked, still in a daze, breathing heavily.

"Come on, the cost for the new hockey arena in the village. The lottery at the café."

"Yeah? So what about it?"

She had her arms folded under her chin, lying on my chest with her face inches from mine.

"They're going to have to sell forty thousand tickets at ten dollars a piece to raise four hundred thousand dollars."

"Yeah, so?"

"So come on, how are those people at the cafe going to sell forty thousand tickets at ten bucks a pop in a little place like this?"

"Well," I said, "first of all they've got eight months to sell them. And they're going to be selling them to all the café's customers, and everyone in town. And they're going to sell them everywhere they go, up and down the highway, places like Dawson, and Whitehorse too, all over. And I'll take a whole bunch south with me this winter. I know lots of people in Phoenix who'll buy tickets."

She smiled and stared into my eyes. I blinked first.

"You know what I like most about you, Brody?"

"What?"

"You're such an easy read."

"What's that supposed to mean?"

"It means you're a lousy liar. So stop while you're ahead, okay?"

We looked at each other for a long time. *She knew*. She knew I knew she knew. There was a scratching at the door. I'd closed it when we came in. I hadn't wanted any competition. I didn't feel like getting up to let them in.

"Stop!" I yelled. Scratch. Scratch. Scratch. They weren't going to stop.

"Stop!" she yelled. They did. Just like that, they stopped. Nothing worse than having an alpha female spend the weekend with you and your dogs. They'd never listen to me again.

"I brought you something," she said.

"Oh yeah?"

When she got off the bed I got to take another good long look, a really good 'up and down'. A bit of 'back and forth' too. Nothing had changed. Maybe a little tanner, that was about it. It was still 'wow' all over. She picked up her backpack in the corner and came back to bed with it, sat down upright against the headboard beside me.

"I see you're still eating that fish."

"What are you talking about?" she asked, digging around in her pack.

"Pilates."

She rolled her eyes and said, "Here, this is for you."

It was a glossy envelope. I opened it. Inside was an airline ticket. I pulled it out. Mr. C.E. Brody. Phoenix to Acapulco. December twenty-fifth.

"Really?"

"We leave Christmas day, if that works for you. Two weeks. You and me and a beach. I rented a Tiki hut. Don't forget your flip flops. I'll meet you at the airport in Phoenix."

"Hey, I'm there. Thanks." We smiled at each other. All of a sudden I couldn't wait for Christmas.

"Sarah?"

"What?"

"How come you never called?"

"Because I was under orders not to call. I almost got suspended because of you."

"Really? Because of me?"

"Yes, really, because of you. But now that this whole thing's over and done with, I can see you now."

"Well, that's good."

"It is, isn't it?" She smiled. We were quiet for a moment.

"Sarah, what did you want with Charlie tonight?"

"Oh, I gave him a bunch of papers to sign. He needs to get pictures taken of him and his boy, then he's got to have everything notarized – don't let him sign anything unless it's in front of a notary – then he has to mail everything by registered mail to Vancouver. He should be a landed immigrant by Christmas."

"That's great!" I sat up and kissed her. "That's fantastic! Thanks! You came through!" I kissed her again.

"I said I would. A promise is a promise, right?"

I nodded and said, "Yes, it is."

"So now I have a question."

"What?"

"Do you trust me?"

"Yeah," I said. "Of course I do. Sure I trust you." I squeezed her hand.

"Good. Then it's time for you to prove it. It's time for you to take a leap of faith."

"A leap of faith?"

"Yes. A leap of faith."

"Okay. What's the leap of faith?"

"What's your first name, Brody? What does the 'C' stand for?"

"Oh, no. No, no, no. No way. I told you already. You call me Brody, I'll call you Sarah, we'll be just fine. We'll know who we're talking to."

She glared down at me, then spun around and straddled me, sitting back on her heels. She cupped her breasts in her hands.

"Do you see these?" she asked.

"Well your hands are kind of in the way."

"C. Edward Brody, if you want to play with these in the ocean at Christmas, you're going to tell me your first name. Okay?"

Damn woman. This was an egregious tactic. Blatant sexual exploitation – extortion of the worst kind – ruthless and categorically unfair. I sighed and looked at her breasts again, then thought about the ocean. She dropped her hands to her knees and stared me in the eyes. I stared at her breasts some more. This was just so very, very unfair. I took a deep breath.

"Alright, I'll tell you," I said, fixated on her chest. Then my jaw froze.

"Brody!"

"Hmmm?"

"What is your first name!"

"Cornelius," I murmured through clenched teeth.

"Cornelius? Is that what you said?"

She had her eyebrows raised and was leaning in for the kill, coaxing a child out of a secret.

"Yes."

"Cornelius?"

"Cornelius."

It started with a twitch at the corner of her mouth, grew to a grin, and blossomed into a smile. Then she laughed. And laughed. She threw her head back and laughed until she cried.

She laughed herself to sleep.

From the Author

What I learned more than anything while writing my first novel was how much help would be required to turn it into a book. I am indebted to the following people and take this opportunity to extend my thanks.

To my father, whose support and enthusiasm for this project never wavered. Thank you, Dad.

To the following people, who were kind enough to read my early manuscripts, and not only gave me encouragement, but were more than gracious when pointing out where I might make improvements: Linda Quinn, Terese Lawrence, Lynn Fimberg, Stan Fimberg, Gordon Denton, Marie Thomas, Jack Hollmeyer, Deirdre Lapp, Joey Baird, Carmel Beck, Suzi Wasmund, Jan Snider and Cindy Williams.

To my sister, Esther, is there anyone you don't know? Thanks for all the introductions to the most interesting people.

To Ernie Bourassa, a born and bred Yukoner, former two term mayor of Whitehorse, and a wealth of Yukon knowledge.

To Wikipedia, now where would a writer be without that extraordinary resource? Kudos to Wikipedia for not selling out, for remaining a breath of fresh air in an internet that's polluted with advertising and pop-ups. Let's all pitch in and help keep it that way. Send them a few bucks every year and we can preserve a special place to learn.

To Mark Dornblaser, photographer extraordinaire, who kindly

provided the image for the cover, and to Aaron Lapp, who made it sizzle with his design.

To Mark Smith, for your dedication to detail and all the hard work to produce a great map.

To Glendon Haddix at Streetlight Graphics, for putting the whole thing together.

To the nice lady at the Canadian Aviation and Space Museum in Ottawa, for letting me 'inside the ropes' for a 'real good look' inside the very first DeHavilland Beaver.

And finally, thanks to the colorful five percent, the pilots, the miners, the prospectors and drillers, and all the men and women of the Yukon who still work outdoors in one of the toughest environments on earth – not because they have to – but because they want to.

May the spirit of the Yukon live on.

About the Author

Ken Baird operated a Yukon gold mine for ten years. A former receiver-manager and private pilot, he now lives in Florida.

Yukon Audit was his first novel. It won the 2016 Indie Book Award for Best Thriller. The sequel and second C.E. Brody adventure, Yukon Revenge, was released in June, 2019.

NOW AVAILABLE

"...a fantastic sequel to Yukon Audit."

—Readers' Favorite

It's been a year since Brody was lucky to escape with his life after a harrowing chase down the Yukon River. A mobster named Kay had been intent on killing him, but after the two men entered a white water maelstrom, only Brody got through. Kay's body was never found, and as far as Brody's concerned, the man drowned. But with two recent murders pointing to Kay, the RCMP aren't so sure about that.

Turn the page to read an excerpt from Yukon Revenge.

ONE YEAR AGO

In desperation the big man in the river grabbed a floating tree and could only watch as his canoe was swept into the rapids.

It bounced off a rock, spun around, rode up a boulder, sailed into the air, and jettisoned the little man at the front. It landed upside down, rolled upright, and stopped momentarily with a ton of water in the hull. Then the current took hold, accelerating it downstream, slamming it into rock after rock, rolling it over and over, purging its precious cargo. Seconds later everything disappeared into a wall of white water: the canoe, the little man, and three styrofoam boxes. Three million dollars was in the Yukon River.

Everything was in the Yukon River.

The tree he was clinging to was thick and heavy, moving slowly and haltingly through the rapids as it toggled from one rock to the next. Its long branches kept it from rotating and he managed to mount and straddle it, raising most of his body out of the frigid water. But time and time again another wave would rise and fall over him, thoroughly soaking him to his skin, inducing a great shudder that rippled down his torso and resonated through his bones. His feet were his greatest concern, he couldn't find a way to keep them out of the water, and they were beginning to feel dead and unattached as a numbing pain crept up his legs. He knew he didn't have long, he could only survive another few minutes before succumbing to the ice cold grip of the river.

He had to get to shore.

Halfway down the rapids, the top of the tree plowed into a narrow gap between two boulders, stopping it dead, hurling him forward into a nest of branches, cutting a deep gash across his brow. With blood in his eyes, he couldn't see what had stopped the tree, but now that it was stationary, the torrential river engulfed him. Flattened to the trunk by tons of water gushing over him, he gasped and thrashed and kicked out at a rock. With a mighty push of his left leg, the tree began to swing to his right in a long slow arc. When it was at right angles to the current, it released from the boulders and began a slow drift sideways, skidding and sliding along a row of rocks toward the right side of the canyon. He turned his head and saw the river bank was not thirty feet behind him, getting closer by the second as the tree tracked across the current. The water between him and the shore was fast and smooth, and though a poor swimmer, he knew this was his one and only chance to survive.

The rocky shore was twenty feet away when he fell more than leapt from the tree, and began windmilling his arms wildly. He realized immediately something was wrong, for as much as he tried to summon his great power, the strength in his body had left him. But though the frigid water might have won his energy, it could never defeat his resolve, and he gasped and thrashed for his life until his hand came down on a rock. He pulled himself forward until he felt another rock, pulled on that one too, then another, and another. When his knees finally scraped bottom, he stumbled to his feet, took a few steps, fell back to his knees, and with the roar of the rapids behind him, crawled onto land.

He would live.

* * *

Ten minutes later the big man had climbed halfway up a rocky bluff and was standing on a narrow ledge. Cold and exhausted, bleeding and shaking, he turned and looked down at the Yukon River. He was at the north end of a pillar of rock about as high and long as a battleship. To his left and right the river rushed past him through two narrow canyons, but in the distance beyond it lay wide and flat and calm. He squinted his eyes against the low sun, and using both hands to shade his face, scanned the sparkling water for any sign of the little man.

What he saw made his blood boil.

A man in a canoe was stopped beside the little man who was in the water. The little man was lying on a white box, clutching it to his chest. The white box he was clinging to was one of the three styrofoam boxes they'd been carrying in their canoe.

Inside the box was a million dollars in cash.

The man in the canoe seemed to be talking to the little man, but then he abruptly paddled away.

Leaving the little man to die.

The big man knew who was in the canoe. It was the pilot who had led them into the rapids. The pilot who would be thinking he had killed them both. But he was wrong about that. Dead wrong. Because only one man would die that day.

The pilot would have to pay for what he did.

But first the big man would make him miserable.

Then he would make him suffer.

Then he would kill him.

ONE

Life is full of mysteries.

Like why would a man with a pickup, a plane, a cabin on the river, and two dogs to keep him company, not be happy?

I was mulling over the possibilities while peering up into a dark deep recess in the car above me.

Another mystery.

It seems there's one in every job, a single nut or bolt that's impossible to access, but has to be removed to change a part.

I wonder why automotive engineers design cars like that. To discourage do-it-yourselfers? To keep car dealers in business? Or is it simply a disdain for mechanics in general?

It was then I caught a whiff of smoke.

Now there was a problem.

In the Yukon we don't have hurricanes, tornadoes, tsunamis, sinkholes, or volcanoes. And on the rare occasion when the houseplants sway a little, well it's hardly what you'd call an earthquake. But when you smell smoke in the air up here, you find out where it's coming from.

Fast.

I left the car on the lift and walked out of my rough timber shop with a wrench in my hand. The wind was out of the south, cool and light and steady. I took a long deep breath. A forest fire in the Yukon is rare in early June, but smoke was on the wind.

Wood smoke.

The dense spruce forest surrounding my shop blocked every view of the horizon, so I headed across the gravel lot to my old Chevy half ton. I dropped the tailgate, got in, and turned the key. The engine started and ran nicely. It had better run nicely, I have the only auto repair business for forty miles and the engine in my truck is my whole advertising campaign.

I dropped the wrench on the seat, wiped my hands on my jeans, lowered the windows, looked in the mirrors, and started counting. One, two, three, four...and didn't get to ten before two Jack Russell terriers came charging out of the woods, leapt into the box, and skidded to a stop at the cab window. I put the transmission in drive, idled out of the lot, and started up the two track lane leading out to the Klondike Highway. A cloud of dust kicked up and followed like it didn't want to be left behind. Branches and bushes scraped the sides of the truck and I made a mental note to do some spring pruning.

Russ and Jack—they're my dogs—were eagerly anticipating some action. They'd each picked a corner of the box and were up on their hind legs with their front paws draped over the sides, craning their necks ahead, filling the big western mirrors with their portraits, surveying the air for anything with a heartbeat.

A minute later we reached the highway. I stopped and waited for the dust to sail past, then got out and looked up and down the empty road. And smelled the air again. The pungent aroma of smoke was even more tangible now, though the sky still clear as a bell.

The source had to be close.

My boys eyed me carefully when I strode out and stopped in the middle of the tarred gravel road. The gold rush city of Dawson is a hundred and eighty miles north of where I was standing—a left turn out of my place—and the city of Whitehorse, the Yukon's capital, a hundred and fifty miles south. That would be a right turn. There are no traffic lights in Dawson but Whitehorse has plenty, probably a dozen by now, and whenever I ever get the urge to see one, it's a two and a half hour drive from my cabin. I generally avoid places with traffic lights, though, so living where I do, near a dot on the map called Minto, in the middle of nowhere as people tell me, well that suits me just fine.

I scanned the horizon in all directions and saw nothing but pale blue sky. Other than the engine idling in my twenty year old pickup, not a rattle or tick in it by the way, there was barely a sound to be heard—a rustle from the trees, the caw of a crow, a chattering squirrel, a whisper of wind.

Just another Monday morning rush hour in Minto.

But with smoke in the air.

Russ and Jack were wary, watching my every move, getting antsy.

"Stay," I commanded, knowing well that neither would even think about jumping out with the motor running, and risk missing a drive down the highway. Unless of course they spotted something with fur and four legs, in which case they'd both be gone in the blink of an eye.

For a good two minutes I stood there in the middle of the Klondike Highway, scanning the sky, sifting the air, waiting and watching. Then I glimpsed a faint plume of smoke rising over the tree line. It was low in the sky to the south. Not far. Probably from the village. I jumped into my truck and spun the tires.

Two minutes later I knew what was burning.

* * *

CPSIA information can be obtained
at www.ICGtesting.com
Printed in the USA
BVHW070130281220
596442BV00001B/53